Dr Ribero's Agency of the Supernatural:

The Case of the Twisted Truths

Dr Ribero's Agency of the Supernatural:

The Case of the Twisted Truths

Lucy Banks

AMBERJACK
PUBLISHING
Chicago

AMBERJACK
PUBLISHING

Copyright © 2020 by Lucy Banks
All rights reserved
Published by Amberjack Publishing
An imprint of Chicago Review Press Incorporated
814 North Franklin Street
Chicago, Illinois 60610
ISBN 978-1-948705-76-9

Library of Congress Cataloging-in-Publication Data
LCCN   2020942244

Cover design: Jonathan Hahn

Printed in the United States of America
5 4 3 2 1

PROLOGUE

Excerpt from A Historie of Spirits, *modern translation*

The war against the Persians was long, bitter, and bloody. Yet, as every good tactician knows, even the most formidable armies can be defeated with supernatural force. And so it was with the battle of Samarqand that the invaders won, with a daemon at their helm.

The Persian ruler Arscaces, realising his inevitable defeat, laid down his sword and knelt at the daemon's feet, begging for leniency, which was granted. And thus Persia was won, and the human world had its first spirit ruler.

The daemon, inhabiting the form of a demigod, was large, bold, and strong. The people of Persia grew to love him and called him Arsaces too; chief of the Parni people. To celebrate his victory, this spirit, this second Arsaces, gave the people a symbol of his respect and admiration: precious coins, declaring him to be a benign autocrat.

However, the daemon could not have achieved such success alone, without fellow spirit assistance.

Chapter 1: A Christmas Visitor

Kester was fully aware that a piñata wasn't capable of human emotion.

However, there was something about its refusal to smash, even after several minutes of vigorous walloping, that convinced him that the papier-mâché horse had a definite air of smugness about it. It was *goading* him, swirling around on its string, and the more he hit it, the more unlikely it seemed that he'd ever break it apart.

"Come on, this is not a pillow fight. Put your back into it, yes?"

Kester glanced at his father, who was stretched out on his leather sofa. He was still wearing the pink paper crown he'd retrieved from a cracker at lunchtime.

"I'm trying," Kester protested, wondering if it would be against the rules to pick up the fire poker instead, which looked far better suited to the task than the plastic baseball bat he was currently wielding. "But the piñata's made of concrete or something, I swear."

"Well, this has been riveting to watch, I must say," Serena muttered from her curled-up position on the armchair. "Why don't you give up, Kester? You've been at it for ages."

Kester yawned, then placed the bat beside the hearth. It was only four in the afternoon, but already the sun was starting to set. The pine trees outside cast steadily lengthening shadows over Ribero's polished wooden floor, almost reaching the flickering amber glow from the fireplace.

On the other sofa, Pamela hiccupped, then leant her head against Miss Wellbeloved's shoulder. "What's for tea?"

"Tea?" Ribero's moustache bristled at the word. "I cook a most magnificent Argentinian Christmas dinner, and you ask for tea?"

"You cooked?" Miss Wellbeloved raised an eyebrow. "I seem to remember preparing most of the vegetables. Not to mention peeling all the potatoes."

"Ah," Ribero wagged his finger imperiously in her direction. "But I did the asado. The fine, meaty meal. *Man* food. And that, as you know, is the most important part."

Mike groaned from his sprawled position on fireplace rug. "It certainly was," he said, clutching his stomach. "If I ate another thing, I think I'd explode like a hand grenade."

Kester grinned. Even though the annoying piñata refused to burst, it had been a good Christmas Day; far better than he'd expected. After his mother had died in the summer, he'd fully expected the festive season to be miserable, not to mention lonely. But here he was, with the father he'd only been acquainted with for the last few months, plus the rest of the team. It felt strangely *right*, somehow, as though he'd known them for far longer.

I feel at home, he realised, with something close to satisfaction.

"Here." Serena rose from the armchair and clicked her fingers in Kester's direction. "If you want a job done properly, get an expert to do it."

Kester reluctantly passed her the bat. "It's not as easy as it looks, you know. In fact it's—"

With one immense thwack, the piñata erupted, spraying a fountain of colourful paper and sweets over the floor. Ribero crowed with delight, and the others clapped enthusiastically. In spite of his earlier protestations, Mike started grabbing at the sweets, shovelling them into his trouser pockets.

Serena turned; bat balanced upon her hip. "You were saying?"

"I probably loosened it up for you," Kester replied as he slumped back on the sofa. "Either that, or it was an exceptionally lucky shot."

"Or you're just a bit feeble?"

He sighed. "Or I'm just a bit feeble. While you're there," he added, pointing at the floor, "pass me a sherbet lemon, would you?"

"What about the beautiful *alfajor* biscuits I made?" Ribero squawked. "I went to a lot of effort. I even ordered some dulce de leche so I could make it like my dear mother used to."

"I'll have some later," Kester mumbled, through a mouthful of boiled sweet.

"I'd be delighted to sample them for you," Pamela offered, and, without waiting for an invite, promptly bustled off into the kitchen.

Relishing the warmth from the fire, Kester reached for his wine and sipped it thoughtfully. It had been snowing earlier, and a few melting remnants of snowflakes stuck stubbornly to the windowpanes. With a sigh of contentment, he closed his eyes, taking in the fuzzy stillness of the room—a welcome moment of calm after all the conversation and games.

"Budge up," Serena ordered and then, without waiting for a response, promptly squeezed in beside him. She poured herself the last remaining drops of the bottle of merlot. "Did Tinker get back to you about the analysis yet?"

Mike groaned. "I thought we weren't going to talk about work today? Come on, take at least one day off a year, Serena, it won't kill you."

"It's *important*," Serena persisted, looking at him with disapproval. "I wondered if Tinker had got in touch yesterday, that's all."

Kester shook his head. A few weeks previously, he'd received a mysterious letter under his hotel door, shortly after he'd narrowly escaped being kidnapped by the Thelemites. Tinker, who seemed to be a man of many talents at Infinite Enterprises, had offered to perform a series of tests on the contents to find out who it was from. Privately, Kester thought there wasn't much point. He was positive it had been from the daemon Hrschni, presumably sent to freak him out even more.

He was, however, curious about what it had meant. *When you're ready to see the other side,* the letter had said, *the key will guide the way.* A small, ancient key had fallen from the envelope too, though what it unlocked was anybody's guess. But this puzzling behaviour was the spirit way, a fact Kester was now very familiar with—especially daemons, who loved communicating with riddles and mysteries.

He shuddered at the memory of encountering Hrschni in Chislehurst Caves. In the few months he'd been working in his father's supernatural agency, he'd encountered all sorts of spirits, but none had radiated the power or authority of the daemon. *The strangest thing,* he thought, *was that Hrschni let me go. He could have seized me after I escaped, but he chose not to. It doesn't add up.*

Miss Wellbeloved leaned forward, breaking his thoughts. The firelight highlighted her cheekbones, making her look even more angular than usual. "I do hope Tinker gets back to us soon," she said seriously. "It's important to gain as much information as possible, especially as Infinite Enterprises' search of the caves yielded nothing."

"That was no surprise," Mike added. "The Thelemites are too clever by half. And too dangerous."

Ribero shrugged. "Not so dangerous, if you ask me. They kidnapped Kester, yes, but lost him soon after. That is just careless, right?"

Kester scratched his head thoughtfully. Since that horrible night, when Anya and the Thelemites had tricked him into entering the labyrinthine network of caverns at Chislehurst, he'd often gone over the events in his mind, trying to make sense of it all. There was so much that didn't add up. They were *missing* something, something important, and it worried him deeply.

"That's enough about work now," Mike said. He sat up, blocking the light from the fire. "This is meant to be a boozy day off, so let's enjoy it. Who's for a game?"

"Is it a drinking game?" Serena asked, with a wry look at Mike's empty glass.

Mike winked. "All the best games are." He grinned as Pamela returned, bearing a tray full of sugary *alfajores*, plus extra wine bottles tucked under each arm. "Aha, here come the fresh supplies."

After the drinks had been poured, Kester raised his glass. "I just wanted to say—"

"That you have never tasted anything as good as my cooking?" Ribero interrupted, waggling his own glass around in response. "That you are so grateful to come here for Christmas?"

"Well, partly that," Kester agreed, with a sheepish grin. "But actually, I wanted to say that it's been lovely spending it here with you all. Not many people spend Christmas Day with their work colleagues—"

"Hear, hear," Mike interrupted. "What were we thinking of, eh?"

"—but it's been really good fun," Kester finished. He clinked glasses with Serena, who smiled.

"It's only because we've got nowhere else to go," she answered, folding her legs neatly beneath herself. "It's not like any of us have family and friends to visit, is it?"

"Well, that is just charming!" Ribero squeaked.

She laughed. "I didn't mean it like that. But it's true, isn't it? We're all waifs and strays, really. Pamela and I are single . . ."

"Which is perfectly fine by me," Pamela added, with a firm nod. "I don't require a man to achieve happiness, thank you very much."

" . . . and Mike's family hate him," Serena continued.

Mike coughed loudly. "I'll have you know, they don't *hate* me," he corrected, shaking his head vigorously. "True, last year they got a tiny bit annoyed at me . . ."

"You got blind drunk and mashed a mince pie on Crispian's head, didn't you?" Serena reminded him.

"Well, the moron deserved it," Mike retorted. "Honestly, I didn't know it was possible for anyone to witter on about investment banking for so long. My brother is such a *massive* bore." He held his hands up, protesting his innocence. "Hey, I was only trying to lighten the mood. And it was funny."

Kester laughed. He'd heard Mike talk about his elder brother Crispian before, and never in good terms. The words *moron, idiot,* and *prat* tended to crop up most often. "Why do you dislike him so much?" he asked, letting the red wine slip down his throat, silken as a caress. "Surely you got on all right as kids?" He thought back to his own quiet upbringing as an only child. He'd always imagined that it would be great fun to have a brother or sister.

Mike snorted. "I dislike Crispian because he's a berk of the highest proportions." Pouring himself another wine, he added, "And he was always picking on me, even when we were young. Mum and Dad think he's brilliant, of course; just because he makes loads of money and has an attractive wife."

"Not that you're jealous or anything," Serena added with a smirk. Mike glared at her, then consoled himself with a handful of Ribero's *alfajor* biscuits.

"So, Kester," Miss Wellbeloved interrupted smoothly, sensing an impending row. "How are you feeling about starting your studies in a few weeks' time?"

Kester groaned. He'd been trying to forget all about it. The official start date of his BA in Spirit Intervention and Business Studies was in the second week of January, and he still hadn't read all the class literature yet. In fact, he was horribly behind with it all and was having palpitations every time the thought crossed his mind. *It doesn't help that the course is run by a terrifying genie,* he thought. *Even though I'm studying online, I'll still be able to see Dr. Barqa-Abu, and presumably she'll be able see me.* Meeting her in the flesh recently hadn't made him feel any less uncomfortable about it all, either.

"I'm sure it'll be fine," he replied eventually. "I just need more time to finish reading *Spirit Intervention for Beginners.*"

"Goodness me, Kester," Miss Wellbeloved exclaimed. "I lent that to you over two months ago. Surely you should have completed it by now?"

"Well, I've brought it with me," Kester replied defensively.

"I was going to carry on reading it today." The statement wasn't entirely true, but he'd planned on at least flashing the book around the room at some point, to show he was still focused on the task at hand.

Ribero tutted. "I hope you are not going to bring shame on our agency." His severe tone suggested that being underprepared for the course was a sin of unimaginable proportions.

"Don't worry," Kester said quickly, "I'll catch up at some point."

Serena sniggered and nudged him over, making more room to spread out in. "You're going to completely bomb at the SSFE, aren't you? I can literally *feel* failure radiating off you, like a bad smell."

"Absolutely not!" Kester snapped back. "Also, do you have to sound so gleeful about it?"

"That's an interesting question," Serena said, musing the point, before adding, "Yes, I think I do."

Well, no wonder no one else wanted to spend Christmas with you, Kester thought grumpily. He knew he was being unchari-table. Serena's mother had committed suicide several years ago, after having been plagued by a spirit. Her father drank himself to death only a few years later, leaving Serena alone, with an under-standably negative attitude towards the spirit world; and indeed, towards people in general. *Still, she could at least try to stop being such a mean git, especially at Christmas,* he concluded, awarding her with his very best glare.

Several increasingly silly games and many bottles of wine later, the fire started to burn low, bathing the room in comforting glow. Pamela and Ribero had already passed out on the sofa, and the latter was snoring like an elephant in labour. Serena seemed to have lost the power of speech, and, after claiming it was too hot,

Mike had removed almost all his clothes, then retreated to the dining room table, where he sat forlornly picking at the remnants of the roast potatoes and carrots.

At midnight, Kester finally rose and shook his father. Ribero woke up with a start, the party-popper balanced on his chest bouncing softly to the floor. He glared upwards at his son; his eyebrows knitted in irritation.

"I'm going to bed," Kester whispered with a nod at Miss Wellbeloved, who had gone to sleep on Ribero's shoulder.

"And you woke me to tell me this?" Ribero hissed. "Go on, off to bed with you, silly boy."

Kester smiled. "I just wanted to say thank you." He bit his lip. "I thought it wouldn't be much fun, spending Christmas without Mum, but it's been great."

Ribero's expression softened. "I am glad you had a pleasant time. That is good to hear." He shifted on the sofa, taking great care not to disturb Miss Wellbeloved. "Now go to bed. Sleep off all that food and wine."

"I will." Kester peered across at the dining table. To his astonishment, Mike was still awake, stoically popping chocolate truffles into his mouth.

"Good night, Mike," he whispered. Mike grunted in response, then resumed eating.

The attic guest room was a bitter cold contrast to the snugness of the lounge. Kester perched on the window seat and peered outside into the woodland beyond. The moon was a milky blob behind the thick clouds, and soft snowflakes pressed against the glass. He touched it briefly, feeling the icy chill against his fingers.

I wonder where Anya is right now. Is she with the Thelemites? He leant his head against the wall, the usual pang of betrayal hitting him like a punch in the gut. The image of her, cosied up to the odious Barty Melville, or the two Thelemite masters he'd met in the caves, Reggie Shadrach and Felix Taggerty, was almost too much to bear. *She's probably forgotten all about me,* he realised ruefully. *I was just a pawn in her game, and now she's done with me.*

He wondered if Anya was still letting the daemon Fylgia inhabit her body. From what he gathered from the others, humans who permitted daemons to live inside them were often rewarded with wealth and success, much like the late Billy Dagger had been, when Hrschni lived within him.

Who could blame her if she did? Kester mused, reaching for his overnight bag to get ready for bed. *It'd be a far more exciting life than the one she'd have with me.*

But still, the thought sickened him. The time they'd spent together had meant the world to him. He'd even lost his virginity to her. Little had he known that he'd actually been sharing the bed with a spirit as well as his girlfriend.

A movement in the wood outside pulled him from his thoughts, a flicker of green like a sickly candle flame, darting through the tree trunks. Lurching forward, he squinted through the window into the darkness beyond, but the thickening curtain of snowflakes blurred his view. *I've drunk too much, and I'm dwelling on the supernatural yet again,* he realised. His head was starting to spin. The most sensible thing would be to get into bed and put it all out of his mind.

Taking off his glasses, he placed them neatly on the bedside table and changed into his flannel pyjamas. The crisp, freshly laundered fabric made him feel instantly cosier. He caught a glimpse of himself in the mirror above the sink, his face looking oddly sharp in the dim light. Recently, he'd been able to see more of his mother's features in his face, especially now that he'd lost a bit of weight. He fastened the last button on his nightshirt and smiled.

I remember how Mother always used to make me special Christmas pyjamas, he thought. Hand stitched, soft to touch, occasionally embroidered with his initials or a little image of a kestrel, the bird he'd been named after. Christmas Day had always been a quiet affair back in their little house in Cambridge, with the same artificial tree, tinsel, and Bakelite gingerbread house that his mother had inherited from her German parents. But he'd loved it, despite the tired glitter of the decades-old decorations, because it had been just him and his mother, and Mildew the cat, of course.

Folding the duvet down, he clambered into bed, relishing the sensation of the crisply tucked cotton sheets against his toes. He was more than ready to go to sleep, thanks to the combination of alcohol, rich food, and nostalgia. Before he knew it, his eyes had drifted shut.

Kester had no idea what time it was when he woke up. It felt as though the whole night had passed, yet a glance at the dark curtains told him that morning was still several hours away.

Without knowing why, he sat up abruptly, skin prickling as though he'd been dunked underneath a cold shower. *Something doesn't feel right,* he thought instinctively, fumbling for his glasses. *There's someone else in here. Something is watching me.*

With that uncomfortable thought in mind, he switched on the lamp and scanned the room. Aside from a dead spider dangling in a web in the corner, he was most definitely alone.

He took a deep breath, aware of his heart thumping against his ribs. "My paranoia is getting ridiculous," he said aloud, more to comfort himself with the sound of his own voice than anything else. A glance at his wristwatch told him it wasn't even two o'clock yet. To make matters worse, an unpleasant, overstuffed feeling in his head suggested that a hangover was looming on the horizon.

He leant over, ready to turn the lamp off again.

Hang on a moment. Adjusting his glasses, he peered into the darkness around the foot of the bed. *What the hell is that?*

A small, off-white rectangle lay on the floorboards, its corner just pressing against the edge of the threadbare rug. Kester felt his breath catch painfully in his throat. He knew what the thing was. He'd seen an almost identical one only a few weeks before. And he knew, when he picked up that little rectangle of white, there would be a red wax seal on the other side, just like the last one.

I don't want another letter from them! he thought, desperation rising in his stomach. *Not now! Not here! Why are they playing with me like this?*

Despite every instinct in his body currently ordering him to turn off the light, pull the duvet over his head, and shiver like a frightened puppy, Kester climbed out of bed. The floor was icy against his feet, and the draught from the window chilled him through his pyjamas. Drawn like a magnet, he bent down slowly, finger brushing the mottled parchment of the envelope.

As predicted, the letter featured the same wax seal, the ancient symbol of the Thelemites. He stroked the surface thoughtfully, aware that his thumb was trembling.

Should I take it to Dad? he wondered. However, he was frightened what might be outside his bedroom door, hiding in the shadows. The fact was, Hrschni or Fylgia could get to him whenever they wanted, regardless of where he might be. When the daemons weren't inhabiting a human, it was easy for them to float through walls, then rematerialise on the other side. But entering houses without invitation wasn't their usual behaviour, or so he'd been told. Miss Wellbeloved liked to remind him that daemons were highly respectful of humans; unless, of course, they were plotting to kidnap them.

He looked at his mobile phone, lying on the bedside table. It wouldn't take too long to phone his father's landline, or he could quickly open the door, shout for help, then shut it again. However, he suspected the others might not take too kindly to being woken up after a day of overindulgence.

Come on, just open it and stop being so cowardly, he ordered himself, then prised the seal apart before he could think of a rational reason not to. This time, no key fell out; only a letter, written on the same thick paper as before.

"*The Ram's head will show you where to look,*" he read aloud. The words hung still in the silent bedroom, and he felt uncomfortably as though he were being watched. "What on earth does that mean?" he muttered.

Flipping the note over to see if there was anything on the other side, he rotated it in his palm, thinking hard. *The Ram's head?* he wondered, easing himself into a cross-legged position on the rug, oblivious to the cold. He vaguely remembered reading about a ram's head in his *Spirit Intervention for Beginners* book, but couldn't remember the context.

"*When you're ready to see the other side, the key will guide the way,*" he murmured, repeating the previous letter's contents, which he now knew by heart. "And now this. Why do they have to be so cryptic?" *More to the point,* he thought, *why are they bothering? Surely if they wanted to lure me back to the Thelemites, all they'd need to do is kidnap me again, like they did the last time.*

It wasn't a pleasant thought. Uncomfortably aware of his isolation from the others, he stood, wincing as both his knees cracked in protest. There was no point in trying to go back to sleep now. Even if he hadn't been so frightened, he doubted he'd be able to stop his mind from going into overdrive trying to figure out what on earth the note could mean.

Instead, he pulled open the door, took a deep breath, and

stepped out into the darkness. Aside from the small circle of light emanating outwards from his doorway, the attic landing was completely black. Kester swallowed, then groped his way to the staircase.

The reassuring grumble of his father's snoring gave him some comfort when he reached the first floor. The sight of Pamela downstairs in the living room, tucked up in a sleeping bag on the sofa, was even more welcome, melting the last of his fears away.

A rumbling grunt reverberated from somewhere in the shadows. "What are you doing up, eh?"

Kester leapt into the air, an involuntary squeal slipping from his lips. To his shock, he saw a broad, naked back, slumped over the dining room table, illuminated only by the tiny lamp in the corner of the room.

"Mike, you scared the life out of me!" he hissed, hand pressed against his chest. "Have you even been to bed yet?"

Mike nodded, then shook his head, then nodded again. "Think I briefly shlept for a bit," he slurred, whilst reaching for another chocolate.

Shlept? Kester thought, then surveyed the row of empty wine bottles in front of him, one teetering precariously on the edge of the table. He had no idea how one human body could hold so much alcohol without malfunctioning entirely.

"Well, don't mind me," he said aloud, as he tiptoed over to the fireplace. "I just need to get something." He briefly toyed with the idea of telling his friend about what he'd found in his room, then decided against it. Given Mike's current state of inebriation, Kester doubted he'd be able to understand anything he said, much less pass useful comment on it.

The leather sofa squeaked loudly as Pamela shifted to one side. As Kester passed, she peered upwards, head emerging from the sleeping bag like a tortoise.

"Everything all right?" She rubbed her eyes, then checked her watch. "What time is it?"

Kester grimaced. "Sorry I woke you. Something's happened and I urgently need to get my *Spirit Intervention for Beginners* book."

Immediately, Pamela sat up in her sleeping bag, caterpillar-like within the swathes of shiny material. "What's happened?" she asked, sounding remarkably awake given she'd been fast asleep only moments before.

Quickly, Kester filled her in on the details.

Pamela's eyes widened as she listened. "Can I see the note?" she asked. Swiftly, she reviewed the contents, then rested back against the sofa with a low whistle. "Wow. What on earth can it mean, do you think?"

"I don't know," Kester replied, nervously chewing his nails. "But it scared the living daylights out of me, I can tell you."

Pamela glanced at the staircase. "I'm not picking up any energies," she said finally. "I'm confident that whatever left this note isn't here anymore."

"Thank goodness for that." Privately he'd felt the same, but he couldn't identify why exactly. It just felt safer, all of a sudden.

"What's going on over there?" Mike's indignant, barely coherent cry startled them both. Kester had almost forgotten he was there, were it not for the regular low rustling as he unwrapped yet another boiled sweet and crunched it in his teeth.

Pamela winked at Kester, then turned around. "Don't worry, lovey," she called, leaning over the back of the sofa. "Why don't you get some sleep instead?" Mike gave her a drunken thumbs-up, hiccupped, then slumped down on to the table top.

"Do you think we should take him to bed?" Kester whispered.

"No, he's happy enough there. He'll be miserable in the morning, but that's another matter entirely. Now, why were you looking for the *Spirit Intervention* book?"

"I remembered something in it about rams' heads," Kester replied, pulling the book open and flicking through the musty pages. "But I can't recall which section it was in."

"Let me save you the trouble." Pamela eased herself out of the sleeping bag and straightened her nightie, which had what looked suspiciously like purple unicorns dancing all over it. "A ram's head is the symbol of Baphomet." She waited, then frowned when he shrugged his shoulders. "Haven't you heard of Baphomet?"

"No, that's why I'm going to study at the SSFE, isn't it? I haven't got a clue about any of this stuff."

She chuckled. "Fair enough. I'll quickly fill you in. Baphomet is typically portrayed as a ram-headed deity, and he's often associated with the occult. Some even linked the ram's head symbol to Satanic ritual."

"That's comforting to know." Kester peered anxiously over his shoulder, half expecting to see something awful creeping up on them both at that very moment.

Pamela waved her hand dismissively. "There's no truth in any of that nonsense, trust me. More interesting, Baphomet features in Aleister Crowley's books."

"Who's he?"

"People always think he started the Thelemites," Pamela explained. "He didn't, of course. He was just one of their more famous members. And he did get rather big-headed towards the end, apparently."

"So, you're telling me," Kester clarified, struggling to follow, "that this ram-headed Baphomet is associated with the Thelemites, right?"

Pamela nodded. "That's right. It's the divine androgene."

"Like androgenous, you mean? Both male and female?"

"Yes." Pamela folded her hands over her stomach. "And more. Light and dark. Life and love." She closed her eyes, and continued softly, "As above, so below."

Kester sighed heavily. "You're getting a bit esoteric for me, Pamela. It is half past two in the morning, after all."

She squeezed his arm. "You know what I'm like, dear. I get very enthusiastic about things like this."

Kester looked back down at the note in his hand, eyes trailing the delicate calligraphy and thick, black ink. The lettering was so perfect it could have almost been printed, but the indentations proved it had been produced by hand. "What do you think they mean," he continued finally, as he rubbed his fingers along the paper, "when they say that the ram's head will show me where to look?"

Pamela shrugged. "I haven't got the foggiest idea."

"Is it foggy?" Mike echoed, head buried deep within his arms. "I thought it was snowing."

"Not anymore." Kester glanced out of the window. The panes were frosted with delicate patterns of ice, but there was no evidence of any fresh flurries. Not that there was any point reporting to Mike anyway, who had promptly nodded off again.

He glanced at Pamela. "Should I be worried about this?"

She chewed her lip thoughtfully, reread the note, then subsided against the sofa with a sigh. "Honestly?"

"Honestly."

"Perhaps a little bit, love. But it's nothing we can't handle."

Kester's gaze travelled to the fireplace, where all that remained was a crumbling husk of ashen log. It seemed symbolic of how he felt; previously warm and lively, now burnt out by the worries of the world. "I suppose I'd better go back to bed," he said finally, looking with great reluctance at the dark staircase. "There's no advantage to us staying awake, is there?"

Pamela leaned over and gave him a hug. "Why don't you sleep down here with us?" she offered, pointing to the throw on the opposite sofa. "Then, if anyone does return in the night, they'll have me and Mike to contend with too."

"I don't think Mike would be capable of putting up much of a fight," Kester said.

Pamela laughed. "You're probably right. But it would be funny watching him try, wouldn't it?"

Mike grunted loudly, then mumbled something in his sleep, as though he'd overheard them. Kester chuckled, then scooped up the woollen throw, which felt pleasingly thick under his fingers. He tucked himself in as best as possible, and gave Pamela a smile, feeling like a little boy again, about to spend the night at a friend's house. She grinned in return, then eased back into her sleeping bag.

"Don't worry, Kester," she said quietly. "I know it's scary. It's worrying for all of us. But no daemon, Hrschni or otherwise, is going to kidnap you again. Not without having to have a bloody big fight with the rest of us."

"Thanks," Kester replied with a yawn. He shut his eyes and tried to relax. *There's no point lying awake, fretting about things,* he told himself firmly. *Even if a spirit did leave a note in your bedroom, they're not here anymore. And if they'd wanted to do anything worse to me, they would have done it already. So calm down and get some rest.*

He knew it was sensible advice. However, the growing unease, nestling deep within him, refused to be quietened. Eventually, after hours of fretting in the dark, he finally fell asleep.

Chapter 2: The Morning After

"Get up! Lazy boy!"

Kester cried out as a hand seized his shoulder and shook it hard. Still lost in his dreams, he imagined the attacker was a spirit, grasping him and dragging him off to some cold, dark cave. "Help!" he shouted, then shot up, eyes wide and unblinking.

Ribero edged backwards, looking rather like someone who'd encountered a worm, only to find out it was a highly venomous snake. "Hey," he said placatingly, palms outstretched. "It was just a little joke, okay? Calm down, please."

Slowly, Kester realised where he was. He took a deep breath, then glared at his father, who was looking distinctly sheepish. "What did you do that for?"

"We need to talk to you." His father perched beside him on the sofa and plumped up a cushion, handing it to Kester by way of apology. "It is nearly midday and we have waited a very long time already."

"Damned right," Serena added, appearing over the back of

the sofa like an inquisitive weasel. "We've been tiptoeing around all morning, waiting for you to stop snoring your head off."

"I told them about last night," Pamela said. Her sleeping bag had been folded up neatly, and she was sipping at a mug of what smelt like strong coffee. "Everyone's very worried, Kester."

Ribero frowned. "Why did you not wake everyone, eh? With news like this, you should have told us all."

"I didn't see the point," Kester replied, still feeling rather dazed. He ran a hand through his tousled hair. "After all, there was nothing we could have done in the night, was there?"

"Mike could have used his Residual Energy Sensor to see what time the spirit left the note," Ribero barked back.

Kester laughed. "Did you see Mike last night? He was in no fit state to do anything." He glanced over at the dining room table to see the man in question, who was now wearing one of Ribero's velveteen smoking jackets and clutching his head with a look of palpable pain.

"Yeah," Mike agreed hoarsely. "And funnily enough, I didn't bring my equipment to Christmas dinner."

"Or indeed to any other occasion where we might desperately need it," Serena snapped.

"Bugger off." Mike glowered at her, then winced again, looking distinctly pale.

A moment later, Miss Wellbeloved emerged from the kitchen with two mugs of coffee in her hands. She placed one in front of Mike, who nodded gratefully before groaning again. The other she delivered to Ribero, who seized it without acknowledgement.

"Would you like a drink, Kester?" she asked, whilst giving Ribero an indignant prod on the shoulder. "I'm sure, unlike your father, you'd actually express some gratitude when you receive it."

"Yes, yes, thank you very much," Ribero grumbled, with more

than a hint of sarcasm. "It is a very good coffee. All the way from Argentina, of course. I share it with all of you, but when do I get the thank you, hey? *Never*." Nodding with self-righteous zeal, he glowered behind the rim of his mug.

Miss Wellbeloved sat down the other side of Kester. "It must have been a horrible shock," she said gently. "But thank goodness it was only a note."

Kester smiled weakly. "I suppose so. But it's worrying how easily they can get to me, whenever they want to."

"Those bloody spirit bastards," Serena said fiercely, as she perched on the armrest of the sofa. "Who the hell do they think they are, playing with us all like this?" She caught sight of Miss Wellbeloved's expression and frowned. "And don't tell me not to call them that, because that's what they are, and you know it."

Miss Wellbeloved looked worried but made no reply.

"I'm not sure it's you that they're playing with," Kester replied, wiggling around to get comfortable. His shoulder muscles ached from his night on the sofa, regardless of how soft the cushions were. "I think they've made it pretty clear that they're after me."

Serena slid gracefully off the armrest and landed beside Ribero, squeezing them all uncomfortably together. "Yes," she agreed, "but when they mess with you, they mess with all of us."

"That's sweet of you to say," Kester said, feeling touched.

"It's not personal," Serena replied sternly. "If I had my way, you wouldn't be in the team full stop. But as you are, I suppose we're duty bound to protect you." Suddenly she flinched, and without warning, slapped a hand against the top of her head.

Kester looked upwards, already knowing that he'd see Serena's little incubus, whirling morosely around her hair. Ever since she'd tried unsuccessfully to trap it, it had dogged her like a lovesick puppy, turning up at the most inappropriate moments.

Instinctively, he gave it a wave. For a moment, he was sure that he caught glimpse of a tiny little hand waving back.

"Don't encourage it!" Serena shouted, and belted her head again for good measure. "It was pestering me last night too. It's taken to trying to sing, but all it sounds like is the most god-awful whine you can imagine. It's like a mosquito crossed with a musical saw."

"Remember, it did fight for your honour against Reggie Shadrach," Kester pointed out. When Shadrach had shoved Serena hard outside Chislehurst Caves, her incubus had leapt to her defence, slapping at the muscle-bound Thelemite with flimsy but no doubt irritating limbs.

Serena slapped her head again, and the spirit plipped out like a light bulb. "Yes, but it's still bloody annoying," she said, as she smoothed down her hair. "Which is precisely what I'm talking about when I say we need to get firmer with spirits. They're taking liberties and it's time to get rid of them all."

"Serena!" Miss Wellbeloved snapped. "What would Dr.Barqa-Abu say if she heard you talking like that?"

Kester could only imagine the fury on the ancient genie's face if she'd have heard Serena's sentiments. He shuddered at the idea. *Dr. Barqa-Abu is terrifying enough when she's in a good mood, let alone angry,* he thought.

"She never liked me anyway," Serena persisted, "so I don't really care what she—"

Ribero coughed meaningfully. "I do not think now is the time to be having this silly fight, no? Let us return to Kester's note."

"Pamela thinks it's to do with Bopomet or something," Kester said blearily.

"Baphomet," Pamela corrected. "And it was only a guess."

"It's a good guess though," Miss Wellbeloved said, standing

up. "I mean, it's directly linked to Thelemite ideology, isn't it? Not that we know what it means about the ram's head showing you where to look. That's very puzzling." She sauntered off to the kitchen.

Kester shrugged. "I have no idea." He leant his head back against the cool leather. *I don't have the energy for this anymore,* he thought, closing his eyes. *In the last few months, I've lost my mother, started a career hunting for spirits, enrolled with a supernatural school, been betrayed by my girlfriend, and been kidnapped by a mad secret cult. What else am I going to have to endure?*

Serena nudged him, startling him out of his thoughts. "You've gone very quiet. Hangover caught up with you yet?"

Kester shrugged. "A little, perhaps." He sighed. "I don't know; I suppose I'm just exhausted by it all. It's been nonstop action since I joined the agency."

"One thing's for sure," Serena retorted, "things have certainly been crazier since you turned up." She caught sight of his crestfallen face and her expression softened. "But that's not necessarily a bad thing, you know. It keeps us all on our toes."

A loud heaving noise pulled their attention to the dining table. Mike, whose complexion had gone from dun white to an alarming shade of green, stood up abruptly. With a horrified look at them all, he dashed out of the room, clutching his mouth with both hands.

Ribero glowered. "Let the vomiting begin, yes?" Judging by the copious retching noises emerging from the downstairs toilet, his conclusion was accurate.

Miss Wellbeloved returned to the room, clutching a freshly brewed cup of tea, which she handed to Kester. "I added several sugars," she said, as she settled back on to the sofa. "You've been looking a bit thin recently, thought you could do with them."

"Thin?" Serena trilled incredulously. "I'd hardly say he was thin. Look at this!" Without warning, she prodded Kester's gut, then gave it a wobble for good measure.

Kester laughed, artfully wiggling out of Serena's grip. "I'd hardly call myself thin either. The spare tyres are definitely still there."

"No, you have lost weight," Ribero declared, and poked Kester's stomach himself to prove the point. "You now have the cheekbone thing, yes?"

Kester stroked his face absentmindedly. "I don't think I've ever had cheekbones in my life."

"I think you look handsome whatever your size," Pamela added, with a jovial wink. "And cheekbones are overrated, in my opinion."

"Can we move on from Kester's cheekbones for now?" Serena said testily. "And address the issue of what we're going to do about this letter from the Thelemites? In case none of you had noticed, this house was invaded by a spirit last night. Am I the only one who has a problem with that?"

"Why use the word *invaded*?" Miss Wellbeloved snapped. "All the spirit did was slip a note under Kester's door."

"Spirit Conduct laws say they're not even supposed to do that," Serena bit back angrily. "Section 2B, 'any entry into human property without invitation is a direct contradiction of—'"

"—I don't think you've quoted that correctly, it's actually— "

Kester coughed, interrupting the pair of them. "Whatever the law is, the main point is that the spirit didn't enter my room, Serena. Nor did it hurt me."

She flashed him a look of disgust. "Don't tell me you're sticking up for them too! For goodness' sake, Kester, they kidnapped you only a few weeks ago, or have you forgotten?"

He sighed, massaging his temples. "It was humans that kidnapped me too, Serena, not just spirits. Anyway, let's leave that aside for the moment and focus on the letter itself. What are we going to do?"

"The sensible thing would be to send it to Tinker," Miss Wellbeloved said. "He can compare the two letters side by side and tell us if there are any discrepancies."

Kester frowned. He knew there wouldn't be. Having held both letters in his hands, having felt the weight of the paper, and its high-quality, textural surface, he felt certain it was the same. Likewise, the red wax seal and the handwriting looked identical.

Miss Wellbeloved reached over to the coffee table and scooped up her mobile phone. "No time like the present," she declared, tapping at the screen.

"You're calling the poor lad on Boxing Day?" Pamela said, with a sceptical look. "That's a bit harsh, isn't it?"

"From what I've heard, Tinker isn't the sort of person who even takes Christmas Day off, much less Boxing Day," Miss Wellbeloved replied. She waved her hand in their direction, indicating that they should be quiet. "Hello, is that Tinker?"

"I can't believe she's phoning on one of his days off," Pamela whispered. Miss Wellbeloved shooed her comment away, then filled Tinker in on the new letter.

"Oh really?" she said suddenly, eyes widening. "That's a bit odd, isn't it?" The others perked up and drew instinctively nearer in an attempt to overhear the conversation. Miss Wellbeloved shifted irritably, then forcibly removed Ribero's head, which was currently pressed against the other side of her phone.

"What's going on?" Pamela mouthed.

Miss Wellbeloved shook her head, then stood up. "Yes, carry on, I'm listening. I'm with the rest of the team, and they're trying to hear what we're saying." She frowned at all of them, before continuing, "They're being quite annoying actually."

"Charming!" Ribero exclaimed, folding his arms.

Miss Wellbeloved fell silent, nodding occasionally and releasing the occasional quiet *hmm*. "Well, thanks for letting us know," she said finally. "I'm not sure what to make of the information, but it's certainly very interesting. Many thanks, Tinker. I'll send the other letter over as soon as possible."

She hung up, then placed her hands on her hips, elbows sticking out at sharp angles. "Will you *please* not do that when I'm on the phone?" she snapped. "It's most off-putting."

"Never mind that, what did he say?" Ribero barked. "Stop with the mystery and tell us."

Miss Wellbeloved took a deep breath. "Well," she began, "it's a bit odd, really."

"Yes?" Serena prompted. "And?"

"The wax seal on the envelope," Miss Wellbeloved continued, "features the Thelemite symbol."

"We knew that already," Pamela said. "It shows the pentagram. What's so odd about that?"

Miss Wellbeloved leaned against the side of the sofa, frowning. "It's the old version of the symbol, not the new."

Kester looked at the others in bafflement. He hadn't known there was more than one version. "Perhaps they just used their old seal?" he suggested. "You know, because they couldn't be bothered to find the new one?"

Miss Wellbeloved shook her head. "No, you're missing the point. They haven't used the old symbol for hundreds of years."

"What's the difference between the two?" Pamela asked.

"You won't believe me when I tell you," Miss Wellbeloved continued.

"For heaven's sake, can you just get on with it?" Serena stood up and started pacing the room like a caged tiger. "This is getting ridiculous. I feel like I'm in the final scene of an Agatha Christie novel."

"I wasn't deliberately trying to be dramatic, Serena," Miss Wellbeloved retorted. "The modern Thelemite symbol is a simple pentagram, just the five-pointed star and the surrounding circle. The old version is the same, but for one key difference. There's a faint etching of a ram's head inside."

Kester whistled. Even Serena was surprised enough to pause her restless pacing.

"Tinker also told me something about the handwriting," Miss Wellbeloved carried on, eyes gleaming. "He said that it was too uniform to have been done by human hands. He believes, judging by the precision of the pen strokes, that it was a spirit who wrote it."

"How can a spirit hold a pen?" Kester asked.

"They can exert a certain level of physical force through energy alone," Pamela explained. "Though it's much harder for them to do it than for us." She nodded at Miss Wellbeloved. "Daemons are particularly good at using energy, which is why they're often capable of touching humans. They can even successfully breed with us, though it's very rare. Lesser spirits don't have the same ability. Normally, they'd just pass right through you."

Kester shivered. He couldn't help it. Even the thought of a spirit gliding through him was unpleasant, not to mention the rest of it. However, Pamela's explanation made sense. He remembered his time with the two daemons, Hrschni and Fylgia, down in the caves. Fylgia had stroked his face, her prickly, skeletal touch eerily cold, but very real nonetheless. *She told me that she'd enjoyed getting to know me,* he remembered, wincing. *She called me a "sweet, innocent thing."*

"What are the children like?" he asked. "You know, the kids produced by a daemon and a human?"

Pamela shrugged. "There haven't been any cases for several decades, not since the new laws came in. I presume they might have some additional powers, but who knows?"

"So," Miss Wellbeloved interrupted, tapping the coffee table, "we now have evidence to suggest it was written by Hrschni. And for some reason, he's choosing to use the old symbol. Just a coincidence?"

"I don't think anything that daemon does is a coincidence," Serena said coldly. "I think he carefully maps out every single thing he does. I don't like it one bit."

Miss Wellbeloved nodded. "I know what you mean. Tinker didn't have much to say about the key, other than it looked Victorian, and he believed it had been manufactured abroad, probably in Italy or France. He's sending the items back to us tomorrow, so we should have them in a few days' time. It goes without saying that we must keep this all top secret. We don't want Hrschni to know our progress, so we must only discuss matters when Pamela has confirmed that no spirits are in the vicinity."

A loud bang startled them, and they looked towards the source of the noise, which happened to be the downstairs toilet door flying open. Mike appeared a few moments later, wiping his mouth and beaming. He strode into the room, then held his arms aloft, like a footballer celebrating a goal.

"I feel much better now!"

"I bet my toilet does not," Ribero muttered darkly. "I hope you cleaned up in there, yes?"

"Mike, you've got some vomit on your jacket," Serena pointed out, nose wrinkling in disgust.

"That is my jacket!" Ribero squawked, flapping his hands in

horror. "I lend you my favourite jacket to keep you warm and you put sick on it. That is revolting!" He then proceeded to launch into a flurry of Spanish expletives, whilst Mike continued to grin cheerfully.

"Put it in the washing machine, it'll be fine."

"It is the finest South American velvet, you do not just 'put it in the washing machine'!"

Pamela placed herself firmly between the two. "Come on, Mike," she said firmly, as she grabbed his arm. "Let's get your proper clothes on, eh? Don't worry, Julio, we'll book your jacket in for a professional wipe down at the dry cleaners."

Ribero watched them hurry out of the room, eyes fixed on them like furious laser beams. "That was my favourite jacket," he muttered, still scowling. "What is he doing now, eh? Going to put sick on the rest of my clothes?"

"Let's hope not," Miss Wellbeloved said, as she hauled him towards the kitchen. "Come on, let's rustle up some lunch. It might wake us all up."

"So people can be sick again, right?"

Kester chuckled, then hastily straightened his face at the sight of the indignant glare from his father. "Some food would be lovely," he added, hoping to take Ribero's mind off the matter. "Do you have any of that nice chimichurri sauce?"

His father brightened visibly. "Yes, of course. My cupboards are never without it, Kester. I will make you a nice sandwich with the leftover steak and some sauce. You will love it."

Miss Wellbeloved winked and then disappeared into the kitchen.

After a sizeable lunch of yesterday's leftovers, the team set about packing their belongings and getting ready to return to their homes. Fortunately, Mike had only managed to mislay one shoe, which turned up outside the patio doors for some reason, but other than that, the afternoon was relatively incident free.

"Hey, we're going to have to plan New Year's Eve, aren't we?" Mike suggested cheerfully, as he opened the front door, backpack slung over his shoulder. "What do you say, Kester? Big booze-up in town?"

Kester shrank back instinctively. "I've never been out for New Year's Eve," he replied, with a nervous tweak of his collar. "I'm not sure I'd be very good at it."

"Good at what?" Mike said with disbelief. "Drinking beer and talking to attractive ladies?"

Kester cringed. Talking to any ladies, whether they were attractive or not, was the last thing he felt like doing.

"Come on, it'll be good fun," Mike pressed on. He turned to Serena. "You'd be up for it, wouldn't you?"

To Kester's surprise, Serena shrugged. "Maybe," she drawled, picking up her neat leather suitcase. "It depends. If it involves you embarrassing me all night, then absolutely not."

Mike grinned leerily. "As if I would? We could invite Luke too, see if he fancies joining us."

Kester smiled at the prospect of meeting up with Luke again, who was always unfailingly cheerful, despite having to work for Larry Higgins, Ribero's sworn enemy and one of the most pompous people he'd ever met. "We should invite Dimitri too," he added, noting with amusement that Mike looked rather less enthusiastic about the prospect of the serious Russian accompanying them.

"The Royal Albert Memorial Museum has got an event on," Serena suggested, leaning against the doorframe. "Some Day of the Dead–themed party, I think."

"You lot will fit right in, then," Pamela declared, as she

squeezed past them. "Now, if you'll excuse me, I've got to go and rescue Hemingway from the next-door neighbours."

You mean, rescue the neighbours from Hemingway, Kester thought, thinking of the oversized dog's tendency to cover unsuspecting visitors with hair and drool. "I'd quite fancy going to the museum," he said brightly. He hadn't had a chance to visit yet, given how busy they'd been over the last four months, but any building dedicated to learning, history, and all things ancient suited him to a tee.

Mike wrapped his arms over Kester's and Serena's shoulders, pulling them in for a tight, rather painful bear hug. "I'll see if I can get tickets," he concluded, before rapping the side of his nose in a knowing way. "I've got *connections* who should be able to help us."

Serena rolled her eyes, pulling away from him. "Yes, because everyone is so desperate to go to a museum for New Year's Eve," she said, then dipped a hand in Mike's trouser pocket, pulling out the keys to the van. "Right, shall we get going?"

"Oi, I'm driving!" Mike exclaimed.

Serena snorted. "No, you're not. You smell like a stale brewery. The police could probably pick up the alcohol fumes a mile off, and the last thing we need is for you to lose your licence. Come on, Kester, let's get going."

Kester grinned, grabbed his overnight bag, then turned to his father and Miss Wellbeloved. "Thank you for a lovely Christmas," he said, feeling suddenly rather emotional. "It's been surprisingly nice."

"Surprisingly?" Ribero repeated, narrowing his eyes. "I will take that as a compliment. Come here." Without warning, he tugged Kester into a fierce embrace and planted a tickly kiss on each cheek. "Remember, work tomorrow. Nice and early, no oversleeping like a lazy teenager, okay?"

Kester groaned. "Okay. See you in the office."

Mike, clearly buoyed by the thought of going out on New Year's Eve, sauntered over to the van whilst whistling cheerfully; he didn't even complain when Serena shoved him unceremoniously into the backseat.

Grinding into reverse, she swivelled around and eyed them both severely. "Don't even think about being sick whilst I'm driving, okay? If anyone feels queasy, give me plenty of notice."

"Yes, dearest," Mike replied dutifully. Serena pursed her lips together tightly, then swung the van around with alarming speed, causing Mike to lurch painfully against the door.

"Oops. Hope that didn't hurt you."

Mike grunted. "You're a mean old cow, you know that, right?"

Kester stared out the window, letting the noise of their bickering wash over him. Gradually the bumpy driveway gave way to smoother roads, and finally, they emerged from the snow-frosted pine trees and out into the open. The whole of Exeter lay beneath them, nestled in the rolling landscape as though trying to conceal itself from prying eyes. Even from here, he could make out the stocky twin towers of the ancient cathedral and the vague twinkle of the river.

And somewhere over the other side of town, he thought, *there's my cold little house. And I bet Pineapple's already returned from visiting his parents, which just makes life that bit worse.* His housemate was infuriating at the best of times and likely to be even more hyperactive than usual after the Christmas festivities.

Finally, the van bounced painfully up the hill and into his road. Serena pulled up outside, twisting around to give him an imperious nod. Mike had nodded off and was emitting muffled snores, like a bear with a head cold.

"Out you get, then," Serena said, with a vague smile. "See you tomorrow morning."

Suddenly, Kester sat bolt upright in his seat. "Green!"

"Excuse me?"

He threw a finger into the air, where it remained, quivering like the tail of a bloodhound. "Green, last night."

Serena frowned. "What the hell are you talking about?"

Kester's eyes widened. Slowly, he lowered his finger. "I saw a flash of green. Before I went to bed, before I found the note."

"Kester, you're going to have to be more explicit than that. I haven't got a clue what you're waffling on about."

He leant forward impatiently, grasping the headrest. "I saw a bright flash of green, in the woods outside the house. I was looking out the window, and—"

"Yes, I get the idea. But what has that got to do with anything?"

Kester sighed. "Fylgia."

Serena looked baffled, then suddenly gasped. "You mean because she's green, right? Why didn't you tell us this sooner? Didn't you think a daemon sighting was something worth mentioning?"

Mike grunted in his sleep, muttered something, then curled into a tight ball against the door, oblivious to the excitement around him.

Kester shrugged. "I totally forgot about it, to be honest. At the time, I thought I'd just imagined it, as I'd had a few too many glasses of wine."

"There's still a chance it was just your imagination," Serena said firmly. "Just because you saw a quick flash of green doesn't prove anything. However," she added, "it is interesting. Perhaps Hrschni's sending Fylgia to do his dirty work?"

"Who knows?" Kester opened the door, letting in a sharp blast of snow-tinged air. "But it's worth keeping in mind, so we know exactly who we're dealing with." He paused, then pulled the door shut again. "Serena, do you mind me asking you something?"

Her eyes narrowed. "Depends what it is."

"Why do you hate spirits so much? I know what happened to your mother, but why do you loathe all of them without exception?"

Serena took a deep breath, rubbing her nose as she pondered the question. "Hate is too strong a word," she said finally. "You make it sound like I want to eliminate them all."

"And don't you?"

She paused, then shook her head. "No. That's not what I want. I'm sure many spirits are perfectly okay, once you get to know them. I just don't see why we need to have them here, with us. They've got their own world. Why can't they stay there?"

Kester grimaced. "Don't take this the wrong way, but what you're saying sounds a bit like racism. Or spiritism, or whatever you call it."

She waved his comment away dismissively. "Oh, I've been called a spiritist on several occasions. It's not true at all. I just think they take liberties. They come into our world and abuse our hospitality—"

"Now you're really sounding like a racist."

Serena cleared her throat defensively. "Kester, if you're just going to attack my views, then you may as well just get out the van now. I'm not in the mood, and I don't have to justify my feelings to you."

Kester held his hands up in apology. "Okay, okay, calm down. I was only asking."

"Well, don't."

He climbed out, then pulled the van door shut behind him. The wind immediately hit him, an icy blast that made his eyes water. He turned to wave goodbye, but the van had already screeched off down the road, presumably with a grumpy-looking Serena hunched furiously over the steering wheel. He waited, watching as it steamed out of sight, issuing the occasional burst of smoke as the gears were changed. *How it passes its MOT, I've no idea,* he concluded, then fumbled in his pocket for his house keys.

The first thing he noticed, stepping into his house, was how cold it was; not much warmer than outside, in fact. However, that wasn't unusual. Since the boiler started to malfunction a few months ago, the house was mostly heat-free, apart from the occasional half-hearted blast from the radiators. What was more unusual was the rectangular parcel sitting on the hallway table, addressed to him. It was wrapped up with aged-looking paper, which immediately roused his suspicions.

This had better not be something else from the Thelemites, he thought, stroking the surface. *I've had enough horrible surprises for one lifetime, thank you very much.* To his relief, the label was printed, which was a definite improvement on the unnaturally perfect calligraphy on the two letters and suggested that it didn't contain anything sinister.

"Pineapple?" he called. The word echoed up the empty stairwell. "Pineapple, are you in?"

A clutter, followed by a cough, answered the matter for him. Sure enough, a few minutes later, Pineapple's topknotted head peered over the bannister. He blinked blearily, then saluted Kester with a strange, complex series of hand movements.

"Yo, my bro! You're back in the hood, innit! That's sterling news, solid gold."

"Er, right," Kester concluded. "Pineapple, did you accept the delivery of this parcel?"

Pineapple nodded, then waltzed down the stairs, loose-limbed as a jellyfish and about as coordinated. "Right on, my homeboy," he declared, tapping Kester's shoulder. "It came on Christmas Eve. Some sweet present from your lady friend, yeah?"

"I doubt it," Kester retorted, then remembered his manners. "Did you have a nice Christmas?"

Pineapple slipped past him, neon pink sweater hanging loosely around his thin frame. "Nah, I don't celebrate Christmas, do I? I mean, nuff respect to Jesus Christ and his brethren, but my beliefs are on a more spiritual plain, you catch my feel?"

"Not in the slightest." Kester scratched his head. "Didn't you go to your parents for Christmas?"

"If by parents, you mean the right-on dudes that brought me into this world—"

"—yes, that's exactly who I meant—"

"Then yep, that's where I went." Pineapple clicked his fingers, winked, then rolled into the kitchen. "Man, I need some nourishment. You got any cereal I can borrow, my brother?"

Kester rolled his eyes, then followed Pineapple into the kitchen. "I'm not your brother, Pineapple. And you can't *borrow* cereal. Once it's passed through your digestive system, there's no way I'm having it back, thank you very much."

Pineapple stared blankly, then let out a raucous hyena-pitched cackle, which Kester took to be a laugh. "Yeah, right on, Kester, right on!" Without waiting for any further response, he rummaged in the cupboards, then drew forth a box of cornflakes, waving it in triumph.

Kester sighed. "When is Daisy back?"

"Ah, she's gone on a journey of the mind and spirit, my friend. Gone to set her soul free." Pineapple nodded, then retreated behind the door of the fridge.

"What's that supposed to mean?"

"She's gone on holiday. With a *man*."

Blimey, Kester thought, surprised and slightly envious. *The bloke's standards must be low if he's willing to put up with her. Why is it that everyone seems to have better luck in love than me?*

After watching Pineapple neck half a pint of milk from the carton before pouring the rest over his enormous bowl of cereal, Kester sighed and retreated to his bedroom, parcel tucked under one arm.

Who the hell is it from? he wondered, throwing it down on his bed. He couldn't think of anyone who would send him a present. *Larry Higgins perhaps?* he thought, then started to laugh. The idea of Higgins even *thinking* of buying Kester a gift was ridiculous. Pressing a finger against the edges, he suspected it was some sort of book. It was certainly the right shape.

Sure enough, as he tore into the paper, he saw a smart, leather-bound cover. "*A Historie of Spirits*, translated by Hamish Bramberry," he read aloud, and rubbed his palm over the embossed surface. "I wonder why anyone would send me this?" Opening it up, he saw a neatly printed note, wedged into the spine.

Dear Kester,

As you know, you are due to commence your studies in a few weeks. I suspect you may find this book useful, and as such, I would like you to read it thoroughly. If necessary, read it several times, until you are familiar with the contents. I hope you are prepared.

Yours sincerely,

Dr. Ark'han Barqa-Abu

Kester scratched his head. "That's a bit peculiar," he muttered to no one in particular. "Perhaps this is a new book on the reading list." Thankfully, it wasn't too huge, otherwise Kester suspected he might have started weeping. He had enough to read as it was.

He idly flicked the book open, reading the first page he came across.

> *The daemon Arsaces ruled honourably for many years. The Parni people grew prosperous under his rule, though none suspected that he was daemonic in nature. Likewise, no one knew that another spirit worked at his side.*
>
> *The great Djinn, one of the most powerful of its kind, had sacrificed much to see the daemon ascend to the throne. Yet, in time, the Djinn began to question its judgement. Although Arsaces was a powerful ruler, his ruthlessness began to grow. The people started to grow fearful. The Djinn feared what might follow in the future.*

"Blimey," Kester whispered, and shut the book with a snap. He placed it on his bedside table. "That'll be some pleasant light reading for the evening, then." Personally, he failed to see how a detailed glimpse into the ancient history of spirits would help him understand how they were today, but he respected Dr. Barqa-Abu's judgement; plus, he was terrified of what she might do if he failed to do as she asked.

He glanced at his phone and sighed at the empty screen. Only a few weeks ago, his phone had been regularly beeping away, full of messages from Anya. Now, the silence was almost unbearable. He wondered what she was doing, then forced himself to stop.

No, he thought, patting the *Historie of Spirits,* reassured by its sturdy front cover. *That's behind me now. No more women. Just work. And trying to stop the Thelemites from taking over the world, of course.*

Chapter 3: The Tulpa

The following morning, Kester awoke to find his windowpanes laced with snow. An hour later, emerging reluctantly from his front door, he discovered that the pavements were coated, making the street look as though it had been wrapped up in a giant marshmallow. Sinking a foot into the virgin snow, he admired the perfect dent his shoe had made, then strode off to work.

Regrettably, the novelty of squelching through the snow soon wore off, and by the time he'd reached the office, with soaking trouser legs and fingertips so cold they'd turned purple, he was positively sick of the stuff.

"It's bloody freezing out there," he declared, stomping off the last mushy remnants from his shoes. Slamming the door behind him, he caught sight of his father, who was rather incongruously standing in the middle of the office, arm outstretched, beaming from ear to ear.

"Surprise! Look what I have got for you."

Kester's gaze followed the length of his father's arm until it reached the item at the end of it, which happened to be a new desk. Small, but certainly serviceable, it was a massive improvement on the fold-up camping table which usually collapsed at least once a day. "Wow!" he squeaked. "A proper desk at last!"

Ribero's face clouded. "I know it has taken us a bit of time, but we wanted to make sure you were sticking around and not doing the swan-off back to Cambridge, yes?"

Kester grinned, then started to take off his jacket. "Thanks. It's great."

Miss Wellbeloved stood up. "No point taking your jacket off, Kester. We've got a job this morning. Only a small one, down in Topsham."

"Oh, really?" Kester felt deflated. He had no desire to go out and deal with a spirit at this time of the morning. "What sort of job?"

Serena emerged from behind her computer screen. "A really quick, easy one," she stated. "A tulpa. Though we've no idea who brought it over here, that's something that—"

"Hang on a minute, I'll have to stop you there," Kester interrupted. "What the heck is a tulpa?"

Serena tutted, gathering her scarf and wrapping it around her neck. "A tulpa is a minor spirit who can only enter this realm if specifically called," she explained, sounding remarkably as though she'd learnt the definition in a textbook. "In the past, humans have summoned tulpas deliberately to do their bidding."

"Like golems," Mike added cheerfully, as he packed his equipment into the rucksack. "Have you heard of them?"

Kester pondered for a moment. "They're the creatures that are made out of mud and then brought to life, aren't they?"

"Sort of," Miss Wellbeloved confirmed. "In the past, humans have created figures out of clay, then invited a tulpa to inhabit it. They called those tulpas golems."

Pamela breezed over, leaving a waft of highly pungent floral perfume in her wake. "This one is a familiar, though," she confirmed, as she reached for her coat. "So it's a bit different."

"What do you mean, it's familiar?" Kester asked.

"*A* familiar, not familiar!" Serena snapped. "God, have you actually read any of the texts you were given for your course?"

Kester glared. "Yes, I have. And I know what you mean now. You're talking about a witch's familiar. I remember them." He suddenly reviewed what he'd just said and blanched. "Hang on, is there a witch involved?"

Serena slapped her forehead. "Dear lord, Kester! No, there is no sodding witch! Just one very little, very inoffensive familiar in the shape of a black dog. It'll be a doddle to get rid of."

"Famous last words," Mike added, with a wink at Kester. "I have to say, I'm looking forward to this. It's a good chance to practice using my new image capturer."

"I thought it didn't work when you tested it out?" Kester asked, obediently following as Miss Wellbeloved led the way out of the office.

"I figured out what I did wrong last time," Mike clarified, seizing the van keys from the nearest desk and jangling them enthusiastically. "Wrong type of digital lead."

"Well, if you buy it off some dodgy bloke on the internet . . ." Serena said.

"I'm working on a tight budget, aren't I?"

They made their way through the dark landing to the back stairs, then out into the car park, where the van sat, already covered in a blanket of snow. In fact, the flakes were falling even harder now, muffling the air and making it seem as though they were standing in a strange, swirling tunnel.

"Your English weather," Dr. Ribero snarled, rapping the side of the van as though it was personally responsible. "You would not get such weather conditions where I come from. It is nasty, cold stuff, don't you agree?"

Kester nodded. *Perhaps that's why I can't stand it,* he thought, as he clambered into the back, *because I've got sunny Argentinian blood in my veins.*

"Are you going to be all right driving?" Pamela asked, leaning over the front seat.

Mike snorted. "Ha. A bit of snow won't stop me. I could navigate this vehicle through a hurricane and it would come out perfectly the other side."

"That's funny, given that you struggle with driving along a normal road without it breaking down," Serena snipped.

Mike delivered an obscene hand gesture in her direction, which she chose to ignore.

"Is the heating working?" Kester asked, already knowing the answer. His trousers were soaked to the knees. Even worse, the snow had somehow seeped right into his shoes, making his toes feel as though someone were torturing them with ice cubes.

"It's only a short drive," Miss Wellbeloved said, giving him a comforting pat.

"Where is it in Topsham?"

"In a pub, down by the estuary," Pamela said, as she settled back down in her seat. Mike whisked the van around and promptly skidded, nearly sending them into the entrance gate. Kester hoped it wasn't a sign of things to come.

Serena rubbed her hands together, then blew on her fingers, her breath coming out in a series of misty clouds. "The familiar hasn't been there long, only a couple of days, apparently. The pub owner has had an absolute meltdown about it."

"I really don't see why," said Miss Wellbeloved testily. "This familiar has been making itself very useful, by all accounts."

"What do you mean?" Kester asked.

"It's taken on a canine form. Bless it, all it's been doing is running around the pub, taking on guard-dog duties."

"It also nipped a customer, let us not forget that," Ribero reminded them from the front seat.

"And then vanished into thin air," Mike added with a chortle. "Fortunately, the customer was blind drunk and thought he'd imagined the whole thing."

"Just a minute," said Kester, trying to figure it out in his head. "So this tulpa or familiar, it's just been loping around the pub like a real dog?"

"Like a helpful dog," Miss Wellbeloved corrected. "Tulpas are brought over from the spirit realm to assist. They're absolutely lovely creatures."

"Are they?" Kester asked incredulously, as he sneaked a look at Serena, who shrugged in a noncommittal manner.

"The big question," Ribero declared, as he spun around in his seat. "Is who summoned it? We do not know the answer, and that is worrying. Not many people can call a tulpa into the world. I am hoping, when we get there, that I can detect some form of intention, which might give us some clues."

They were all momentarily distracted by a sudden acceleration as the van lost its grip and went skidding down a hill, hurtling through the snow at an alarming rate. Mike gripped the wheel and jiggled the brakes at the bottom, finally grinding to a halt. He looked alarmingly pale.

"So much for driving through hurricanes, eh Mike?"

"Shut your face, Serena. It's not my fault that the roads are bloody—"

"Anyway," Miss Wellbeloved interrupted deliberately, seemingly unfazed by the incident. "Now we know we're not about to drive into the river, let's continue. Julio is right. The mystery is who brought the tulpa here in the first place. As far as I'm aware, nobody knows the complex rituals involved to call up a familiar anymore."

"Unless another spirit did it?" Serena suggested.

"Maybe," Miss Wellbeloved concluded. "These are strange times we live in, and anything is possible. Let's see what we discover when we get there."

They arrived at the pub over half an hour later, after a series of perilous skids and much swearing from Mike. Fortunately, the snow had finally stopped, leaving the sky a dirty white, like a wrung-out dishcloth. Indeed, the whole landscape, including the surrounding buildings and estuary, looked as though it had been drained of all colour. Kester took a moment to take it all in, breathing in the crisp air, before realising that his trouser legs were getting wet once again, thanks to the snow drifts around his ankles.

"Shall we?" Ribero declared grandly, pointing at the entrance. "This should not take long." He hung back whilst the others went past him, waiting for Kester.

"My boy," he said in a low voice, as he checked that the others weren't listening. "I would like you to try to open the spirit door, okay?"

Kester groaned, shoving his hands even more deeply into his pockets. "Dad, you know I have very little control over it. I wish I did, but I don't."

"Just give it a go, right? Remember what you did last time, when you got rid of the Scottish fetch."

"We were being chased by a furious bull then. It was a little bit different."

Ribero's nose wrinkled. "So, it will be easier this time, maybe?" He swallowed suddenly, then winced. Kester noticed that his hands were shaking.

"Are you okay?"

"Ah, I am fine. It is the Parkinson's, nothing more." Ribero attempted a smile, then marched through the entrance. Kester wasn't convinced but didn't pursue it any further. He knew his father didn't like talking about his condition.

Right, here goes, he thought, mentally preparing himself for the spirit. *At least this one looks like a dog and not like a terrifying creature from another dimension. That's a good start.*

It was dingy inside, and the darkness was even more pronounced, thanks to the nicotine-stained ceiling and varnished tables, not to mention the dark wooden panelling on the walls. A clattering noise behind the bar drew their attention. Two seconds later, a thin head popped up, followed by an equally lean body, clutching a tea towel and a pint glass as though his life depended on it. He looked at them nervously, eyes flitting from person to person.

"Mr. Nancarrow?" Miss Wellbeloved guessed as she stepped forward, hand extended. The man stared at it for a few moments, then grasped it quickly.

"Are you the agency?" he whispered in a high-pitched, quavering voice. "I do hope you are. These last few days have been quite unbearable."

"Why is that?" asked Miss Wellbeloved, in a bristly tone. "Presumably the spirit has been no problem, has he?"

The man shook his head, then nodded, then promptly shook it again. "I haven't slept a wink," he said finally, as he placed the glass on the bar. "I keep hearing it padding around down here, growling every so often. It's the most menacing sound I've ever heard."

You clearly haven't encountered many other spirits then, Kester thought wryly. *Have a go with a screaming banshee, a murderous fetch, or a plotting daemon, that should change your mind.*

"May we ask you a few questions before we start?" asked Pamela. Mr. Nancarrow nodded, though his expression suggested he'd rather do anything but discuss it.

Serena stepped forward. "These spirits are called into existence by someone. Any idea who might have done it?"

He shook his head. "I don't know anyone who hates me enough to inflict this on me."

Miss Wellbeloved sighed, then glanced at the others. "Familiars used to be welcomed by humans in the past," she clarified. "It wouldn't have been sent by anyone who disliked you, trust me."

"Why would anyone welcome a thing like that?" the man wailed, fixing a beseeching gaze on each of them in turn. "One minute it's small; the next, big as a pony! It keeps popping out at me, even when I'm on the toilet! It's given me horrible tummy problems, I can tell you. I'm too frightened to go most of the time."

Kester stifled a laugh. "That must be unpleasant," he said, with as much sympathy as he could muster.

"However," Miss Wellbeloved continued, with a warning stare in Kester's direction. "Be assured, this spirit means you no harm. He just wants to help you. He'd probably make an excellent guard dog, you know."

"It doesn't feel like it," Mr. Nancarrow stated urgently. "It was looming over me in my bedroom last night. I nearly wet myself with fright."

"So, the bladder is working fine, even if the bowels are not, right?" Ribero said with a wry smirk. Miss Wellbeloved glowered at him.

"Can you tell us about the time it first arrived?" Serena asked, nimbly perching on the nearest barstool.

The man frowned. "We first noticed it at closing time a few days ago. It bounded into the bar, big as a horse, ran around for a bit with its tongue hanging out, then tore off back to the kitchen."

"Did you follow it?"

"Of course I did!" Mr. Nancarrow said indignantly. "I thought it was a real dog, didn't I? It certainly looked like one, before it disappeared before my very eyes."

Serena stroked her chin thoughtfully. "Who else was here? Did you hear anyone chanting strange words, for example?"

He shook his head.

"What about peculiar lights? Did you see anything like that?"

Again, the barman shook his head, then paused. "I did see an odd-looking light the next day," he said slowly. "But to be honest, I thought it was because I was tired. I didn't get a wink of sleep, as you might imagine."

Serena looked excited and gave Kester a meaningful glance. "What sort of light? Was it a particular colour?"

I see what she's getting at, Kester suddenly realised. *She's trying to find out if Hrschni or Fylgia are behind this. But why would they bother? What's the connection?*

"It all happened very fast, as I was carrying the carton of eggs for the day's breakfasts," Mr. Nancarrow said thoughtfully, hoisting his thinning fringe away from his eyes. "There was a bright flash of red light by the oven, then it vanished. I thought I was getting a migraine or something."

Serena gave the others a triumphant look and mouthed one word. *Hrschni.* Kester sighed. It was certainly a strange coincidence, but it still didn't add up. Why would the Grand Master of the Thelemites summon a pleasant spirit like a familiar?

"Why don't you keep him?" Mike offered, as he fished out a metal contraption. He flicked the switch on the side, and it omitted a soothing hum in response. "Familiars are useful, you know. You'd never need to worry about getting burgled again."

Mr. Nancarrow shook his head. "No. I want it gone. Can you make that happen?"

Ribero took the man by the arm and led him to the nearest barstool. "I tell you what," he suggested kindly. "Why don't you go upstairs, and we will take it from here? It will not take long, not with a minor spirit like this."

Mr. Nancarrow smiled weakly, then pointed at the corridor that led out to the back of the pub. "How do I know that *thing* won't be waiting for me upstairs? Can one of you come with me?"

"No, we're all needed here," Serena snapped. "Just scream if you need us."

They waited until the thin man had trotted fretfully out of sight, then sighed collectively.

"Dear me, it's so much easier when they're a bit more open-minded about spirits, isn't it?" Pamela said as she started to pace around the tables.

"We mustn't forget that people are frightened by what they don't understand," Miss Wellbeloved reminded her, as they watched Mike pour the rest of his equipment onto the bar.

Kester twiddled his thumbs fretfully. Even though the familiar was meant to be a nice spirit, he didn't fancy being caught anywhere on his own with it. Especially if it really was the size of a small horse. "What do you want me to do?" he asked hesitantly, hoping he'd be given an easy task.

"Go exploring," his father ordered. Kester noticed that his hands were shaking quite badly now, regardless of how tightly he pressed them against his stomach.

"Can I take someone with me?"

"I'll come with you, love," Pamela said kindly, and laced an arm through the crook of his elbow. "I'll be able to detect a familiar a mile off. I'm already picking up strong energies."

Mike brandished his equipment in the air like a gunslinger saluting a victory. "I'm going to get to work with my image capturer. Who knows what I might catch on camera, eh?"

"Probably nothing at all," Serena said scathingly. "Delivering zero results is something of a speciality of yours, isn't it?"

"Serena, you come with me," Miss Wellbeloved said anxiously, sensing yet another argument looming on the horizon. "Mike, you go with Julio."

"I am looking for spirit intention," Ribero said, with a click of the finger in Kester's direction. "That is what I do. You know that, right?"

"You have mentioned it before," Kester replied. His father always seemed very prickly about his talents and went to great lengths to ensure everyone knew exactly what they were. Reluctantly, Kester followed Pamela through to the kitchen. His nerves weren't helped by Pamela calling out canine endearments every few seconds.

The small kitchen was scrupulously clean. Stainless steel glistened in the harsh fluorescent light, and the floors, though pocked with age, were buffed to a high shine. It was a sharp contrast to the ancient bar area, which seemed to have been extracted directly from the Tudor times. They patrolled the room, both attuned to its unnatural quietness. Kester didn't like it one bit, but then, that wasn't unusual. Even the mere mention of a spirit tended to freak him out, let alone being trapped in a building with one.

After a few minutes, Pamela froze. Then she held a hand up to stop Kester in his tracks. "I think puppy wants to play," she said softly. Kester groaned and instinctively looked over his shoulder. *Oh god, please no,* he thought, and resisted the urge to squeeze his eyes shut.

Before he had a chance to scream, an enormous black mass of *something* leapt at them both, freezing the air in its wake. Kester stumbled blindly backwards and staggered against the dustbin, knocking it against the wall with a metallic clang. Before he could recover, the *thing* bounded over again, a mass of thick limbs, burning eyes, and dense, writhing fur. Then, as swiftly as it had appeared, it vanished again with an audible pop.

"Help!" Kester bellowed instinctively, grasping at Pamela for dear life. "I didn't like that at all!"

Pamela laughed, then gently prised his fingers from her arm. "Don't be alarmed," she said. "He's just being friendly. Let me get Miss Wellbeloved."

A few seconds later, Miss Wellbeloved scurried in, closely followed by the others. "Have you spotted it?"

Pamela nodded. "Oh yes, and it's still here, watching us. It wants to play."

Mike chuckled. "I should have brought a ball or something to throw."

As though responding to Mike's comment, the air suddenly shimmered. With another imploding pop, the familiar appeared again; this time racing along the work surfaces, trailing a faint black mist as it went. It hurtled towards them with the force of a steam train, and Kester instinctively ducked, diving behind Pamela's reassuringly solid back.

"Kester, now is time to do the door thing, yes?" Ribero called out over the phantasmal padding of the familiar's paws, which sounded like a series of muffled lead weights pounding over the steel units.

Kester peered over Pamela's shoulder, saw the familiar loping alarmingly in their direction, then cowered back down. "Nope, I don't think it is, actually!"

"Kester, you are being a big coward! Stand up and be a man this instant, please!"

Serena snickered. "Shall I get the water bottle?"

Ribero waved her aside, then dodged nimbly as the familiar bounced past him and sailed into the dark corridor beyond. "No, this is Kester's chance. I want to see him open the door. I know he can do it." He pointed at his son, firm as a master with a particularly naughty pet. "Go out there on your own and get on with it, okay?"

"No, not okay! Why on my own?"

"Because then you will not get stage fright!"

Miss Wellbeloved coughed. "Perhaps he's right, Kester. It can't hurt to have a go. The sooner you master the skill, the better."

Kester shrank back behind Pamela's shoulder, summoning up the most vehement head shake he could muster. "I don't want to be alone with that *thing,* thanks very much."

Ribero tutted and folded his arms. "This is a little tulpa, right? A friendly familiar. Not some big scary spirit. Get in there and stop doing the pillock thing."

"I'm not doing the pillock thing, I'm merely protesting about the fact that—"

Mike ambled over, grasped Kester's arm with a friendly but firm grip, and escorted him to the corridor. "Come on, mate. Once you've sent the familiar back, we can start thinking about lunch. I don't know about you, but I'm starving."

Serena rolled her eyes. "It's only ten o'clock, Mike."

Kester removed his arm and glared at them all. "Fine," he agreed slowly. "I'll have a go. Not that it'll do any good. If that familiar kills me, it's all your fault."

"It won't kill you, dearie," Pamela said with a laugh. "It might knock you over if it's excited enough, but you won't experience any lasting damage."

You rotten sods, Kester thought mutinously, as he marched out towards the bar. Even now, he could hear the eerie, slobbering noises of the familiar as it barged its way around the tables. It sounded uncannily like a dog but for the whistling echo of each pant, not to mention the deadened thump of misty paws against the floorboards.

"Hello doggy?" Kester said uncertainly, as he poked his head around the door. For a glorious moment he thought the familiar had vanished, until a moment later, when it leapt out from underneath a table and raced cheerfully towards him. Kester resisted the urge to either yelp or run away, and instead, focused on the air in front of him.

Come on, where is a spirit door when you need one? he thought, struggling to tune the noise of the phantom dog out. *This is getting ridiculous. Just appear for me, just this once? Please?*

But as he'd anticipated, nothing happened. The room remained resolutely spirit door free, and the familiar was still rollicking around the room with all the energy of a small cyclone.

Kester's shoulders slumped. It was no use. *Why can't I do this, Mum?* he thought. *I bet you didn't have this embarrassing problem. I'm such a failure.*

No, you're not. Even though he recognised the other voice in his head as his own, it seemed to come from another place, deeper within him. It reminded him painfully of her.

What would she have done now? Kester wondered, as he dived behind the bar to avoid the familiar's relentless whirl around the room. *How would she have got the door to open?* He tried to imagine her standing beside him. *She wouldn't have faltered or doubted herself,* he thought. *She would have just got the job done with no messing around.*

Suddenly, quite without him noticing it, the air began to shimmer. Kester's eyes widened, then he started to laugh. *I don't believe it,* he thought, feeling almost delirious with triumph and relief. *It's opening. What did I do differently this time?*

Perhaps you just believed you could do it, the deeper voice reminded him. He nodded, aware that he was conversing silently with himself, but not caring one bit. *I'm doing it!* he thought triumphantly. *I'm making it happen again!*

He watched as the air started to tear, shining with a strange wetness, like a gaping wound. The door opened a little wider, revealing a seething mass of darkness beyond. Kester concentrated hard, willing it to open even wider. The familiar ceased its mad bolting and froze, head cocked to one side, red eyes fixed on the door with interest. Then, as though pulled by a magnet, it paced towards it, growing smaller in size with every step, before finally slipping through without a sound.

Kester sighed with pleasure, and at once, the door sealed itself. An outburst of wild applause startled him from his trance.

"I knew you could do it!" Ribero's strident tones rung from the narrow corridor walls, and a moment later, his hand connected with Kester's back in a mighty swipe of pride. Kester blushed and took a deep, shuddering breath.

"I'm amazed," he muttered, as the others ushered him down on to the nearest barstool. "It was much easier that time. I just thought of Mum, and what she would have done."

Pamela leant against the bar. "Perhaps that's the key," she suggested, rubbing her chin. "Maybe she's the magic ingredient that helps you to achieve it."

Ribero grinned. "This is a good day," he declared. "And to celebrate, I am taking you out for a meal this lunchtime."

"Excellent!" Mike declared, with an appreciative pat of his stomach. "I could do with a big feed up, I'm starving."

"Not you," Ribero barked. "Just Kester. I am not made of money. You will go back and process the images you captured. I want to see what you found."

"If you found anything at all," Serena added with a smirk towards Mike, who looked decidedly disappointed.

After relaying the good news to Mr. Nancarrow, who they'd found cowering upstairs beneath his duvet, they returned to the van and headed back into the city. Kester found it hard to stop smiling. In the last few weeks, he'd been living under a cloud of gloom, devastated by Anya's betrayal and terrified that Hrschni would come for him again. Now, he felt like he had something to hope for again—that he actually might not be as useless as suspected.

His father chose the location for lunch, and to Kester's surprise he selected a pub overlooking the cathedral rather than the little Cuban cantina down the road, which he claimed was as close to Argentinian cooking as he could get.

They settled themselves in the window seat. Relaxing against the chair, Kester took in the view of the huge cathedral as his father went to order, admiring the squat solidity of the grey granite towers and crumbling stonework. A few people ventured across the green, braving the cold, their faces obscured by thick woollen scarves. The pub, by contrast, was gloriously warm, and the air hummed with the low buzz of conversation and laughter.

Ribero returned, then plunked a wine glass in front of Kester, who stared at it in surprise.

"Bit early in the day for that, isn't it?"

"It is never too early if you're celebrating," Ribero declared, and clinked their glasses together before Kester could protest. "And we have a reason to celebrate, eh? You did good today, my boy. Very good indeed. Now you are officially a member of our agency, you see?"

Kester blinked. "What, you mean I wasn't before?"

"Ah, you know what I mean." Ribero winked, then gestured outside. "This is an excellent view."

"It is," Kester agreed.

"You know this pub has an interesting history?"

Kester shook his head. "I could tell it was old, but I don't know anything else about it."

Ribero nodded secretively, then pointed at a small door by the bar. "Go down there," he whispered, "and you will find a skeleton. Left over from the plague."

Kester raised his eyebrows. "A real skeleton? That's sinister."

"Pah, it is not," Ribero said indignantly. "Boy, you just came face to face with a familiar, how can you say a little dusty skeleton is scary?"

Kester laughed. He supposed his father did have a point. "So," he continued eventually, as he twirled his glass between his fingers. "Here's to me finally getting the hang of being a spirit door opener."

"Yes," Ribero agreed, smiling wistfully. "I remember Gretchen doing it for the first time, you know."

Kester sat up straighter. "What happened?" he asked. He knew very little about his mother as a young woman and never liked to ask, given that she'd had an affair with Ribero when he had been engaged to Miss Wellbeloved.

Ribero eyes softened at the memory. "It was at the SSFE. We had studied it in class, you see, and your mama, well, afterwards, she told me that she thought she could open spirit doors." He chuckled. "I didn't believe her. Not at first. No one could open spirit doors, or at least, no one we knew. It was a rare gift."

"What happened next?"

Ribero slapped his thigh and laughed loudly. "She went and opened one! A few weeks after, when we found a little spirit outside the college, down a little dark alleyway. The air opened up and the spirit passed through, as though it was the easiest thing in the world. Gretchen, she was wonderful, yes?"

Kester smiled. "She really was. I still miss her so much." He cleared his throat and took another gulp of wine, feeling it cruise through him in a pleasant, relaxing wave. "Did everyone get very excited that she could do it? Open spirit doors, I mean?"

Ribero shook his head. "She told no one. Not at first. Jennifer knew, of course. They were best friends back then." Kester noted that his father had the good grace to look ashamed.

"So, you kept it a secret?"

"Yes." Ribero nodded. "We had all planned to work for Jennifer's father's agency, and we knew that with a spirit door opener we would be the best agency in the country. We wanted to keep it a surprise, to get us ahead of the competition."

Kester sighed heavily. "I suppose I can understand that." He chewed on a fingernail, thinking hard. "Did she manage to master it right away?" *Was she better at it than I was?* he added silently, suspecting that she probably had been.

"She practiced whenever she could," Ribero stated. "And she got good very quickly. She could do it in a few seconds, just like that." He clicked his fingers to emphasise the point.

"Wow." Kester could imagine his mother deftly unzipping the air, forcing the spirit through the opening, then closing it tightly behind. She had always been such an efficient, practical person.

He presumed she must have adopted the same no-nonsense approach when dealing with spirits.

"But hey," said Ribero, interrupting his thoughts. "We are not here to talk about your mother's achievements. We are here to talk about you, Kester! This is a great day, yes? Great news for the agency!"

Kester grinned. "I suppose so," he said. "It certainly felt good to be able to do it. Can I ask one more question though?"

Ribero tilted his head to one side. "You with the questions. You are inquisitive."

"Did Mum always know she could open spirit doors? I mean, when she was a child?" He waited patiently as his father pondered the question.

Finally, he spoke. "I think perhaps so," he said quietly. "There were times when your mother and I were . . . alone. When she confided the secrets to me, you see?"

Kester shuddered involuntarily. He didn't want to think about those *alone* times. Although he'd come to terms with the fact that Ribero and his mother had once been romantically involved, he didn't want to dwell on it. "Go on," he said eventually.

"She told me she had the nightmares, when she was a little girl. That she was always scared of doors. She thought that nasty things would come out at her. Then," Ribero paused and sipped his drink, "she got older and she realised. Those doors were not nightmares. They were *real*. But nobody explained to her what they were."

Kester took a deep breath. "That's amazing," he said. "It's almost exactly what I experienced when I was young. I *hated* doors. What I don't understand is, why did Mum never explain it to me?"

Silence fell. Ribero gazed out of the window, focusing on

something in the distance. "I cannot answer that," he said finally. "Your mother, she had a lot of secrets. There were things that Jennifer and I did not know, and we were closest to her. If you want me to guess, I would say she was trying to protect you, maybe?"

"Perhaps." Kester joined his father in staring out of the window. Something didn't quite make sense about it all. He remembered all those nights as a child, sitting frozen in bed, weeping because he'd seen a door in the air. And all his mother had ever done was hold him tightly and tell him it was just a dream. *I believed her,* he thought. *But as a door opener herself, why did she hide the truth from me? She was always so honest.*

"Hey," Ribero muttered, as he placed a hand on Kester's own. "Sometimes, it is not good to dwell on the past. Especially when you will never know the answer." He looked up, then nodded cheerfully to the other side of the room. "Aha. Here is our food. I ordered you lots, because you need to be fattened up like a little piggy, yes?"

Kester brightened at the sight of two plates full of bacon baguettes and chips, looking pleasingly huge and greasy and giving off a wonderfully tantalising smell. "That'll do the job nicely," he replied, and patted his stomach.

However, the feeling of disquiet still played in the back of his mind. *Why did Mum lie to me?* he thought, as he bit into the bread. And more worryingly, he felt the nagging suspicion that she had been hiding something more from him all along.

CHAPTER 4: THE PARTY AT THE MUSEUM

New Year's Eve proved to be the coldest day so far, with the forecaster on Miss Wellbeloved's radio announcing that temperatures would plummet to below freezing as the day drew on. The snow had stopped, and instead, a thick layer of impacted frost smothered every conceivable surface, giving Exeter's high street a bleak, unwelcoming appearance. Even the Christmas decorations looked pathetic and downcast, as though waiting for someone to remove them and forget about the festive season for another twelve months.

"Goodness me, it's so dark outside," Pamela chimed, peering out of the window. It was only four o'clock, but already the sky had turned dusky over the roofs, a thin wisp of grey cloud passing over the moon, which was already bright in the sky. She blew on her fingertips and rubbed them together. Even the office's snug central heating couldn't fully block out the icy breeze squeezing through the window frames. "That'll put a damper on your New Year's plans, won't it?"

Mike glanced up from his laptop, then smirked. "Nothing will put a damper on this evening's events!" he crowed, pointing at Kester and Serena in turn with a leery wink. "We're going to party like we've never partied before. Isn't that right, you two?"

Kester smiled weakly. "Um, yes. I suppose so. It is in a museum though, so I presume we won't be able to party *that* hard."

"Oh, you'll be partying, Kester, mark my words. It's too late to get cold feet now." With those ominous words, Mike ducked back down to his laptop. Serena caught Kester's worried frown and mouthed *Ignore him.*

Kester returned to his work. He'd been trying to wade his way through the *Historie of Spirits,* mainly because he was terrified about what Dr. Barqa-Abu might do to him if he couldn't recite it word-for-word by the start of term.

Although archaic, the book was an interesting read; stories of ancient Persia, Mesopotamia, and Greece. *Sort of like Herodotus's work,* he thought, as he idly flicked forward a few pages. *But with fewer daring generals and more plotting spirits. Fascinating.* It surprised him how far back spirit history ran, and how much more accepting humans had been of spirits back then. However, he still wasn't quite sure why the djinn had sent it to him, and not just added it to the recommended reading list along with all the other texts. It was strange, to say the least.

Well, she knows I'm still clueless about the spirit world, he reasoned. *This is probably her way of telling me to brush up fast.*

An exultant yelp from the vicinity of Mike's desk drew his attention away from the book. Even Ribero emerged from his office, cigarette smouldering in hand, to see what the noise was about.

"What is going on? It sounds like a dog is being tortured out here, yes?" He took a contemplative puff on his cigarette, then leaned against the doorframe.

Mike flapped his arms at them all. "Get over here and look at this."

They gathered around and peered curiously over his shoulder.

"This better not be some silly video you've found on Spirit-Net," Serena said, as she leaned on the back of Mike's chair. "Honestly, I don't know why you watch them. That last one with the poltergeist knocking over an old lady wasn't even remotely funny."

"That was pure gold," Mike said distractedly, then fiddled with a piece of equipment connected to his laptop. "However, this isn't a SpiritNet video, you'll be pleased to hear. It's something far better. Just you wait."

Kester examined the equipment more carefully, then exclaimed. "Hey, that's your image capturer, isn't it? The one you took with us on the Topsham job, when we got rid of the familiar?"

Mike winked. "Top marks for Kester. You're absolutely right. What's more, I've managed to get it to work."

"It only took you three days. That must be a record for you," Serena said scathingly.

"Well, better late than never." Mike adjusted his computer screen to give them all a clear view, then leant back, beaming with ill-concealed glee. "You won't believe this. Watch."

He pressed play, and at once the screen filled with an image of the pub in Topsham; the bar area and the surrounding tables and chairs were immediately identifiable. The colours were vague and hazy, but other than that, the picture quality was surprisingly good. They watched, holding their breaths collectively, as the camera panned around the room, focusing in on tables and barstools.

After a few minutes, Serena tutted. "Well, this is a riveting bit of footage, isn't it? I do love a good tour of an empty pub."

Mike wagged a finger in her direction. "Shush, woman. Wait for it."

"Is it coming soon, Mike?" Miss Wellbeloved looked at her watch in consternation. "I've got a few things I need to finish before the end of the day."

"Blimey you lot, could you show a bit of patience?"

They returned to silence, watching the screen as the camera continued to pan around the room. Occasionally, Ribero's legs or Pamela's bottom obscured the view, but other than that, there was nothing of interest.

Suddenly, a red shape flashed across the screen before disappearing as rapidly as it had appeared. Mike whooped triumphantly, then hit the pause button, sending the screen into immediate jittery stasis.

"There!" he yelled as he turned to face them all. "Did you see it?"

Kester looked back at Mike, impressed. *My goodness,* he thought. *Has his equipment actually worked for once?*

"Rewind it, quickly!" Ribero barked. A long cylinder of ash from his forgotten cigarette dropped to the floor. No one noticed.

Obediently, Mike rewound the footage, then played it again in slow motion. As the red form began to speed across the camera, he hit pause once more.

The others gasped in unison.

"Mike, that's *amazing,*" Pamela breathed, leaning heavily over his shoulder. "I can't believe it. You've caught that spirit perfectly."

Mike's grin grew even wider. "I know," he replied smugly. "It's flipping phenomenal, if I do say so myself. What do you think, Serena?"

Serena shrugged her shoulders. "I think if you swell up with any more smugness, you might burst," she said witheringly, before adding, "but I do think it's impressive. And I think we all know who that spirit is, don't we?"

Kester shivered. Of all people, he certainly should know who it was. Although the image was blurred due to the incredible speed the spirit was moving at, the overall shape was unmistakable, the snaking, sinewy form instantly recognisable. *Hrschni.*

"The big question is," he said, looking seriously at them all, "what was he doing there?"

Ribero and Miss Wellbeloved gave one another a worried look, which they hastily tried to conceal from Kester.

"Perhaps he's just checking up on you?" Miss Wellbeloved said hesitantly.

"Or just following all of us, yes?" Ribero added, with a comforting pat on Kester's arm.

Kester took his glasses off and polished them on his jumper. He appreciated his father's sentiment but suspected it wasn't true. Hrschni wasn't interested in the rest of the team. He'd made it pretty clear that Kester, and Kester alone, was his target.

But why would he follow me to the Topsham job? he thought, frowning. *Why not try to kidnap me again? What's he up to?*

"It doesn't make much sense, does it?" Serena said, reading his mind. "He was obviously there with us, so why stay hidden? Did he want to see you open the spirit door with his own eyes, perhaps? What's his reason for it all?"

"I dunno. Why send Kester two weird letters with cryptic clues in them?" Mike added. "Why send him a rusty old key? None of it makes much sense, does it?" He spun his chair a hundred and eighty degrees, so his knees bumped into their legs. "Anyway, the important thing is, my equipment *works.* I invented it. Infinite Enterprises will have to take notice of me now."

"Oh, I see," Serena drawled, as she folded her arms pertly across her chest. "*That's* the thing you're worried about, is it? Having Infinite bloody Enterprises notice your skills as an equipment designer."

Mike's face fell. "Not at all. You've got me all wrong."

Ribero chortled and smacked Mike on the back, knocking him uncomfortably forward. "Ah, I would not worry, Serena. I do not think Infinite Enterprises would be interested in hiring someone like Mike."

"Why not?" Mike barked.

"Because most of your equipment does not work, you silly man."

"And," Serena added, warming to the conversation, "you drink too much and embarrass yourself horribly when you're inebriated."

"And you wear a baseball hat with the Lego logo on it," Miss Wellbeloved chimed in.

Pamela tittered. "Yes, and you do suffer from terrible wind from time to time."

"You're a fine one to talk!" Mike squawked. "And I don't see what that's got to do with anything anyway!"

Still laughing, the others returned to their desks. Kester gave Mike a sympathetic look, noticing that he looked rather deflated. "I thought it was impressive," he said quietly. "You should post the video on SpiritNet. I bet it would get loads of likes."

Mike muttered something while casting a dark look at the others. Kester was fairly sure it wasn't complimentary.

They worked the remaining hour in silence before Miss Wellbeloved finally coughed, and rapped her watch for good measure.

"Off you go, everyone," she declared, then nodded at Serena, Mike, and Kester. "I suspect you'll all want to get ready for your big party tonight."

"It's not a big party," Serena corrected. "It's quite a sedate, mature event, I've been told."

"Now you tell me." Mike threw his leather jacket on and closed his laptop. "I didn't sign up to go to some old person's evening out, thank you very much."

Serena sighed and tugged her gloves on. "I didn't mean it like that. It's a classy event. That means cocktails and canapes, not beer and dry-roasted peanuts." She paused, then looked at Mike dubiously. "You're not going to humiliate us, are you?"

Mike grinned in response.

"I like canapes," Kester piped up, as he switched his computer off. "What time are we meeting?"

"Luke's coming down for half-eight," Mike said, heading for the door. "And apparently, sodding Dimitri's coming too, which is a shame."

A ghost of a smile tugged the corners of Serena's mouth. Mike glared at her, then stalked out into the dark landing.

The temperature outside was every bit as cold as the weather forecast had predicted. Kester paced home swiftly, eager to get out of the biting wind and into a nice hot shower. Sadly, his dreams of warming himself were scuppered when he realised that the boiler had packed up again, dowsing him in a deluge of freezing water instead. Thoroughly grumpy, he was briefly tempted to avoid going out altogether, but he could imagine what Mike's reaction would be. *He'd probably march up here and drag me forcibly out of the house,* he realised, as he opened his wardrobe and agonised over which shirt to wear.

A series of raps at his bedroom door made him swivel round in alarm. A second later, the door creaked open, and Pineapple's familiar wobbling topknot poked through the entrance, followed swiftly by his beaming face.

"Yo, you going out?" Pineapple eased into the room like oil oozing through a pipe, then studied Kester's clothes with open scepticism.

Kester scratched his head and pulled out the nearest shirt. "Yes. Why?"

Pineapple pursed his lips together and nodded approvingly. "Nah, that's cool, man. Real cool. Where you going?"

Oh god, I can see where this is heading, Kester realised, as he self-consciously tugged off his dressing gown and slid the shirt over his back. "I'm just going out with my work colleagues," he said quickly. "To the museum."

"You is going to the RAMM for New Year's Eve? That's pure crazy, bro. Why there?"

"What's the RAMM?"

"RAMM, man. Every local calls it that. It stands for Royal Ancient Museum Mojo. Or something sweet like that."

"Royal Albert Memorial Museum," Kester corrected absent-mindedly, dabbing at his neck. He'd caught himself shaving and was now worried that he was going to be left with an ugly red welt under his chin. *Not that anyone will be looking at me,* he thought wistfully. *No one ever notices me.* He thought of Anya and mentally added, *Unless they want to abuse my trust and betray me, of course.*

"It's a ticket-only event," he clarified, spotting Pineapple's hopeful expression. "All sold out. Where are you going?"

Pineapple shook his head sadly. "Ah, it's proper sacrilegious, you know? I was going to a rave—a pure sweet rave up in the woods. But it's been cancelled, and now I'm out of action. Do you feel me?"

Kester shook his head. "Not really. Isn't Daisy back yet?" Daisy normally buddied up with Pineapple for social events, providing double the idiot power at any venue they attended together.

Pineapple collapsed on Kester's bed with a mournful expression. "No. I got a postcard from her this morning. She's still in Thailand with her new man-lover, getting frisky under the Asian sun, proper tight, yeah?"

"If you say so." Kester finished buttoning his shirt, then examined the overall effect in his mirror. It wasn't *that* impressive, but it wasn't offensive either, which was about as good as he could hope for. *Perhaps I should even wear a pair of jeans,* he thought, feeling a little adventurous. Normally he relied on his trusty slacks, but to celebrate his slimmer figure, he'd treated himself to some jeans a few weeks back. Thus far, he hadn't dared to wear them.

"Yo, Kester, are you listening to me? I'm not feeling the love, bro!" Pineapple folded his arms, topknot quivering mutinously.

Kester turned around. "Look," he began, as kindly as he could. "You can't come with me to the New Year's Eve event at the museum. You haven't got a ticket, and it's not your sort of thing anyway. Sorry."

Pineapple sighed elaborately, then rolled off the bed. "I'm gonna hit the town anyway," he declared grandly, a single finger hovering in the air to emphasise the point. "All on my own. Right? You dig?"

"I dig very much indeed," Kester replied, as he ushered his housemate out of the door. "Good luck with that. You'll need a coat, it's freezing outside." *Mind you, can't be colder than in here,* he thought, giving his broken radiator a cynical kick.

Even Kester felt he might have underestimated the coldness of the evening. By the time he'd reached the entrance of the museum, he was frozen to the core, teeth chattering and the tips of his fingers tingling painfully. He surveyed the crowd standing outside the doors with a sinking heart. *I don't believe it,* he realised, looking down at his outfit, then comparing it to everyone else's. *I completely forgot it was fancy dress.*

Suddenly, a black leather glove clamped down on his shoulder, startling him. To his horror, a skull-painted face loomed over him, beaming widely.

"Kester! Where's your costume?"

Kester realised with a sense of relief that it was Luke. Another skulking skeleton lurked behind him, which he guessed must be Dimitri; though under the face-paint, it was difficult to tell. He shrugged, feeling rather embarrassed.

"I totally forgot we had to dress up," he explained, gesturing impotently at his shirt. "I thought I was going to a lot of effort wearing a pair of jeans."

"Well, you're looking good," Luke chimed, and wrapped an arm over his shoulder. "I wouldn't worry about it. C'mon, let's go in. Mike texted us earlier, he's already inside."

"Probably getting started on the cocktails, I should think," Kester shouted, struggling to make himself heard over the noise. He nodded to Dimitri, who nodded severely in response, holding his hand out stiffly to be shaken.

"This is not my usual sort of thing," Dimitri declared, eying the entrance as though it contained a dangerous bomb. "But it is nice to come out, I suppose."

"It's good to see you," Kester said. He actually meant it was good to see Luke, who he was very fond of, and somewhat less good to see Dimitri, but there wasn't really any polite way to express this. Dimitri, however, seemed to recognise Kester's insincerity, and narrowed his eyes accordingly, before stalking past him up the stone staircase.

Luke laughed, then tugged Kester towards the entrance, nudging their way through throngs of loitering people drinking, talking on phones, or smoking cigarettes. "It's so good to see you," he said cheerfully, as they showed their tickets at the door. "I want to hear all about what's been going on. Sounds like it's been pretty crazy."

Kester shook his head as they stepped into the central atrium. A dual staircase swooped elegantly to the left and right, with an imposing statue of a man mounted in the centre. *That must be Prince Albert himself,* he realised, as he took in his surroundings. "It's nice in here, isn't it?" he shouted, ducking beneath a stray piece of bunting hanging down from the ceiling.

Luke nodded appreciatively. "Yeah, you English know how to do a good building, I'll give you that. Let's go find the others." Dimitri had already stormed ahead and was now only just visible over a sea of heads.

"Kester, my main man!"

Kester turned instinctively towards the source of the booming greeting to see Mike, propped up happily against the bar. Judging by the smeared face paint and cheerful expression, he'd already had a few drinks. Beside him, Serena twitched irritably, her narrow face obscured by heavy makeup.

"Who have you come as?" Kester asked, overwhelmed by her thick black lashes, which looked uncannily like spider's legs.

"I'm a mistress of the dark," she snapped. "Isn't it obvious? It's good to see you've made an effort."

"Hey, Kester's come as a murderous psychopath," Luke said, as he prodded Serena playfully. "They look just the same as everyone else."

"It is a Day of the Dead party, not Halloween," Dimitri said sniffily, then proceeded to order a drink without offering anybody else one.

Mike rubbed his stomach then belched reflectively. "Well," he announced, "I've come as a proper skeleton. A rather handsome one, if I do say so myself."

"And you're the *only* one who says so. Trust me," Serena retorted. Mike wrapped a hand around her waist and pulled her closer, much to her obvious horror.

"Ah, you love me really, you old cow," he bellowed, and planted a wet kiss on her cheek. Serena's expression of total mortification made the rest of them burst into laughter, even Dimitri.

The music changed, and Mike's face lit up. Releasing Serena, he thrust his drink up into the air. "I love this tune!" he howled, much to the alarm of everyone in the near vicinity. "Come on, let's dance!"

"I do not dance," Dimitri scowled, before Mike seized his arm and dragged him forcibly onto the dance floor. Luke shrugged, then ambled over to join them, leaving Kester standing awkwardly beside Serena, who was still rubbing furiously at her cheek.

"I cannot *believe* he did that," she stuttered, shooting pure daggers of rage in Mike's direction. "It's so unbelievably rude of him."

"It was only a little kiss," Kester said, as he ordered a drink. "I wouldn't get so worked up about it, if I were you."

"Yes, well you're not me, are you?"

"Thank goodness," Kester muttered quietly, then mooched off quietly, drink in hand. The last thing he wanted was to listen to Serena ranting on about Mike all evening. He watched the others for a while, feeling envious at their complete lack of inhibition. Mike and Luke were currently waltzing across the floor, and even Dimitri was dancing, though in a strangely robotic manner.

How wonderful, Kester thought, *to just dance like that, without caring about what anyone else thinks!* By contrast, he was feeling highly self-conscious about his choice of outfit, and he suspected he was attracting attention for all the wrong reasons.

"Not thinking of joining in, then?" The clipped voice beside him sounded as though it had come from another era, with its nasal, clipped tones. Kester turned and found himself staring at an unusually short man, with a head so wrinkled that it could have passed for a walnut. A furry little wisp of white hair protruded from his scalp like smoke from a bonfire, but other than that, he was entirely bald.

"Er, no," Kester bumbled, nearly spilling his drink. "I'm not much of a dancer, I'm afraid."

The man chuckled, then nodded wisely. "Nor I. My dancing days are long behind me." He patted Kester's arm in a friendly manner, then began to retreat. "I'm Dominic Clutterbuck, head of the RAMM, I'm just chatting to everyone to ensure they're having a good time."

"Oh, you're the head of the museum?" Kester repeated, surprised. "What a fantastic job. I'd love to do something like that."

Dominic Clutterbuck laughed again, his tiny shoulders bobbing with the exertion. "It is good fun, yes. I think I probably should have retired years ago, but I like it here too much, you see. Anyway, pleasure to meet you. Here, please take my card."

"Nice to meet you too," Kester replied, as he watched the man weave deftly through the crowds, chatting to various other people. *What a pleasant chap,* he thought as he sipped at his cocktail, casually reading the business card in his hand. *Professor Dominic Clutterbuck, Head of the RAMM, Exeter.* He frequently noticed how friendly people were down in the southwest. Even the old dear in the local post office liked to call him "my lover," which had bemused him initially, but now he'd grown rather fond of it.

Suddenly, he choked. Twin rivulets of alcohol jetted from his nose as he looked back at Dominic Clutterbuck, who was now almost hidden from view, concealed behind row after row of people. He spluttered wildly, then frantically tried to get the attention of the others.

Luke ran over immediately, and, without warning, walloped Kester's back with a full-force blow that knocked his glasses askew. Squealing with surprise, he hastily retreated when he saw Luke's hand rising again.

"No, I'm fine, honestly! There's no need."

"What's the problem then?" Luke asked, smoothing down his hair. "I thought you were choking to death."

Kester glanced over his shoulder again, but the head of the museum had now completely vanished.

"What's occurring?" Mike said, wrapping an arm over Kester's shoulder. "Come on, get on the dance floor!"

"It's the ram's head!" Kester gasped, and waved a futile hand in the direction of the crowd behind him. "The ram's head! It doesn't mean the animal; it means the museum!"

Mike scratched his ear, looking thoroughly perplexed. "Kester," he said seriously, "have you taken something? Because you're acting really odd."

Kester rolled his eyes. "As if I would," he retorted. "Listen to me carefully. The mysterious note that I got at Christmas, the one that said *The ram's head will show you where to look,* you remember?"

"Of course I bloody do," Mike said, looking mildly put out. "What are you getting at?"

"What if it means the R-A-M-M? The Royal Albert Memorial Museum? What if I'm meant to talk to the head of the RAMM?"

Mike shrugged, looking at Dimitri and Luke. "Could be, I suppose. But honestly, Kester, do you ever shut off from work?"

Dimitri nodded approvingly. "That is good detective work," he drawled. "You are like Sherlock Holmes. What are you going to do now, then?"

Kester smiled gratefully, then pointed behind him. "I literally just spoke to the head of the RAMM. He's called Dominic Clutterbuck. I guess I'd better find him and see what else he has to say."

"What if you're wrong?" Luke said, looking worried. "You don't want to give anything away, you know."

"I'll be subtle," Kester replied. "Leave it with me."

Mike snorted. "So much for a fun night out. Go on then, enjoy yourself. I'm off to dance again."

Luke clasped Kester's shoulder. "You want any company?"

"No, I'll be okay." Kester glanced at Mike, who had already slid into the centre of the dance floor and was currently trying to get a blonde woman to waltz with him. "You'd better keep an eye on him instead." He looked over at Serena, who was still standing by the bar, glowering at Mike with open fury. *Oh dear,* he thought, as he attempted to squeeze through the crowds of skeleton-painted people. *Mike's in big trouble if that expression is anything to go by.*

To his frustration, Dominic Clutterbuck seemed to have disappeared entirely. He scoured the main room, searching from corner to corner, though the general darkness and strobing lights weren't helping much. *Typical,* he thought. *Why couldn't it be a tall person I'm searching for? They're easier to spot.*

Easing his way around the corner, he moved through to another room of the museum. There were less people here, and Kester felt instantly soothed by the displays of prehistoric bones and broken pieces of pottery. He approached the entrance to the next room, then noticed it was barred by a piece of velvet rope. A member of staff, clad in black suit and tie, shook his head firmly at Kester's approach.

"It's okay, Rick, I believe the young gentleman is looking for me."

The familiar clipped voice echoed from the room beyond, and

shortly after, the short figure of Dominic Clutterbuck appeared by the darkened doorway.

"I'm sorry," Kester stuttered, now rather unsure what to say. "I hope you don't think I'm stalking you. I just wanted to ask you a question."

The man nodded as though he'd expected nothing less, then gestured to Kester to climb over the roped barrier.

"Do come through," he said warmly, as he made room for Kester to stand beside him. "It's quiet in here, and it will be much easier to discuss things." Without waiting for Kester to respond, he trotted stealthily through the high-ceilinged room, past row after row of dimly lit glass cabinets.

"It's amazing in here," Kester breathed, as he peered eagerly at the medieval carvings, paintings, and other knickknacks on display. "I've been waiting for a chance to visit."

"Ah yes," Dominic agreed, as he led them around a corner and into a slightly smaller space with a simple bench next to the wall. "Exeter is a veritable treasure trove of history and secrets. I believe you're starting to realise that already, aren't you, my dear boy? Indeed, you must have guessed that I was waiting for you tonight."

Kester followed the old man's lead and settled beside him on the bench. "So, I take it you know what I'm going to ask you?" he said quietly, aware that even when speaking in lowered tones, his voice echoed around the space.

Dominic smiled and turned to Kester, fixing him with a pair of extraordinarily alert blue eyes. "Yes," he agreed, "but I need to hear it from you. There are certain steps that one must follow, you see."

"I was told that the *ram's head would show me where to look*," Kester replied. He felt a little self-conscious, especially under the ceaseless inspection of the old man's gaze. "And I suddenly realised that it might be you. Because you're the RAMM's head, of course."

The old man nodded. "That is correct. Now, what did you want to ask me?"

Kester felt lost for words. *What do I want to ask him?* he thought, as he looked at the surrounding displays for inspiration. *I spent so long figuring out the meaning of the ram's head that I hadn't thought about anything else!*

"Well," he said slowly, clearing his throat and hoping for the best. "I was given a key, a few weeks before Christmas. It came with a note, that said when I was ready to see the other side, the key would guide the way. Do you know what that means?"

Dominic exhaled heavily. "All I know is the next step, Kester. I don't know what follows."

Kester looked at him. "Are you a Thelemite?" *Am I in any danger here?* was his other silent question. His concerns must have shown in his face, as the little old man sat up straighter and shook his head.

"I am aware," Dominic replied eventually, "that you've had some problems with the Thelemites recently."

"You can say that again," Kester said in a low voice. "I hope you don't think I'm being rude, but how can I trust you, if you're one of them?"

Dominic twiddled his thumbs gently in his lap, looking for a moment as peaceful as a reclining Buddha. "There is no way I can convince you to trust me," he said finally, in a strange, almost conversational tone. "We choose our paths in life, and we must follow where our heart leads us."

Kester thought about it for a moment. *I've come this far,* he realised, as he leant his head against the cool stone wall. *I may as well continue. Anyway, this doesn't feel like Hrschni's work. I can't say why not, it just doesn't seem like his style. Perhaps there is more going on with the Thelemites than I realise.*

"You're lost in your thoughts," Dominic said with a chuckle. "That happens to me all the time, you know."

"I'd like you to show me the next step," Kester said quickly, before he could rationalise a way out of the decision. "I need to know."

The old man nodded solemnly. "Very well. In that case, here is another note from your mysterious benefactor." He reached inside his inner pocket and pulled out an envelope, which was identical to the last two. "I don't know what it says," he continued seriously, "I have not read it, and nor do I wish to. My part in this is done, for now."

"Why is it always puzzles and secrets?" Kester asked, as he scrutinised the calligraphy on the front. "Can't it ever be obvious?"

The old man looked at him earnestly. "You already know the answer to that, I believe."

Because it's daemons we're dealing with here, Kester thought. *That's how they operate. Through riddles and codes.* "Is it some sort of test?" he asked, rubbing the paper reflectively. "Do I need to prove myself?"

"Perhaps."

"Should I read it now?"

Dominic shook his head. "No," he replied firmly. "Go. Enjoy your evening with friends. Life shouldn't be serious all the time, you know."

Kester smiled. "I don't seem to have much to be cheerful about at the moment, unfortunately."

The old man rose and patted Kester on the back. "You remind me of myself as a younger man. All work and no play. Remember, when you can see only shadows ahead, that means there is light just behind you."

"I'll keep that in mind," Kester replied. "This has been strange, but it's been nice meeting you, nonetheless."

"Good luck." The man gestured back the way they'd come, then added, "I'm returning to my office now. Happy New Year to you, young man." With that, he seemed to melt away, his footsteps echoing loudly as he disappeared into the darkness. Kester watched him go, biting his lip nervously, and then pocketed the mysterious envelope.

He returned to the crowds in the main hall, feeling oddly disconnected from all the celebrations. An endless sea of brightly painted faces swam before him, laughing, cackling, spilling drink over the floor. He scanned the dance floor, but there was no sign of the others, only a huge, rowdy mob of sweaty figures grinding and bouncing to the music.

To his relief, he soon spotted Luke and Dimitri perched on chairs near the bar, deep in conversation about something.

"Where are Mike and Serena?" he asked breathlessly, as he crouched down to speak to them. Dimitri shrugged noncommittally, though looked rather nettled.

Luke grimaced. "Mike had a go at Dimitri, then stormed off. I've no idea where he went. Serena marched after him."

Kester whistled, eyes widening. "Blimey. Sounds like I've missed all the drama. What was it all about?"

Dimitri threw his hands expansively in the air. "I have no idea. All I did was talk to Serena and then Mike goes crazy. He is not right in the head, I think."

Kester laughed. "Mike's probably a bit jealous of you. I wouldn't worry too much—he'll have forgotten all about it in the morning."

"Yes, but I might not have," Dimitri growled, glaring at the dance floor.

"So you don't know where they've gone, then?" Kester asked. "I've got some important news I need to tell them. You too, as it happens."

"You found something out?" Luke replied, leaning across to hear Kester better. "What happened? Did you talk to the old guy?"

Kester quickly filled them both in on what had happened. Dimitri and Luke stared at him, then looked openmouthed at one another.

"It's like a murder mystery book!" Luke exclaimed, with a noise that was halfway between a laugh and a snort of amazement. "Why aren't you going to open the envelope now? I wouldn't be able to stop myself."

Kester pondered the idea, then shook his head. "No, it's probably better if I wait," he said, and patted his pocket to check the envelope was still there. *After all,* he thought, as he looked up at the ceiling, *there might be CCTV cameras watching my every move for all I know. It's safer if I review it when I get home.* "I'm going to search for Mike and Serena," he announced, standing up. "I hope they're not having a raging argument somewhere."

"I hope Serena is giving Mike a piece of her mind," Dimitri said huffily. "He was very rude to me, you know."

Kester smirked. "Oh, I'm sure she is." *Serena has no problems giving Mike grief,* he thought silently. *Don't you worry about that.*

He moved through the museum as quickly as possible, skirting around huddles of laughing people and trying to avoid being accidentally elbowed, nudged, or knocked over as he went. The music was unnecessarily loud in his opinion; pumping, throbbing beats that echoed throughout the building.

Where the heck have they gone? he wondered. They weren't

in the entrance hall, and they didn't seem to be on the staircase either. Confused, he went back into the main building.

This is a bit strange, he thought, the first small burst of worry blossoming in the pit of his stomach. *They wouldn't have left without telling me, would they?* He checked his phone, but there were no messages.

Finally, as he explored the quieter parts of the building, he spotted what looked like one of Serena's legs, poking out at a strange angle from a darkened corner. *It must be her,* he thought, as he studied the foot in question. *No one else wears heels that high.* Creeping forward with trepidation, he peered around, then gaped in open amazement at the tangle of limbs before him.

His initial thought was that Serena was throttling Mike, and that he was trying to prise her away. Then he realised what was actually going on and gasped. At the sound, Mike and Serena sprang apart like fighting dogs under a water hose and immediately set about straightening themselves up.

"Oh my goodness!" Kester bellowed, clutching his mouth in shock. "I can't believe it!"

"It's absolutely not what it looks like!" Serena shouted, smoothing down her bob. "Don't draw any conclusions at all!"

"You were . . . you were snogging each other!" Kester said, then started to laugh. He simply couldn't help it. In fact, he wasn't sure which was funnier, Serena's look of unadulterated mortification, or Mike's bleary-eyed, boozed-up grin.

Serena whacked Kester across the stomach, then levelled the full force of her most hostile stare at him. "We were not *snogging*," she hissed, emphasising the word to demonstrate her revulsion at the thought. "I had something in my eye and Mike was having a closer look for me."

"With his tongue?" Kester said, with a raised eyebrow.

Mike chuckled, then fell silent when he caught sight of Serena's expression.

"Listen," she continued frantically, as she dragged Kester away. "Don't you even *think* about telling anyone, okay? It meant absolutely nothing. And it was all Mike's fault, of course."

"Naturally," Kester agreed. "By the way," he added, as he pointed at her hair, "do you realise your incubus is back? He looks a bit put out."

Serena swore and ruffled her hair anxiously, peering into the air above her. The incubus, who was looking very morose indeed, nimbly avoided her prodding fingers and bounced towards the back of her head, casting furious looks in Mike's direction.

"It needs to vanish now!" Serena barked, as she looked with panic at the people around them. "If anyone sees it . . ."

"Ah, I wouldn't worry," Mike said, as he lolled along beside them. "You've given them enough of a show as it is."

With an explosion of fury, Serena walloped him across the back. "Don't, Mike! Just *don't*, okay?"

Without saying another word, she stalked off, heels clipping furiously across the polished floor. Kester looked at Mike, then burst out laughing again.

"Well," he concluded, as he slid a supporting arm around Mike's waist, who was already starting to lurch in an alarming manner. "I didn't see that one coming."

Mike hiccupped, then winked. "I did," he slurred, and gave his chest a triumphant pat. "She's always loved me, she has. She couldn't contain herself anymore."

"If you say so," Kester replied, shaking his head with disbelief. *Who would have thought it, eh?* he mused, as he led Mike back to the bar. *What a night. A meeting with the RAMM's head, another strange envelope, and Mike and Serena sharing a moment of passion.*

Just another weird and wonderful day in Exeter, he thought, suddenly feeling more cheerful than he had in a long time. *Heaven knows what tomorrow will bring.*

Chapter 5: The Hunt for the Painting

The next day, Kester awoke, eyes gritty, the taste of stale rum lingering unpleasantly in his mouth. Instantly, his eyes travelled to his bedside table. The envelope Dominic Clutterbuck had given him was still there, propped neatly beside his glass of water.

He sat up and winced as his head started to pound. Pulling the note out of the envelope, he read it once again.

The painting points the way. To find the answer, you must be held to ransom.

"What the hell does that mean?" he wondered aloud. If anything, this was the most obscure clue he'd received so far. *Which painting? And where am I supposed to start looking?*

Kester put it carefully back in the envelope and took a long drink of water. As far as he'd been aware, he hadn't even had that much to drink the night before, though obviously the cocktails had been more potent than he'd realised.

He dimly remembered Mike tumbling over on the dancefloor, then lying there like an upended tortoise until two irate bouncers had hauled him to his feet. *Had he been kicked out?* he wondered, trying to remember what Mike's reaction had been. He vaguely recollected some shouting going on, so it was entirely possible.

As for Serena, Kester had no idea where she'd disappeared to. After being caught in that embrace with Mike, she'd stalked off, and they hadn't seen her for the rest of the evening. *Probably knowing her, she'd stormed home to sulk on her own,* he thought uncharitably. *I wonder what she's going to be like in the office tomorrow? And, how much teasing can I get away with before she actually murders me?*

His gaze drifted to the pile of books lying on his desk, and he groaned. Although he'd read most of the texts for his Spirit Intervention and Business Studies course, he still felt woefully underprepared. The *Historie of Spirits* still lay on the top of the pile, looking distinctly unappealing in the watery winter light. *I'm meant to start the course in a few days,* he realised with a sinking feeling. *How on earth am I going to manage it with everything else that's going on?*

Even a huge sausage sandwich for breakfast failed to lift his spirits. Nor did it alleviate his hangover, which was even more unfortunate. Feeling distinctly out of sorts, Kester watched television for an hour or so, decided that there was absolutely nothing on, then grabbed his jacket and headed outside.

Reaching for his phone, he quickly dialled Miss Wellbeloved's number.

"Kester, I didn't expect to hear from you today!" Judging by her chirpy tone, Miss Wellbeloved clearly hadn't drunk nearly as much the night before as Kester had.

Quickly, he filled her in on the evening's strange events, deliberately leaving out the part about Serena and Mike's clandestine kiss. There was a long pause whilst Miss Wellbeloved processed the information, so long that Kester wondered whether his phone had gone dead.

"Are you still there?"

"Yes, still here," Miss Wellbeloved said finally. "Just trying to work out what the clue might mean."

"I know," Kester agreed, as he quickened his pace to keep warm. "It's rather random, isn't it?"

Miss Wellbeloved sighed. "I'm not sure what the Thelemites are playing at here. Hrschni's already proved he has the power to kidnap you. Why bother with all these clues?"

"Do you think he's testing me, to see if I can figure it out?" Kester asked. The bitter air was freezing his throat, and he was starting to regret his decision to go for a walk.

"Perhaps it's some sort of rite of passage," she mused. "The Thelemite initiation process involves a series of puzzles."

"What, you think he's trying to initiate me?"

"I don't know," Miss Wellbeloved admitted. "But I don't like it. Where are you going? You sound like you're walking somewhere."

Kester glanced around him. The street was entirely deserted. Presumably most people had done the sensible thing on New Year's Day and stayed warm inside. "I just needed to get out," he said finally. "I've got too many things to think about, and I hoped a stroll would clear my head."

"You mean, you've got a hangover?"

Kester grunted. "Perhaps a slight headache. Nothing compared to what Mike is experiencing, I shouldn't think."

There was a pause. Kester sensed that Miss Wellbeloved was pondering something. She often fell quiet for extended periods of time when thinking, oblivious to the fact that others were waiting patiently for her to speak.

"Kester?" she said finally, in a wheedling voice.

"Yes?"

"I've had an idea. It's probably nothing, but it'll give us some-thing to do today, at the very least."

He frowned. "What did you have in mind?"

"Well." She cleared her throat. "We're looking for a painting that points the way, right?"

Kester sighed. He could sense where this was going. *So much for a day off,* he thought, as he kicked at a pile of dirty snow. "Go on."

"The museum has a gallery. Quite an extensive one, actually. I wonder if the painting we're looking for will be in there?"

"You want us to go hang out in a gallery on our day off?" Kester licked his lips, which were already tingling painfully in the cold air. He thought about it. *There are worse ways to spend your time, I suppose,* he rationalised. "Will it be open today?" he asked, picking up his pace.

"Yes," Miss Wellbeloved confirmed. "They're open virtually every day of the year. Shall I meet you there? It won't take me long to walk over. Your father can come too; the air will do him good."

"Oh, he stayed with you last night, did he?" Kester shuddered involuntarily, imagining Ribero's expression; suave and annoy-ingly smug.

"Yes, Kester, he did. Is that okay with you?" Miss Wellbe-loved's tone was distinctly bristly.

He coughed awkwardly. "Fine, of course." *It's not really,* he thought. *In fact, it freaks me out that my father's getting more action than I am.* "I'll see you in a bit," he added aloud, then hung up.

Apart from one person walking their dog, the streets were empty as he walked into town. However, to his surprise, the museum was busy when he arrived, with families going in and out of the entrance doors. To his even greater amazement, all the decorations from the previous night had been completely stripped away—making it seem as though the event had never happened at all.

He loitered in the entrance hall, idly watching as people made their way up and down the staircase. *I wonder if Dominic Clutterbuck is in today?* he thought, glancing around. *I don't suppose he'll give me any more clues though; the whole thing seems to be steeped in secrecy.*

"Aha, it is the boy!" He saw a hand swishing into his periphery, followed by his father's beaming face. "You had an interesting evening last night, yes?"

Kester smiled. "You could say that. I take it Miss Wellbeloved told you about the letter?"

Miss Wellbeloved peered over Ribero's suede-jacketed shoulder. "I certainly did. Are you ready to examine some paintings?"

"I suppose so," Kester said, wrinkling his nose. In all honesty, he was finding it difficult to muster much enthusiasm for the task. "I could do with a cup of tea first though."

"Paintings first, tea later." Ribero grasped Kester's arm and tugged him down the corridor to a set of doors, which swung smoothly apart at their approach. "Let us see what we can find out, right?"

They sauntered into an open space far airier and more modern than the rest of the museum. Kester sighed with satisfaction at the sight of the vast whitewashed walls, interrupted only by the artwork itself. It was a haven of peace and contemplation, which was exactly what he needed.

At once, Miss Wellbeloved began poring over the paintings, squinting at all the descriptions. "It would help if we knew what we were looking for," she muttered as she adjusted her glasses.

"Kester, would you mind repeating the clue again?"

"The painting points the way," Kester recited obligingly. *"To find the answer, you must be held to ransom."*

"Why ransom, I wonder?" Miss Wellbeloved straightened, then moved on to the next one. "Perhaps we're looking for a painting of a highwayman?"

Kester frowned. "That seems a little far fetched." Suddenly, he noticed that his father was still standing by the door, grasping the wall.

"Are you all right?"

Ribero waved him away, face contorted with pain. "It is nothing. Just a cramp, yes?"

"That's not good," Kester whispered, glancing back to Miss Wellbeloved. "When did it start?" He knew that his father's condition caused cramping from time to time, and he suspected it happened more regularly than Ribero let on.

"Ah, it does not matter." His father took a deep breath and briefly closed his eyes. "I will be okay in a few minutes. You go on, I will catch up, okay?"

Kester shook his head firmly. "No. Come on, let's take you to the café." He caught Miss Wellbeloved's eye, who nodded in understanding, her expression full of concern.

"This is silly," Ribero spluttered, as Kester led him back out into the busy corridor. He shrugged Kester's hand off his arm and glared at the floor. "I am not an old man; you do not need to fuss at me."

"You *are* an old man," Kester reminded him. "And you have a medical condition. So, you need to sit down for a while and recover. Understood?"

Ribero swore in Spanish, then winced again, clutching at his legs. Finally, he nodded. "Fine, you win."

Kester grinned. "That must be a first." Leading Ribero into the busy café, he placed his father gently onto the nearest chair. "Wait there, I'll get you a coffee."

"Make it strong," Ribero barked. "And South American. None of this other rubbish."

Sighing, Kester quickly ordered the coffee, then requested a chocolate cake for good measure. *Oh well,* he thought, as he carried it back to the table. *If he doesn't eat it, I'm sure I can force it down.*

"Do you want me to sit with you?" Kester hovered close by, keen to know how Miss Wellbeloved's search was going but equally worried about his father. Not to mention hopeful that he might be able to have a bit of cake.

Ribero shook his head. "No, you go." He pointed at the door. "The cramp is going now, anyway. I will join you in a few minutes, yes?"

"Are you sure?"

His father nodded, then grimaced again, massaging his legs. "It will be better soon. Do not worry."

Kester gave him one last reassuring pat on the back, then headed back to the gallery. He hated seeing his father like that. *I know he's getting older,* he thought, *but it's awful to see him so frail.* He wondered if his father was getting worse, then hastily quelled the thought. If Ribero's health continued to deteriorate, there was a large chance he'd be called upon to take over the agency, and that prospect didn't even bear thinking about.

To his surprise, Miss Wellbeloved had already finished in the first room and had made her way to the smaller room next door. Her thin, straight-backed figure cast a discordant shadow against the white wall.

"Any luck?" he asked, peering at the picture in front of her.

She shook her head. "Absolutely none whatsoever. Unless I'm missing something obvious, the clue doesn't relate to any of these paintings."

Kester took off his glasses and polished them thoughtfully on his jumper. "So, what now, then?"

Miss Wellbeloved smiled. "Don't panic, there's another gallery area upstairs. I suppose we'll have to start looking there. How's your father?"

"In pain, by the looks of it." Kester followed Miss Wellbeloved out through another set of doors which led to the main atrium of the museum. "Should I be worried?"

She shrugged. "I'm not sure, to be honest. He's just as secretive about his health with me as he is you, Kester."

They trudged up the long flight of stairs and emerged on a landing which appeared to be some sort of temporary shop selling pencils and notebooks. An elderly woman at the desk smiled at them obligingly, then looked rather disappointed as they moved straight into the gallery.

"What have the doctors said?" Kester persisted, refusing to believe that Miss Wellbeloved didn't know anything. His instincts told him that the pair were concealing the facts from him, like protective parents sheltering a child.

She squeezed his arm. "Kester, you'll have to speak to your father, okay? He knows far more than I do. Now, shall we look at these paintings?" She studied the sign on the wall. "These are apparently local painters."

Kester scanned the room, then nodded approvingly. "Some of them are pretty good, aren't they?"

"You sound surprised," Miss Wellbeloved said. "Believe it or not, talent does exist outside London, you know."

He laughed, then commenced pacing around the room, scrutinising each painting in turn. Rural landscapes, Victorian etchings of Exeter's quayside, portraits of stuffy-looking gentlemen in military regalia—nothing that looked even remotely related to their clue. *Perhaps we're looking in entirely the wrong place,* he thought, as he stuffed his hands even deeper into his pockets. *But how can we be expected to know where to start? There simply isn't enough to go on.*

Miss Wellbeloved eventually caught up with him. Hands on hips, she sighed loudly. "I suppose it was a bit of a stab in the dark, wasn't it?"

Kester slumped onto the nearest bench. "This is craziness. We're on yet another wild-goose chase, and we haven't got a clue what we're looking for, or why we're even looking."

"I know." Miss Wellbeloved positioned herself neatly beside him, eyes still restlessly roving the walls. "But what else can we do? The government have made the Thelemite case a top priority, which means we have to act on every lead that we get."

"But something doesn't quite add up," Kester replied, as he rubbed his eyes wearily. "We're missing something."

Miss Wellbeloved smiled. "Honestly, the number of times I've heard you say that, Kester. Mind you," she added, "you've never been wrong. What do you think we're missing?"

Kester glanced around the room to check they couldn't be overheard. "Well," he began, "let's look at the facts. Hrschni kidnapped me. He was planning to imprison me in a secret cave so he could tap into my spirit door opening abilities. Right?"

"Agreed."

"So," Kester continued, warming to the topic, "why has he suddenly backed off? He's had numerous opportunities to kidnap me again. It wouldn't be hard for him, would it? After all, he's a daemon. He can sneak around without detection."

Miss Wellbeloved nodded. "Go on."

"Instead, he's playing games," Kester said, slapping his leg with frustration. "He's sending me these strange little envelopes filled with cryptic clues. And that makes no sense at all. It doesn't help him to achieve his goal, does it?"

"No." Miss Wellbeloved nibbled on a finger, frowning with concentration. "You're absolutely right, it doesn't. What do *you* think is going on, then?"

Kester shrugged. "I only wish I knew. It's been driving me mad." He gestured angrily to the paintings. "I almost feel like screwing the envelopes up and throwing them away, along with that silly key. Why should I play along with him, after all?"

Miss Wellbeloved leant over and gave him a nudge with her shoulder. "It must be frustrating, not to mention worrying." She straightened as an elderly couple entered the room, then flashed a warning look in Kester's direction. "However," she continued in a whisper, "what else have we got to go on? You know how important this case is to your father. If we crack this one, it'll put our agency right back on track."

"If this is about his constant need to beat Larry Higgins . . ." Kester began loudly. Miss Wellbeloved shushed him anxiously, nodding at the other people in the room.

"It's not just that," she muttered. "You know how tight money is. We need to succeed if we're going to survive. Infinite Enterprises are controlling more and more of the spirit sector, and it's only a matter of time before they start moving to the southwest. In fact," she added, "the only reason we're still in operation is because we have something they don't."

"What's that?" Kester asked, intrigued.

"You! A spirit door opener." She studied him carefully, then sighed. "You really don't understand how rare your gift is, do you?"

Kester shrugged. "Mum had it too, so I presumed it wasn't *that* rare."

Miss Wellbeloved watched the elderly couple move into the next room, then exhaled loudly. "That's because it's genetic," she explained patiently. "But that doesn't mean it's common. Back in the old days, your kind would have been called shamans, witch doctors, or warlocks. They were revered not only because they could open spirit doors but because they were integral to creating sun gates."

"The permanent doors to the spirit world? I thought no one knew how they were made."

"They don't, not anymore. But some of the world's ancient scriptures suggest that a spirit door opener is required to complete them."

Kester studied her closely. "You don't think Hrschni would know how to make one, do you?"

She shrugged. "I've wondered the same thing. It would explain why he wanted to kidnap you. But not why he let you go."

"Maybe I was a disappointment to him." He laughed wryly. "After all, I'm not very good at it."

"Don't put yourself down; you've got a rare, incredible talent. Back in the old days, spirit door openers like you were worshipped for their powers because very few people *had them.*"

"Shame I don't live in the old days, then," Kester quipped. "I could do with a bit of worshipping."

She pursed her lips. "Be serious, please. Your mother was better at it, I'll grant you, but nonetheless, you have the ability."

"Where did Mum get it from?"

Miss Wellbeloved sighed, then gave him an affectionate squeeze. "Sometimes, it staggers me how little you know about your own family. Gretchen's father was a door opener too."

"I know hardly anything about my grandparents," Kester said. "Other than the fact that they fled to England during the war. Mum told me they had to hide in someone's barn for ages to avoid detection."

"That's right," Miss Wellbeloved said. "Gretchen's parents' history was fascinating. German Jews, stuck in the middle of the Second World War. It must have been awful for them." She dabbed her eyes. "I can even remember the night we talked about it. We'd had a lot to drink. The only way to get your mother to open up about things was to feed her lots of alcohol."

"Yes, she never liked to talk about herself much," Kester agreed with a rueful smile. He remembered, with bitter clarity, countless evenings sat by the fire with his mother, Mildew the cat on his lap, as they chatted about their day. However, he'd learnt at an early age not to press her about the past. Her obvious discomfort at discussing it meant that he'd simply got out of the habit of asking.

"So," he pressed, "did she know that her dad was a door opener?"

"Yes, though I don't think she realised the extent of his powers until he died," Miss Wellbeloved said. "Your mum had only been at the SSFE for a few months when she found out he didn't have long to live." She paused, then studied Kester intently. "Sorry, I should remember I'm talking about your grandfather here."

"It's okay," Kester said. "I didn't know him, so it doesn't upset me. When did Mum realise that she had spirit door opening abilities too?"

Miss Wellbeloved shrugged. "Good question. Gretchen never really talked about it. However, her parents probably suspected what she was capable of—otherwise, why would they have sent her to the SSFE? But I don't think she realised the extent of her ability until her father told her, on the night he died."

Kester sat in silence, taking it all in. *There was so much I didn't know about her,* he thought, torn between sadness and frustration. *And now, I can never ask her. It seems unfair, somehow. At least her father told her his secrets before he died. She didn't do that for me.*

A brisk cough startled him from his thoughts. Ribero stood by the doorway, devilish grin in place. "Let me guess," he declared, as he stomped across the floor. "You have solved the mystery already, right?"

"Wrong," Kester replied with a grin. "There's not a single painting in here that relates to being held to ransom. No highwaymen, no images about bribery, not even any pictures featuring money. We've hit a dead end."

Ribero twirled his moustache, glaring around the room as though expecting the relevant painting to somehow magically appear. "That is not good," he said finally. "Maybe another gallery, right?"

Kester nodded. "How is your cramp?"

His father's eyes glittered dangerously. "It is gone. And it was no big deal, okay? So, no making a mountain out of a molehill."

"Did you finish the cake?" Kester asked.

Ribero grimaced. "It was too sugary, not such a good flavour. I put it in the bin. Next time, get me a pastry. I like those much better."

Kester frowned, trailing after his father as he marched back out of the room. *I could have enjoyed that cake,* he thought gloomily. *Still, I suppose it would only ruin my diet.*

"What now?" Miss Wellbeloved asked. Light poured in from the atrium windows above their heads, a sharp contrast to the dark gallery they'd emerged from. "Should we try any other galleries, do you think?"

"Are there any other galleries?" Kester asked.

"I have absolutely no idea." She stuffed a hand in her pocket, yanked out a tissue, then blew her nose loudly. "We could look it up on my phone, couldn't we? See if there are any others in town."

Kester shook his head. A wave of tiredness hit him like a lead pillow, and at present, the only appealing option was going home and climbing back under his duvet. "I don't see any point," he replied. "I think we need to rewind a bit. Return to the start and try to figure out the best course of action."

"Remember, time is not our friend," Ribero said seriously. He placed a hand on Kester's shoulder, dark eyes fixed on him with hawkish intensity. "We must make progress, yes? Otherwise, no payment for us. It is that simple."

"We could search for other cases," Kester said weakly. "Like the familiar in the Topsham pub. Nice, easy ones like that."

Ribero rolled his eyes, dragging Kester towards the stairs. "They will not keep us going, you see? We need high profile cases. Then we get our reputation back and we get better paid jobs. We have to, do you understand?"

"I do," Kester said heavily. "And I'm sure we'll get to the bottom of this Thelemite case in the end. Just give me a while to think about it." He marched onwards, shoes clattering on the polished stairs. "That's all I ask. A day or so to review all the information so far. Okay?"

His father muttered something under his breath but was silenced by a look from Miss Wellbeloved. "Fine," he agreed eventually. "But then you get on with it."

"Why is it my responsibility?"

"Because you are the spirit door opener and know more about Hrschni than anyone else!" Ribero exclaimed, hands extended to the ceiling in furious protest. "This is not difficult to comprehend, right?"

"All right, all right." Kester pursed his lips together. There was more he was tempted to say, but now probably wasn't the time to say it. "I'm going home, then. I'll see you in the office tomorrow."

"Don't you want a cup of tea?" Miss Wellbeloved gestured to the café, which had become even busier than before.

Kester surveyed the crowd of young children shouting by the counter and shook his head. "I think I'll pass."

Miss Wellbeloved gave him a brief hug. "Go and get some sleep then," she said. "I hope your hangover is better in the morning."

He laughed weakly. "So do I. It's unfair, I didn't even drink that much."

Exiting the building, he was immediately assaulted by a brisk wind which swept his hair around his face in a most irritating manner. Struggling to pull his fringe out from behind his glasses, he nearly stumbled down the entrance steps, then promptly managed to walk into someone's back.

"I do apologise!" Kester said instinctively, as he tugged his glasses off to release his trapped hair. "I wasn't looking where I was going, and—"

"Hello, Kester."

Kester's apologetic smile froze, faltered, then died. Anya stood before him, blonde hair covered in a woolly hat topped with the biggest pom-pom he'd seen in his life. His heart thudded painfully in his chest. He opened his mouth, closed it, then promptly opened it again.

"Hello." The response was strained, not to mention embarrassingly high-pitched. *Act cool!* he ordered himself sternly, not trusting himself to look her in the eye. "If you'll excuse me, I have to go home and—"

"Kester, I know you must hate me." She trotted beside him,

keeping pace despite his attempts to speed up. "But please, just give me some time to explain things . . ."

He shook his head. The first blossoming of anger, raw and painful, expanded in his chest. "No, I don't want to," he replied tightly. "And you know perfectly well why not."

"You don't understand!" She grasped his arm, saw his expression, and promptly dropped it again. "It's not how you think it is."

He dared a glance at her face, then wished he hadn't. *She's lost weight,* he realised. Her cheekbones were unusually prominent, and her eyes hollow with shadows. However, that was nothing compared to her ravaged, desperate expression. *I wish I could just wrap her in my arms and tell her everything will be okay,* he thought, then steeled himself. He knew it could never be okay again, not after her betrayal. *I won't be fooled by her. Not this time. Not ever again.*

"Can we talk?" Anya persisted. "I could buy you a cup of tea, perhaps a bacon sandwich?" A hint of a smile tugged her lips but disappeared as soon as she met his gaze. "Please, Kester?"

He sighed, then pulled his jacket up firmly. "Absolutely not. And Anya?"

"Yes?"

"Don't *ever* talk to me again. I mean it." With those parting words howling in his head, he stalked away, refusing to look back. There was no way of knowing for sure, but he could almost feel her eyes burrowing into his back as he strode quickly along the pavement.

Should I go back to her? A sharp prickle of a tear caught the corner of his eye, and he wiped it away furiously, ashamed at his weakness. Every part of him ached to run back, to forget everything and just be *with* her again. But he knew it could never be the same. Their relationship was broken beyond repair.

Finally, curiosity got the better of him. He peered over his shoulder, anticipating the sight of her, rooted to the spot, staring sadly after him. However, she was nowhere to be seen. Crowds milled around, peering into windows, chatting, smiling as they gossiped on the phone. But Anya had vanished from sight.

The full weight of it all settled agonisingly within him, a suffocating pressure of misery and dismay. *And rejection,* he thought, jaw tensing. *She didn't even try to run after me. She walked away, just like she did last time.*

Should I have listened to what she had to say? he wondered. *Or would it have just been more deception?* He sidestepped absentmindedly around a mother fussing over her baby in a pram. *Have I missed the only chance to make things right again with her?*

Overhead, the first specks of rain started to fall, a freezing fuzz of moisture that threatened to turn into sleet at any moment. He straightened, filled with sudden resolve.

I was right to walk away, he reassured himself, fighting to smother down the desire to cry. *She's nothing to me now. After all, she's a Thelemite. And that means she's part of their horrible games.*

CHAPTER 6: TINKER'S FINDINGS AND RIBERO'S REVELATION

"I don't believe it." Mike's wail echoed around the office before being muffled as he sank his head into his arms. Judging from the rhythmic thumping, he was presently banging his forehead against his desk.

Pamela popped out from behind her computer, alert as a bloodhound. "Problem, dear?"

Vague mutterings emanated from the region of Mike's elbow. Kester raised an eyebrow, then got back to reading the *Historie of Spirits*. It wasn't uncommon for Mike to have meltdowns from time to time, particularly when one of his pieces of equipment exploded.

Finally, Mike raised his head. "Crispian," he announced, then sighed dramatically.

"Your brother?" Pamela looked up again, curious. "Oh dear, is he all right? I hope nothing bad has happened to him."

Mike growled under his breath, with an expression that suggested he disagreed. "The bastard's coming down to stay with me."

Serena chuckled. "But you hate each other. Why would he come to stay with you?"

"His bloody wife has left him," Mike continued. "Apparently Crispian was getting frisky with his secretary, and Margot found out. Now he wants to *get away from it all* and lick his wounds, the daft prat." He gestured angrily at his computer. "He's sent me an email telling me he's coming down tomorrow."

"Ah, that'll be nice," Pamela said as she rose and walked over to the stock cupboard. "Maybe you can patch up your relationship while he's here."

"Fat chance." Mike fumed at the screen as though it were personally responsible. "He'll spend all his time figuring out new ways to put me down." He sighed, then slumped his head in his hands again. "He always makes me feel so *rubbish* about myself."

"Oh diddums," Serena said. "Having to cope with your big brother. How will you survive?" Since New Year's Eve, she'd been even pricklier towards Mike than ever, and the atmosphere in the office was nothing short of hostile.

"You try living with him," Mike snapped. "See how long you last."

"I don't know," Serena replied, as she casually inspected her fingernails. "I thought the photo of him that you showed us a while back was quite cute."

Mike pursed his lips so tightly that they vanished. As he opened his mouth to retort, Kester quickly interrupted.

"Does anyone know what time Tinker's calling?" Earlier that morning Miss Wellbeloved had emailed Tinker, asking him to phone them, but so far they hadn't heard anything.

"Who gives a toss what time Tinker's—"

"I got an email from him a few minutes ago," Miss Wellbeloved replied smoothly, ignoring Mike's baleful stare. "He said he'll call as soon as he can; he's busy working on something at the moment."

Kester sighed, then returned to his book. He wanted to ask Tinker some more questions about the mysterious key he'd received from the Thelemites. *Oh well,* he thought, glancing at the clock, which seemed to have either got stuck or was going even slower than usual. *I may as well get on with preparing for next Monday instead.* The start of his university course was approaching fast, and he felt woefully underprepared.

Sighing, he continued reading.

> *The Djinn realised that the daemon king Arsaces, though powerful, was not a benevolent ruler. The daemon's vision of a united world, an existence between the spirit and human realms, was drifting into a chaotic dictatorship. The Persians grew frightened, sensing their master's terrible ambitions.*
>
> *The Djinn waited and watched. Mindful of its position, it assisted the daemon outwardly, but inwardly, plotted. "His plans must not come to fruition," it decided, and silently, it amassed an army of its own to conquer him.*

"Has anyone else read this *Historie of Spirits* book?" Kester asked finally, looking up. It was quite a fun story, but he couldn't really see how it related to spirit intervention.

Pamela glanced over. "Yes, it was a recommended text back when I was studying at the SSFE. I don't remember much about it, to be honest. Why?"

Kester cleared his throat, then closed the book. "I just wondered why Dr. Barqa-Abu sent it to me. It's all about a djinn; I wonder if that's why she likes it?"

"Remind me again?" Pamela asked, as she swivelled in her chair.

"It's just about some daemon who becomes ruler of the Persians with the help of a djinn, but the djinn is actually plotting behind his back. Or something like that, anyway."

Miss Wellbeloved looked over. "I think I remember that story. To be honest, Kester, I wouldn't worry too much about it. I doubt that book will be covered much on the syllabus; there are a lot of experts who believe it's all made-up nonsense anyway. Heaven knows why Dr. Barqa-Abu felt you should read it, I thought it'd come off the recommended reading list a long time ago."

Kester laughed. "It's probably to help me brush up on my knowledge. There's still so much I don't know." He paused, then ran his fingers thoughtfully along the book's cover. "I'm dreading Monday, you know."

Miss Wellbeloved smiled. "You'll be fine. As for Dr. Barqa-Abu, her heart is in the right place, even if she's intimidating at times."

At times? Kester thought, with a rueful grin. *Try all the time. Even hearing that djinn's name scares me.*

"She won't be as intimidating as my brother," Mike moaned.

"Oh Mike, give it a rest, would you?" Serena retorted. "He's your sibling for goodness sake, not the Antichrist."

"You don't know him like I do. Honestly, he's—"

"—a perfectly normal guy whom you're jealous of because he's more successful than you are?"

Thankfully, the phone rang loudly, cutting Mike off midexpletive. Miss Wellbeloved quickly scooped up the receiver, then nodded.

"Hello Tinker, thank you very much for calling us." She waved at Kester to come closer. "It wasn't me who wanted to talk to you, actually; it was Kester. Hang on, let me pass you over."

Kester grabbed the phone.

"Hello there." Tinker sounded every bit as flustered and timid over the phone as he did in person. "I take it you have some further questions about the key, is that right? I should tell you that—"

"Yes, I did," Kester interrupted. Although he'd only met Tinker a handful of times, he knew better than to let him continue waffling on. "As you already know, I received another envelope, this time from the head of the local museum."

"Most mysterious," Tinker said, sounding rather breathless. "I can only presume that the gentleman in question is also working for the Thelemites, and perhaps has been awarded the task of—"

"Yes, you're probably right." Kester winked at Miss Wellbeloved, then settled himself on the corner of her desk. "Anyway, we're desperately trying to uncover more clues here, and I wondered if you could tell us anything more about that key?"

Tinker cleared his throat. "As it happens, I can. I got in touch with an antiques expert in Camden, and he had a look at it for us. He said that the pattern was unusually ornate and suggested it dated from the 1800s. He also verified that it was Italian. In fact, quite remarkably, he was able to tell us precisely which workshop manufactured it, due to the hallmark on the side."

"Really?" Kester was surprised. He had no idea that hallmarks were so specific. "Which workshop was it, then?"

"The key would have originally been made to unlock an ornate box," Tinker continued. "And these boxes were crafted in a place called Gardone Riviera, in Italy. Their craftsmanship is apparently very well known across the world, you see, and—"

"Gardone Riviera?" Kester frowned. The place sounded familiar. *Has someone mentioned it recently?* he wondered.

"Yes, I'm afraid I haven't got around to finding out where that is, but that's where the key is originally from, anyway." Tinker coughed loudly. "Not that it's probably much help, as these ornate boxes were sold across the globe."

"What about the paper itself or the ink?" Kester asked. "Anything unusual about them?"

"The paper is unusually high quality," Tinker replied carefully. "It's obviously expensive. But there are no distinctive features to tell us anything further, I'm afraid. The same applies for the ink."

Kester nodded. "I see. Thanks, Tinker. I'm not sure whether the information will be useful or not, but you never know."

"That's quite all right. Cardigan said if you could keep us all informed if there are any developments your end, that would be most appreciated, and—"

"Of course," Kester interrupted. He smiled at the thought of Cardigan Cummings; large, implacable, and astonishingly calm, even in the face of adversity. He hadn't spent a lot of time with him, or his colleague, Ian Kingdom-Green, but he'd enjoyed working with them both and sometimes wished they had more opportunity to work together. However, being up in London meant they were difficult to reach, and most communication was done over the phone.

Putting down the receiver, he sighed heavily and headed back to his desk. The others were looking at him expectantly.

"Well?" Miss Wellbeloved asked.

Kester pointed at his father's office. "Should I wait for Dad to wake up?" He glanced at the clock. It was still another fifteen minutes before Ribero was due to emerge from his daily nap.

"Good heavens, no," Miss Wellbeloved said. "Come on, tell us what you found out."

Quickly, Kester related what Tinker had told him. "Does Gardone Riviera sound familiar to any of you lot?" he asked, looking around. "For some reason, it's ringing bells for me."

Serena tucked her hair neatly around her ear, frowning in concentration. "I know what you mean. But I can't imagine why we would have heard of it. It's not like we ever deal with Italian spirits, is it?"

Kester clicked on his computer keyboard, bringing the screen to life again. "I'll type it in online, see what I can find out about it." The internet whirred through its usual machinations, but he was so used to its pitifully slow pace by now that he hardly noticed.

"Here we go," he said finally, as he scanned the screen. "Gardone Riviera. It's apparently a small tourist resort, located on the western shores of Lake Garda in Italy. It's in the province of Brescia, and its most famous attraction is the *Il Vittoriale del Italiani*—"

"I'm certain you didn't pronounce that right," Serena interrupted.

"That hardly matters, does it?" Mike growled. "God, woman, you always have to *pick* at everyone—"

"I'm merely saying that—"

"My goodness!" Kester leapt backwards so forcefully that his glasses fell askew across his nose. "That's it! Of course, how could I have forgotten!"

"Here we go again," Mike said wryly. "Kester's had one of his detective moments. Go on, Sherlock, what have you uncovered this time?"

Kester shoved his glasses back into position, then beamed at them all. "Do you remember the Bloody Mary case?"

"Of course we remember it," Serena snapped. "The spirit nearly killed me. How could I forget?"

"And Mike practically burned the house down," Pamela added.

Kester nodded. It had only been a few months since the Bloody Mary case, but so much had happened since then that it felt like a lifetime ago. *I was so naive back then,* he thought, as he recollected his blind fear when they'd entered the house on Colleton Crescent. The mesmerising, menacing eyes of the Bloody Mary, concealed in the portrait of a green-dressed woman, still haunted him from time to time.

"How does the Bloody Mary case relate to this?" Miss Wellbeloved asked, with a perplexed look in his direction.

"The painter!" Kester exclaimed. "Do you remember the painter who created the portrait of the green-dressed lady? He'd lived in Italy for a while—that's where he made the painting. Don't you remember? We found a website that told us all about the house he'd lived in. That was in Gardone Riviera, I'm sure of it."

Mike folded his arms sceptically. "It's surely just a coincidence. I can't see how that painter would link to the Thelemites."

Kester sank back into his seat, brow furrowed. "No, I suppose you're right," he concluded as he leant back and regarded the ceiling. "After all, Gardone Riviera is a fairly popular resort. I suppose lots of people have been there."

"I haven't," Serena snapped. "I never get to go anywhere nice; I don't make enough money." She glared balefully in Miss Wellbeloved's direction, expression suggesting that she held her solely responsible.

A deafening bang reverberated from wall to wall. Ribero stood, framed in the doorway, hand still poised against his open door, which was still quivering from the impact. His face was ashen.

"Gosh, are you all right?" Pamela instinctively bustled over and clasped him by the shoulder. She looked over at the others, who looked every bit as surprised as she did.

Ribero opened his mouth. His lip was quivering. "I . . . I do not think that I am . . ."

"What's that?" Serena shouted. "We can't understand you; you're slurring your words."

Kester leapt up at the sight of the confusion in his father's eyes. "Dad, why don't you come back into the office?" he suggested, guiding him gently backwards.

Ribero faltered, eyes glazed and fixed on the floor. "I . . . I woke and now I do not know . . ."

Kester shook his head quickly at the others, stopping their inevitable questions. "It's okay," he said carefully, as he steered Ribero into the cosy confines of his office. "Let's sit you down, you'll feel better in a few moments." *At least, I hope he does,* he thought with silent alarm. He'd never seen his father this bad before. His speech was incoherent and barely audible, but it was the panic and bafflement in his expression that worried Kester more.

Closing the door behind them, Kester coaxed his father into his armchair, then poured a glass of water. Ribero sighed, reached to take the glass, then removed his hand quickly.

"I cannot hold it," he whispered, eyebrows knotted. "My . . . my hands. You see?"

Kester nodded, crouched down in front of his father, and clasped his hands between his own palms, fighting to keep them steady. "It will pass," he said calmly, and stroked rhythmically with his thumbs. The skin felt loose and malleable, a smooth blanket coating the knobbly skeleton beneath. Finally, the trembles subsided.

"What happened?" Kester said finally. "Did you wake up too quickly? Is that what brought on the attack?"

Ribero closed his eyes, head dropping to his chest.

"Are you okay? Do you want me to get you a doctor?"

Ribero shook his head, and then, to Kester's horror, let out a sob. "I am so old, Kester. And the Parkinson, it is taking me over."

Kester clasped his father's hands even more tightly, massaging them as though boosting his circulation would somehow raise his spirits. "Come on, Dad, don't talk like that. You're just having a bad episode, that's all. You'll be okay in a moment."

Ribero sighed, an expression of terrible resignation. "It has been bad for a few weeks, Kester. And now my speech is going. I am . . ."

"You're what?"

His father slumped back against the headrest. "I am frightened."

You can't say that. Kester scanned Ribero's face, hoping to see a sign of his usual good humour or at least his bluster. *You can't be frightened. Because if you're frightened, then that means you're going to say you can't continue running the agency any more, and that would be terrible.* "What are you frightened about?" he said finally.

"That I am not capable, yes? That I am failing. That I am letting you all down."

"You're not letting anyone down." Kester eased his knee out. The bone popped loudly as he moved to the swivel chair. "Honestly, we all understand that you sometimes feel a bit poorly."

"This is more than *a bit poorly*!" Ribero shouted, fist slamming down on the table beside him. "Kester, I have the Parkinson, and it will only get worse! Do you not understand, silly boy?" He waved wildly at the door. "And they don't know. You know. Jennifer knows. But the others, they have no idea."

"Then tell them," Kester said quickly. "They won't think any less of you. Plenty of people live with Parkinson's, Dad. It's not a life sentence."

"Then why does it feel like my body is a prison, eh?"

Kester chewed his lips. He had no answer. *How can I tell him everything will be all right when I don't know that myself?* "Is it time for . . ." he began, then faltered.

Ribero looked up, eyes bright as a fox. "Yes."

"You don't know what I was going to say!"

"You were going to say, is it time for you and Jennifer to take over."

"And your answer for that was *yes*?" Kester was horrified. He'd always presumed his father would cling to his leadership until the bitter end. This shaking, wild-eyed man, shrunken into the folds of his leather armchair, was a horrible contrast to the suave, leonine gentleman that usually occupied the space.

Ribero nodded slowly. "I think it is time. I will still come to the office. I have nowhere else to go. But you and Jennifer will take over the agency."

Kester closed his eyes, letting the full impact of the words hit him. "I wish you'd reconsider," he muttered finally. "I don't think I'm ready for this."

The room fell silent. His father reached for the glass of water and sipped it, fingers still trembling. "You must be ready," he concluded simply. "We have no other choice. I cannot make all the decisions when I am like this, okay?"

No, not okay, Kester thought glumly. *About as not okay as you can get. How the hell am I expected to run a supernatural agency which I only joined a few months ago, whilst also studying an online degree? Not to mention the fact that I know virtually nothing about spirits. It's a recipe for disaster.*

"Jennifer will take on most of the responsibility," Ribero said, guessing his thoughts. "You will learn from her. Help her. Then, when you are ready, the agency will be yours."

"If I must," Kester said heavily.

"You must. You need to change your name too."

"What?" Kester's head jerked up. "Why would I want to do that? I like the name Kester." *Don't say he wants me to name myself something Argentinian like Juan or Felipe,* he thought. *I'd feel like a right imposter.*

"Not the Kester part!" Ribero snorted. "You need to become a Ribero. We are called Dr. Ribero's Agency of the Supernatural. That cannot change."

Kester sighed, then folded his arms, trying to figure out the best way to placate his father, who was getting more worked up with every passing second. "It can still be called that," he suggested gently. "But I'm not changing my name. My mother was a Lanner. I'm staying a Lanner. And that's the end of the matter."

A knock at the door prevented Ribero from answering, which, if his thunderous expression was anything to go by, was fortunate. A moment later, Miss Wellbeloved poked her head around the door.

"May I come in?" she said quietly, then without waiting for an answer, slipped inside and silently shut the door. "We're all very worried. Are you feeling any better, Julio?"

Ribero flapped a hand in her direction, face red with indignation. "I am telling the boy his responsibilities, Jennifer, and he is saying no. I am not happy."

"I accepted the responsibility of taking on joint management of the agency," Kester flared. "I didn't agree to changing my surname!"

Miss Wellbeloved stifled a smile and moved over to the desk. "I don't believe Kester is under any contractual obligation to become a Ribero, Julio."

Ribero grunted, arms folded. "It is a nice surname. I do not see the problem."

Miss Wellbeloved sat down on the corner of the desk, then studied him intently. "Have you decided that you can no longer run the agency? Is that what this conversation is about?"

Ribero exhaled loudly. "Yes," he replied. "That is what we were talking about. I can no longer trust myself. Not when I am like *this*." He gestured to himself, face full of disgust.

"I see." Miss Wellbeloved glanced at Kester, eyes softening. "And how do you feel about this?"

Kester shrugged. He wasn't sure how he felt about it, to be honest. It was inevitable that this day would come, but now that it was here, it filled him with anxiety, dread, and a vague hint of excitement. *I certainly don't feel ready to take it on,* he thought, *but I doubt I ever will. So it may as well be now.*

"If Dad needs to take a break from it all," he began, still watching his father's hands tremble violently in his lap, "then I'll do what I can to make life easier. But don't give me anything important to do. You know I'll bodge it up."

Miss Wellbeloved smiled. "You're far more capable than you give yourself credit for. However," she continued, as she placed a steadying hand on Ribero's shoulder, "I'll take on the bulk of the management duties. And as I once said to Kester, we can explore the option of merging agencies."

"What?" Ribero's head shot up as though yanked by a string. "What agency? What is this?"

"Well," Miss Wellbeloved began slowly, steeling herself for the inevitable outburst. "Kester and I discussed the possibility of joining forces with another supernatural agency. We would win more high-profile jobs if we pooled our talents with someone else."

Kester looked at his father and winced. Ribero's cheeks had gone a worrying shade of maroon.

"And who do you plan joining forces with, eh?"

"Larry Higgins," Miss Wellbeloved replied smoothly, though the anxious flitting of her eyes revealed her nerves. "I spoke to him a while back and he wasn't against the idea."

"Never! Never! Woman, what are you doing to me? This is my agency, you cannot—"

"Julio, you've always said it was my agency really. My father wanted it to be run by a male, but those sexist views are dated. It's time I started to have more input into this agency's future, and now is a good time to start."

Ribero puffed out his cheeks, grasping the arms of his chair to contain himself. "This is *treason*," he spat finally, then looked over at Kester, who was doing his best to make himself invisible in the corner. "Did you know about this?"

"Um, Miss Wellbeloved might have mentioned it a while back," Kester admitted. "But we only talked about it briefly, nothing was finalised."

"So you are in this together, right?" Ribero clasped a hand over his mouth, then started to mutter wildly in Spanish, shaking his already tremoring hands towards the ceiling. Miss Wellbeloved met Kester's eye and cringed.

"Perhaps we should continue this conversation another time," she suggested calmly, "when you're a bit less overwrought. I must say, I thought you'd be a little less dramatic about it."

"The Higgins is my sworn enemy! You know this! He is a *pig* in man's clothing! He is a turd upon my shoe! He is a—"

"—Yes, I get the point," Miss Wellbeloved interrupted quickly. "We know you don't like him. However, he's the only other agency left in the south aside from Infinite Enterprises. If we don't join him, we'll end up going bankrupt and you know it."

"Then join the Infinite bloody Enterprises then! Anyone but the Higgins!"

"As if Infinite Enterprises would want to join us!" Miss Well-beloved scoffed. She smoothed back her hair, which had unravelled from her bun, giving her a slightly crazed appearance. "Dear me, Julio, Infinite Enterprises are a multimillion-pound organisation with over one hundred employees. They wouldn't bother with small fry like us."

Ribero unleashed a cry that sounded uncannily like a cat in heat, then slumped back against his chair, eyeing them both with open fury. "You have betrayed me both," he whispered, and rolled his eyes as though in agony. "My heart, it feels such *pain* at this. You wait until I am vulnerable, yes? Then you *pounce.*"

"Oh, for goodness sake!" Miss Wellbeloved exclaimed, finally losing her patience. "Nobody has pounced on you! It was you who asked us to take over the agency, so now we're going to do what's best for us all! We should have done this years ago."

Ribero suddenly pitched forward and stabbed at her with his finger. "Fine," he hissed, brows furrowing dangerously low. "But I will have nothing more to do with it. You hear me? You do this, and I will *never* come back."

"Dad, just calm down," Kester said placatingly. "You've misunderstood our intentions. We want the agency to survive, and if we carry on as we are now, it won't."

"It sounds like you have already made your decision." Ribero pursed his lips, moustache wrinkling furiously under his nose. "There is nothing more to be said. I will leave now."

"You're not going anywhere," Miss Wellbeloved said urgently, and grasped him by the shoulder. "Come on, Julio, I didn't say we'd definitely merge agencies. I merely said that we needed to explore our—"

"You said *enough,*" Ribero said heavily. He stood awkwardly, grasping the corner of the desk for balance. "I will get the taxi home. You do not need to worry about me driving."

"Dad, don't go," Kester continued, but he could see from the expression on his father's face that any protest was futile. With one last wounded glare, Ribero spun on his heel and stormed out of the office, slamming the door. Miss Wellbeloved stared after him, mouth hanging open. They remained motionless for a minute or so, taking time to register the severity of the situation.

"That didn't go very well," Miss Wellbeloved said finally, and slumped into Ribero's vacated armchair, pressing her head wearily against the headrest.

"Perhaps it wasn't the right time to bring it up?" Kester suggested gently. He wanted to run after Ribero and talk him round, but he suspected there wouldn't be much point. By now he knew better than to try to calm his father when he was in one of his rages, especially if the anger was caused by Larry Higgins.

Miss Wellbeloved sighed deeply and stroked the leather armrest. "Perhaps not," she admitted. "But when would have been a good time?"

Kester shrugged. "I don't know," he said. "Do you really think it's the best thing? Joining with Larry Higgins, I mean?"

"I think so," Miss Wellbeloved replied. "I've been through the figures, and if we carry on the way we're going, we'll run out of money within a year."

"Gosh," Kester said. "The problem is, though," he continued, trying to be as diplomatic as he could, "you know Dad hates Higgins. This is about the worst thing that could happen to him."

"I know, Kester!" Miss Wellbeloved snapped. She shook her head angrily. "Don't you think I've discussed it with him on several occasions? Every time I bring up the fact that we're running out of money, he buries his head in the sand! If he'd have addressed the problem several years ago, we wouldn't be in this position now!"

"Couldn't you take out a loan?"

Miss Wellbeloved laughed bitterly. "There's no way we could pay it back. In my grandfather's day, the agency had the respect of all the banks in town. Now look at us."

"But you said yourself, times are difficult now. It's far harder to make a living as a supernatural agent, because spirits are now less believed in and more disliked than ever."

She shrugged. "Perhaps. There are only so many excuses we can make, though." Straightening, she pounded her fist against the chair. "I'm pretty sure Larry Higgins is our only hope, unfortunately."

Kester rubbed his temples. *I understand where she's coming from,* he thought, as he studied her in silence. *But I'm worried about the solution she's come up with.* "You'll have to make sure Higgins doesn't have too much control," he said finally.

"Absolutely," Miss Wellbeloved said firmly. "There's no question of him seizing this agency, if that's what you're worried about."

Isn't there? Kester wondered. The Larry Higgins he'd become accustomed to was greedy, pigheaded, and belligerent to a fault, and he could well imagine the man trying to take things over.

"Very well," he nodded finally. "Shall I try to pacify Dad, or shall you?"

Miss Wellbeloved smiled faintly. "We may as well both have a go," she said. "Honestly, it's worse than having a baby."

Kester imagined how the conversation might go, with his father ranting and raging for hours on end. *And I don't fancy my chances at calming him down,* he thought. *Not one bit.*

CHAPTER 7: CONVERSATIONS AND REVELATIONS

The first session of Kester's course didn't get off to an auspicious start. Only hours before his first evening session he discovered that his laptop had stopped working, and even after Mike had fiddled about with a screwdriver for an hour, it still refused to switch on.

Fortunately, Pamela offered use of her computer, with the promise that she'd stay out of the way whilst he was studying. When Kester arrived at her house later that evening, he discovered that the promise didn't extend to Hemingway, her exuberant, hairy dog who immediately set about coating him in a shower of enthusiastic slobber.

"Cup of tea?" Pamela asked, as she peered around the dining room door.

Kester looked up and shook his head nervously. "No thanks, it'll make me need another wee." The last thing he wanted was for Dr. Barqa-Abu to think he had bladder issues or something.

Pamela peered over his shoulder at the clock on the computer screen. "Only a few more minutes," she muttered, ignoring Hemingway as his tail thumped rhythmically against the chair leg. "It's impressive they can do it all online these days. It's lucky you're being taught by a djinn and not any other spirit; most spirits can't tolerate technology."

"Does it hurt them?"

"It can. It certainly messes up the broadband speeds, I can tell you. But ancient djinns like Dr. Barqa-Abu are skilled at managing their energy, unlike the others. We had a case where a ghoul got into a call centre once. Absolute chaos, it was. Exploded computers everywhere."

"Did you enjoy studying at the SSFE?" Kester asked, changing the subject. He welcomed the distraction. Staring at a blank computer screen, waiting for a terrifying djinn to come into focus, wasn't his idea of fun.

"Yes, very much," Pamela said wistfully. "It was the first time I realised I wasn't a freak, and that there were other people like me."

Kester smiled sympathetically. "I take it your parents weren't very supportive of your talents?"

"Ah, they did their best," Pamela replied. "But Dad was a vicar, you see. So, having a psychic as a daughter wasn't very convenient." She reached down and patted Hemingway's head, who writhed gleefully in response. "Come on, you mangy mutt, we need to leave this boy in peace."

Kester tickled Hemingway behind the ears, then wished he hadn't when he saw all the sticky dog hairs attached to his fingers. "I'll see you both later then," he said, with a reluctant glance at the computer. Of all the things he fancied doing after work, this was very low down on the list.

Just as the dining room door clicked quietly shut, the computer came alive with a welcome message flashing across the screen. Kester gulped, then clicked the button to join the session.

At once, Dr. Barqa-Abu appeared on the screen, her familiar misty form weaving restlessly to and fro. Even though her face wasn't yet clear, Kester could sense her impatience.

"Are we all present?" she asked finally, in a voice of gravel and wind. Kester could see a few smaller images across the bottom of the screen, which he presumed were his classmates. All of them were nodding, and, to his relief, most looked as worried as he felt.

The djinn nodded, her features briefly coming into sharp relief, before tapping a skeletal finger on her desk. "I have reviewed your essays," she began, and whirled closer to the screen. "For the most part, they were satisfactory. Not particularly good, but they showed some basic knowledge of the subject, which is a start."

Kester sighed with relief. He'd only just managed to submit his on time, which was hardly surprising given how busy they'd been at work. *At least I haven't bombed the first test,* he thought, as he tapped his pen against his notepad. *Perhaps there's hope for me yet.*

"I hope you have all taken the time to familiarise yourself with the syllabus," the djinn continued smoothly, black eyes simmering in their direction. "I will not waste time explaining the modules. The lessons will be divided between myself and Dr. Ryland Quincy, who will be taking the business studies classes. I, of course, will be covering spirit intervention."

Without any further preamble, she launched into an initial definition of intervention and the basic processes involved. Kester took notes frantically, struggling to keep pace with her ceaseless speech, which rose and fell hypnotically, like shifting sand in a dune. The other students interrupted at various intervals to ask questions, leaving him quite in awe. *I'd never dare to ask anything,* he thought, as he flicked over to the next clean page in his pad. *She scares me far too much, and, knowing my luck, I'd accidentally ask something horrendously stupid or insulting.*

The grandfather clock chimed softly behind him, causing Hemingway to bark from somewhere down the hallway, but Kester scarcely noticed. Indeed, he was surprised when Dr. Barqa-Abu eventually paused, ceased weaving for a moment, then announced it was the end of the first lesson.

"That was quite interesting!" he exclaimed, completely forgetting he could be heard.

Dr. Barqa-Abu's eyes narrowed. "I am glad you approve."

"Oh, I didn't mean that I expected it to be boring," Kester added quickly, aware that the other students were listening with great interest. "I just—"

"Now is not the time for feedback," the djinn hissed. "Class, please note that your next session will be in four days' time, with Dr. Quincy. You may now log off."

As Kester's hand reached towards the mouse, the djinn quickly added, "Not you, Mr. Lanner. I would like to talk to you."

His heart sank. *What have I done wrong?* he wondered, as he watched the djinn circle around on the screen, curling as smoothly as a python. *I bet it was my essay. She's just waited until the end to tell me off about it.*

She waited patiently until the other students had logged off, then fixed her empty gaze on Kester. "How are you?" she asked eventually. Her voice was almost kind.

"Um, very well, thank you?" he replied uncertainly.

Dr. Barqa-Abu ran a bony hand over the surface of her desk. "I presume that is not true. I have heard about what happened to you with the Thelemites in Chislehurst Caves."

"I suspected you might have," Kester said. He paused, waiting for her to continue, but she remained steadfastly silent. "I suppose it did rattle me a bit," he admitted finally. "I don't like the thought that Hrschni can get to me whenever he wants."

She nodded severely. "He was always unpredictable. I've been reminding the government of this for centuries, and they persist in ignoring me."

"Did you know Hrschni, then?"

The djinn made a harsh, grating sound, which might have been a laugh. "I used to. We have come into contact on many an occasion. The most recent being 1945."

Kester smiled. "That doesn't sound that recent to me."

"It's a drop in the ocean for the higher order of spirits."

Of course, he reminded himself. *A few decades are nothing to these guys.* "What was he like back then?" he asked, curious.

"He was inhabiting the body of a great war hero," Dr. Barqa-Abu said, "named Captain Monty Fletcher. There is plenty of information about Captain Fletcher online, though of course none of it recognises the fact that he was actually housing a daemon."

Kester vaguely remembered Curtis Philpot saying something about it in the past. "Fylgia fought in the war too, didn't she?" he asked. "Wasn't she a code breaker or something?"

"That is correct," the djinn said evenly, then commenced her ceaseless weaving once more, floating in and out of focus before his eyes. "We all worked together to fight the Nazis."

"Why do spirits get involved with human wars?" Kester asked. "Why not just stay out of it?"

Dr. Barqa-Abu paused. "Because we cannot leave you to destroy yourselves," she said finally. "It is against our nature."

"Oh." Kester pondered that for a moment. "Aren't spirits tempted to let humans wipe themselves out? After all, most humans don't treat you very nicely, do they?"

The djinn sighed. A glitter of emotion sparked her eyes, just for a moment. "That is only a recent thing," she replied. "We hope that one day, our relations will return to the way they were."

"What do you think Hrschni is going to do next?" Kester asked anxiously. Despite his instinctive dread of his professor, there was something about her that he trusted implicitly. *And she can't help looking so scary,* he realised. *Appearances aren't everything. I should know that more than anyone.*

Dr. Barqa-Abu looked at the clock on the wall behind her. "I must log off in a moment," she said eventually. "To answer your question, I do not know what the daemon will do next. But I think you will be safe. I do not think Hrschni wants to hurt you, if that is what you are concerned about."

"No, I don't think he wants to hurt me either," Kester agreed. "I don't suppose I could ask you one more question, could I?"

She flitted impatiently. "Very well. One final question."

"I received another letter from the Thelemites," he said quickly. "You may already know about it. It says: *The painting points the way. To find the answer, you must be held to ransom.* I can't figure it out at all, do you have any idea?"

The vaguest hint of a smile briefly tugged her lipless mouth before vanishing back into an unreadable mist. "It sounds," she said solemnly, "like the sort of riddle you may already know the answer to. Perhaps there's a word in there that means something to you? A word you've heard before?"

"I don't think so. I've been puzzling it over for ages and haven't got anywhere with it."

"I am certain you will solve the mystery and that the journey it will take you on will help you to see things more clearly."

Before Kester could question her further, Dr. Barqa-Abu shook her head. "It is late. Good night, Kester."

He nodded. "Good night. And thank you for your help."

She bowed, and the next minute, the screen was black. Kester shut the video app down and sat back in the chair, looking thoughtfully out of the window. A moment later, he heard the door creak open.

"How did it go?" Pamela's head appeared around the door, followed closely by Hemingway's.

"Okay, I think," Kester replied absentmindedly, still mulling over the djinn's mysterious last words. "I didn't embarrass myself, which was a good start."

Pamela sat on the saggy sofa beside him. "Good for you. Would you like anything to eat or drink? I made a very tasty lemon drizzle cake, and it's just come out of the oven."

Kester sniffed appreciatively. "It smells wonderful. I'll pass for now though, thanks. It's getting a bit late."

"More for me and Hemingway." At the sound of his name, Hemingway woofed appreciatively before leaping up on the sofa like the world's largest, hairiest mop.

"I asked Dr. Barqa-Abu about that weird clue," he said finally, as he stood up to leave. "You know, the one about the painting and being held to ransom."

Pamela leaned forward. "What did she say?"

"Not much. She said there might be a particular word that meant something to me, and that the journey would help me see more clearly, whatever that means."

"That's a strange thing to say." Pamela scratched the dog's tummy. He had stretched out so much he covered the entire sofa. "Almost like she knows something."

"There's no way she could, is there?"

Pamela shrugged. "You never know with djinn. They're secretive creatures."

"What do you mean?" Kester stuffed his notepad back into

his satchel and grabbed his coat. "Are you suggesting Dr. Barqa-Abu knows more than she's letting on? Could she be working with Hrschni? She said she knew him."

Pamela shook her head. "Not a chance. She's against what he's doing; she's made that very clear."

Kester recalled Dr. Barqa-Abu appearing out of nowhere in the cramped surveillance van in Whitby. It was thanks to her secretly entering the Thelemite lodge there that they'd found out valuable information about what Hrschni was up to. "What are you suggesting, then?" he asked, as he slung his jacket on.

"Djinn just *know* things," Pamela said simply. "They don't give much away to anyone else, but there's a lot going on in *here*." She tapped her forehead meaningfully, then flinched as Hemingway launched himself at her face, seeing it as an opportunity for a lick.

Kester smiled and patted the dog on the head. "If you say so. I'd better go, it's getting late."

"Are you sure you don't want to stay the night? I don't like the thought of you walking home in the dark."

"I'll be fine." Kester started to head towards the door. "Nobody ever notices me anyway. I'll just melt into the background like I normally do."

He stepped out into the cosy hallway, giving Pamela a cheery smile as he opened the front door. Icy winter air immediately circled in, making him miss Pamela's snug central heating even before he'd left the house.

"Thanks for letting me use your computer."

Pamela giggled and rubbed his arm affectionately. "Don't be silly, love. It's nice to have the company once in a while."

She waved him down the garden path and then shut the door, taking the last of the warmth and light with her. Kester tugged his jacket lapels as high as they would go, the chill air already stinging his eyes. *Roll on, spring,* he thought gloomily, crossing the road. *Except knowing this country, it won't get warm until at least July, and then it'll only last a few days before raining again.*

As though responding to his thoughts, a fleck of moisture landed on his nose, followed closely by another. Kester looked up to see the first stripes of rainfall illuminated by the streetlight.

You've got to be kidding me. Literally the minute I step out of the house? He picked up his pace as the rain fell harder; the deft specks of water swiftly transforming to big, soggy plops.

"Oh, this is just perfect," he muttered crossly, as he made his way up the hill. Thankfully, Pamela's house was only a fifteen-minute walk from his own, but given the heaviness of the down-pour, he was likely to be soaked when he arrived back home.

As further insult, the rain ceased the moment Kester put his key into the lock of his front door. Rolling his eyes skywards and shaking off the worst of the moisture, he stepped into his house. It even felt warm for once, though he suspected that was just in contrast to the horrible weather outside.

Pineapple poked his head around the lounge, alert as a meer-cat. "Yo, Kester," he greeted, hand suspended in salute. "Man, you been swimming or something?"

"Yes, that's right, I dived into the river for a laugh," Kester snapped sarcastically, stripping his jacket off.

"Jeez, that is pure bad for your health, you know? You don't want to go river swimming in the winter, that's crazy."

Kester studied Pineapple, then opened his mouth indignantly. "Hang on a minute, is that one of my shirts you're wearing?"

Pineapple plucked at the garment on his chest, then grinned. "I was keeping it warm for you, brother."

"Well don't!" Kester squawked, waving in Pineapple's direction. "Give it back now."

"Aw, just let me keep it a little while," Pineapple implored, hands pressed together. "I ain't got no other clothes, you feel me?"

"You've got plenty of other clothes, what are you talking about?" Kester had seen the extent of Pineapple's wardrobe, and most of it was lurid, tie-dyed, or made of shiny plastic.

Pineapple shook his head. "Nah, I proper messed them up."

Oh god, do I want to know? Kester thought, as he leaned heavily against the stair bannister. "Go on then," he said finally, against his better judgment. "Tell me what happened."

"It was on the internet, like," Pineapple began, warming to his story. "I follow MC Funkadonkey online, and he always has proper nice tips for unique clothing, yeah?"

"Was this the same guy who recommended splashing food all over your top?" Kester asked warily.

Pineapple brightened. "Yes! That is the man! Have you seen his videos?"

"No." Kester sighed. "Go on. What great tip did he have for you today? Smearing your clothes with excrement? Dropping them down the toilet for an authentic smell of rankness?"

"Nah, nothing like that. His video shows you how to use a lighter to make your tops crazy fried, like you've survived a fire or something."

"Why would you want to look as though you'd survived a fire?" Kester was genuinely baffled—and also had a horrible idea where this story was going. Come to mention it, there was a suspicious aroma of burnt fabric coming from the direction of the kitchen.

Pineapple nodded sagely, oblivious to Kester's look of alarm. "It's the look at all the raves, man. MC Funkadonkey calls it 'volcano-clubwear.' Proper smooth."

"So, let me guess," Kester said wearily. "You've burnt all your clothes."

His housemate at least had the good grace to look sheepish. "Most of them," he corrected. "It was harder to put out the fire than I realised, bro."

"At least you didn't burn the house down," Kester said, as he walked towards the kitchen.

"Only the kitchen unit." Pineapple's voice trailed behind him, just as Kester spotted the singed surfaces by the oven. "And it's only a bit damaged. No one would notice, would they, man? Proper sweet."

Kester groaned. The kitchen unit, which wasn't in the greatest condition to begin with, now boasted three large blackened patches, plus some unsightly bubbles of partially melted plastic. *I'm just going to pretend I can't see it,* he told himself firmly, as he strode to the fridge. Instead, he poured himself a large glass of wine and returned to the lounge.

"Don't say anything else, please," he said firmly to Pineapple, as he turned up the volume on the television. "You can keep the shirt for now, but don't even *think* about stealing any of my other clothes, okay?" He paused, then poured a substantial amount of the wine into his mouth. "And don't you *dare* burn anything else either."

"Got you loud and clear, my brethren." Pineapple sat silent for a few minutes, then promptly began to talk again. "By the way, got an email from Daisy. That sugarcoated sweetheart is on her way home, you feel?"

"Really?" Kester said, fighting to keep the complete lack of interest out of his voice. *Oh, good,* he thought morosely, as he half-heartedly watched the soap opera on television. *Two oddballs for the price of one. Normal service resumes.* "When is she back?" he asked.

"In two days' time. Her Romeo broke her heart in two, so she is downbeat and seriously sad. Not cool."

"Well," Kester said cheerfully, as he settled himself more comfortably into the sofa. "I'm impressed he put up with her for as long as he did, to be honest."

"She said he'd promised to take her all around Europe. France, Paris, Italy—"

"Paris *is* in France."

"Yeah, yeah, all France, yeah."

Kester looked outside the rain-coated window. "I could do with a bit of Italy right now, I can tell you."

"Right," Pineapple nodded, and folded himself into a cross-legged position. "Somewhere hot, man. Where the sun beats down and you don't need clothes."

"You still need clothes in Italy," Kester corrected him. "You can't just stride around naked, you know."

"Yeah." Pineapple closed his eyes and tilted his head towards the ceiling. "Proper blissful, you are right."

Kester sighed and returned his gaze to the television. *Being anywhere warm at the moment would be nice,* he thought, as he drained his glass. He was tempted to pour another, but he knew that would make getting up for work tomorrow even harder. *Perhaps I should save up and go on holiday. Not that I know much about Italy, apart from Gardone Riviera, and even that I only know about thanks to that Victorian painter and the green-dressed ghost.*

"Ahh!" Kester leapt up in his seat. His glass tumbled to the floor, missing the tiled hearth by inches.

Pineapple's eyes shot open. "You all right, man? That's some proper crazy look you've got there."

"Robert Ransome!"

"Eh?" Pineapple stared bovinely in his direction. "Is that someone you know?"

Kester scrabbled to his feet and nearly trod on the wineglass in the process. "Where's my phone?" he said wildly, as he patted his pockets. "I need to find it!"

Ignoring Pineapple's incoherent suggestions, he stormed out into the hallway and patted down his soaking jacket. Sure enough, his phone was still nestled in his inner pocket, slightly misted from the moisture but otherwise in full working order. He fumbled for the right number as he marched up the stairs, then pressed the phone to his ear.

Miss Wellbeloved answered after only a few rings. "I was about to go to bed, is everything all right?"

"Is Dad there with you?"

Miss Wellbeloved snorted. "Not a chance. He's still not speaking to me. Why are you calling, Kester?"

He dived into his bedroom and pressed the door closed behind him. "I think I've figured out the clue. You know, the one about being 'held to ransom.'"

"Really?"

"Yes." Judging by the silence, Kester could tell he had her full attention. "You know Tinker said the key came from Gardone Riviera in Italy?"

"Of course, why?"

"And I mentioned the painter, the one who created the green-dressed lady painting that the Bloody Mary hid in. I said that I remembered he'd been to Gardone Riviera, because we'd found it out while working on the case. Do you remember?"

Miss Wellbeloved chuckled. "How could I forget? That's one case I won't forget in a hurry."

"Yes," Kester continued breathlessly, "but we all forgot his name, didn't we?"

Miss Wellbeloved paused. "Go on," she said slowly. "Remind me."

"It's Robert Ransome. *Ransom.* Do you see?"

"Gosh!" Miss Wellbeloved spluttered down the phone. "*The painting points the way!* And then the clue says about being *held to ransom*! Kester, you absolute genius, you've done it again!"

Kester beamed. It felt nice to have someone tell him he was good at something for a change. "Dr. Barqa-Abu helped," he admitted. "It was something she said this evening that made me think of it."

"I think we need to revisit the gallery in the RAMM, don't we?" Miss Wellbeloved suggested. "I'll phone Pamela and ask her to look after things in the office tomorrow, and you and I can go there first thing in the morning."

"I should probably phone Dad," Kester said. "He needs to know too."

Miss Wellbeloved paused. "Absolutely. Only . . ."

"What?"

"Well, don't be too offended if he gives you the cold shoulder. Your father has a tendency to sulk at times."

Kester weighed it up in his mind. "We can't just give up on him, though, can we? Especially as he's going through such a tough time?"

"You're absolutely right," Miss Wellbeloved agreed. "Just make sure you're well prepared when you call him, okay?"

He laughed. "I'm sure I can handle it. I'm getting used to his mood swings."

After hanging up, he promptly dialled his father's number, excitement still firing through him. It might come to nothing. They might not be able to find a painting by Robert Ransome. But it was the best lead they'd had in a while, and it was one step closer to finding out what Hrschni was up to.

Finally, Ribero answered the phone. Kester was immediately struck by how frail he sounded.

"Dad, it's me," he began, keeping his voice as calm and authoritative as possible. "I've worked out what the latest clue from the Thelemites means, and I wanted to—"

"I do not care, Kester."

Kester's mouth dropped open. "What do you mean?" he said stupidly. "Look, if this is about what was said earlier in the office—"

"Of course it is! You cannot imagine how I feel, uncaring boy!"

Kester pulled the phone away from his ear, momentarily stunned by the force of Ribero's reaction. *Well, Miss Wellbeloved warned me he'd be sulky,* he thought, *but I wasn't prepared for this magnitude of anger.* "Calm down," he replied weakly, already well aware that the comment wouldn't go down very well.

"Calm down? I am betrayed by my own son and my oldest friend! How do you expect me to calm down, eh?"

"You betrayed Miss Wellbeloved a long time before she betrayed you!" Kester fired back, then immediately regretted it. The deafening silence from the other end of the line revealed just how badly his comment had been received.

"That was *different,*" his father hissed finally. "And how *dare* you use that against me! That was a cruel blow."

"I'm sorry," Kester replied, massaging his head. This was going even worse than he'd imagined. "But you need to stop attacking Miss Wellbeloved. It's not fair."

His father spat something in Spanish which he suspected was an expletive or two. "You tell me what is fair? You? Who has only been with us a few months? You do not understand these things, Kester!"

"And yet you're happy to leave me in charge of the whole agency!" Kester shouted back. "You can't have it both ways, Dad! You can't keep calling me stupid and ignorant, and then tell me

I'm qualified to manage your entire business! And you cannot keep attacking the woman who stuck by you even after you cheated on her!"

Ribero gasped. Kester took a deep breath. He knew he'd said too much.

"You do not know what it was like back then," his father whispered finally. The fight had suddenly left him, and he sounded fragile and hurt again. "I loved them both. And I did not mean to hurt Jennifer."

"I believe you," Kester said. "So, why not do this for her now? Let her take control of the agency again and let us merge with Larry Higgins."

"But it is *the Higgins*." His father sighed. "I cannot work with that man."

"You won't have to work with him," Kester said. "We'll keep you two apart. We'll get a solicitor to handle it to make sure it's all fair. And, if we work well together, there's a chance we'll start to win big contracts."

"But I will have to *see* him all the time. I do not want to look at his fat face, no? It makes me sick."

Isn't it time you just got over it? Kester thought with frustration. He knew that they'd hated each other at university, but it was decades in the past, and it seemed rather silly to let the feud continue. "You won't see him that often," he said placatingly. "Most of the time, we'll be working from Exeter, he'll be working from his offices in Southampton or Essex."

His father mused over it for a moment.

"I cannot be happy about it," he declared finally. "But I know I must do this for Jennifer. It should have been her agency, and I do not have the right to stand in her way."

Kester smiled, silently congratulating himself on his parent-management skills. "That's wonderful," he replied. "I know she'll be relieved. And don't worry. It'll all work out fine. It's better than the agency shutting down, isn't it?"

Ribero paused. "Yes. Jennifer's father trusted me to make a success of it. I could not live with myself if it failed."

"Just out of interest," Kester asked, shifting into a more comfortable position on the bed. "Why do you feel you owe him so much?"

"I do not know where I would be without the kindness of the Wellbeloved family." Ribero cleared his throat and paused. "When I arrived in this country, I had nothing. No money. I could only speak a few words of English, yes? I got in with a bad crowd. I did things I was not proud of. And I ended up badly hurt. In hospital."

"Really?" Kester sat up. "I had no idea. What happened?"

"Mr. Wellbeloved, Jennifer's father, was on a spirit job at Plymouth Hospital, where I was recovering. He spoke with me and realised my gift. It was a fortunate thing. And it turned my life around, yes?"

"I can imagine," Kester said. "So, they took you in?"

"I lived with the Wellbeloved family for two years before going to study at SSFE," Ribero finished. "By then, I was very in love with Jennifer. She was not only beautiful, she was also kind. It was her who taught me English."

And you broke her heart by sleeping with my mother, Kester concluded silently. He now understood the enormity of the debt Ribero owed Miss Wellbeloved and wondered how his father could even sleep at night. *To repay such kindness with such cruelty,* he thought with sudden anger. *How could he do it?*

"I am tired," Ribero said, interrupting his thoughts. "It has been a long day. Good night, my boy."

"Good night," Kester said automatically, and hung up. He

mulled over the conversation, imagining his father as a teenager, arriving in an unknown country, thousands of miles from home. It was only after a few minutes that he realised he'd completely forgotten to mention what he'd discovered earlier.

Oh well, he concluded, as he headed back downstairs again. *Some things are more important. And getting Dad to see sense was perhaps the most important thing of all.*

CHAPTER 8: A STRANGE ENCOUNTER

Kester stepped into the museum, glad to be out of the cold. Miss Wellbeloved had just phoned in a state of complete disarray and told him that she wouldn't be joining him after all. From what he could tell, it was something to do with a burst water pipe in the office, which had apparently leaked all over the floor during the night. *I'm lucky to be out,* he thought. He could imagine how irate the rest of the team were at this moment and didn't much fancy being a part of it all.

The old man at the reception desk gave him a welcoming smile and brandished a brochure in his direction. "Do you want a map?" he croaked, then promptly exploded into a succession of coughs. "I must say," he added, "you're very keen. We've only just opened."

"No, I'm all right thanks," Kester replied, as he hoisted his bag over his shoulder. "I know where I'm going."

The man beamed before breaking out into another round of spluttering. Kester quickly moved to avoid the shower of saliva that accompanied it. The last thing he needed right now was to catch a horrible winter cold.

To his delight, the gallery upstairs was completely deserted. The arched ceiling and white walls made the space feel almost ecclesiastical, and he adjusted his steps accordingly, adopting a more reverent pace to suit the mood. It was the perfect way to soothe his restless spirits and offer some respite from the ceaseless barrage of questions racing around his brain.

Silence accompanied him as he walked from painting to painting, giving him the chance to examine each one without interruption. The art mainly focused on scene after scene of dramatic Devon landscapes and windswept coastal images, but he couldn't find anything that had been painted by Robert Ransome.

It must be here somewhere, he thought, frowning. *There's no way I interpreted the clue wrongly. It makes perfect sense that the painting would be in this museum.*

He kept on looking. Finally, to his relief, he found the painting he was searching for. Robert Ransome's artwork wasn't much to look at: an innocuous oil painting that was darkened and mottled with age, dominated by a gilt frame that was far too large and ornate. Biting his lip with excitement, Kester leaned closer and read the description beside it.

> Lake Garda by Sunset, *Robert Ransome, 1842.*
>
> *Ransome is best known for* Haytor by Twilight, *as well as his detailed Devon landscapes. However, this painting is notable in that it is one of the few surviving works from his time spent in Gardone Riviera, Italy (1841–1845). The painting depicts the villa in which Ransome lived, which overlooks scenic Lake Garda.*

Kester felt a prickle run over his spine. He shivered. *So, that's the villa where Robert Ransome painted the horrible portrait of the green-dressed lady.* He felt an irresistible urge to touch the canvas, to connect in some brief way with the artist. However, the sad truth was that two hundred years stood between them, and he had no way of ever knowing the man's secrets.

"Why couldn't you have written a diary, like anyone else?" he muttered quietly. "That would have made this a lot easier." Scrutinising the image, he thought back to the clue. He was sure he'd found the right painting but wasn't sure what to make of it.

Let me think this through. Kester paced to the bench in the middle of the room and sat down heavily, eyes still fixed on Ransome's artwork. *Tinker tells us that the mysterious key is from Gardone Riviera,* he mused. *We then get a clue, which we think leads to the painter, Robert Ransome. And here's a painting, showing Gardone Riviera. Is that where we need to look next?*

He pulled out his phone, quickly took a photo of the canvas, then texted Miss Wellbeloved to keep her updated. At present, Kester couldn't tell what any of it meant, but he felt certain they were getting somewhere.

After a quick perusal of the rest of the galleries to check he hadn't missed any of Ransome's other works, he zipped up his jacket, ready to go back into the cold. It was probably still pandemonium in the office, but he knew he couldn't avoid it forever. He wondered just how much swearing and cursing had gone on in his absence.

He felt a tap on his shoulder and jumped.

"I do apologise," a woman's voice said smoothly. Kester turned and gasped. It was Parvati Chowdhury, one of the prominent members of the Exeter Thelemite Lodge; her petite height and piercing eyes made her immediately recognisable. The last time he'd seen her was at Chislehurst Caves, just after she and her group had kidnapped him.

"You?" he spluttered, instinctively stepping away. "What are *you* doing here?" *More to the point,* he thought with rising panic, *is Hrschni still inhabiting your body?* If the daemon was still inside her, he could be in serious danger. The place was empty, and he knew no one would get to him in time if he was attacked.

Parvati stuffed her hands into her jacket. "We need to talk."

"There's no way I'm talking to you," he hissed. "And if you lay a *finger* on me, I'll shout the place down, I swear."

Parvati held her hands out, palms open in supplication. "I'm not going to touch you. Nor will I hurt you in any way. I merely want to speak to you."

He peered at her intently, unsure how to respond.

"Who am I talking to, anyway?" he said finally, trying to seek out the spark of brightness that gave away the presence of a daemon. It was difficult to tell with the stark museum lights reflecting off her pupils. "Are you Parvati, or Hrschni?"

She nodded slowly. "The latter. Parvati has kindly granted me use of her physical form for this meeting."

Kester gasped. "We are *not* having a meeting. How dare you even suggest it, after what you did to me?"

"That's what we need to discuss," Hrschni continued smoothly. "I came to apologise. My actions were crude and ineffective."

"They were threatening and horrible!" Kester said, more loudly than he'd intended. His voice echoed off the walls. *He's got a nerve to approach me like this!* he thought. *But, more to the point, can I make a run for it, or will he hunt me down?*

Hrschni studied Kester's face carefully, then nodded. "I understand your emotions."

"I doubt that very much."

"Nonetheless, I need to talk to you, and if we cannot talk civilly, we will have to find some other way to have the conversation."

"Is that yet another threat?" Kester's eyes narrowed. "I know what you're like, sneaking around. It was you at the pub in Topsham, wasn't it? When we got called out to deal with the dog spirit."

"The familiar," Hrschni corrected. His expression wrinkled in confusion. "How did you know I was there?"

"Mike captured a flash of red with his video camera," Kester replied. "What I want to know is *why*?"

Hrschni sighed. "Might we go and get a coffee in the café downstairs? Parvati's throat is dry. I believe she is coming down with a cold."

Kester looked at the daemon incredulously, then started to laugh. "You want me to sit down and have a drink with you, as though nothing ever happened? Don't you realise you're the country's most wanted spirit?"

Hrschni waved a hand delicately in the air. "That's because no one comprehends what I'm trying to achieve. Which is why I'm here. I need *you* to understand."

"I don't want to understand, thanks." Kester moved towards the exit. "I'm leaving now. If you try and stop me, I'll . . . I'll open the spirit door."

Parvati's face creased, as though trying to supress a laugh. "Kester, I know you haven't got that level of control yet. That's why I released the familiar in that pub. I wanted to see how well you could manipulate your gift."

"So it was you who released the familiar? Oh, this gets even better!" Kester shouted. "What the hell are you trying to do? Make the world even more chaotic than it is already? Or are you just focusing on making my life difficult?"

"Have a drink with me," Hrschni repeated. "Please. You have my word that I will not harm you in any way."

"As if I'm going to trust *your word*," Kester spat.

"I assure you that a daemon's word is their bond. We have a strict code of conduct, and once we make a promise, we do not break it."

Kester bit his lip. He had no idea what to do. A quiet, quick trip to the museum had suddenly turned into something altogether more worrying; a situation that he didn't know how to handle. He wondered if he could somehow send Miss Wellbeloved a text without the daemon knowing but couldn't think of any way to do it.

Hrschni waited patiently, folding Parvati's arms across her body.

"Fine," Kester said finally. He wasn't sure that he was doing the right thing, but at least with Hrschni here, in plain sight, there was a chance they could capture him. At the very least, he could try to find out more about what the Thelemites were up to.

Hrschni gave a low bow, then gestured to the door. "After you."

"No, you lead the way," he replied. There was no way he was letting the daemon walk behind him. Even though Hrschni had promised not to harm him, he still didn't trust the daemon one bit.

Parvati's petite body marched confidently down the staircase, heels rapping smartly as she went. A man peering at the archaeological finds downstairs paused to give her an admiring glance, which brought a wry grin to Kester's face. *If only he knew he was eying up one of the world's most dangerous spirits,* he thought. *Mind you,* he added silently, *it's probably worse to agree to have a drink with him. What the hell am I doing?*

"Tea or coffee?" Hrschni paused in front of the counter, then gave the waiter a winning smile. "Do you have any herbal teas?"

"I'll have a normal tea," Kester said firmly and looked anxiously around the café. It was too quiet for his liking. A few more people nearby would have made him feel a lot safer.

"Slice of cake?" Hrschni asked.

"Don't push it," Kester hissed back. "I'm not going to be here long. You've got ten minutes exactly."

Hrschni nodded. "Very well."

They sat at the farthest table, which Kester was glad to see was nearest to the door leading out into the main museum. Indeed, if he craned his head around the doorframe he could just about see the coughing old man, who was now standing by the entrance. *Not that he'd be much use if things turned nasty,* he realised. *Unless he's able to cough all over Hrschni and infect him with some particularly unpleasant germs.*

"So," Hrschni began, as he raised the cup to Parvati's lips. "Shall we begin? If I only have ten minutes, I feel I should be as concise as possible."

Kester nodded. "Fine."

Hrschni took a deep breath. "As I said before, our conduct towards you has, thus far, been unfortunate. We were desperate to discover the extent of your talents, and we went about it the wrong way. I doubt you'll forgive us, but I hope, after this conversation, you might understand why we acted that way."

"You used my girlfriend as bait to lure me to a deserted cave." Kester put his cup back down firmly. "Why on earth would you think I'll ever understand what you did?"

"I know." The daemon rapped a knuckle thoughtfully against the table top. "It was poor conduct. But let me explain." He paused, as though waiting for Kester to interrupt, then carried on.

"There hasn't been a proficient spirit door opener in operation for *years,* Kester. The last was your dear mother, and then she disappeared into early retirement. You were our only hope."

"You knew my mother?" Kester's eyes widened.

Hrschni nodded. "Let's not get into that now. All you need to know is that your mother wouldn't help us."

"Why would you expect me to help you, then?" Kester shook his head in disbelief. *For such an intelligent spirit,* he thought, *he really is deluded.*

"Because without us, *you* wouldn't be here," Hrschni hissed, eyes alive with indignation. He glowered, eerily present behind Parvati's face, then calmed immediately. "But never mind that. I want to tell you the *real* story, Kester. Not the falsehoods the government feed you. The truth."

"And what's that?" Kester pushed his tea away. There was no way he could drink it, not when his stomach was clenched with tension.

"Once," Hrschni began, sitting straighter in the chair, "the world was a very different place. There were permanent spirit doors in place, which we called sun gates. Far more spirit door openers too, who welcomed spirits into the human realm. We cared for humans, and they cared for us too. We told them the secrets of the world, and they taught us how to be inventive, cunning, and powerful."

"I know, Miss Wellbeloved already told me," Kester replied.

"Then, things started to change." Hrschni closed his eyes, as though the memory pained him. "Man invented machinery. After that, technology. Humans decided they didn't need spirits anymore and started to block us out. Spirit door openers had no need for their talents, and they began to die out. The old, established spirit doors were blocked for good. Soon, we became obsolete in your world."

Kester pushed his glasses up his nose. "So why not go back to your own world? Why linger in ours, if you're not wanted?"

Hrschni winced. "Because the world used to be *better* than this, Kester. Don't you see? Yes, mankind now has appliances, computers, the internet, and mobile phones. But they've lost themselves. We were a vital part of you, and you've blocked us out. You've lost your *spirituality*. And we spirits have lost something too."

"Or maybe humans just don't need you anymore," Kester replied uncertainly. "Maybe we've moved on, and it's time for you to do the same."

"I don't think you believe that. Not really." Hrschni leaned back, fingers knotted tightly in front of him. "In fact, I think you're more sympathetic to our cause than you're aware of."

The waitress started clearing the table behind them, and they lapsed into an uneasy silence, studying one another over their cups of tea.

"I understand why you want spirits to be allowed back into this world," Kester continued, once the waitress was out of earshot. "But I can't condone your methods. You act like terrorists: threatening the government, breaking into Infinite Enterprises, kidnapping me . . ."

Hrschni sighed. "And you think your government are innocent? Are you really that naive?"

"What's that supposed to mean?" Kester placed his cup carefully back down on the table. "They're just doing their job, which is keeping humans safe."

"Is that what they tell you?" Hrschni raised Parvati's eyebrows. The eyes beneath sparkled with frightening intensity. "Is that the lie that they feed you?"

"I don't know what you're talking about." It felt suddenly

much hotter in the room, with much less air to breathe. Parvati's eyes almost seemed to swell, their dark, ferocious energy drawing him in like a magnet. The daemon leaned closer, hands folded neatly across the table.

"What do you think Infinite Enterprises *do* with all the spirits that get delivered to their headquarters?"

Kester drew back. He wanted to look away, but the pull of the daemon's eyes was too powerful. "They send them back to the spirit world, via the door," he said slowly. "Everyone knows that."

"Everyone *thinks* that," the daemon corrected. "Sometimes, if the spirit is lucky, that's what happens. But what about repeat offenders? Those who keep coming back to the human realm, even though they've been deported before?"

"I don't know." Kester felt flustered. "Just keep sending them back, I suppose?"

The daemon snorted. "Really? Is that *really* what you think happens to them? I thought you were cleverer than that."

"What do they do to them, then?"

Without warning, Hrschni reached over, seizing Kester by the hand. "They *destroy them*, Kester."

Kester tried to pull away, but Parvati's hand gripped his own like a steel clamp. "I don't believe that for one second," he muttered.

"I'm not lying. Daemons don't lie."

Heart racing, Kester finally managed to wriggle his hand free. He glared at the daemon. "You're saying that they *kill* the spirits? Why on earth would they do that?"

Parvati's lips tightened. "One less spirit to worry about, I presume."

Kester felt dizzy. It couldn't be true. The suggestion was preposterous. But he'd never actually asked what happened to the spirits after Mike dropped them off in water bottles at Infinite Enterprises HQ. He'd always just presumed they'd be sent back to the spirit realm. *Why do I never think about things more carefully?* he thought furiously. *Mother always said I focused so much on the details that I forgot the bigger picture. Is that the case here? Have I been blind to what's been going on? Or is Hrschni lying?*

"There's no way Miss Wellbeloved would let that happen," he said eventually. His hand was shaking slightly, and he steadied it against the reassuring warmth of the cup.

"Agreed," the daemon said evenly. "Miss Wellbeloved understands spirits in a way that most other humans don't. Her father was the same. I doubt she would have been told the truth."

"My father wouldn't have known either!" Kester spat. "If it's true, of course, which I'm not sure it is."

Parvati cleared her throat carefully, then looked him in the eye. "Are you sure that your father doesn't know about the killings?"

"What's that supposed to mean?" Kester's jaw tightened.

"I'm merely saying," the daemon said mildly, "that you've known your father for a few months. I've known of him for years. I know what he is and isn't capable of."

Kester stood up, pushing the chair back with a loud squeal. "Your ten minutes is up," he said coldly. "I don't know what you thought you'd achieve with this conversation, but it hasn't worked. I don't believe anything you've said."

The daemon shrugged, then stood too, delicately repositioning the chair under the table. "All I ask," he said quietly, "is that you think about what I've told you. The world isn't always so black-and-white, Kester. It comes in many shades of grey, and you need to adapt your thinking accordingly."

"Please don't contact me again," Kester said firmly, as he threw his bag over his shoulder. "No more creeping around or following me. It certainly won't make me sympathetic to your cause if you do."

Hrschni made Parvati's body bow, then fastened the buttons on her coat. "Very well. I believe, in time, you may change your mind. When you do, I think you will know where to find us."

Kester shook his head with disbelief and opened his mouth to make a retort. However, the demon spun on Parvati's heels without another word and walked back through the café; a tiny, formidable figure that seemed to make the surroundings duller by comparison.

What just happened? he thought, rooted to the spot. *And what am I meant to make of all that?* He pulled his phone out and dialled the office number, but no one answered. He suspected they were all still busy sorting out the burst water pipe. *I suppose I'd better go back and join them.* He was reluctant to do so. Even though he doubted what Hrschni had told him was true, he felt uncomfortable even thinking about it. *As if they'd just destroy spirits,* he thought, as he crossed the reception atrium and opened the heavy doors leading outside. *That's ridiculous. It's the twenty-first century, not the 1800s. The death sentence was phased out years ago.*

When he arrived back at the office, out of breath from walking so fast, he encountered the anticipated chaos. A swift survey of the scene revealed Mike, head wedged under the radiator and soaking wet, Pamela and Miss Wellbeloved obligingly handing him tools, and Serena, crouched on a chair to prevent her shoes from getting wet. The carpet looked sodden, and Kester wondered about the integrity of the floorboards beneath. The building was certainly decrepit enough to fall down without warning.

"What happened?" he asked, wearily removing his jacket. He knew he needed to tell them about Hrschni as soon as possible but sensed this probably wasn't the right time. Mike swore at the top of his voice, then walloped the underside of the radiator. The metallic clang boomed around the office like a klaxon.

"Sod this thing!" he bellowed, wiping his face, which was covered in moisture. "You'll have to call a plumber, Miss W. It's beyond my ability to fix it."

"I thought you could fix anything?" Serena said, idly spinning the chair around. She looked entirely unfazed by it all, and Kester could tell she hadn't lifted a finger to help.

"Machinery, yes. Leaking pipes, no." Mike fiddled around with his screwdriver, then cursed loudly. "It's totally rusted through. It needs replacing, not patching up."

"We can't afford that." Miss Wellbeloved tapped the side of the desk, looking anxious. "And we really can't afford a plumber either."

Pamela wrapped an arm around her shoulder. "I've got some sticky tape, if that'll help?"

Mike sat up, banged his head against the radiator, and swore again. "No, of course it bloody won't! Having said that, there's some industrial duct tape in my drawer. That might do for now, while I think of another solution."

Kester obligingly headed over to Mike's desk. The sheer variety of things stuffed in the drawer was quite fascinating. He wasn't sure what Mike intended to do with a bamboo incense stick holder or a metal owl ornament, but he wanted to find out. After a lengthy rummage, he finally found the duct tape and brought it back over.

"I've got something very important to tell you all," he said in a low voice, watching Mike struggle to wrap the tape around the pipe.

Miss Wellbeloved instantly brightened. She leant against the desk expectantly. "Good news about the painting?"

"Yes," Kester said slowly. "But there's something else. Something more important. I spoke to Hrschni."

The others froze, mouths open. Mike sat up swiftly, banging his head once again. This time, he forgot to curse.

"What?" Pamela was the first to break the silence. "What do you mean, *spoke to him*? Are you okay? Did he hurt you or anything?"

Kester shook his head. The initial shock was wearing off, and he felt the first fragments of fear creeping into his stomach. Hrschni's words still echoed in his head, potent as poison, and although he didn't believe the daemon, he felt somehow polluted by just having heard it. "We had a cup of tea together," he said with a nervous giggle, which came out more as a high-pitched shriek. "He didn't threaten or harm me."

"What did he say?" Miss Wellbeloved asked, fighting to recover herself.

"That I was a naive idiot," he replied bitterly. "That the government are doing things that we're not aware of. I presumed he was lying."

"I doubt it," Pamela said, folding her arms. "Daemons don't lie. It's in their code of conduct. They might manipulate the truth at times, but they don't outwardly deceive people."

"What did he say the government was doing?" Serena asked, stepping off the chair. The carpet squelched under her foot.

Kester rubbed his chin. "He said they were destroying spirits who kept flouting the rules, via Infinite Enterprises. But that can't be true, can it?"

Miss Wellbeloved gasped. "Surely not." She looked at the others. "They've denied euthanizing spirits several times in the past. They wouldn't *dare* carry out secret exterminations, would they?"

Mike stood up, knees cracking with the exertion. "If a daemon says that's what's happening, then it might well be the case."

Miss Wellbeloved swallowed hard, opened her mouth to speak, then stormed across the room instead, clasping her hands around her stomach. "No. I can't believe it. Hrschni must be manipulating the truth somehow. We mustn't take what he says at face value."

"That's true," Serena agreed. "He'll probably say anything to get Kester to join his cause."

"But what if it's true?" Miss Wellbeloved looked back, face crumpled with anxiety. "What if Infinite Enterprises are simply disposing of spirits that don't abide by the rules?"

"They wouldn't," Pamela said. "They wouldn't dare. If word got out, there'd be riots. Imagine the reactions of the spirits in residence here, not to mention those in the spirit realm?"

"My father was always suspicious of the government," Miss Wellbeloved continued. She looked suddenly haggard, as though the news had caused her physical harm. "At the Thelemite meetings he heard a few terrible rumours, but they were never proven."

"Well, let's not jump to conclusions," Pamela said sensibly. "It's worrying, but we won't get anywhere by speculating. What else did he say, Kester?"

Kester sat down on the sofa, which was a reassuringly safe distance from the leaking radiator. "He said something *really* odd— he implied that without him, I wouldn't be alive. What do you suppose that's about?"

Miss Wellbeloved frowned as she sat down next to him. "I can't imagine. How could he have ever possibly saved your life? That sounds preposterous."

"I think I would have remembered." Kester tugged at his trouser leg thoughtfully, then sighed. "I can't make any sense of it all. What was Hrschni trying to achieve? He's not stupid, he must have known I wouldn't trust anything he said."

"Quite." Miss Wellbeloved sank her head against her hand. "I feel like we're sinking in quicksand. There's simply too much to worry about."

And where's my father when you need him? Kester thought, looking at their worried, exhausted faces. *How are we going to manage without him to hold everything together?*

"I need to tell you about the painting too," he said aloud. Quickly, he outlined the details about Ransome's scene of Lake Garda, the same villa where he painted the green lady's portrait.

"The Thelemites are clearly trying to get you to search for something in Italy, aren't they?" Serena said, hopping onto the edge of the nearest desk, polished toe gleaming in the light.

"You might be able to get us all a free trip to Lake Garda!" Mike exclaimed. "I could do with a bit of winter sun."

Miss Wellbeloved snorted. "There's no way the government would pay for us all to go, unless there was good reason. However," she added, glancing back at Kester, "it's entirely possible they might want to send a few people to check it out."

"Really?" Kester brightened. He'd never even left the country before. Travelling by aeroplane was daunting, but he supposed it wouldn't be anything compared with facing spirits on a daily basis.

"Here's a question though," Serena said, interrupting his thoughts. "Why is Hrschni bothering to do this little treasure hunt? You know, all these clues, leading to Gardone Riviera?"

Pamela folded her arms. "What do you mean?"

"Well," Serena continued, "he's just spoken to Kester. He's been bold, open, and transparent. No riddles at all. So why bother with all the rest of it?"

"I'm not sure it was an entirely riddle-free conversation," Pamela pointed out. "After all, it's made all of us rather confused."

Serena shrugged. "Whatever. But the fact is, it doesn't add up.

Why be so upfront in the museum, then so secretive with all these random clues and old keys?"

Kester nodded slowly. She had a point, and it was something that had been niggling him for some time. "I agree. It almost makes me wonder…"

"Wonder what?" Miss Wellbeloved leaned closer.

"Whether the clues are coming from Hrschni at all." Kester frowned and looked at the others. "What if someone else is sending them?"

Mike laughed. "Christ, this is getting more complicated by the day. Who else would? Anyway, the envelopes had the official Thelemite stamp on them, didn't they? That big old red wax seal, remember?"

"They did," Miss Wellbeloved agreed, chewing her fingernail. "However, don't you remember what Tinker said about the wax seal?"

"Remind us," Pamela said, listening intently. They fell silent. Even the leaking radiator seemed to have been momentarily forgotten, despite the fact it was releasing an ominous hiss from the other side of the room.

Miss Wellbeloved nodded. "He told us that it was an older version of the seal. Not the one they use nowadays. Could that be significant, do you think?"

"Who knows?" Kester sighed heavily. He liked solving puzzles, but this was overwhelming. "Let's focus on one thing at a time, shall we?"

"Who died and left you in charge?" Serena snapped. "I don't recall you getting to give the orders, thanks very much."

Kester glanced at Miss Wellbeloved, who grimaced. "We do need to tell everyone about what's happening to the agency at some point," she said quietly. "Perhaps we should get it over and done with."

Before she could continue, an abrasive succession of beeps and vibrations erupted from the direction of Mike's desk. Mike immediately leapt up and galloped over, fumbling in the mess for his mobile phone. He held a finger up to the others, then answered.

"Hello?" His face remained in a fixed grin, before falling abruptly, like a deflating soufflé. "Oh, it's you. What do you want?"

The others looked confused. Mike shook his head, then started pacing around his desk. "What do you mean, *you've arrived*? You're not meant to be here yet!"

"What's going on?" Pamela whispered to Serena, watching Mike with fascination. Serena shrugged.

"No, I can't bloody come and pick you up, I'm at work!" Mike continued, oblivious to the rest of them. "You'll just have to walk to my house. I'll meet you there later." He rolled his eyes furiously, then leant on the desk. "I sent you the address the other day. If you've lost it, that's your own fault."

He hung up, then glared at the others. "Crispian," he said, by way of explanation.

"Oh dear." Miss Wellbeloved winced.

"Maybe it'll turn out better than you think?" Pamela suggested helpfully.

Mike growled with frustration, before being drowned out by another, more alarming sound. With a violent hiss, the duct tape around the pipe suddenly exploded outwards, showering the surrounding carpet with a fresh spray of water.

Kester hastily ran over, along with the others, desperately trying to stem the flow. Only Mike remained, still hunched over his desk, glowering in indignation.

CHAPTER 9: DRINKY-POOS AND UNEXPECTED GUESTS

The next few days passed swiftly with a commotion of activity in the office. A plumber arrived, mended the radiator with a lot of complaints about the age of the heating system, then left again. The carpet was still wet, leaving the office bathed in an unpleasant aroma of damp. Serena pointed out that there were a few tiny mushrooms sprouting in the farthest corner, but Pamela claimed they'd been there for a while, just no one else had noticed them yet.

While this was going on, Miss Wellbeloved busied herself with phone meetings to both Infinite Enterprises and Larry Higgins, discussing details of the case and the merging of the agencies. Kester could tell after her conversations with Higgins that she was worried about her decision, especially given that Ribero was still refusing to come into the office. However, it was too late to back down now. Higgins gleefully announced that he'd get in touch with his solicitor, and the day after, a letter came through the post, detailing the provisional terms of the two agencies coming together. Miss Wellbeloved put it to one side, muttering that she'd look at it "when she could bear to."

The most recent conference call, between herself, Larry Higgins, and Cardigan Cummings, drew her into the snug confines of Ribero's office. The rest of the team heard nothing from her for over an hour, until she emerged at nearly five o'clock, red-faced and decidedly dishevelled.

"This is all very exhausting," she announced to them all and promptly returned to her own desk, slouching over her laptop in a defeated manner that was very out of character.

"What did they say?" Kester asked, turning away from the screen. He'd been attempting to work on the latest essay for Dr. Barqa-Abu but wasn't having much luck.

Miss Wellbeloved wiped her eyes. "They agree that we need to send a team to Gardone Riviera. Bernard Nutcombe's approved the plan, and they'll fund four people to go."

"Who is it?" Serena's head poked up over her screen, alert as a dog that had got a sudden whiff of steak. "Please say it's me. *Please.*"

"No, it needs to be me," Mike interrupted, stuffing a bundle of wires back into his desk. "Crispian is driving me crazy. If I don't escape soon, I'll probably end up killing him."

Kester grinned. They'd already heard plenty about Mike's brother, Crispian, who was staying at Mike's to escape from his ex-wife. So far, Crispian had managed to break Mike's games console, snap the handle off the shower, and accidentally drop tomato pasta all over the lounge carpet. Needless to say, Mike wasn't impressed.

Miss Wellbeloved shook her head. "No, it needs to be representatives from each agency. So it'll be Kester, Dimitri, Ian Kingdom-Green, and Lili Asadi."

"Why them?" Serena whined, flicking her computer off. "Who picked the people, anyway?"

Mike grunted. "Yeah, and why two people from Infinite Enterprises? That's not fair, is it?"

"You two can enjoy your honeymoon in Italy at a later date." Pamela swung her coat over her shoulders and winked. "Plenty of time, young lovebirds."

"Please shut up, Pamela. You're making me feel sick." Serena gave Mike a look that would have killed lesser beings on the spot, before collecting her coat from the back of her chair.

"When are we going then?" Kester asked. Excitement rose in his belly. He had no idea what it was like being in an aeroplane, let alone in another country.

Miss Wellbeloved stood, yawning loudly. "Cardigan suggested that you leave in a couple days' time. It'll only be for two days or so. You know how tight the government are when it comes to money."

"Yeah, I bet it'll be a budget airline," Serena added, as she pulled open the door, letting the cool air into their warm office. "Let's hope it doesn't crash."

"You said that as though you meant the exact opposite," Kester said accusingly. Still, he refused to let her negativity get to him. Even though the Italian trip would undoubtedly involve some unpleasantly scary investigations, it was still exciting.

"Who's coming down the pub?" Pamela scurried after Serena, coat billowing behind her.

Mike brightened. "Yeah, all right then. That means I don't have to go home to that colossal prat."

"That's no way to talk about your reflection, Mike."

"That's the worst joke you've ever made, Serena, and that's saying something."

They ventured out into the cold, eager to get to the pub as soon as possible. Kester didn't much like this time of year. Christmas was over, and the world seemed to be left in a dreary stasis, like it was just waiting for someone to get it revved up again.

The pub was mostly empty, aside from Bill the barman, leaning on the bar and studying his phone. He looked up as they came in and beamed.

"Hello, you fine people! What can I get you today? No Dr. Ribero with you?"

"No, he's in a big sulk," Miss Wellbeloved explained, as she ordered a drink. "I'm sure he'll snap out of it soon."

Bill made himself busy pouring their drinks, then leaned in conspiratorially. "I'm glad you've all come in, actually."

"Why's that?" Mike tested his ale, then smacked his lips appreciatively.

"Some tosser came in about an hour ago, sat at the bar, and wouldn't stop talking," Bill explained, as he passed Serena a bag of ready-salted crisps. "The guy is an absolute git of magnificent proportions."

"Blimey," Mike said, surprised. "He must be bad if you're saying that, Bill."

"He's driving me crazy." Bill looked over his shoulder. Through the toilet doors, they could hear the dim sound of a hand-dryer blasting away over unseen hands. "Uh-oh," he added, "looks like he's on his way back."

The door swung open, and a tall man swooped out. He reminded Kester of someone, but he couldn't think who. His dark hair was so tightly slicked to his head that it looked like a plastic helmet.

"Goodness, look who it is!" The man stopped, hands suspended dramatically in front of him.

"Oh god," Mike muttered. "You cannot be serious."

"Mike, I thought you said you were coming straight home after work?" The man's voice was polished and slimy, like oil slipping over a rock.

Serena stared, then burst out laughing. "I don't believe it. *This* is your brother?"

Bill clamped a hand over his mouth and promptly made himself busy at the farthest end of the bar. Kester caught Pamela's eye and wished he hadn't, because her incredulous expression only made him want to laugh even more. Mike, by contrast, looked as though he might combust on the spot.

Crispian, oblivious to his brother's mortification, smiled toothily, then seized Serena's hand and kissed it. Her eyes widened.

"You, fair maiden," he began, "must be Serena. I have heard about you, though Mike failed to mention what a beauty you are."

Serena extracted her hand, mouth still half-open with shock. "I doubt Mike ever has anything nice to say about me, to be honest."

"Look mate," Mike barked, stepping forward. "Why are you here?"

"For the same reason *you're* here, one presumes." Crispian winked, then smoothed a hand over his immaculate hair for good measure. "To indulge in a little drinky-poo or two."

Bill snorted, then hastily turned it into a cough. Mike's face reddened.

"Might I join you all?" Crispian slurred, tripping slightly as he collected his drink from the bar. "I'd love to find out more about what you all do, Michael's ever so secretive about these things."

"*Michael?*" Serena repeated loudly, clearly enjoying every second of Mike's discomfort.

"Absolutely. Michael St. James Smythe." Crispian saluted sloppily, oblivious to the fact that Mike looked as though he was about to murder him.

"What did you say his middle name was?" Pamela shifted closer, eyes alight with amusement. "Sinjems? What sort of a name is that?"

"It's spelt *St. James*," Mike said miserably. "Now, if you'll excuse me, I'm tired of being the butt of your amusement, so I'm going to drink my pint quietly in the corner and ignore you all."

"I thought your surname was Smith?" Kester called after him. He felt sorry for Mike, but at the same time, the sight of his face, getting more enraged by the second, was quite funny.

"Smythe, Smith; same difference." Mike banged his drink down on the table, no doubt imagining it was Crispian's head. "Anyway, if you think my middle name's a giggle, ask him what *his* is! Go on!"

Crispian smirked. "I have no shame about my middle name, Michael. It's Tottingley. After my grandfather."

Miss Wellbeloved pressed her fingers against her mouth. She was the only one who managed to successfully supress a grunt of laughter.

"Hang on a minute," Serena continued, winding a path through the crowded tables to where Mike was sitting, still glowering at them all. "You always pretend to be a wide boy. Are you actually a posh toff?"

"No, I am not!"

"Did you go to a private school?"

Mike's brow dropped so low, he looked positively gorilla-like. "No, I sodding didn't, all right?"

"It was a pretty good grammar school, though," Crispian chorused from the bar. "One of the best in the country. I got all A-grades, naturally. Michael didn't do quite so well."

"Bugger off!" Mike hunched over his drink, turning his body away like a child having a particularly ferocious strop.

"So," Serena continued, settling down on the bench beside him, ignoring his discomfort, "you're the black sheep of the family, then?"

Crispian grabbed his glass and wobbled unsteadily across the floor to join them. "A big, black elephant, more like. Michael couldn't have disappointed our parents more if he tried."

"I managed not to shag my secretary and destroy my marriage though," Mike barked back, fingers clenched around his pint glass.

"Mainly because you aren't married and presumably don't have a secretary either?"

Mike's growl of rage was almost deafening. "Look, if you're going to keep winding me up, I'm leaving, all right?" He raised his pint and downed it in five swift gulps.

Crispian held his hands up in protest, eyes wide and innocent. "Goodness me, you are in a mood, aren't you? Now, shall I buy you another drink to apologise? In fact, let me buy you all a drink. Then I can find out more about what you actually do."

Miss Wellbeloved's lips tightened. "That's quite all right, I've only just started my—"

"I insist!" Crispian smacked her hard on the back, then trotted back to the bar, ambling along like an arthritic dog. Mike looked at the others and groaned.

"Shall we go somewhere else?" he hissed, as he studied Crispian at the bar. "We could sneak out now while he's ordering, then go to the White Hart instead?"

Serena shook her head, eyes gleaming. "No, I'm enjoying your brother's company, Michael *Sinjems* Smythe."

Mike buried his head in his hands and refused to emerge,

despite Pamela's best attempts to coax him out of hiding. The others made themselves comfortable, watching Crispian with curiosity. *I can see why Mike dislikes him,* Kester thought, observing the slicked hair, the expensive shirt, and the general look of entitlement and privilege. However, it was amusing to know that Mike didn't have quite the humble upbringing he pretended to have.

Eventually, Crispian returned with a tray of drinks, which teetered alarmingly in his grip. "Righty-ho," he murmured, before lowering himself on the nearest stool. His bottom missed entirely and he ended up sitting on Miss Wellbeloved's lap instead. However, he didn't seem to notice, not even when she unceremoniously shoved him back onto his own seat.

"So," he began, with a smile that was presumably meant to be charming but looked rather deranged. "Let's begin. What *is* your company, exactly? What does it do?"

"None of your business," Mike rumbled, from the confines of his arms. "I've told you several times to stop asking."

Crispian smirked. "Mike said it's something to do with technology?"

"Something like that," Serena spluttered. "Though Mike mostly maintains our website."

"I *do not!*" Mike's head shot up, livid as a bear awoken from early hibernation. "I make valuable contributions to the agency, and you know it!"

Crispian leaned forward, pitching his chin on his fingers. "Aha. An *agency.* What sort of agency, exactly? A marketing agency? Advertising? Technology development?"

"We're an investigative agency," Pamela chimed. The others glared at her. "What?" she said defensively. "That's what we do, isn't it?"

"We work in the private sector, partly investigative, partly developing new technologies for our clients," Miss Wellbeloved said smoothly. "Mike's a very valuable part of the team."

"Is he?" Crispian looked incredulous. "Ah well, there's a use for everyone, isn't there?"

Mike muttered something, then slumped down on the table again.

Throughout the course of the evening, it became apparent that Crispian wasn't going anywhere anytime soon. However, given that he was quite happy to buy every single round of drinks, nobody was complaining too much, and even Mike started to perk up after four pints of ale.

Finally, after several more beers than he'd intended to drink, Kester looked at his wristwatch. To his surprise, it was already half-past nine. *No wonder the pub's filled up so much,* he thought, eyeing the crowds of drinkers squeezed around tables and standing around the fireplace.

"I'd better head off soon," he announced, as he tugged at his shirt collar. It was surprisingly hot, despite the freezing temperatures outside. "Especially as we've got work tomorrow."

"No. No, no, *no.*" Crispian draped a drunken arm over his shoulders and pulled him in tight. "You should stay, Lester! Stay!"

"It's Kester."

"That's a darned peculiar name, isn't it? Lester suits you far better."

Serena sighed deeply and patted Kester on the elbow. "Come on, I'm going too. You can walk me home."

Kester laughed. "You only live over the road."

Serena nodded meaningfully at Crispian and winked.

"I think I'll join you," Pamela said, as she heaved herself out from the tight space between the bench and the table. "Hemingway hasn't had a run-around all day. I really should take him for a walk at least."

"Hang on, don't leave me here with him!" Mike pointed venomously at his brother, who pretended not to notice.

"Aren't you living with him?" Miss Wellbeloved said, as she wrapped her scarf around herself. "You either have to endure him here in the pub or back at your place, presumably?"

"I might make him sleep in the car instead," Mike said, then poked Crispian in the stomach. "The amount you've drunk, you'll probably vomit all over my carpet or something. At least in the car, I won't be able to smell it."

"You're a *fine* one to talk," Crispian slurred.

Kester bit back a laugh. Excessive drinking obviously ran in the family. He stood up, making way for the others to walk past him. "It's been fun," he said brightly, as he slipped into his jacket. "I think we needed a night off, after all the stress of the last . . ."

He faltered. Someone had opened the door, letting in a stiff blast of cold air, but that wasn't what had made him stop. Instead, it was the *who* that had rendered him speechless. Blonde hair. Grungy top. The cute, crooked smile that always made his stomach turn to water. *Anya.*

Serena followed his gaze, then gave a low whistle. "Oh boy." She squeezed his arm. "Are you okay?"

Kester took a deep breath. "It's fine," he said stiffly. "It's not as though I haven't bumped into her before. In fact, it seems to be happening a lot recently."

I wonder if I can slip out without her noticing me? he wondered. He couldn't face the thought of having another argument, especially not after four pints of beer. However, even as he was planning his escape, her head turned, fixed on him, and nailed him to the spot.

She raised an uncertain hand, then lowered it again. The girl beside her, who Kester presumed might be her housemate, looked over in confusion. Kester felt his face redden and wished he could sink through the floor and disappear.

"Come on, Kester," Serena whispered firmly. "We'll just leave. You don't have to say a word to her."

"Yes," he said distantly. He didn't know if it was the effect of the alcohol or Anya herself, but for some reason, he couldn't take his eyes of her. *Why does she have to be so beautiful?* he wondered. *Why can't I just get over her?*

Pamela nodded to Serena, and the pair grabbed an arm each, practically lifting him out towards the door. Anya's eyes widened, then she stepped forward.

"Wait, please!"

"Sweetheart," Pamela said, in as kind a voice as possible, "I don't think he wants to talk to you. It's been a long, tiring week."

"It has," Kester mumbled, rubbing his head.

"Just for a few minutes, please?" Anya looked pleadingly at Kester. "I won't take up a lot of your time. I just need to tell you something, something really important. Things went badly wrong at the caves. It wasn't supposed to happen like that, and—"

"I don't think he wants to hear it," Serena said icily, tightening her arm around Kester's.

"But you must let me speak! You think I'm working for Hrschni, but I'm not!" Anya's lower lip wobbled, eyes starting to gloss with tears. Kester had to look away.

Miss Wellbeloved sidled up quickly. "Remember you're in a public place!" she hissed, eyes flitting over the surrounding crowd. "You mustn't speak about things like that!"

Anya ignored her and grabbed Kester by the arm. "There's bigger things going on here than you realise, Kester. I'm willing to risk it *all* to tell you. But you have to give me the chance to talk."

"You? You're just Hrschni's mouthpiece!" Serena snapped.

"And you've hurt Kester enough."

"I'm not Hrschni's mouthpiece! That's where you're badly wrong."

"Ladies, please!" Miss Wellbeloved whispered urgently. "We're getting looks." Indeed, Anya's housemate was staring with open curiosity, and a few people nearby had paused their conversations to listen.

"I just need to tell you something, please."

"I don't see what you could possibly have to tell me," Kester replied tightly. The pleasant evening had suddenly turned into something darker, something unbearable, and he wanted to leave as soon as possible. Her proximity tormented him, especially when he remembered the ease with which he used to touch her. Now, a wall of remoteness stood between them, and there was no way to break through.

"It's the book! Read the book, you'll find the answers, and—"

Kester nodded. "I told you before," he said, in as firm a voice as he could muster. "I don't trust you. I don't want to speak to you. Now, if you'll excuse me, I'm going home."

Anya let out a loud sob, causing the rest of the room to fall into a shocked silence. She scanned his face with an expression full of such hurt it made his chest ache. Then, to his horror, she turned and ran out of the door. Her housemate gasped, but before Kester could say a word, she'd raced off too, giving him one final glare before she left. Kester felt his cheeks burn, aware of the judging gazes currently boring into him from the surrounding drinkers.

Pamela rubbed her eyes. "That was a nasty scene."

"Goodness me, things kicked off a bit there, didn't they?" Crispian stumbled over, then draped himself over Kester's shoulders. "I wouldn't worry, my old mucker. Plenty of fish in the sea, and all that."

"Shut up, you moron," Mike barked. He looked around himself. The pub was still suspended in eerie silence, hanging on to their every word. "Hmm," he concluded, then nodded to the others. "We'd better leave, I think."

They stepped out into the cold. Kester instinctively scanned the alleyway for Anya, but it was deserted. Whichever direction she'd fled in, she was out of sight now.

"Are you all right?" Miss Wellbeloved tapped his arm, startling him. "What an upsetting thing to happen. You must be feeling dreadful."

Kester shook his head. "I'll be okay. It's inevitable that we'll bump into each other from time to time. After all, Exeter's not a big city, is it?"

"Well, I'm off home," Serena announced, then glanced wryly in Crispian's direction. He was currently leaning against the wall and looking rather unwell. "Michael Sinjims Smythe, I suggest you get your brother home before he pukes up everywhere."

Mike groaned. "Do you think anyone would mind if I just left him here for the night?" He nudged Crispian tentatively, who snorted, staggered, then promptly lurched down on to his knees.

"Best get him to bed," Pamela suggested, wrapping herself tightly in her coat. "Speaking of which, I'll bid you all good night."

"Good night, everyone," Miss Wellbeloved added, massaging her head. "I don't know about the rest of you, but I need a good glass of milk and some indigestion tablets before bedtime. Too much alcohol really doesn't agree with me."

Kester said goodbye, watching as the others headed off to their homes. He felt oddly removed from the events of the evening and numb to the blistering cold of the night. It all felt suddenly unreal, which he suspected might have something to do with the quantity of beer he'd drunk.

I wonder what book Anya was talking about? It had been a strange thing to say. Had she left a book at his house when they were seeing one another? He certainly hadn't seen anything lying around. *What could she have meant?* He soldiered on up the high street, ignoring the leery hoots of drunken men staggering out of the neighbouring bar.

Maybe she was a bit tipsy, he reasoned. *Maybe the whole horrible confrontation was because she'd had a few too many to drink at home before coming to the pub.* However, she certainly hadn't seemed drunk. It was all very odd, not to mention unsettling.

When Kester arrived home, the first thing he noticed was that the front door was open. The second thing was that Pineapple was waiting anxiously behind it, framed by the hallway light like a skinny, day-glo angel. He sighed when he spotted Kester, flapping his hands urgently to hurry him along.

"What on earth is the matter?" Kester stepped inside, brushing his feet off on the mat. "Why were you waiting for me?"

Pineapple took a deep breath, then sat heavily on the stairs. Kester waited, watching him in confusion. *What the hell's the matter with him? Why's he being even more weird than usual?*

"Some sinister, bad juju going on here, man," he whispered eventually, fingers gripping the bannister. "Sinister, *bad juju.*"

Kester sighed. "To start with," he began, leaning on the telephone table, "you're going to have to explain what 'juju' is. Then, you'll need to tell me what happened."

"Juju," Pineapple repeated, eyes glassy. He tugged at his top, wrestling it around his hand like a dishcloth. "Bad vibes. I saw something *bad,* Kester. Something *horrible.*"

"Like what?" Kester was intrigued. He didn't think he'd ever seen Pineapple without his usual inane grin.

Pineapple shook his head, first slowly, then more energetically, like a small child trying to block out a bad dream. "I don't know what it was," he mumbled. "A flash of something. A figure. It saw me then disappeared."

"Excuse me?" Kester knelt down beside him, attention now fully engaged. "What did you just say? A *flash*? A *figure*? Which disappeared afterwards?"

"Yeah. I came out of my bedroom, and saw it, clear as a solid bell, coming out of your room." Pineapple clutched his stomach and groaned. "It had a *face*, I swear it."

"So, let me get this straight." Kester leaned forward and seized Pineapple by the shoulder. "You saw a flashing creature, with a face, in my bedroom?"

Pineapple nodded miserably. "That's pure correct, man." He wiped his face, expression full of silent pleading. "What's going on with me?"

"When did it happen?" Kester frowned, sitting down on the floor. He knew what the creature sounded like, and he wasn't happy about it. *So, now I've got daemons nosing through my home,* he thought, gazing up the stairs, half expecting to see Hrschni hovering at the top. *This has gone too far. I thought they weren't allowed to enter people's homes without invitation. Doesn't it go against their code of conduct or something?*

"Oh, man." Pineapple interrupted his thoughts, stuffing his head between his knees. Kester noticed he was shaking. "Oh man, this is so *bad*. I don't believe in ghosts, it's all made up, right?"

Kester allowed himself a wry smile, given that Pineapple's gaze was currently fixed at the stairs beneath his head, and he couldn't be seen. "Yes, of course. I mean, come on. A flashing figure? That's not even possible, is it?" *If only you knew,* he thought.

"So, I didn't see anything, right?" Pineapple sat up again, eyes full of hope.

Kester shook his head. "It was probably something you ate," he said lamely. "Too much cheese can make you hallucinate, you know."

Pineapple brightened. "I did eat some mouldy bread. Mould must be proper drug-like, yeah?"

"Oh, definitely." Kester helped his housemate to his feet and patted him awkwardly on the back. "Don't worry, everyone gets scared sometimes. I won't tell anyone."

"Proper smooth." Pineapple tugged his top back into place and smiled sheepishly. "I went total nuclear there, didn't I?"

"Whatever that means, yes, you did a bit," Kester agreed. "Are you going to be all right down here while I'm upstairs?" *I want to check whether anything's been taken,* he thought. *Thank goodness there's nothing important up there.*

Pineapple nodded, topknot wobbling as he staggered into the kitchen. "Sure, man. Pure sweet. I'll make myself some toast, yeah?"

"Just don't use the mouldy bread!" Kester darted up the stairs, wondering if Hrschni was still in the house, if indeed it had been the daemon at all. *There's still a chance Pineapple was just imagining things,* he rationalised, as he stepped into his bedroom. *Though to be fair, he's not exactly gifted in the imagination department.*

His first thought, surveying his single bed and desk, was that nothing had been taken. It all looked exactly as he'd left it—orderly, clean, and slightly spartan, which was just how he liked it. Then he spotted something, something so obvious he wondered how he'd missed it before.

"What on earth is going on here?" he whispered, adjusting his glasses. His copy of *A Historie of Spirits,* which he'd left neatly by his computer, had been moved to the bottom of the bed, lying open. He touched the page, frowning.

"Pineapple?" Kester stalked out again, hanging over the bannister. "Pineapple, did you move any books in my room?"

Pineapple's head appeared around the corner, peering up at him. "Nah, mate." His eyes widened. "Why, what's happened? Does that mean there *was* a ghost, moving things about in your bedroom? Ah man, that's total not-cool, that's—"

"No, nothing like that." Kester shook his head quickly. The last thing he needed was for Pineapple to get hysterical again. "It's nothing to worry about, go back to your toast."

He returned to his room, chewing his finger thoughtfully, eyes fixed on the pages. Whoever had left it open had obviously done so for a reason. Finally, he settled himself on the duvet and started to read.

Arsaces, leader of the Parni people, daemon in human form, was unaware of the plot laid out against him. For the Djinn outwardly feigned friendship, whilst gathering an army in secret.

The ancient clan of the Parni was split in two; those who followed the chaos of Arsaces, and those who fought to preserve the world as it was. At last, the war was declared, the battleground laid out, and the Djinn revealed its true intentions. Arsaces was heartbroken at the treachery of his oldest friend, then angry. A daemon, when enraged, is a formidable foe, but so too is a Djinn.

The battle was fought for thirty days and thirty nights; a bloody, vicious war with many casualties on both sides. At last, Arscaces, now defeated, crawled from his human body, and fled back to the spirit world, taking many followers with him.

The Djinn worked hard on restoring peace to the land, and creating unity between man and spirit.

Kester looked up. He thought about what he'd read, then reread it again, just to be sure. Then he began to smile.

"I think I know why you sent me this book, Dr. Barqa-Abu,"

he whispered, as he gathered it protectively against his chest. "You're working directly against Hrschni, and this story parallels what you're doing right now."

But who had broken into his house to open the book at the right page? He couldn't imagine Dr. Barqa-Abu doing such a thing, and it made no sense for Hrschni to do it. Kester sighed, placing the book carefully on his bedside table.

It's always the way, he thought, as he patted the front cover reflectively. *When one mystery is solved, another mystery is always ready to take its place. But surely things can't get any more tangled than they already are, can they?*

CHAPTER 10: ITALIAN INVESTIGATIONS

The Lake Garda visit was arranged with astonishing speed, which Miss Wellbeloved assured Kester was very normal whenever Infinite Enterprises was involved. Within twenty-four hours, the flights had been booked, the accommodation arranged, and everything set in place for their trip to Gardone Riviera.

On the day of the flight, Miss Wellbeloved accompanied him to the airport, more to settle his nerves than anything else. Before he passed through check-in, she patted his shoulder and gave him a proud smile.

"You'll be fine," she said, glancing at the line of people waiting to go through. "Flying is as easy as anything, you'll see."

Kester clutched his suitcase, feeling as nervous a small child going to school for the first time. "I thought Dad might have come too," he muttered. "I know he's not feeling great at the moment, but it wouldn't have been too much effort to see me off, would it?"

Miss Wellbeloved laughed. "You're going to Italy, not the moon. Besides," she added, rolling her eyes, "he's still hell-bent on punishing us both, isn't he?"

"Probably." *Though I wish he'd just get over it,* Kester added silently. Although his father was talking to him again, he'd been distinctly frosty, particularly when discussing the trip to Italy—not to mention the prospect of working with Infinite Enterprises and Larry Higgins again. Putting the thought from his mind, Kester fumbled in his pocket to check he still had his passport to hand. "I suppose I'd better go through," he concluded lamely.

"Yes." Miss Wellbeloved hugged him briefly, then stepped back to admire him. "You know, you look very grown up, Kester."

"I'd hope so. I mean, I am in my twenties," he pointed out.

She smiled. "Yes, I know. I'm just proud of how far you've come. Anyway, you'd better get on. Remember, you'll be the last to arrive, but Ian Kingdom-Green said he and Lili Asadi would be waiting at the airport for you."

Kester took a deep breath. "I'll see you in a few days then?"

"Absolutely. Good luck."

He watched her leave, then turned to the windows. The sight of the aeroplanes did nothing to calm his nerves, nor did going through passport control and finding himself scrutinised with alarming intensity by the officer. Finally, he entered the departure lounge, where he promptly buried his head in a book and hid from all the other people around him.

The plane took off without incident. After a while, he started to enjoy the sight of the landscape laid out like a patchwork quilt below. Even the in-flight meal was surprisingly edible, though he wasn't sure if it was a hash brown he was eating or particularly rubbery scrambled egg.

After a while, he closed his eyes and settled back into his seat. It seemed like only a few minutes later that a tinny voice broke through the peace; the pilot was announcing their impending arrival to Verona Airport. Kester immediately sat up and peered out of the window. The plane dipped steadily through the clouds until finally it emerged over a seemingly endless landscape of fields in varying shades of brown and beige. *Goodness, it's dry out here,* Kester thought. He'd been expecting turquoise Mediterranean seas and glittering beaches, not this parched scrubland. In fact, it looked exactly like England, only with a lot less greenery.

The plane touched down, and Kester joined in the scramble, fighting against a growing sense of panic. *What if Ian and Lili aren't there to meet me?* he wondered, as he stumbled down the metal steps and out into the open. *What if I'm stranded here in a country where I can't even speak the language?*

The large, airy terminal calmed him, as did the realisation that his suitcase had made it to Italy too. To his even greater relief, he saw the familiar faces of Ian and Lili waiting casually for him on a pair of plastic seats, as though they hung out in foreign airports all the time.

At the sight of him, Ian Kingdom-Green smiled, a beam of gigantic, affable proportions. Gallantly seizing Kester's bag, he smacked him on the back with the force of a colliding steam train. "Good to see you again!" he shouted, oblivious to the surprised looks of the people surrounding them.

"Hello, Kester." Lili was more reserved but welcoming nonetheless. "We've hired a car, and Gardone Riviera is only half an hour away. Are you ready?"

"Who's driving?" Kester asked, following them out of the door. It was chillier than he'd thought it would be.

"Me, of course," Lili answered, with an incredulous look at Ian, who failed to notice. "Our hotel is right at the top of the hill; it's got great views of the lake."

They crossed the road and entered a cramped multistorey

carpark stuffed to the brim with rental cars. Apart from one sleepy-looking man sitting by a desk, they were the only ones there. Lili gestured to a tiny car, parked tightly between two vans. "That one's ours."

Kester squeezed himself through the impossibly narrow gap between their car and the next, then was faced with the task of trying to get comfortable in the virtually nonexistent backseat. Matters were made worse when Ian swooped in, drove the seat back in one fluid motion, and pinned Kester's legs against his stomach.

"That's not going to make you uncomfortable, is it?" he asked, peering over his shoulder.

Kester shook his head, then attempted to ease one leg out from beneath the other. "No, not at all," he squeaked in response.

They set off. Despite his discomfort, Kester was fascinated by the changing landscape outside the window. Gradually, commercial buildings and garish billboards gave way to a greener, more luxuriant setting; and finally, he caught his first glimpse of the lake.

"It's so big!" he breathed, unable to believe his eyes.

Ian Kingdom-Green sighed, sweeping a hand at the expanse of water and nearly hitting Lili in the process. "Ah, the beauty of the Italian lakes," he declared, eyelids batting as though the mere thought was too much for him to bear. "You should see them in the summer months. Such spectacular scenery, Kester!"

"I can imagine," Kester said politely.

As they drove on, the road slowly shifted closer until they were driving along the banks of the lake itself. A few lone sailboats bobbed on the choppy waters, sharp and spectral in the shifting fog. They began to pass through villages and towns, a succession of elegant crumbling villas and stylish promenades.

"Not long now," Lili said finally, over the rhythmic click of the car indicator. "I asked Dimitri to buy us some lunch, so let's hope he's done it."

Kester patted his stomach reflectively at the mention of food. "Where's the villa then?" he asked, as they entered Gardone Riviera. "The one that Robert Ransome lived in?"

Ian pointed down towards the lake. "It's a delightfully run-down old property," he explained, as the car swept up a steep hill. "We haven't had a chance to visit yet, but we've been informed that it's brimming with spirit activity."

Kester's stomach lurched. "Why? The Bloody Mary hasn't lived there for ages!" *And it's not fair,* he added silently. *No one told me that I'd have to investigate a house "brimming" with ghosts.*

Lili forced the car into a lower gear, cursing under her breath as it struggled upwards. "It's what we call a magnet," she explained patiently. "When a house is inhabited by a spirit, then left empty for several years, it's only natural that other spirits move in. It's a nice, quiet place for them to live."

"Oh, good," Kester said weakly. All the warm, happy feelings he'd had about Italy were already fading at the prospect of dealing with a herd of supernatural beings. *Why me?* he thought, so lost in his thoughts that he hardly noticed the car pulling through the gates and into the hotel car park. *Why do I have to cope with such unpleasant things?*

He looked up. The hotel loomed ahead, pastel pink walls fronted with ornate, crumbling pillars, and row after row of windows looking out to the lake below. Wisteria trailed a lazy path over the plaster façade, its blooms mostly faded in the cooler climate. "It's *beautiful*," Kester gasped, eyes lingering over it all. The quiet dignity, the sense of timelessness; it was everything he'd ever dreamed an Italian hotel would be.

"It's pretty dated inside," Lili corrected.

Ian nodded, unbuckling his seatbelt. "But divinely poetic decor, my friend. One can almost feel the lingering aura of the artists and writers who must have dwelt within its walls."

"Or the holiday-makers looking for a getaway on the cheap." Lili opened the door and stepped nimbly out. "Come on. We've got three rooms on the upper floor with cracking views."

Kester lugged his suitcase across the gravel driveway and through the swinging doors, which parted reluctantly under the pressure of his hand. The man at reception raised his head, gave them a laconic nod, then resumed staring at his phone. Lili smirked, pointing towards the lift.

"It's a pretty sleepy place," she explained as the polished brass doors squealed open. "Even in summer, apparently. Most people head up to the north coast."

The lift churned and clicked as it hefted them upwards. Kester couldn't help but feel excited by it all. *I'm in a foreign country!* he thought, thrill blossoming in the pit of his stomach. *I managed to fly in a plane and get here all by myself!*

With a melodic ting, the lift doors slid open, revealing a narrow corridor ahead. They paced along it, their shoes squeaking across the polished floor, until finally they reached the door at the end.

"Dimitri had better have remembered that I wanted a margherita pizza, nothing else," Lili said, rapping smartly.

"Dear me, where's your sense of culinary adventure?" Ian declared.

"It gave way to my overwhelming hunger," Lili said, as the door swung open. Dimitri peered through the gap, looking even more vampiric than ever with dark circles under his hooded eyes.

"I did get you the pizza, do not worry," he barked, ushering them in. "I heard you through the door. I got the pizza, and some special cheese. It is local. Very nice as well, according to the girl in the shop."

"Please tell me you got some artisan breads and regional wine to accompany it?" Ian swooped into the room, deposited his coat on the nearest chair, and stretched.

Dimitri grinned. "I always bring the wine. Don't worry about that."

Kester dropped his suitcase to the floor, taking in the sight before him. The room was simple, basic even, but had a charm that he couldn't quite put his finger on. Perhaps it was the shutters flanking the window, or the mottled sofa and chairs. Even the bed's frilly divan had a rustic appeal to it.

"Your room is through there," Lili pointed. "These two are adjoining. Mine is the other side of the corridor."

"So you will not be kept awake with snoring," Dimitri said, striding to the coffee table and laying out the food.

"I don't know," Lili said thoughtfully, seizing her pizza with the speed of a diving gannet. "I snore pretty loudly sometimes."

"Am I sharing with anyone?" Kester sat down, looking longingly at the food. It suddenly seemed a long time since he'd eaten on the plane.

"No," Ian said, offering Kester some of the bread. "Dimitri and I are happy to bunk up in here. You can have a room all to yourself, like Lili."

Kester tucked into the food. A peaceful feeling had settled over him like a comforting blanket, and he was reluctant to spoil the moment. *I'm really in Italy, eating Italian food!* he thought, studying the lump of cheese in his hand. It all felt a bit miraculous, which was silly, given how many people flew abroad all the time.

"We thought we'd start the investigation tonight," Lili said, mouth full of food.

"What?" Kester snapped immediately out of his reverie. "Tonight? Really?"

"There is no time to waste," Dimitri announced darkly, picking a burnt piece of crust off his bread. "We only have a few days; we must make each moment count. And tonight is perfect, as it is a full moon."

"Why is that important? Do spirits like a full moon?" Kester asked.

Dimitri laughed mirthlessly. "No. It is easier for us to see where we are going."

"Less chance of anyone falling into the lake," Lili added, reaching for another chunk of cheese. "We'll have an hour or so to freshen up, then get the equipment together and head down there."

"We're not staying at Ransome's villa *all* night, are we?"

Lili raised an eyebrow. "Possibly, Kester. It depends what happens, really. I take it you've remembered the key that the Thelemites gave you?"

Kester nodded defensively. "Of course. Why, do you think the chest it belongs to will still be in the villa, after all these years?"

"Who knows?" Lili shrugged. "It might have been looted long ago. Or it might be still hidden there. My guess is that the Thelemites wouldn't have given you that key unless you were meant to use it, though."

Kester shivered. He didn't like the prospect of poking around in a haunted house for a spooky old chest. "How many spirits do you think will be in the villa?" he asked, in what he hoped was a suitably casual voice.

Dimitri grinned, eyes gleaming with amusement. "Are you worried, Kester?"

"I'm a little bothered by the thought."

Lili brushed the crumbs off herself, then belched behind her hand. "There are probably quite a few," she said seriously. "The records say the villa's been empty since Ransome left. That's well over 160 years, plenty of time for the spirits to make themselves comfortable."

"And invite a few friends to stay," Dimitri added, cracking his knuckles.

"Maybe you could use your spirit door opening prowess to send a few of them back to the spirit realm?" Ian suggested, with a yawn. "The Italian government will probably be most grateful."

"I'll see what I can do," Kester said weakly.

After lunch, he ventured into his room, which was smaller and darker than the other. However, it had an austere delicacy that appealed to his senses, and the bed felt comfortingly like his old bed, back in his childhood home. He plumped up the pillow and rested his eyes for a moment, wishing he could have a quick siesta before getting to work.

No such luck, he thought, as he listened to Dimitri and Ian stomping around next door. With a sigh, he hefted himself up and clambered into the shower, which released a diminutive dribble of unenthusiastic water down his back. However, it was warm, which was a step up from his horrible shower back in Exeter.

Once he'd changed into his clothes, he heard a smart rap at the door.

"Are you ready?" Lili barked, before he'd even had a chance to open it properly.

"Probably not," Kester answered. Ian and Dimitri were already with her, laden down with huge rucksacks, which he presumed must hold all the equipment. He pointed. "Do you want me to carry anything?"

"Sure do," Dimitri said with a grin, and gestured to another enormous bag, sitting on the hallway floor. Kester groaned, then hoisted it reluctantly on to his shoulder.

"What have you got in here?" Kester staggered under the weight. "Rocks or something?"

"That bag holds all the surveillance kit," Lili said primly. "Don't worry, you only have to carry it to the car."

"Is it really all necessary?" Kester followed them reluctantly, back already aching with the strain.

Lili smirked. "Oh *yes*. Just you wait and see. This is how Infinite Enterprises conducts an investigation."

"We like to do things *properly*," Ian clarified grandly as he pressed the lift button.

Dimitri caught Kester's eye and winked. They both knew what the implication was, that their agencies were inferior in every way. Which, he had to concede, was probably true.

Once they were downstairs in the lobby, Dimitri hung back, waiting for Kester to catch up.

"So," he began, carrying his bag with enviable ease, "how do you feel about our agencies joining forces, eh?"

Kester rolled his eyes. "It's not how I feel about it that's the problem. Dad is *furious*."

"Oh dear." Dimitri gallantly held open the door for Kester to pass through. "Larry is very pleased. I think he is especially pleased because he knows Ribero is not." They crossed the car park and dumped the bags next to the car.

"It'll be nice to work with you all," Kester added, massaging his neck. *Well, perhaps not Larry,* he added silently.

Dimitri smiled. "Yes, I am looking forward to it. It is a good thing for all of us. It makes our agencies more powerful." He leant over and patted Kester on the back, in a manner that managed to be somewhat sinister.

Lili flapped a hand at the car door, foot rapping on the gravel. "Are you two going to spend all day chatting, or can we get going?"

"I do not want to go in the back," Dimitri said firmly. "It is very uncomfortable."

"Shall I?" Ian offered kindly, despite the fact he was about a foot taller than the rest of them.

"Goodness me, it's only a five-minute drive!" Lili started to laugh. "Look, Kester and Dimitri, you're the shortest. In you both get."

They crammed themselves into the car, which, given it was already stuffed with bags of equipment, was quite a challenge. Finally, Ian managed to lever the front door closed, wedging them all in like whelks pressed between two rocks.

"Let's hope it's not a bumpy ride," Lili remarked, looking enviably comfortable in the driver's seat.

Regrettably, it was worse than bumpy. After descending at breakneck speed down the hill, Lili proceeded to navigate through a succession of tiny, winding roads, bouncing and jiggling them all with unbearable ferocity. Finally, she pulled up beside a rusted set of gates and turned to look at them all.

"This is it!" Lili opened the door without waiting for a response, then rapped on the roof to hurry them along.

Kester unfolded his legs, which had a serious case of pins-and-needles. He wrestled himself out of the car and stared at the looming gate with growing disbelief.

"I don't think that building could look more haunted if it tried," he muttered, leaning against the car.

"Ah, come on, my lad." Ian chuckled. "It's just a bit run-down, that's all."

"A bit?" Kester looked incredulously at the sight in front of him. Rusted gate aside, the property was almost totally hidden by dense pine trees, which hung drunkenly over the ornate fence. The house itself wasn't any better, with black, empty windows staring out in silent accusation.

Lili peered through the crusted railings and wriggled the lock tentatively. With a piercing shriek, the gate lurched open, teetering precariously on its hinges. She turned to the others and grinned. "Looks like we're in business."

"Are we allowed to go in?" Kester squeaked. "We shouldn't trespass, you know."

Ian placed a hand firmly on Kester's shoulders and led him forward. "Don't worry," he said soothingly, "we've got permission from the necessary authorities. It's all taken care of."

"I don't feel taken care of," Kester mumbled mulishly, aware that he was being ridiculous, but unable to stop himself.

Dimitri stalked in after Lili, carrying two rucksacks this time, as though to prove his strength. "This place has some serious energy," he muttered, with a satisfied nod. "It is like a house I once investigated back in Moscow. Full of spirit activity, so strong you can feel it a mile off." He beamed and marched up to the front door.

Kester groaned. *They're actually enjoying this,* he thought grumpily. *To them, this is like Disneyland.* "It's getting rather dark, isn't it?" he commented, looking over his shoulder to the bottom of the quiet road, where the lake lapped quietly.

"It's only going to get darker," Lili said, twisting the handle of the front door. The protesting scrape of swollen wood echoed through the dark passageway beyond. "Ah, would you look at that?" She flung the door open and beamed at them all. "They obviously sent someone over to unlock it earlier, just like they said they would."

"It would have made things tricky if they had not," Dimitri said, nose pointing in the air as though smelling the breeze. "Hmm. It is as I thought. Plenty of supernatural activity inside. The spirits are listening to us now."

Kester took a deep breath. Although spirits no longer scared him quite as badly as they used to, he still wasn't comfortable with the idea of spending the night with a whole rabble of them. *Oh well,* he thought, stepping into the building. *This is what you do for a living, after all. And it's not like you haven't had time to get used to it.*

"Gosh, what a malodorous pong!" Ian threw down his bag and thrust his hands on his hips, looking rather like a Shakespearean actor about to launch into a soliloquy. "A few air fresheners wouldn't go amiss, would they?"

In the dim evening light, Kester watched the others as they scanned the hallway. He hardly liked to look at it himself. There had obviously once been ornate yellow wallpaper on the walls, but now it hung in sad tatters, like peeling skin. The tiles underfoot were coated with thick dust, which clearly hadn't been disturbed for years.

"Why hasn't anyone ever bought this place?" he whispered. He knew there was no need to whisper, but it felt like the atmosphere called for it.

Lili shrugged. "The local council sent over a file which said a few people did try to purchase it, many years ago. But the sales all fell through."

"Because of the atmosphere, I suppose," Dimitri added. He rummaged in his bag and pulled out a large flashlight. "Shall we get started?"

Kester took a deep breath. There was an unpleasant feel to the house, and it wasn't just the decay and stench either. He had the horrible sensation of being watched; as though there were eyes at every corner, surveying his every move. *Which makes sense,* he told himself sternly, *given that there probably are. They just haven't made themselves known yet.*

They went through to the living area. Things weren't any better in there. In fact, if anything, they were considerably worse. The marble fireplace had crumbled at the sides like a weather-worn gravestone, and the two velvet sofas, which might have once been elegant, now lay haphazardly on their backs. The curtains lay unnaturally thick, weighted down with dust, and the cornicing had flaked and cracked, giving the room a diseased appearance.

An easel was still propped up in the corner. It was the only thing that was undamaged in the room, and its varnished wooden frame gleamed in the flash of Dimitri's torchlight. Kester touched it thoughtfully. He could imagine Robert Ransome working at it, diligently painting the lake before any of the troubles had started. *You mean before the Bloody Mary found him,* he reminded himself.

"Right," Ian boomed, clapping his hands. "Lili and I will proceed with setting up the surveillance and monitoring equipment. Might I suggest that you two explore the rest of the house? Dimitri, you're our resident psychic, if you could give us an official report, that would be most welcome."

"Yes, I was about to do that anyway," Dimitri growled. Kester resisted the urge to laugh. The Russian obviously didn't like Infinite Enterprises taking charge any more than he did. *But they are the bigger agency,* he thought rationally, as he stepped over the tattered rug and headed through to the neighbouring room. *They're the ones that collaborate directly with the government, not us.*

The next room was smaller than the living area, with two huge bookcases leaning against the wall. Kester ran a finger along the book spines, leaving a trail in the thick dust. "It could do with a clean, couldn't it?"

Dimitri paused and held a hand up for Kester to be silent. Finally, he nodded. "There are at least two other spirits in here with us," he muttered, eyes searching the ceiling. "Not hostile. Just wondering why we are here."

Kester looked anxiously upwards. "Well, it's a fair question, I suppose."

"They are lesser spirits," Dimitri said confidently. "They will not cause us any harm. They just want us to not pay attention to them."

"That won't be a problem at all."

Dimitri chuckled. "Good." He opened the door at the end of the room, which led out to the hallway again. Kester followed him quickly. He wasn't too bothered by the thought of two nonhostile spirits, but he didn't much fancy being left alone with them either.

"Ah, the kitchen." Dimitri disappeared through a doorway, then poked his head back out. "There is a lot more activity in here. Watch out."

Before Kester had a chance to process the comment, something large and metallic whizzed through the air, straight towards his head. He ducked with a scream as it clattered off the wall behind him.

"What was that?" he hissed, still crouched in a ball on the floor. "And what the hell *threw* that?"

Dimitri reached down, grabbed Kester by the armpit, and hoisted him unceremoniously to his feet. "A common poltergeist," he announced, then collected the object from the floor, which happened to be a dented saucepan. "Don't show you are afraid. They throw more things if they think it scares you."

"Difficult not to be scared when you've got heavy items being lobbed at you," Kester snapped. He scanned the rest of the room, trying to identify any other objects that could potentially be used as projectile weapons.

"Hmm." Dimitri wandered over to the aged oven and slid a hand above the surface, fingers quivering in the air. "This poltergeist is trying to tell us something. I don't know what, I don't speak Italian. He says *non sei l'artista. Non sei l'artista.* Over and over."

"Do you think that means something like *you're not the artist?*" Kester guessed, excitement rising in his chest.

Dimitri shrugged and stuffed both hands in his pockets. "It could be, yes. I think I heard the name Ransome, so it would make sense."

Kester edged around the room, keeping a close watch on all moveable items. His heart was only just starting to recover after the shock of the saucepan. "Do you think the poltergeist doesn't like us?" he asked reluctantly.

"Poltergeists don't really care either way about us humans," Dimitri explained, as he gestured out of the room. "They are simple spirits, very reactive. They like to surprise us, but it's not personal. Do you understand?"

"I think so." Kester followed Dimitri gladly out of the room, hoping there wouldn't be more poltergeists waiting for them upstairs.

"How are you both doing?" Lili called out from the living room. From halfway up the stairs, Kester could just make her out, her arms draped with a serpentine mess of wires.

"Kester nearly got hit with a saucepan," Dimitri shouted back. "Nothing serious."

"There are definitely plenty of spirits with us," Ian added casually. "But we've opened the curtains and the view of the lake is splendid. You really should see it."

"Maybe later," Dimitri barked, as he continued up the stairs.

The upper floor was even more decrepit than downstairs. In one room, a wall had started to crumble down, revealing a jagged square of evening sky, which cast a milky light on the rough floorboards. The main bedroom still contained an old bedframe, plus a burst mattress, which slumped beside it as though it had given up all hope.

"I suppose this is where Robert Ransome slept," Kester whispered. There was something unspeakably *melancholy* about the room. It wasn't just the desolation of it all. The air hung heavy with a sense of despair and loss, and Kester could well imagine the artist's turmoil as he struggled to resist the Bloody Mary spirit. He wandered to the other side of the room, where a simple dresser stood against the wall. The mirror on top of it was smashed. Kester shuddered.

"Have you found anything interesting?" Dimitri wandered over to him, making him jump.

Kester shook his head. "Only this mirror. I remember reading that Robert Ransome broke every mirror in the house, presumably in an attempt to stop the Bloody Mary from showing herself. It didn't work though."

"It is strange," Dimitri murmured, running an absentminded hand over the dilapidated cupboard. "The spirits do not come into this room. I do not know why. They pass by along the hallway but do not enter."

"Perhaps it feels too sad," Kester suggested.

Dimitri nodded. "Yes. Perhaps you have a bit of the psychic in you too, Kester. You pick up the emotion of the place. That is impressive; I do not know any investigators with more than one skill."

Kester joined him by the cupboard, tracing a finger over the detailed carvings that decorated the door. *It must have once been a beautiful piece of furniture,* he thought, sighing at the splintered wood. *But time breaks everything down, sooner or later.*

He opened the door, which squeaked sharply on its hinges. Half expecting to see Ransome's old clothes still hanging up, he was instead greeted with an empty, musty space, which Dimitri helpfully illuminated with his flashlight.

"No one's opened this in a while," Dimitri commented, wrinkling his nose.

"I know," agreed Kester, "it smells like a tomb." *And I feel unnervingly like a grave robber,* he added silently, casting a glance over his shoulder. He brushed a dense cobweb aside and peered in. There was a large box sitting in the bottom, squat and ornately decorated, from what he could tell.

The chest! His hand flew instinctively to his trouser pocket, where the key still rested, reassuringly heavy. *Could it be the one we're looking for?* he wondered, heart racing. *Surely not, after all this time?*

"Look!" He crouched down quickly. "Shine the light on this, let me have a proper look."

Dimitri obligingly tilted the light, then whistled. "You think it might be Ransome's chest? The one that matches your key?"

Kester shrugged. "We mustn't get our hopes up. It's probably just an old box with nothing in it." However, he couldn't stop his stomach from fluttering. There was something about the chest, with its ornate iron hinges and smooth polished lid, that made him think they'd hit the jackpot. He tested the lid gingerly, but it didn't budge.

"Try the key," Dimitri suggested helpfully.

Kester brought the key into the beam of light. Its surface glinted darkly.

Here goes nothing, he thought, pressing it into the delicate lock. To his astonishment, it fitted. To his even greater amazement, it turned easily, as though it had never been separated from the chest in the first place.

"It's the right chest!" he squealed, unable to contain his excitement. "Shout for Lili and Ian, quickly!"

Dimitri raced out into the hallway and bellowed down the stairs, taking the torchlight with him. Kester was too excited to care. He noticed that his hands were shaking, but he clasped on tightly to the key nonetheless, scared to let go in case it didn't work a second time. He didn't dare open the lid, for fear of what he might find inside.

The other two clattered up the stairs in a cacophony of footsteps, the beam of light announcing their return.

"Is it really the chest?" Lili stepped forward, ducking down to kneel beside Kester.

He nodded. "It's unlocked. Shall I open it?"

"Good god, man, yes!" Ian exclaimed, hopping from foot to foot behind him. "Come on, this is what we came for, isn't it? The surveillance is low priority compared to this!"

With trembling fingers, Kester prised the lid open. Dimitri shone the light directly into the chest, and they all peered in.

"Letters," Lili breathed, clutching Kester's arm.

"Quite a few, by the looks of it." Kester stared, almost frightened to reach in, as though touching the envelopes would make them disintegrate. "What should we do?"

"Pick them up!" Ian said excitedly, hammering a fist on Kester's shoulder. "Read them! Come on, I'm desperate to know what they say!"

Do these letters hold the clue to all the mysterious goings on? Kester wondered, as he reached in. *Or are they just another trick, left by the Thelemites to mess with our minds?* The pile of letters felt oddly warm to touch, their surfaces smooth and porous. He pulled them out and placed them carefully on his knees.

"Who are they addressed to?" Dimitri asked, then shone the light helpfully down so Kester could read the writing.

"Let's see." Kester picked up the top envelope and read aloud. "Captain Monty Fletcher. That's strange, the name sounds familiar. Does anyone else think so?"

Ian clicked his fingers, eyes alight with triumph. "Of course it's familiar. It's the person Hrschni inhabited, during the war. Well, I never. Of all the things I was expecting we'd find here . . . Are they all addressed to him?"

Kester looked down again. "No. This one's addressed to . . ." He faltered, then stopped. His eyes widened. *It's not possible,* he thought, reading again. *There's no way this is possible. It's a trick.*

"What's up?" Lili scooped the envelope from his hand and held it up to the light. "Mr Gerhard Lanner. Hang on, that's—"

"—my surname," Kester finished heavily. He sat back on the floor, unable to take it in. "It's also my grandfather's name. And I'm fairly sure that was his address in Germany."

After taking a deep breath, he began to read.

CHAPTER 11: OLD FRIENDS

11 November 1944

> *My dearest Gerhard,*
> *Safe passage has been prepared for you and your wife. You need not worry about anything; we will ensure you are well protected throughout the journey. I trust that your English is now good enough for you to live comfortably in England; hopefully these letters will help you to practice in the meantime.*
>
> *Let me reassure you that when you arrive there, you will have accommodation and food. I do not forget those who are my friends, and I will make it my personal responsibility to ensure not only your comfort, but your safety.*
>
> *I know you and your dear wife have been through considerable trauma. Concealment from the Nazis hasn't been easy, and I know you've watched many of your friends suffer. The good news is, your own suffering will soon be over. I cannot leave details in this letter for*

obvious reasons. We will get a message to you the usual way.
   Yours in fondness,
   Monty

***

25 November 1944

   Dear Monty,
   You are most kind. A thousand times I thank you. We owe you a debt that can never be repaid. I can leave no details in this letter, but please be assured, we received your notice, and we are prepared for departure at the agreed time.
   I only hope England is a safer country than this. My beloved homeland has been turned upside down, and my people called vermin. When I arrive on English soil, I will burn the humiliating armband. I will stamp on its ashes. Never will I let anyone persecute me again. I pray my other Jewish friends are kept safe too. Though they do not have the guardian angel that I have.
   I look forward to meeting with you again, my dear friend. And yes, we have been practicing our English. It is much better than it was, as I hope this letter proves.
   Sincerely,
   Gerhard

***

8 July 1946

   My dearest Gerhard,
   Thank you for your recent letter. I am delighted to hear that you

are enjoying your home in Cambridge; I told you that it was a fine place to live. Some of the greatest minds in history have studied there, and the air is rich with learning and knowledge.

With regards to our agreement, we need to discuss the matter further. It isn't prudent to do so via a letter; instead I shall visit you personally, in a few days' time. I know you said I was always welcome in your house, and I shall now make the most of this kind invitation. Do not worry, I will not alarm you and your wife, I will appear as the Captain, as is appropriate.

In the meantime, I implore you to remember our agreement. We made a solemn pact; a pact not just as two beings, but as brothers. I know you are a good man, Gerhard, and your concerns are valid. But do not allow these to overrule what you know in your heart to be true. Remember what you learned in the war. It is better to be united than divided.

We cannot delay any further. I look forward to seeing you.
Your dearest friend,
Monty

***

14 July 1946

Dear Monty,
Firstly, please allow me to express my deepest regret at the way our last meeting ended. It breaks my heart to think of our difference of opinion, and I know you are angry at me.

That is why I must explain myself to you now. The words were stuck in my throat the other day, and I could not express my feelings. Perhaps, by writing it in this letter, it will become clearer.

I know we had an agreement. You would help me and I would

help you. But dearest Monty, when I made this agreement, I did not understand what you were asking for! I believed you wanted me to use my gift to open a single door, to allow easier passage for those who were like you. I didn't realise you wanted to tear a hole in the world.

You must understand, what you are proposing to do is madness. Without proper controls between your people and ours, there will be chaos. Terror. Perhaps worse.

Please believe me when I say that I never meant to disappoint you. I owe you my life, my wife's life. I will never forget what you have done for us. I implore you to write back to me swiftly, otherwise I shall not sleep easy.

Your devoted friend,
Gerhard

***

8 February 1964

Dear Gerhard,

I can only imagine how shocked you were last month, when I arrived at the hospital. It has been many years since we saw one another, and our last words were not kindly spoken. And of course, my appearance is now greatly transformed.

I wanted to congratulate you and your wife on the birth of your little girl, and I hope the flowers and gift reached you safely in the post. She is a beautiful thing. I took the liberty of following your wife one day along the high street and watched your daughter in the pram. So alert! So intelligent! I could feel the power radiating from her, and I am certain she has your gift. She will go on to do great things, I am certain of it.

Last time we spoke, you made your feelings clear regarding the *opening of the door and the union between your people and mine. One last time, I beg you to reconsider. Your talent can change the world. You and I could become great beings. Together, we could herald in a new age.*

I will visit you soon. Even if you do not agree, we must be friends again. You are too valuable to me, and these years without your company have been a trial.

Fondest wishes,

Monty (should I now sign off as Billy?)

***

19 March 1964

Dear Monty,

I want you to know that I have reviewed your kind offer. For many nights, I've thought about it, especially now that I am a father and have new responsibilities. It is tempting, I cannot deny that. You offer me the world, and I feel too humble to take it. I am, after all, only a man.

But I cannot. I still feel that, whilst your intentions are noble, your approach is not. I cannot speak plainly in this letter, but you must know what I am referring to. Your "people" and mine; we cannot connect anymore. The world is changing, and we are all changing with it. You and I are exceptions to the rule—thanks to my strange door-opening gift. But we are few and far between. The rest of this planet? It will not take so kindly to those you seek to unleash upon it.

I was also concerned about your veiled threat. Nothing was said explicitly, but it was there, hidden in each word. My daughter Gretchen is the dearest thing in the world to me. She has nothing to do with our old pact, and you must not try to make use of her in the future. I forbid it. Please, for the love of our old friendship, do not give up on me and turn to her instead. I know you can be very persuasive.

As for those trying to thwart your plans? Monty, I swear I know nothing of this. I may not be actively helping you to achieve your goals, but I give you my word, I would never work against you. In all honesty, I think you are being paranoid.

Perhaps it is better if we desist contact. Please think kindly of me. I know you feel I've let you down, but remember this—I shall always believe you to be the noblest of creatures, with a bravery and strength that is astounding. I am convinced your intentions are good. But I am not convinced you are going about things in the right way.

Ever your friend,
Gerhard

Kester put the final letter down, hands trembling. The others waited, gathered around him silently. Somewhere far away, a motorbike revved its engine, reminding them all that there was a world out there, beyond this strange, watchful villa.

"Wow." It was the only word Kester could muster, and he knew it wasn't a very good one. He rubbed his face, then looked at Lili. "Wow."

"The plot thickens," Ian said quietly, as he shifted himself into a more comfortable position. "The question is, what does it all mean?"

"I wonder why he didn't just sign himself as Hrschni?" Kester asked, touching the letters again, as though to reach out to his grandfather through the paper. His mind was buzzing, struggling to take in the enormity of what he'd just read. How was it possible that these letters should end up here, just waiting to be read by him? There was a bigger picture here, but no matter how hard he tried, Kester couldn't see it.

I never knew my grandfather, but my mother always spoke so highly of him, he thought, his mind drifting back to childhood conversations. Or rather, curious questions, which his mother had often left unanswered. *So many mysteries, even in my own family. How much more is there that I don't know?*

Lili touched him gently on the arm, bringing him back to the present. "I guess Hrschni was being cautious," she said, as she picked up the top letter again, eyes travelling over the words. "After all, if the letters had been intercepted, people might have wondered who the hell would have a name like that."

"But . . ." Kester began, then stopped. He was struggling with it all, his brain unable to process the magnitude of the evidence put before him. "My grandfather? And Hrschni? How is that even possible?"

Dimitri patted Kester on the back. "It must be a big shock. But it makes sense. Hrschni was interested in your grandfather because he could open spirit doors. Then you come along, and you have the same gift? Of course he wants to make use of you too."

"But he *helped* my grandfather," Kester said weakly. He remembered his mother talking about her parent's escape from Germany during the war, though as with everything, she never went into too much detail. *And I never thought to ask,* he thought, anger swelling in his heart. *Why am I so stupid? If I'd have pressed her, I'm sure she would have told me. Or would she?* Kester bit his lip. Perhaps he didn't know his mother nearly as well as he thought he did.

Lili rustled the letters, snapping him out of his thoughts. "Daemons can be kind too, you know."

"That's correct," an unfamiliar voice agreed.

The four of them jumped as one, instantly alert, eyes scouring the room.

"Who's there?" Lili said, getting to her feet. Kester gathered the letters and pressed them to his chest.

Ian stepped forward, motioning to Dimitri to shine the torchlight around the room. "That was a spirit voice," he hissed to the others, then nodded at the Russian. "What do you pick up, Dimitri? Who's in here with us?"

"There's really no need for that," the same voice murmured. The air at the foot of the bed started to quiver, shimmering like a wave of heat before gradually forming into something solid.

Kester exhaled with relief. He'd already worked out who it was, even as the air reassembled itself into the familiar, whirling form. "Dr. Barqa-Abu," he said as he stood up.

Lili gasped. "I had no idea you'd been called in for this case. My apologies."

The djinn spun closer, a single skeletal hand emerging from the glimmering mist. "There's no reason you would have known, Lili. Because I *wasn't* called in, you see."

"Gosh." Ian ran a hand through his mane, eyes hollow in the shine of the torch. "So, without meaning to sound rude, why are you here, madam?"

"I think I know," Kester said in a small voice. He remembered the *Historie of Spirits*, left open in his room. "Dr. Barqa-Abu, you've been trying to tell me for a while, haven't you? That you're a key part of this?"

Dr. Barqa-Abu's face came into focus. Her mouth tilted slightly at the edges, in what might have been a smile. "I know it seems that we've been playing games with you, Kester. But you had to solve the puzzle for yourself, in order to understand."

Kester held the letters in front of him. "But I *don't* understand," he said bitterly. "I don't know why Hrschni and my grandfather were friends. I don't know why my mother never told me anything. And I don't know why you couldn't just tell me about this from the start."

The djinn sighed, a dry sound like breeze rustling a sand dune. "You are right to feel angry and hurt, Kester. Once again, people have kept you in the dark. That's why I'm here now. To finally enlighten you."

"Please, enlighten all of us," Ian chimed in. "I'm feeling just as confused as this young chap here."

"Very well." Dr. Barqa-Abu shifted restlessly, becoming invisible for a moment, before solidifying into a misty, narrow form. "Kester, these letters explain Hrschni's interest in you. He's been following your family for decades, as he believes you're his best hope."

"But I'm not, and I won't help him!" Kester said. "Please tell me you're not on his side too, and you're just here to try to convince me?"

Dr. Barqa-Abu shook her head. "No. Did the *Historie of Spirits* teach you nothing?"

Kester cast his mind back to the ancient story. The daemon, inhabiting a human body and conquering a land. His friend, the djinn, working undercover to stop him. The penny dropped. His mouth fell open. "Are *you* the djinn in the story?" he asked, scarcely able to believe it. The tales in the *Historie of Spirits* dated back centuries, but then, his father had told him that Dr. Barqa-Abu was thousands of years old.

"I am," Dr Barqa-Abu confirmed. "And Hrschni was the daemon."

"Well I never!" Ian exclaimed, slapping his thighs in amazement. "I just thought those stories were all made up!" He opened his mouth to laugh, then spotted Lili's disapproving face and thought better of it.

"Hrschni was your friend?" Kester asked. His head was whirling, threatening to come apart at the edges with it all. "But how? Why? And what happened after?"

The djinn faltered for a moment, her face becoming far clearer. He thought he saw a downturned mouth, black eyes glittering with sadness, before she became vapour once again, swirling around them. "The djinn and the daemons are among the most ancient orders of spirits," she began. "Back then, Hrschni and I were close. We both loved the human realm and used to travel with the nomadic people, helping them whenever we could."

Kester sighed. He didn't know if it was the smooth, dusty quality of her voice, or the words that she used, but he could imagine it clearly. Two powerful spirits journeying across an endless desert with their family of humans. *Perhaps things were simpler between spirits and people back then,* he thought.

"But Hrschni wanted so much more," Dr. Barqa-Abu continued. "He wanted the spirit and human world to be as one, without barriers. He used his powers to amass an army, a vast number that believed he was right."

"What about you?" Dimitri asked hesitantly.

"He lured me in to begin with," Dr. Barqa-Abu admitted, hovering for a moment as though remembering. "He's very convincing, as you know. But the more I considered it, the more I realised what a dangerous notion it was. I tried to reason with him, but he couldn't see it my way at all. I had to stop him."

Kester leaned heavily against the cupboard, wiping his eyes. It was all starting to feel rather surreal. "Surely you couldn't have stopped him all by yourself? I know you're a powerful spirit, but so is he."

"I was working with another daemon. To this day, Hrschni has no idea she plotted against him."

"She?" Kester whispered. "Do you mean . . . Fylgia?"

Lili whistled. "No way. The daemon who's working with Hrschni now? The one who inhabited Kester's girlfriend's body?"

Dr. Barqa-Abu nodded. "Yes, Fylgia. We joined forces to stop Hrschni back then, and we're still working against him to this day. This madness has to end. He's too close to succeeding."

"But hang on," Kester said, waving the letters in front of her. "Why show me these? They explain that Hrschni's been trying to cash in on my family's talents for decades, but they don't show him as a bad spirit. In fact, quite the opposite. He saved my grandfather's life." *That's what Hrschni was talking about, that day in the museum,* Kester suddenly realised. *When he'd said "without us, you wouldn't be here." It's true, I do owe him my existence after all.*

"That's the point, Kester." A hint of Dr. Barqa-Abu's usual impatience resurfaced in her tone. "He's not evil. Despite the fact we hardly speak anymore, I still regard him as one of the greatest spirits that ever existed. And for what it's worth, I wish I were still his friend. But he's gone too far, don't you see? If he succeeds, it will be a disaster. For *everyone.*"

Lili shivered, wrapping her arms tightly around herself. "I have a question," she said. "Why couldn't you tell Kester this earlier? Why push the notes through his door? Why give him clues to follow?"

"And why bring us here to Italy?" Dimitri added. "Not that I am complaining, it is very nice. But still."

The air around the djinn shimmered brightly, before dimming. She turned, her black eyes coming into sudden, sharp focus. "It's a fair question," she said slowly. "First, Fylgia has been the one leaving the clues. And you know what daemons are like with their riddles. It's a part of their nature."

"That's certainly true," Ian muttered.

"Second," Dr. Barqa-Abu continued, ignoring the interruption, "would you have believed us, if we'd simply blurted it out to you? Your head was already a mess after the kidnapping in the cave. We felt you would trust us no more than you'd trust Hrschni. You needed to journey to this point by yourself, so you could see the bigger picture. The story of the Thelemites is a long and complex one, but you need to gain understanding of it if you're going to help us protect the human world."

Kester coughed. "You talk about trust. Speaking honestly, I'm not totally convinced I trust you now."

The djinn nodded, acknowledging the point. "Third, the clues were designed to get you thinking. To make you understand that this is not a black-and-white matter. It's complex. It comes in shades of grey. It's tempting to always seek the villain in your line of work, but in this case, there is no villain. Not really."

"But why bring us here?" Dimitri persisted. "Why did you store the letters at Robert Ransome's house?"

"He was a Thelemite too," Dr. Barqa-Abu explained. "Like the rest of us, he was initially entranced by Hrschni. He believed that the daemon was right to want to unite the two worlds, and he was willing to help. Especially when Hrschni helped him to gain popularity in the artistic community."

Kester looked at the others in amazement. *Robert Ransome, a Thelemite?* But he supposed it made sense, in a strange sort of way. "Was that why he encountered the Bloody Mary?" he asked, seeing the room with fresh eyes. *Perhaps it wasn't an accident,* he thought. *Perhaps the Bloody Mary was summoned on purpose.*

Dr. Barqa-Abu glided closer, studying him intently. "I think you understand," she said quietly. "It was Hrschni who brought Robert Ransome to this country. He paid for the young man to stay here. He introduced him to all the right people. For a while, Ransome was the talk of the town. Of the whole lake, perhaps."

"Let me guess," Ian interrupted, arms folded. "In return, he had to help Hrschni? Was he a door opener too?"

"Not him," the djinn corrected. "His childhood sweetheart, Constance Pettifer. A lovely young woman, as I remember, though I only met her once. Ransome later married her, but she died soon after."

"Robert Ransome was married to a spirit door opener?" Kester could hardly believe what he was hearing.

Dr. Barqa-Abu nodded. "That's why he was a part of the Thelemites. He'd grown up with a girl who could invite spirits in and out of the world at will. And because he loved her, he accepted it as normal. That's why he allowed Hrschni to encourage Constance to open a spirit door, here in this villa."

"Constance came here?" Kester scratched his head. "I thought she stayed back in England?"

"She came to visit him, just the once."

"And opened the spirit door?"

The djinn nodded. "I wasn't there, of course, so I don't know exactly when she did it. But I do know it happened, and I believe the Bloody Mary slipped through it."

"And made poor Robert Ransome's life an absolute misery, I would imagine," Ian said gruffly.

Kester nodded. He already knew the rest of the story. The smashed mirrors. The trapping of the spirit in the painting shortly after. The horrible impact when the spirit escaped; both for Emmeline in the 1890s and for Isabelle Diderot in Exeter, only a few months ago. *How can Hrschni not see how devastating it would be if spirits like the Bloody Mary were allowed to roam freely?* he wondered. For such an intelligent spirit, he was staggeringly blind to the truth.

Dr. Barqa-Abu stilled for a moment. Her bony hands knotted anxiously before disappearing into the mist of the rest of her. "Fylgia told me that Hrschni took it badly. Very badly indeed. After the problems with the Bloody Mary spirit, Robert Ransome and Constance swore not only that they wouldn't help the Thelemites but that they wanted nothing more to do with Hrschni. And so, he lost another treasured friend."

"You'd think he would get the message," Dimitri remarked grimly. "He needs to listen to those who love him."

The djinn smiled slightly. "You are right. However, this is the situation, and we must deal with it as best we possibly can."

Kester glanced out of the broken window. The sun had now completely set. However, Dimitri had been right about the full moon, which was already casting a glow across the floorboards, before coming to an end on the sunken mattress. "What do you propose?" he asked, relaxing his grip on the letters. He hadn't realised he'd been clutching them so tightly until now.

Dr. Barqa-Abu shook her head, shifting from side to side. "We have a plan, but we can't discuss it yet. I am confident we're not being overheard here, but we need to finalise details before starting. And we need to know if you'll help us."

More secrecy? Kester wasn't surprised, somehow. *This is what you should expect when dealing with supernatural beings,* he realised. "I believe that what you're doing is right," he said slowly, looking at the others for support, "and that Hrschni needs to be stopped. But it depends on what plan you're proposing."

"Can I take that as a provisional yes, then?" Dr. Barqa-Abu shimmered slightly, then settled into virtual invisibility.

Kester paused. "Yes. For now."

"And the rest of you?" The djinn floated around the room, studying them all intently.

"It's a big yes from me; that's what I'm hired to do," Lili said firmly.

Ian nodded. "Yes. Myself also."

Dimitri paused, looking at Kester, then nodded too. "It must be done," he said seriously. "Though I feel for this daemon. He is full of good intentions, wrapped up in a bad idea."

"He's not the first, and he won't be the last," Dr. Barqa-Abu said crisply. She wheeled around in a violent circle, then stopped, sharp features coming into vision once more. "So it begins, and now I must depart. Thank you for understanding."

I'm still not sure I do understand, Kester thought, shoving his glasses up his nose. He nodded. "I guess I'll see you next week for the lesson?"

The djinn's mouth twitched. Again, Kester was fairly sure it was a smile, but he never liked to presume anything with the notoriously prickly spirit. "Yes, I will see you then," she said, before adding, "and I will be expecting your essay. I hope it is of a good standard."

I haven't even written it yet! Kester thought with sudden panic. "Can't I have an extension, because of all this?" he asked lamely, already knowing what the answer would be.

The djinn shook her head. "Out of the question. Oh, and one thing before I go. Something I think you should know, Kester."

"Yes?" He wasn't sure he wanted to know. His head was already stuffed with enough craziness as it was.

"Your girlfriend, Anya. She—"

"—what about her?" he interrupted, a little too defensively.

The djinn sighed. "When she allowed Fylgia to inhabit her body, she did it to stop Hrschni. But also to protect you. Fylgia promised that you wouldn't come to any harm."

"Oh," Kester replied. He couldn't think of anything else to say. Then he thought about it some more, and his frown cleared. *"Oh.* I see." Suddenly, in spite of the gravity of the situation, not to mention the spookiness of the house, he felt much happier.

Dr. Barqa-Abu flittered abruptly, then started to fade into invisibility. "We'll talk soon," she said, before plipping out of the room entirely.

They looked at one another, each with identical expressions of shock, confusion, and the vague beginnings of excitement.

"I think we're finally getting somewhere," Lili said finally, breaking the silence. She strode across the room, then gestured to them all to follow. "Come on, we may as well pack up. We've got what we came for, haven't we?"

"I'd say more than we came for, actually," Ian announced, with a theatrical wiggle of the eyebrow. "It appears we may be closer to stopping Hrschni than we think."

Kester smiled, then paced after them down the stairs. It had been a productive evening, as well as enlightening and disturbing in equal measures. However, he couldn't dull the nagging sensation in the pit of his chest, the anxious churning that suggested it wouldn't be as easy to capture Hrschni as the others might think.

Chapter 12: The Signing of the Contract

"You have to tell us more than that." Serena snapped her fingers in Kester's eyeline, trying to galvanise him into action.

However, she wasn't having much luck. Kester had arrived home from the airport, after a delayed flight, at two in the morning, and work was the last thing he wanted to do. His eyes felt as though someone had rubbed salt in them, then chucked in a load of gravel for good measure. Even the dim wintry light coming in through the office window was giving him a headache.

"I've told you everything already," he protested, slumping over his desk. "Well, as much as I can remember, anyway."

"What was the hotel like?" Pamela asked, nursing a cup of tea on her lap. "Was it posh?"

Miss Wellbeloved tutted. "I fail to see how that's important. More to the point, how do you feel about it all, Kester? Finding out that your grandfather and Hrschni were friends must have been an awful surprise."

Kester looked at the letters, which were currently piled on the corner of his desk after the others had perused them thoroughly. He tapped them, then sighed. "It was a shock," he admitted. "But not because of any personal feeling I might have towards my grandfather. I mean, I never even knew him; he died before I was born."

Mike reached over and took another biscuit from the tin. "What was it then, mate?"

"I don't know," Kester replied. But deep down, he knew exactly what was bothering him. *These are yet more details of my life that I never knew about because Mum never told me.* It was embarrassing to admit how little he knew about his own family.

"So," Miss Wellbeloved said briskly, finishing off the rest of her tea. "The big question is, what now?"

Kester shrugged. "Wait for instructions, I suppose." He glanced around the room. "Do you think we should be careful what we say, in case someone's listening?"

Pamela followed his gaze, then laughed. "Oh, dearie me, no spirit's going to slip my attention, don't you worry. We can talk freely. And you can tell me what the hotel was like regardless of whether anyone else is listening. Was breakfast included?"

"Pamela, *please* can you stop focusing on the hotel?" Miss Wellbeloved exclaimed. "Kester, would you rather talk about it when you've had a chance to wake up a bit? Larry Higgins and his team are coming later this morning to go through a few more documents before signing the contract. They'd probably be interested to hear what you've got to say too."

Kester resisted the urge to groan. A meeting with the self-satisfied Higgins was not his idea of a good time, especially when his head felt as though someone had rammed half a tonne of concrete inside it. He opened his mouth to reply, but any attempt at speech was soon blocked by a deafening bang, followed by a recognisable snort.

His father stood at the entrance of the office, resplendent in a dapper grey suit. The door still vibrated from the force of its collision with the wall. He pointed at each of them, then grinned.

"I am back!"

"Yes, we can see that," Miss Wellbeloved acknowledged, straightening her hair.

Ribero's face fell, and he crossed his arms, mutinous as a child. "Hey, it is a big deal for me to be here. You should look a bit happier, yes?"

Pamela winked at Miss Wellbeloved, then enveloped Ribero in a hug. "Good to have you back, love," she said enthusiastically.

Ribero prised himself away, looking slightly mollified by the gesture, but rather more crumpled than before. "And the rest of you?" he continued, scouring the room. "I would have thought my only son would have been more pleased to see me."

Kester stood awkwardly. "Does that mean you're not angry anymore?"

"Hmm." Ribero stalked across the carpet in four swift steps, nudged Mike out of his seat, and promptly placed himself down in the vacated chair. "My feelings are still hurt because you betrayed me. But I *missed* you all; you are my family. This business is all I have. So, I am back."

"That's nice," Miss Wellbeloved said, with a small smile. "I should probably tell you that we've got Larry Higgins coming in an hour or so, by the way."

Ribero's face darkened. "The Higgins? In *my* office?"

"Is it still your office?" Miss Wellbeloved's lips tightened. Kester could tell that she wasn't going to let him off the hook that easily.

Ribero sighed elaborately, then placed his hands on the table. Fortunately, they weren't shaking. In fact, Kester thought he looked better than he had done for a long time. *Clearly retirement works for him,* he thought, *even if hasn't acknowledged that he's actually retired yet.*

"I know, I know," his father said eventually, with a generous smile. "I have passed the business on to Kester, and so—"

"What did you say?" Serena screeched, straightening abruptly.

"Kester," Ribero repeated patiently, oblivious to the warning gestures being made by Miss Wellbeloved. "I have now signed the business to him. He is your official boss."

Oh no, Kester thought with a groan.

Serena's face reddened. "Since when? He can't run this agency! He's about ten years old!"

"Nearly twenty-three, actually," Kester corrected.

She glowered at him, as though he was personally responsible for every single problem in her life. "He's only been here five minutes!"

"Five months."

"He's . . . he's a cowardly, dithering moron!" Serena bit her lip, smoothed her hair, then looked apologetic. "Not that I don't like you, of course, but—"

Kester shrugged. The words *cowardly* and *dithering* were probably fair enough. *Moron* seemed somewhat harsh, but then, Serena was clearly working herself up into something of a rage. "If it makes it any easier," he said, as placatingly as possible, "I didn't ask Dad to pass the agency on to me. And—"

"And Kester won't be running it officially until much later," Miss Wellbeloved interrupted. "I'll be in charge until he's ready."

Serena folded her arms and glared. "Yes, but it'll still be *his,* won't it? It doesn't seem very fair to me."

"What do you mean, not fair?" Ribero snapped. "The agency belongs to me, so I give it to my son and heir, yes?"

"Son and heir?" Serena rolled her eyes. "What about giving it back to the person who it belonged to originally? It was Jennifer's father's agency to begin with!"

"That's what I said," Kester added, then wilted under Ribero's glare.

Miss Wellbeloved rested her chin on her fingertips, fixing Serena with an earnest gaze. "So," she began, "what *exactly* do you have a problem with, Serena? Let's be frank, now."

Serena glanced at Mike, who shrugged. Her stare then shifted to Pamela, who smiled sympathetically. "It just seems," she began, toying with her nails, as though seeking the answer in their gleaming red polish, "it just seems that . . ."

"Yes?"

"You're all so focused on Kester and his amazing ability that you've totally forgotten the rest of us exist." Serena took a deep breath, then retreated into her chair. "So now you know how I feel. How *we* feel."

Miss Wellbeloved scratched her head. "Mike, Pamela, do you feel the same?"

Mike snorted, rubbing his nose. "I'm not angry about it," he said slowly, fumbling for the right words. "But I've started thinking I'm *never* going to get promoted. I mean, there's nothing to get promoted to, is there?"

"And I think this puts huge pressure on Kester's shoulders," Pamela added, with a kindly pat on Kester's arm. "He's ever so young, Julio, and it's a lot to ask of him."

"It certainly is," Kester said. He smoothed down his shirt, then met Serena's gaze. "For what it's worth, I didn't want any of this. Perhaps we should look into a more cooperative solution, so that we all have equal shares in the agency?"

"No, we will not do that!" Ribero barked, fist bouncing energetically on the desk. "It is bad enough you share it with the Higgins, let alone make everyone boss!"

Miss Wellbeloved coughed. "I seem to remember you agreeing to pass the agency on, Julio," she reminded him sternly. "Which means executive decisions will be made by myself and Kester."

"Nothing is signed yet! I am still in charge."

"Oh, for goodness sake!" Miss Wellbeloved's eyes narrowed to beady slits. "You cannot keep ducking in and out of the agency at whim. I understand you're unwell, but this uncertainty is playing havoc on my mental wellbeing!"

"What's wrong with you?" Serena interrupted.

"He's got Parkinson's disease," Pamela said solemnly.

Ribero whipped round, sharp as a greyhound. "How did you know? Did Jennifer or Kester—?"

"No, it was obvious," Pamela replied, giving his shoulder a comforting squeeze. "You should have just told everyone, though. No one would have thought any less of you."

Serena's mouth opened and closed like a goldfish. "I had no idea," she said. "I'm ever so sorry. It all makes more sense now."

"I didn't even notice anything was wrong," Mike added.

"Yes, I have the Parkinson," Ribero announced grandly. "So, now you all know. But no sympathy. No treating me like an old man, okay? I am fine most of the time. Just a bit shaky some days."

"You *are* an old man, Julio," Miss Wellbeloved reminded him, but her voice was gentler than her words suggested. "Now, let's leave the topic of who's running the agency for now, shall we? Larry and his team will be here soon, and we need to present a united front. Agreed?"

The others nodded. Serena gave Kester a tight smile, which looked more like a grimace. He understood her anger but wished it wasn't directed at him. *It's not my fault that Dad keeps using me as an obstacle to her ambition,* he thought. Joining forces to run the agency cooperatively seemed like a good idea to him, providing they didn't all drive each other mad with their differing opinions.

They resumed work at their separate desks, though the atmosphere was noticeably frostier than usual. Dr. Ribero disappeared into his office, even though technically he'd handed the office over to Miss Wellbeloved. Miss Wellbeloved resumed her position at her old desk with a sigh.

An hour later the phone rang, startling them all—especially Kester, who'd been about to doze off. Pamela, who happened to be nearest at the time, scooped up the receiver.

"Good morning, Dr. Ribero's Agency, how can I—oh, hello Larry, how are you?" She winked at the others, then mimed an angry face, which suggested Larry's greeting had been less than friendly. "Yes, you're in the right place," she said a few moments later, then winced. "Oh dear, the entrance to the car park is rather tight, isn't it? I hope you didn't scrape it too much. Do you want us to come down and fetch you, or are you okay to come up? It's the door right in front of where you're standing. It's already unlocked."

She put the phone down. "Gosh, someone doesn't sound like he's in a good mood."

Miss Wellbeloved looked up. "When does Larry *ever* sound like he's in a good mood?"

"Has the daft old bugger damaged his car on our fence post?" Mike asked, gleefully rubbing his hands together.

Pamela tittered, then covered her mouth. "Don't start. You know I'm terrible when it comes to getting the giggles around Larry."

"Probably because he's such a monumental wally."

A cacophony of stomps and muttered swearing announced

that Higgins and his team were just outside the office. Sure enough, a few seconds later the door swung open, slamming into the wall and nearly knocking all the coats off their hooks in the process.

"What a bloody shambles your office is!" Higgins stood in the doorway, rotund and furious, arms digging firmly into his generous sides. "Ridiculously narrow entrance to the car park, horribly pungent staircase, and then we come up to find it's pitch black! No way to run a business, no way at all."

Without waiting for a response, he stalked in, closely followed by Luke and Dimitri, who looked mortified by their boss's conduct.

"It is a very nasty scratch on the car," Dimitri confirmed, giving Kester a little wave. "Not pretty."

"Darned right it's not pretty," Higgins said, hovering in front of Miss Wellbeloved's desk like a large, angry hornet. "That'll *ruin* my insurance premium. Absolutely *ruin* it."

"Oh dear," Miss Wellbeloved said brightly, before springing to her feet. "How about I make us all a nice cup of tea, eh?"

"I'd rather have a freshly percolated coffee with cream, if that's not too much to ask."

"I'm afraid it *is* too much to ask, Larry," Miss Wellbeloved replied. She already looked exhausted. "But I'll see what we've got in the cupboard."

Larry marched from desk to desk, eying the surrounding walls as though they'd been smeared with excrement. "Hmm, it's a bit of a hovel, isn't it?" he said eventually. "Still, I suppose you have to make do with what you can get, don't you?"

"Yeah," Mike agreed, with a gleam in his eye, "I mean, your soulless office must be a nightmare to work in, but I respect you for sticking with it."

Luke sniggered, then hastily covered his mouth.

"Let me get the spare chairs from the stockroom," Pamela said and bustled off to join Miss Wellbeloved. The others stared at one another in awkward, appraising silence.

"Is the old git in?" Higgins said eventually, thrusting a dismissive finger in the direction of Ribero's door.

"If by *old git* you mean Dr. Ribero, yes he is," Kester confirmed, hoping his dad couldn't hear. The idea of the two old men battling it out this early in the day wasn't an appealing one.

Pamela emerged, obscured by the pile of plastic seats in her hands. "Here we are!" she said, plonking them unceremoniously in the centre of the room. "Grab a seat, and we can start our little chat."

"Little chat? This isn't a cosy coffee morning," Higgins muttered, seizing the top chair and yanking it to the ground. Luke and Dimitri followed suit, as the others wheeled their desk chairs into a rough circle.

"There, very nice," Pamela declared, nodding with approval at them all.

"Not really the same as a proper meeting room, is it?"

Luke beamed at them all. "I think it does the job just fine. We can all talk better when there's not a big table in the way, can't we?" He gave Kester a thumbs-up, and Kester dutifully returned the gesture.

Finally, Miss Wellbeloved joined them, staggering under the weight of an enormous tray of tea. "I've got some homemade cake too," she said, nodding at the Tupperware box.

"What flavour?" Kester asked, eying the box suspiciously. He knew what Miss Wellbeloved's cakes were like, and they usually involved at least one unpleasant health product in the ingredients.

"Pistachio," Miss Wellbeloved said curtly, before adding, "and avocado and courgette," under her breath.

Higgins coughed purposefully, arms folded over his gut. "Let's move on from the cake, shall we?" He clicked his fingers at Luke, who sighed, then rummaged in his bag, pulling out a folder full of papers. "We've had the contracts drafted out, so all that remains is for you to check them over and—"

"Larry," Miss Wellbeloved interrupted, hand hovering in the air. "I don't mean to be rude, but this really isn't the best way to start a merger."

"What's bloody wrong with it?" Higgins looked around the room, indignant as a bantam cock.

"It's a bit . . ." Miss Wellbeloved faltered.

"Yes, it's a *little* bit . . ." Pamela unhelpfully added.

"It's a bit *cold,* mate," Mike concluded. "If we've got to work together, we need to get started on the right foot."

"And what did you have in mind?" Higgins asked, looking flustered.

Mike shrugged. "Dunno. Trip down the pub?"

"No, Mike, *not* a trip down the pub," Miss Wellbeloved said hastily. "Things don't always have to revolve around alcohol, you know." She patted down her hair, which was already starting to unravel from its bun. "I mean, let's discuss this in a more *human-like* manner."

Higgins looked at Luke and Dimitri, who shrugged. "Very well," he said eventually, straightening his shirt. "How has your morning been, Jennifer?"

Serena giggled, then hastily straightened her expression.

"Yes, very pleasant," Miss Wellbeloved replied smoothly. "Kester was filling us in on the details about Gardone Riviera."

"I've already had the full briefing from Dimitri," Higgins retorted, eyes still narrowed in Serena's direction. "Sounds like it was a very fruitful trip."

"Gosh, how did you give him a full briefing?" Kester asked Dimitri, rubbing his eyes. "I can't even manage to stay awake, let alone talk business."

Dimitri's hand flicked over his trousers in a single debonair sweep. "I am always a professional, Kester." He nodded in Serena's direction, who turned immediately pink. Mike's mouth set into a mutinous line of irritation.

"Yeah, so it sounds like the Thelemites are broken in two," Luke said, legs extended in front of him. "One team supporting Hrschni and his crazy-assed ideas, the other working to stop him."

"Which is presumably why those letters you received had a different wax seal on them," Pamela said, prodding Kester's stomach to wake him up. "To show they were from the Thelemites who remained loyal to the old ways, not Hrschni's new plans."

Kester jumped. "What letters?" Then his tired brain caught up—the letters he'd found pushed under his door, with the clues on them. Tinker had told them that the wax seal featured an old version of the Thelemite symbol, not the modern one. *So even then, Fylgia and Dr. Barqa-Abu were trying to leave us clues,* he realised. *Not very obvious clues, admittedly, but clues nonetheless.*

"Dear me, someone is rather dopey today, aren't they?" Higgins sneered, then hastily adjusted his expression at the sight of Miss Wellbeloved's disapproval. "Anyway, now it should be a case of getting Dr. Barqa-Abu to hand us Hrschni, then it's all done and dusted."

Mike scratched his head. "I doubt it's going to be as easy as that."

"It never is," Serena groaned, stretching catlike over the back of her chair.

"So," Higgins said firmly. "Niceties over, shall we get down to business? As I said, the contracts are all here, ready to be signed, then we can—"

"We'll probably need Dr. Ribero present for this," Miss Well-beloved interrupted hastily.

"I thought the silly old sod had already handed the business over to you?"

An enormous bang alerted them all to the fact that Ribero had finally decided to emerge. Eyes blazing like two embers of coal, he stood framed in the doorway, a majestic finger hovering furiously in Higgins's direction.

"Who are *you* to call me a silly old sod, eh? At least I am not the size of a pregnant elephant, eh?"

Higgins bristled. "Elephant I may be, sir, but at least I don't cower in my office like a timid woman, hiding away when—"

"Less of the negative female comparisons, please," Pamela chimed, nibbling a corner of one of Miss Wellbeloved's cakes.

"I am not like the timid woman!" Ribero marched out, door slamming behind him. "I merely reside in my office because I do not want to have to look at your face."

"Believe me, your ridiculous face does nothing for me either."

Miss Wellbeloved sighed, then reached across for Higgins's folder, plucking it nimbly from his hands. "I'll just start looking over the contracts, shall I?" she announced, over the top of Ribero's muttering. "Then when you two have finished your silly argument, you can look over them too."

Higgins wiped his chin, eyes still glinting dangerously in Ribero's direction. "I assure you, I'm quite finished. I wouldn't waste my time on this—"

"And I would not waste *my* time with this big fat watermelon of a man," Ribero concluded, sweeping over to Miss Wellbeloved, then peering down at the documents with revulsion. "Now, are you sure that this is the right thing to do, Jennifer?"

Miss Wellbeloved glanced up. "Yes, perfectly sure, thank you, Julio."

"You do not suspect that this might be a very big terrible mistake, no?"

"No, I'm quite sure it's what we should do."

"You are not thinking that—"

"No, quite sure!" Miss Wellbeloved rummaged through the papers with overzealous urgency, steadily moving them further away from Ribero, who was now bent almost double over her shoulder in an attempt to read them. "Look, Julio, will you *please* give me some space? It's impossible to concentrate with you lurking around me like a bad smell."

Higgins smirked. Ribero's face twitched uncontrollably.

"I remind you, Jennifer, that it is still my company, and—"

"And you asked Kester and I to take it over," Miss Wellbeloved replied smoothly, pressing him firmly away. "Now, this company merger is a group decision, of course, and—"

"And no one else wants to merge with the Higgins, right?" Ribero straightened, hands on hips, moustache bristling with indignation.

"I personally think it's a sensible idea," Pamela said, reaching for another slice of cake.

"Makes sense to me," Serena added.

Mike and Kester looked at one another, then shrugged.

"Well." Ribero's lips pursed tightly, trembling slightly at the edges. "I see. *I see.*"

"See *what,* you blethering old idiot?" Higgins's brow furrowed. "There's nothing to see. Apart from seeing that this is how you run a successful business, which probably isn't something you're familiar with."

Miss Wellbeloved gave everyone an overly bright smile, which didn't fool anyone. "Shall we read through this together?"

"Count me out, I don't do legal documents," Mike said, standing up.

"Mike's still on picture books," Serena whispered loudly to Dimitri, who sniggered.

"We don't need to look at it either," Luke declared, rearranging his legs and taking up even more space on the carpet. "Do we, Dimitri? We might as well take a look around. Mike, you want to give us the tour?"

"What, all three rooms?" Mike raised an eyebrow. "Yeah, if you want to kill a minute or two, sure."

Kester remained with Miss Wellbeloved, only pretending to glance through the contracts. The words swam on the page like black tadpoles, but he didn't think it mattered too much; the others were clearly handling it. *I should probably be more bothered,* he realised, eyelids drooping again. *Given that it's going to be my company one day. But right now, I haven't got the energy.*

Finally, Miss Wellbeloved placed her pen back in her cardigan pocket. She handed the contract to Higgins, who stuffed it back into his briefcase like a bomb about to detonate. He coughed, then extended a hand.

"I believe this is the moment we shake hands to seal the deal?" he suggested, nodding at everyone else as though to remind them of the importance of the occasion.

Miss Wellbeloved paused, then accepted his hand. "Absolutely. I'm sure it'll be a pleasure working together."

"I'm bloody not," Ribero snarled, leaning against the wall. "I want you to know that I think this is a very bad idea."

"Really? I hadn't realised," Miss Wellbeloved replied through tight lips. "Anyway, we'll probably still be operating as two separate entities for the most part, won't we, Larry?"

Higgins glanced at Ribero, eyes narrowing. "We certainly won't be spending too much time down here, that's for sure. Exeter's a pokey little place, isn't it?"

"No," Ribero muttered, crossing his arms. "It is because you have no appreciation of good things, yes?"

Higgins ignored him, scooping up his briefcase with a flourish. "Well," he proclaimed, clicking a finger in Luke and Dimitri's direction. "I'd like to say it's been a pleasure, but as ever, it's been a trial. However, we've got the documents signed and that's the main thing. It's probably better if we discuss the logistics over the phone tomorrow."

Miss Wellbeloved glanced at Ribero, who mutinously looked away. "Yes, that's probably for the best," she agreed faintly.

"So, we've joined forces, hey?" Luke declared, clapping Mike on the back.

"Yes indeed," Higgins said smugly. He glared in Ribero's direction, then paused for dramatic effect before adding, "whether certain individuals like it or not."

Chapter 13: Snaring a Daemon

Only two days later, the letter arrived that Kester had been waiting for. As with the others, it was pushed underneath the door; though this time it was his own bedroom, where it remained until he awoke late Saturday morning.

He tore it open, wondering what cryptic clue he'd have to solve this time. However, for once, the note from the Thelemites was refreshingly clear.

The Head of the Ram will convey the plan.

Kester scratched his head, sat back down on the bed, and pondered. What exactly were Dr. Barqa-Abu and Fylgia planning? Why go to such lengths to maintain secrecy? *And why did it have to be a weekend?* he wondered, folding the letter carefully back into the envelope. *Couldn't we stick to office hours, just for once?*

Trudging downstairs in his slippers, the first thing he noticed was that it was cold. Being cold wasn't unusual in his house, given that the boiler packed up at least twice a week, but being glacial certainly was. The second thing he noticed, with rising alarm, was that the front door was ajar. The third, which upset his tidy nature and horrified him in equal measures, was that there were dirty footprints across the carpet.

Ignoring the temptation to race back to his bedroom and cower beneath the duvet, Kester grabbed the nearest weapon to hand, which happened to be an umbrella. Given that it was a handbag-sized, fold-up umbrella, it was unlikely to be much use, but Kester thought at least he could open it up with a snap in the intruder's face, or maybe clobber him or her over the head with it.

He edged into the kitchen and gasped. A dirty, hunched figure stood in front of the fridge, illuminated by the murky light. With a high-pitched squeak, Kester lunged forward, the butt of the umbrella bouncing uselessly off the burglar's back.

"Ow!" The figure turned, hand wrapped around a lump of cheddar cheese.

"Oh!" Kester gaped, momentarily lost for words. *Is that Daisy?* he wondered, surveying the dishevelled person in front of him. He swallowed hard. "Sorry, I had no idea you were back. You . . . er . . . you left the front door open and—"

Daisy, who looked far thinner, filthier, and more serious than she had done previously, gave a sob and threw herself into Kester's arms. Not knowing quite how to react, Kester patted her awkwardly before prising her gently away.

"What happened?" he asked, plucking the cheese, which happened to be his, from her hand.

"Oh, Kester," she said, grabbing some kitchen towel and blowing her nose. "Oh, it's been *so* terrible. Caleb *dumped* me in Thailand and I didn't have any money, so I had to *work* to get home!"

"Gosh, work, eh?" Kester echoed. He knew how much Daisy detested any form of labour.

She honked into the tissue again, then clutched the countertop. "I can't believe I *trusted* him, Kester. Men are such *horrible* creatures, they really are."

"Not all men," Kester said defensively.

A clatter of feet drew their attention to the stairs.

"Yo, Kester!" Pineapple's voice wafted through the hallway. "What's with the door open? We having a party or something? That's sweet, man, but we got to put the heating up if the door's staying open, it's proper cold, innit?"

A party at eleven AM? What planet does he come from? Kester thought. "Daisy's back," he shouted, then put the kettle on. Patiently he made the tea whilst Pineapple hurtled in like a racing neon ferret and wrapped himself around Daisy. *They'd make a good couple,* he thought, feeling uncomfortable as they remained tightly embraced. *A weird couple, but good nonetheless.*

"Daisy, proper solid! I have missed your smile, girl. Total sweet like a flower."

"Ah, Pineapple, I'm so glad to see you!" Already Daisy was looking more like herself and less like a dejected tramp. "Can we go out tonight, please? I need to take my mind off everything. It's been an awful few months."

Pineapple's grin was so wide it made him look even more deranged than usual. "Yes, total cool! There's a foam rave in some woods somewhere, and—"

"A foam rave?" Kester said incredulously. "In a wood? In winter? Really?"

"Yeah," Pineapple persevered. "Total foam mentality. In some woods somewhere."

"Do you actually know where?"

Pineapple shrugged. "Nah, just some woods. We'll find it, just keeping our ears to the ground, listening for the vibes, right?"

That means they'll end up down the local pub, Kester thought. He handed them their teas, then gave Daisy a smile. "It's nice to have you back," he said. "Sorry about attacking you with an umbrella."

Daisy hugged him, nearly spilling his drink. "Don't worry. If my auras had been in top form, I would have been able to avoid it. But I feel so *damaged* at the moment, all my emotional chakras are out of line, and . . ."

Kester extracted himself from her arms and neatly sidestepped out of the kitchen. "I'll leave you two to talk chakras," he said, "while I close the front door before we all turn into ice."

Slamming the door shut, he walked back to his bedroom, glad that at least he couldn't feel the wind whipping around his pyjama-clad ankles anymore. *I suppose I'd better get myself prepared for a trip to the museum,* he thought, glancing at the envelope lying on his desk. *Though goodness knows what Dominic Clutterbuck will tell me this time.* He thought back to his meeting with the tiny manager of the RAMM on New Years' Eve. Already it felt like ages ago.

After swiftly yanking on whatever clothes came to hand, Kester trundled off into town. He was feeling strangely buoyed by the prospect of heading to the museum and finally getting to the bottom of what was going on. He just hoped it wasn't going to be a case of yet more clues, dead-ends, and red herrings to navigate his way through.

Pressing through the crowds, he made his way down Gandy Street, remembering the first time he'd been here, last year. *So much has changed since then,* he thought, with a sense of nostalgia and regret. He'd lost a mother, only to inherit a father weeks later. He'd got a new job, in the world's strangest profession. He'd made new friends, who had become like family. Got his first girlfriend, then lost her a few weeks afterwards. Travelled to Scotland and Italy, been kidnapped, bagged several spirits along the way, and encountered a daemon of unimaginable power.

I wonder if you ever experienced craziness like this, Mother? he thought, as he pushed open the heavy museum doors. *Or was life simpler back then?* He realised, with abrupt, crushing sadness, that he'd probably never know. All his life, he'd never thought to ask his mother the questions that *really* mattered, and now it was too late.

The man at the reception desk smiled obligingly as he approached.

"Is Dominic Clutterbuck in?" Kester asked, looking up at the airy atrium above him. In the alcove on the staircase the stone statue of Prince Albert gazed indulgently over the visitors arriving below.

The man nodded, tucking his grey hair behind her ear. "He's up in the office. Do you have an appointment?"

Kester began to shake his head, then paused, thinking of the letter. "He'll be expecting me," he said finally. "My name's Kester Lanner."

The man turned, dialled on the phone behind the desk, and muttered a few words down the line. Finally, he smiled. "Go right up," he said. "It's to the right, past the bird and insect rooms."

Kester made his way up the imposing staircase. A few children padded energetically along the landing above, but other than that, it was quiet. *Peaceful,* Kester realised, allowing himself a moment to soak up the surroundings. *I could do with a bit more of this.*

He found the office door nestled at the end of a dimly lit corridor. After knocking, he waited patiently. A minute later, the door swung open, revealing Dominic Clutterbuck's short, stocky figure. "Do come in," he said, stepping aside.

Kester entered the sparse office with its neat little desk and surrounding bookshelves. "I hope I'm not keeping you from your work."

Dominic shook his head. "This is far more pressing than any museum matters. But first, do you have something to show me?"

Rummaging in his pocket, Kester pulled out the letter he'd received the night before, waiting as the other man scrutinised it carefully.

"Very good." Dominic straightened, then gestured to a pair of sofas in the corner. "Shall we?"

"I understand why we need to be secretive," Kester said, glancing around as he sat, "so how do you know we're not being overheard here? I mean, there could be several spirits in here with us and we wouldn't know it." In fact, he detected something in the air, though couldn't figure out exactly what. It was a little like a vague electric current running somewhere nearby.

The old man's eyes crinkled with amusement. "You're absolutely right. In fact," he continued, as he sat down, "that leads me to an important introduction. Fylgia, would you step forward?"

Kester's mouth dropped open as the air close to his arm started to ripple before solidifying into the familiar form of the glowing green daemon. She curled through the air towards him, dragon-like in the gleam of the winter sun.

"Good morning, Kester."

He rose instinctively, glasses nearly falling off his nose. "I didn't know you'd be here," he stuttered. He wasn't sure how he felt about it either. Although he realised that she'd been working as a double agent, gathering information on Hrschni, he couldn't forget the fact that she'd tricked him so badly. *Nor the fact that when I thought I was alone with Anya, I was actually snuggled up to her too,* he thought with a grimace.

Fylgia stilled, sensing his emotion. "I owe you an apology," she said quietly. "I understand that you and Anya have split up, and that my actions were partly responsible."

"Pretty much entirely responsible actually." Kester crossed his arms, determined not to be intimidated.

"Do you understand why it was done?"

He looked down at the floor. "Yes. But that doesn't make it easier to accept." Thinking back to his behaviour towards Anya in the pub, he was horrified to remember how she'd run out weeping afterwards. *I thought I was justified at the time,* he thought, blushing. *But actually, I should have listened to her.* "Anyway," he said aloud, keen to get off the subject, "I presume you're going to tell me the plan now. Do you want me to give the others a call, so they can be here too?"

"No," Flygia replied. "That won't be necessary."

Dominic leant back in his seat. "The information we're about to give you is for your ears alone."

"But why?" Kester stared at them both. "The others will want to be kept up to speed, not to mention Infinite Enterprises and—"

"Just hear us out," Dominic interrupted, gesturing at the daemon.

"Hrschni has no idea that I've been operating against him for many years," Fylgia began, twisting through the air like a restless ribbon on the breeze. "We've tried to find other ways to put a stop to all this nonsense, but—"

"—it's gone too far," Dominic finished. "All the Traditionalist Thelemites realised that when Hrschni kidnapped you in the caves."

"Traditionalists?" Kester echoed.

"Those who want to preserve the old ways," Dominic explained. "We believe in building relationships between spirits and humans. We don't believe in opening the floodgates and letting the two worlds collide without restraint."

"How many of you are there?"

Fylgia floated closer, until the heat of her shimmering form warmed his cheek. "Not as many as we'd like. We've had to maintain total secrecy for fear that we'd be discovered. Hrschni's rage would be terrible if he found out."

Kester mulled it over. If it was only a few isolated figures against a well-established organisation, it sounded risky.

"Okay," he said, taking a deep breath. "What's the plan, then?"

"We want to use you as bait." Fylgia faded into invisibility, letting the words settle into the silence around them.

Kester's eyes widened. He waited for an explanation but didn't get one. "You're kidding," he said eventually, shaking his head. "I'm not a lump of cheese that you can place on a mousetrap, you know. And the letters I found in Italy proved that Hrschni had once helped my grandparents. It's hardly right for me to repay him with trickery."

"For what it's worth," Fylgia said, "I knew your grandfather too. Trust me, he would not want Hrschni succeeding with his plan." Her body shivered into solidity, her long, angular face coming into sharp focus. "Your grandfather was a wonderful man," she added, looking upwards. "When I spent time with you recently, I was astounded at how alike you both are. The same sweet innocence, the same raw, unbridled talent."

"Let's not talk about you spending time with me," Kester replied briskly. "At the end of the day, I thought you were Anya. If I'd have known, then—"

"I think you enjoyed it," Fylgia said with the hint of a smile. "In fact, I *know* you did. You are better matched to spirits than you realise, Kester."

Kester fell silent, aware of the atmosphere of anticipation, which pressed against him with disquieting intensity. "Won't it be dangerous?" he said finally, changing the subject. "I'm not comfortable with putting myself in a position where I could get hurt."

Dominic raised a hand. "Hear us out, Kester. You wouldn't be in any danger. You're far too precious to Hrschni."

"He's one of the most powerful spirits in the world. Of course I'd be in danger. Anyway, how could I possibly bait him? What do you mean?"

"We mean," Fylgia continued, sliding through the air, "that you would get in contact with him. Gain his trust. Then you would arrange to meet at a designated place, draw him out into the open, and we would catch him."

Kester frowned. The thought of such a powerful spirit being caught like a common poltergeist was deeply unpleasant. "I'm not sure I like the idea of deceiving someone like that," he said slowly, twisting his hands in his lap. "It doesn't feel right."

Dominic's expression softened. "I'd heard much about your good nature," he said. "And I commend you for it. However, in this instance, you must think of the greater good. If Hrschni manages to find a way to open a permanent door between the spirit world and ours, chaos will break out. Imagine Exeter High Street overrun with ghouls and banshees. Imagine them flooding into every school, every office, every home in the city. Can you conceive how terrible it would be?"

"Yes," Kester said softly. He knew that what they were saying was true but still couldn't shake the niggling feeling that something wasn't quite right.

"So, will you help us?" Fylgia added. She reached towards him, grazing her skeleton-spindly fingers against his arm. "Please. We need your assistance. You're the only human who can bring Hrschni out into the open."

"Can't you do it?" Kester asked.

"No. He would question why I would want to bring him to an unsafe location. For the most part, he hides in the Thelemite headquarters. When he goes out, he seldom tells anyone. He's very cautious."

So that's that, then, he acknowledged with an inward groan. *It's me or no one.* "Fine," he said, closing his eyes briefly. "I'll help you to do it."

Dominic and Fylgia glanced at one another, with a look that Kester couldn't interpret.

"That's good news," Dominic said, shaking Kester's hand. "Well done."

Kester stood. "Where do I start, then?"

"You'll need to get a message to Hrschni," Fylgia said, hovering uncomfortably close. "Send it via Anya; that should be convincing enough. She's agreed to keep helping us, albeit reluctantly."

"Can't I just email him?" Kester replied with a nervous chuckle.

Fylgia shook her head. "We avoid the internet whenever possible, especially as we often cause it to malfunction."

"But Dr. Barqa-Abu's mastered it?"

"There are always exceptions to the rule. The djinn are skilled at reducing or growing their energy as required. But even she doesn't find it entirely comfortable. She mourns for the days when she could teach her lessons without the use of technology."

Kester shrugged. "A letter, then." He started walking to the door, suddenly eager to get out in the open again. There was something suffocating about Fylgia's presence, and even the intensity of Dominic's unblinking stare was starting to rattle him.

"Tell Hrschni that you want to discuss things further," Dominic advised. "And remember, this is just between us, for the time being. Nobody else must know."

"Why the secrecy?"

"All it would take is one misspoken word down the pub, one comment in the street, and Hrschni may start to suspect us. Then the whole operation would be in jeopardy."

"Not to mention us," Fylgia added. "The secrecy won't be forever. When the time is right, your agency will be informed."

Kester allowed himself to be led to the door, his mind reeling. He watched dumbly as Dominic swung it open, letting the cooler air of the museum inside. "I trust you to be convincing," the small man whispered as Kester stepped out.

Turning, Kester opened his mouth to ask Fylgia another question only to see that she'd vanished. *Of course she has,* he chided himself, looking around. *It'd hardly go down well if the museum visitors saw a bright green spirit floating around in there.*

"I presume we'll speak soon," he muttered.

Dominic gave him a flash of a smile, then quickly closed the door, leaving Kester staring at the blank wood in amazement and panic.

I just agreed to pass a message to Hrschni via Anya, he realised, making his way back down the stairs and into the main atrium of the building. *Which means I've got to talk to Anya again—if she'll even want to talk to me, that is.*

He pictured the scene: him knocking on the door to her narrow terraced house, her slamming it in his face. Or perhaps bursting into tears, or shouting abuse at him. Either way, he couldn't imagine it going well. Still, he'd agreed to do it, so there was no getting out of it now.

And I don't even want to think about meeting Hrschni again, he thought, exiting onto the brisk, chilly street. *Let alone deceiving him.* He wished he'd had the chance to discuss it with Miss Wellbeloved first but understood the need for secrecy. Too much was at risk.

"Why does everything have to be so difficult?" he muttered, tugging his scarf out of his bag and wrapping it around his neck. With a low groan, he stepped out onto the pavement and started walking home.

He hadn't got far when a loud chuckle resounded close to his ear. He flinched, half expecting a spirit to attack him on the spot, then realised with relief that the voice had been human.

"Why so glum?" The voice asked, accompanied by a resounding slap on Kester's left shoulder. Kester turned to see Crispian, grin stretched wide across his face, decked out rather incongruously in a shiny pinstriped suit.

"Hello," Kester said without enthusiasm. "What are you doing here?"

Crispian's cheeks reddened. "Just taking a walk, that's all," he said, folding his arms. "You know, having a stroll and enjoying the atmosphere."

"In a suit?"

"Yes indeedy, in a suit. That, sir, is how I roll."

Kester frowned. "Well," he said, picking up his pace, "have fun."

"Hang on a moment," Crispian said, grasping his arm. "I don't suppose you know where Buller Building is, do you?"

"Buller Building?"

Crispian's cheeks went from pink to a vivid shade of crimson. "It doesn't matter. Forget I mentioned it, it's only a—"

"Oh, *that* Buller Building," Kester interrupted. He remembered where he'd seen it now, a big sign just off the high street, with another sign underneath: JOB CENTRE. "Are you looking for a new job then?" he asked, curious.

Watching Crispian's face fall was a bit like watching a puppy after it'd accidentally wet itself on the floor. "I might be," he mumbled, shifting from foot to foot. "In fact, yes, I believe I am."

"But I thought you had an amazing career back in London?"

"I did. But, er, I don't anymore. It transpires that they don't take too kindly to employees sleeping with their secretaries."

Kester smirked. "It's the biggest cliché in the book, isn't it?"

"Yes, thank you for pointing that out." Crispian released his grip, leaving Kester free to walk. "It's all rather embarrassing, but a man must do what a man needs to be done, isn't that right? And I will make a success of myself again, I guarantee you. Success is my middle name, you see."

"If you say so," Kester replied. "Look, Buller Building is just down the high street and then left. You can't miss it; the sign's enormous."

"Righty-ho. Thank you. And, er . . ."

"Yes?"

"Perhaps you could not tell anyone about this, okay?" He looked nervously over his shoulder. "The thing is, Michael doesn't know."

"You mean Mike."

"Whatever. Promise you won't mention it?"

Kester nodded, and then watched Crispian scurry away into the distance. He wondered what he was playing at. *I doubt Mike will be too impressed when he finds out his brother is looking for jobs down here in Exeter,* he thought as he started to walk back home. *But I won't be the one to break open that particular hornet's nest. Let Mike find out on his own.*

Checking his phone, he noticed that he had a voicemail from Miss Wellbeloved. Quickly, he pressed the phone to his ear.

"Kester, it's me," her familiar voice trilled. "Sorry to bother you at the weekend. Your father is causing problems at the office, and I'm at a loss as to what to do. Pamela's tried talking to him but it's not helping much. Would you be able to pop over if you're around?"

He sighed, tucked the phone back in his pocket, and promptly changed direction, heading down the alleyway that led to the office. *What's the silly old man doing now?* he wondered, forcing himself to take a deep breath. Given how anxious he was about Hrschni, not to mention Anya, he really could do without the added complication.

The back door was unlocked as usual, and Kester slipped into the darkness, climbing up the stairs two at a time. He could hear the shouting before he'd even reached the top step, followed by a crash; presumably something being hurtled across the length of the office.

Reluctantly, he opened the door and stepped inside just as Miss Wellbeloved stormed out. They collided with earth-shattering force before both reeling backwards.

"Goodness me!" Miss Wellbeloved exclaimed, her glasses askew. "Whatever were you thinking, sneaking in like that?"

Kester pressed a hand against his chest to steady his racing heart. "I had no idea you were there. Are you all right?"

The door to Ribero's office suddenly swung wide, unleashing the usual plume of cigarette smoke. Ribero himself stood in the doorway, bristling with fury. "Do not ask her if she is all right!" he exclaimed, shaking a fist. "Ask me! I am the one who is wounded."

"Wounded?" Miss Wellbeloved spun around on her heel. "Your ego may be wounded, but that's all."

Kester rubbed his temples. He noticed Pamela in the corner, looking as though she were trying to make herself invisible. "Can someone please tell me what the hell is going on here?" he asked. "Coming into work at the weekend isn't my idea of fun."

"Nor mine," Miss Wellbeloved snapped. "Your father is in the midst of a temper tantrum, and—"

"I have a right to be in a tantrum!" Ribero interrupted. "You have given my office to the man I detest the most! Who would not be in the tantrum?"

"Hang on a minute," Kester said wearily, stepping between them both. "Who? What? What's happened?"

Miss Wellbeloved took a deep breath then smoothed her hair, which had come loose in a frizzy halo around her forehead. "Larry Higgins asked if he could use Julio's office space on the rare occasion that he comes down here. So naturally, I said that—"

"You told him to help himself to my private space!" Ribero barked. "My office, where I go to relax and to work, which is filled with all my things! You give him this place to use as his own!"

"For crying out loud," Kester murmured. "Look," he said in as authoritative voice as possible, "Dad, Larry won't be using your office very often. On the days that he's in, you can stay at home." He held up a finger, silencing Ribero before he could start ranting again. "Now, can we all please lock up and go home? This is ridiculous."

"Agreed," Miss Wellbeloved chimed in. "Except there's a problem with that. Julio won't leave."

"I will defend my office," Ribero said, thrusting out his chest. "You may take my beloved agency, but you will not take my private space."

This would be comical in any other circumstance, Kester thought, surveying his father with a mixture of irritation and vague pride. He could see Ribero's hurt, buried deep within the bravado and bluster, and felt sorry for him.

"Come on," he said, putting a hand on his father's shoulder. "You know this is silly. We understand that you don't like the fact that we've merged with Larry Higgins's agency, but you know why we did it, don't you?"

"It was either that or go out of business," Pamela said cheerily, standing up. "That's the harsh reality, my love."

Ribero's shoulders slumped. "I know," he muttered. "But I do not have to accept it easily, do I?"

"It'd make life simpler for us if you did," Miss Wellbeloved snapped. "Why don't you think of someone else for a change?" Without waiting for a reply, she turned to Kester and threw him the keys. "Can you lock up?" she said pleadingly. "I've had about as much of this man as I can take today."

"Hey," Ribero said, scuttling forward. "Do not be like that. I did not do it to upset you, I did it because—"

"You did it because you're incapable of seeing past your own emotions," Miss Wellbeloved said, tugging on her coat. "You did it because you never stop to consider how all of this might be affecting *me*. I'm tired of it, Julio. Do you understand?"

His face fell.

Say something nice, Dad, Kester silently urged him, as Miss Wellbeloved marched towards the door. But before his father could open his mouth, she'd departed, closing the door quietly behind her.

Ribero slunk to the nearest desk, where he sat, head pressed against one hand. "I do think of other people," he said eventually, looking up at Kester.

Pamela sighed, then picked up her handbag. "Perhaps not often enough," she said, patting him on the back as she walked past. "Have a good weekend, both of you."

The quiet of the office was overpowering in their absence. Kester watched his father as he plucked an imaginary piece of fluff from his trousers, hands shaking with increasing urgency. He wondered if he should confide in him about what had happened earlier in the museum, but he remembered what Dominic Clutterbuck and Fylgia had said. Without Pamela's psychic abilities, there would be no way of knowing if their conversation was being listened to by unseen ears or not. It was simply too risky.

"What?" Ribero asked, breaking the silence. "You are giving me a hard look."

Kester said nothing, then shook himself. "It doesn't matter," he said as he helped his father to his feet. "Come on, let's get you home."

CHAPTER 14: SETTING THE COGS IN MOTION

Kester had always dreaded doors of any kind as a child. At the time, he'd presumed it was a bizarre phobia, though now, he wondered if it was to do with his gifts as a spirit door opener.

There was nothing even vaguely sinister about Anya's front door. However, that didn't stop his stomach from twisting uncomfortably at the sight of it. What would she say when she saw him? Would she slam the door in his face? He had no idea what to expect, and that made him even more nervous.

Here goes nothing. He knocked briskly, arranging his features into an expression of nonchalance. The letter to Hrschni rested in his pocket, small and seemingly innocent under his fingers. But he knew that the contents would lead to a chain of events over which he'd have little control.

He waited. The door remained resolutely shut. Then, out of the corner of his eye, he noticed the net curtains twitching in the living room window. A few moments later, the door eased open. Anya stood before him and stared.

Her cheeks were hollow and her expression wary. *She's suffered,* he thought, shuffling on the spot. *I could have stopped that, if I'd just listened to her. But then, she did drag me into a cave and leave me to the mercy of the ruthless Thelemites.*

"Can I help you?" She sounded neither inviting nor cold, just exhausted.

He attempted a smile, lips stretched uncomfortably over his too-dry teeth. "Can I come in?"

"Why? You made your feelings very clear when we last saw each other."

He shrugged lamely. "I've learnt a few things since then. But I can't say much right now."

With a sigh, she stood aside to let him enter. He studied the surroundings surreptitiously, curious to finally see where she lived. It was uncannily like his own house, with the same narrow Victorian hallway, the same dated wallpaper, even the same smell; a combination of damp and last night's dinner.

"Kester," she began, gesturing towards the nearest sofa, "if you're here to get angry at me again, please don't. I'm not in the mood to—"

"That's not why I'm here," he said quickly, pulling out the letter. "I need you to deliver this for me." He looked at her significantly. "*I know.* About what happened. Do you understand?"

Her eyes widened. She opened her mouth to speak, then closed it again. He understood why; there was no way of telling if they were alone or if a spirit was with them, silently listening to their conversation.

"Does that mean that you forgive me?" she asked.

Kester rubbed his nose. "I don't know, to be honest. For now, I need you to make sure that *he* gets this. Tell him that I need to speak to him."

"What's going on here? Why do you—"

He shook his head. "It's best if you don't know too much."

Reluctantly, her hand closed around the envelope. "I see. Well, I don't see really, but I understand that this is important. I'll get it delivered as soon as I can."

Now all I can do is trust her, Kester thought, as the room fell silent again. He'd trusted her in the past and it hadn't worked out well; but now wasn't the time to let his hesitancy get the better of him. He picked at a bit of thread on the armrest, feeling more uncomfortable by the second. "I suppose I'd better go," he said finally, without looking at her.

"Is that it? You don't want to talk about anything else?"

"What is there to talk about?" He bit his lip. The words had come out harsher than he'd intended. "I mean," he said, more gently, "we can't really talk, can we? Not about the truth, anyway."

"But you know that Fylgia shared my body, and—"

"Yes, I know that now." He glanced meaningfully around the room, indicating that caution was needed. Anya frowned but nodded nonetheless.

A floorboard creaked, followed by the sound of footsteps walking across an unseen room above. *Her housemate,* Kester realised, taking it as his cue to stand. "I'd best be going." He finally dared to meet Anya's eye. "I've got an essay to write for my course and it's in soon. If I don't get it done there'll be hell to pay."

A hint of a smile played on her lips. "Sunday is meant to be a day of rest."

"There's never any rest for me. Work's a nightmare too." Kester grinned, forgetting himself, then promptly stopped. "Anyway, I'll leave that letter with you."

He felt the weight of her disappointment as he walked to the hallway, and the hurt in her eyes when he turned to face her was almost too much to bear. *But she hurt me,* he reminded himself, as he pulled the door open. *She hurt me more than anyone ever has before, and even though it wasn't all her fault, it still happened.*

"Did you want to meet up sometime?" she asked, after he'd stepped out into the cold. "Maybe for a coffee? Or tea? I know how you like tea."

Kester paused. The word *yes* rose in his throat, desperate to emerge, but he swallowed it down quickly. It was so tempting to agree, to try to go back to the way they'd been before all of this had happened. But the past couldn't be undone so easily, and he knew if he wasn't able to get over it, there wasn't any prospect of a future together.

"I'm not sure," he said lamely. "I mean, it's not that I don't understand why you did what you did, but the fact is—"

"—the fact is that I put you in a dangerous position," Anya finished for him.

"And you lied to me, though I know you didn't have a choice," he concluded flatly. "Those are pretty big things to get over, you know. All those times when I thought it was just you and me alone, and actually . . ." He let the words drift unsaid. There was no point voicing them, they both knew how awful it was.

Anya nodded. "I just feel so *frustrated,*" she said finally. "Because none of this was my fault, and I did it to protect you."

"Shh," he reminded her quickly. "Don't say anything else. We can't speak about this, do you understand? Not until it's all over."

The air seemed to swell with the unsaid, all the words that were desperately trying to erupt out of them both. Kester extended a hand and patted her awkwardly on the arm. "It'll all come right in the end," he said, with more confidence than he felt. "But for now, this is the way it has to be."

Walking down the path, he heard the door close behind him.

The sound made him wince. Visions of a different ending raced through his head as he trudged home: Anya racing into his arms, him breathing in the scent of her hair as he held her close. *None of this is fair,* he thought, kicking furiously at the pavement. *I didn't ask for any of this. Not my mother dying. Not my father recruiting me to a company that forces me to face fear every day. Not falling in love and being manipulated by daemons. Why can't I just have a normal life?*

He thought of his quiet existence in Cambridge, before his life was thrown into chaos. Back then, the most exciting thing in his life was the daily trip to the local shop to buy some snacks for an evening in front of the television. It had felt safer, but he had to admit it had also been a lot less interesting.

I suppose that's it, he concluded, as he reached his house. *If you're going to live your life, you have to be prepared for some surprises along the way.*

He pushed his front door open to see Daisy, waggling the phone receiver in his direction.

"It's for you, dummy!" she said, grabbing his hand and forcing him to take it. He noticed that she was already looking more like her old self, with a series of brightly coloured clips pushing her hair into all sorts of bizarre positions.

"Who is it?" he asked.

"He did say, but I've forgotten. He sounds grumpy. And a bit of an old bossy-boots too."

Kester put the phone to his ear just in time to hear an explosive "I heard that!"

Oh god, Kester thought, sinking onto the bottom stair. *Just what I need. The Higgins.* "Hello, Larry," he said quickly, cutting off the rant mid-sentence. "Why are you calling me at home?"

"Jennifer gave me your number. She said she didn't want to

have to deal with the issue anymore," he replied, then sniffed. "And yes, it is urgent, before you start reminding me that it's a Sunday."

"Okay." Kester rubbed his head, wondering if the day could possibly get any worse. "Why don't you tell me what's wrong?"

"It's your oaf of a father. He's sending me vile emails, saying that I'm not allowed to use his office, and that he'd rather—"

"This again?" Kester interrupted. "I've already spoken to him, only yesterday in fact. Just ignore him, he'll come around."

The tension over the line was palpable. Kester steeled himself for the next onslaught.

"The thing is," Larry continued, warming to the argument, "when I signed the contract, I believed that it would be yourself and Jennifer that I'd be dealing with. Nobody said anything about that old git being involved. I thought he was out of the picture."

"That *old git* is the same age as you," Kester reminded him, "and he's my dad. Put yourself in his position. He's finding it hard to let go of the agency, which is understandable." *And he detests you with a passion,* he added silently.

Larry tutted. "He was always the same, even back at the SSFE. Always wanting more, always expecting others to make allowances for him. I've never liked the man. If it wasn't for Jennifer, I'd have nothing to do with him ever again."

Kester smiled. Larry's lingering affection for Jennifer was obvious, though it didn't seem to make him act any more pleasantly towards her. "Look," he said placatingly, "just bear with Dad for now. He'll come around; he always does. Who knows, you might end up being friends."

The strength of Larry's snort made Kester wince. "Are you joking? The day I buddy up to that temperamental tit is the day I die, mark my words. If this continues, I'll be exploring ways to terminate the contract. Then what will become of Ribero's precious agency, eh?"

Kester narrowed. It was painfully tempting to retaliate, but he knew from experience that it wouldn't get him anywhere. "Fine," he said heavily, looking at his watch. "I'll make sure Dad understands. And Larry?"

"What?"

"For the sake of Miss Wellbeloved, for the sake of me, for the sake of *everyone* involved, can you try to be civil to him, at the very least?"

"Not an option," Larry barked imperiously. "I leave it with you to resolve this, young Kester. Or face the consequences."

The phone went dead. Kester stared at the receiver for a few seconds, then rested his head in his hands. He could well imagine the sort of emails that his father had been sending Larry, and the number of insults that were no doubt contained within. *You're not making this any easier, Dad,* he thought, as he climbed the stairs. His head felt like it was going to erupt under the pressure of it all, and this was one issue he could really do without.

After an afternoon spent working on his essay, then a night of tossing and turning, Kester was in no mood to go to work the following morning. When he finally arrived in the office, he found that matters were made worse by the obvious tension, thanks to his father's continued mutterings about *that pig Higgins*.

"I've never fantasised as much about retiring as I have these last few days," Miss Wellbeloved groaned, after yet another heated discussion with Ribero.

Kester looked at her in alarm. "Don't even joke about it," he replied. "There's no way I'm taking on this agency on my own. Not with Larry Higgins breathing down my neck all the time."

"And I don't want to have you lording it over me as my boss,"

Serena chimed, eyes flashing over the top of her laptop screen. "However, much as I'd love to outline all the reasons why you'd be useless at the job, we've got more pressing matters to think about. I've just had an email from Curtis Philpot."

Kester slumped at his desk. A message from the government could only mean one thing; more pressure about the situation with Hrschni. *If only I could just tell them what Fylgia and Dr. Barqa-Abu are up to,* he thought wistfully. He understood why they needed to operate in secrecy for the final part of their plan, but still, it made things awkward.

"What does he want?" Miss Wellbeloved walked to Serena's desk and peered over her shoulder.

"An update, basically. Also, something's happened at Infinite Enterprises that he needs to alert us to." Serena scowled. "What update are we going to give him? That we're no closer to finding out where Hrschni is or what he's up to? Or that Kester's being cagey about what's really going on?"

"Hey, I'm not being cagey!" Kester sat up straighter, cheeks reddening.

Serena smirked. "Come off it. Since you came back from Italy, you've been *weird*. It's something to do with those letters that you found, isn't it? The ones between your grandfather and Hrschni."

"What do you mean? I've shown you the letters; I told you what Dr. Barqa-Abu said. What more do you want to know?"

"I'm not sure." She cocked her head, examining him intently. "But I'm convinced you're not being straight with us."

Kester opened his mouth to retaliate, then caught Miss Wellbeloved's eye. *She knows something's up too,* he realised, noting her expression. *She's just choosing to trust me, unlike Serena.* Besides, he couldn't argue with Serena's instinct. She was right—he was concealing things from them, but only because he'd been told to do so. He desperately wanted to tell them the plan that Fylgia had outlined to him, but knew that complete secrecy was imperative, at least for now.

Serena beckoned him over. "Curtis has asked one of us to give him a call," she said, pointing at the screen. "Why don't you do it, Kester?"

"Me? Talk to Curtis Philpot?" Kester shook his head. "That's not a good idea."

"Why not?" Miss Wellbeloved raised an eyebrow.

"Yeah, if you're planning to run this agency, you need to get used to talking to people like him," Serena added.

Kester looked entreatingly at the others. Mike was too busy tapping away at his keyboard to notice, and Pamela merely slurped at her cup of tea and stared out of the window.

"It'll be good practice," Miss Wellbeloved insisted. "Go on, off you go."

"What, now?" Kester stared, sighed, then took his phone out of his pocket. He could tell there was no point in arguing.

Curtis Philpot answered after only a few rings, leaving Kester momentarily lost for words. The others leaned closer to listen, and Kester moved away to the stock cupboard. It might be dingy and cramped in there, but at least he could talk without distraction.

"Mr. Philpot," he began, "it's me, Kester. From Dr. Ribero's Agency—"

"Yes, I know who you are." Curtis sounded terse.

Perhaps I've pulled him away from some serious governmental business, Kester thought. Then he remembered that this case was considered pretty important too, given that it involved protecting the world from an entire population of spirits. "I'm calling to give you an update," he said, in his most efficient voice. "Just like you asked for."

Curtis laughed. "I wasn't expecting it to be you who delivered it, but go on. Tell me what's been happening."

Kester took a deep breath. The last thing he wanted to do was to inadvertently give away something he shouldn't. Quickly, he filled Curtis in on the key events of the last few days. "I think we're making progress," he said, hoping the government official wouldn't press him too hard. He wasn't terribly good at keeping secrets.

The answering sigh echoed down the line. "It doesn't sound like it, if I'm being perfectly honest. In fact, in spite of uncovering those letters in Italy, it sounds like we're no nearer to capturing Hrschni than we were before."

"Trust me," Kester said. "I have confidence it won't be too long."

"The thing is," Curtis went on, "you've only had limited dealings with this daemon. You don't know how clever he really is. If you think you can pull a fast one on him, you're sadly mistaken."

I don't think I can, Kester thought, *but I'll wager a fellow daemon and a djinn might be able to.* Aloud, he said, "We can only do our best."

"That's all very well, but we've had another incident at Infinite Enterprises, and we suspect Hrschni might be behind it. It's rather unsettling to realise that he can enter places like that with ease."

"What happened?"

"Nothing dramatic," Curtis replied. "We found evidence of intrusion in one of our most heavily guarded rooms, but we're not a hundred percent sure that it was him."

"What was in the room?"

Curtis paused. "That's classified information."

"Don't you think we should know? It might give us some clues as to what he's up to."

"I'm afraid my lips are sealed. All you need to know is that it's vitally important, top secret information. The sort that could have devastating impact if it got out."

Kester thought back to his last meeting with Hrschni, when the daemon had suggested that spirits were being executed in secret within the walls of Infinite Enterprises. He'd dismissed it as nonsense at the time, now he found himself wondering if that was what Curtis was referring to.

Surely not, he corrected himself. *More people would know. There'd be uproar among the supernatural agencies. Wouldn't there?*

"Mr. Philpot," he said cautiously, "may I ask you a question? If you have the time, that is?"

"Go on then," Curtis replied eventually. "Make it snappy though, I've got a call coming through at any moment."

"What do you do with the spirits, once the agencies have delivered them to you in the storage units?"

"Or water bottles, in your case," Curtis chuckled.

"Yes, or that. What happens next?"

"You know what happens. Infinite Enterprises have a state-of-the-art spirit door, and we use it to send the spirits back to their own realm."

Kester detected a note of guardedness in the other man's voice. "I know," he pressed, "but what about repeat offenders? Spirits who keep coming back into this world, regardless of how many times you send them packing?"

Curtis coughed. "We just keep popping them back through the spirit door. They get the hint in the end, trust me. Why are you asking, anyway?"

"I was just curious," Kester said, as innocently as possible. He was sure it was only paranoia, but he couldn't help wondering why the government official was being so prickly about it. It certainly wasn't the sort of response he'd been hoping for.

He sat in the darkness of the stock cupboard long after Curtis had hung up, deep in thought. Something felt *off* about the whole situation, and he wasn't sure what. Finally, he composed himself and returned to the main office.

"Good, you've finished," Pamela said, pressing past him. "I can make us all a cuppa now. Want one?"

"No," Kester said absentmindedly, then glanced at Miss Wellbeloved. "Have you got a moment?"

"I have," she said, quickly standing. "It's something important, judging by your expression. What's happened?"

"Tell us all!" Serena demanded, joining them. "Come on, we're a team, not *The Wellbeloved and Lanner Show*. We have a right to know."

Quickly, Kester outlined what Curtis had told him about the break-in at Infinite Enterprises. Pamela stuck her head out of the stock cupboard, just as the kettle finished whistling on the tiny hob. "That sounds worrying," she chorused, pouring the water into a row of mugs. "Hrschni's up to his old tricks again, no doubt."

A moment later, she bustled out, placing a tray of steaming drinks on Mike's desk.

"I asked Curtis Philpot about what they did with spirits after we'd delivered them," Kester muttered.

Serena reached for her mug. "Why? You know what they do."

"Was this because of what Hrschni told you?" Miss Wellbeloved asked, looking concerned. "As we said before, I'm sure it can't be true. We'd know if spirits were being executed. It just wouldn't happen, Kester; not in this day and age."

Kester chewed his lip. "You're probably right," he said. "But then, didn't you say that daemons didn't lie?"

"They like to play with words," Mike reminded him, shutting

his laptop with a loud bang. "A daemon won't lie to you, but that doesn't mean they're definitely telling you the truth either. They're clever like that."

Kester smiled weakly and sipped his tea. He was sure that they were right. After all, they'd been working in this industry for a lot longer than he had. *So why does it feel like something's badly amiss here?* he wondered. *And that it's all going to erupt in our faces if we don't figure it out in time?*

CHAPTER 15: SECRETS AND ASSIGNMENTS

"The thing is with women," Mike slurred, slamming his pint glass onto to surface of the table, "is that they're so hard to please. You think you're doing something right, then bang, it turns out you're getting it all wrong."

Kester raised an eyebrow, keeping his eyes fixed on his grandfather's letters. He'd brought them to the pub in the hope that a few glasses of wine might give him a fresh perspective on them, but thus far he was feeling just as bemused as ever. Mike's continual ranting about the opposite sex wasn't helping.

"Oi. You're not listening."

"I'm trying to work," Kester replied, shuffling along the bench to get out of the range of Mike's prodding finger.

"That's not work. Reading old letters isn't work. Talking to me about important matters, that should take priority." With a sanctimonious nod, Mike polished off the remainder of his drink. "Right, do you want another one?"

"I haven't finished my first."

Mike rolled his eyes and stomped off to the bar. Kester took a deep breath and then reread the letters again.

Just how well did my grandfather know Hrschni? he wondered, putting them down. *And did my mother know him too?* The letters suggested that Gretchen had been protected from the daemon, but who could say? *After all,* he thought to himself, *if Hrschni has a passion for spirit door openers, he'd hardly leave Gretchen alone just because my grandfather asked him to. Or would he?*

"This is so confusing." Kester waved the letters at Mike as he returned.

"What is?"

"All of this. The fact that my grandfather knew Hrschni. That Infinite Enterprises might be lying about what they do to spirits after we've dropped them off. That we're standing on the precipice of something huge, and if we don't tread carefully, things could get very messed up indeed. Don't you worry about it?"

Mike puffed out his cheeks. "We've just got to keep chugging on, haven't we? I mean, our job is to collect spirits and ship them off to their own world. That's as far as it goes. Don't take on too much responsibility, mate. It's not good for you."

Kester thought about what Fylgia and Dr. Barqa-Abu had asked him to do. *How can I not take responsibility?* he wondered, watching as Mike poured the entire contents of a bag of dry-roasted peanuts into his mouth. *If I don't, who will?*

"Aren't you worried about what Hrschni's got planned?" he persisted. "Imagine the craziness of a world full of spirits. All hell would break loose."

"Or people might adapt," Mike suggested. "Now come on, drink your drink. It was you who suggested the pub, and you're being no fun at all."

"I told you I wanted to work."

"I thought you were only saying that because Miss W was listening in."

"No, it was . . ." Kester trailed to silence as he became aware of a head peering over the back of their bench. On closer inspection, the head looked rather delighted about something.

Crispian, he realised, with a sinking heart. *How long has he been here? And more important, how much of our conversation did he overhear?*

A moment later, Crispian sidled around to their table, placing his own drink firmly beside Kester's own.

"I knew it!" he said triumphantly, squeezing in beside them on the bench. "I *knew* your job was more interesting than you were letting on."

"Piss off, Crispian," Mike muttered. "I've had it up to here with you."

"Spirits, eh? Well, well, well. No wonder you didn't want to tell Mummy and Daddy about it. I can understand the secrecy, I mean—"

"Keep your bloody voice down!" Mike looked around in alarm, though thankfully it seemed that most of the other pub-goers were immersed in their own conversations. "Anyway, we have no idea what you're talking about, so if you don't mind, could you—"

Crispian waggled a finger in front of Mike's face. "Don't play the innocent with me. I've long suspected that you were involved with something like this. Why didn't you tell me?"

"Why would I do that? It's hard enough being in the same room as you, let alone having to engage in conversation."

"I'm not surprised that you ended up working with spirits," Crispian blundered on, oblivious to Mike's increasingly reddening cheeks. "After the experiences we had as children, it makes perfect sense that you'd seek out the occult."

Mike snorted. "For god's sake, don't make it sound like we grew up in a haunted castle."

Crispian winked at Kester. "It wasn't quite a castle but *was* a pretty grand house, to be fair." He turned to Mike, mouth twitching with ill-disguised amusement. "So, what is the exact nature of your job? Do you catch spirits, is that it?"

"Mike looks after our website," Kester added helpfully, then quailed under the force of Mike's glare.

"I also design state-of-the-art technology, thank you very much. Not," he said meaningfully, "that it's any of your business. So kindly butt out and don't breathe a word of this to anyone. If word gets out, our agency could be in serious trouble."

Crispian's eyes glittered dangerously. "And what will you give me in return?"

"How about," Kester interrupted, "I don't repeat what you told me the other day in town? You know, when you were looking for a certain building?"

Crispian adjusted his collar. "Ah, yes. Now, about that, I'd like to emphasise that I—"

"What's all this about?" Mike leant over, splashing beer all over the table as he did so. "What building? Don't tell me that you're looking for a place to live permanently in Exeter."

"No. Well, at least, not quite yet."

Mike's eyes narrowed. "What do you mean, *not quite yet*?"

"I haven't found employment yet, but once I have, I shall start looking for—"

"Employment? Here?" Mike looked as though about to explode at any second. "What about your job back in London?"

"Yes, about that," Crispian began, fingers working even more frantically at his shirt. "I lost my job a while ago. I'm officially unemployed. So I thought I'd live down here for a while—get to know my little brother a bit better. What do you say?"

"I say that sounds like a bloody nightmare," Mike raged. "Bugger off back to the capital where you belong."

"That's rather hostile."

"Not nearly hostile enough, as far as I'm concerned. When I think about what a total git you were when we were growing up—"

"I'm going to head off." Kester started to gather up the letters. He had no desire to sit in the middle of a family argument, particularly now that they were drawing curious gazes from the surrounding tables. "You two carry on, don't mind me."

"Don't leave me with him!" Mike pleaded, grabbing Kester by the sleeve. "I can't be held responsible for my actions."

"Mike, he's your brother." Kester pulled away. "Surely you can manage to be civil?"

"I want to hear more about this spirit agency," Crispian said, settling against the seat. "Come on, fill me in on the details. Tell me *all* about it."

Kester groaned inwardly. It was a disaster that someone like Crispian had found out about the agency, as he clearly was no better at keeping secrets than an overexcited toddler. *Still,* he thought, as he headed towards the exit, *there's nothing we can do about it now. We'll have to just hope for the best and pray no one believes him if it gets out.*

The air felt even icier than it had done earlier. He briefly entertained the idea of hailing a cab but decided against it. His salary still hadn't been paid and he didn't like to chase it up, especially as things were so stressful in the office.

He scuttled quickly through town, which was eerily silent due to the bad weather. By the time he'd arrived back home, his fingers were red raw and his nose dripping like a leaky tap. *At least I can climb under the duvet when I get in,* he thought, pushing open the door.

It took him a moment to register the astounding level of noise blaring through the house, then another moment to realise that the hallway, lounge, and kitchen were full to the brim of people that he didn't know.

Kester paused. He entertained the idea of going back outside, reopening the door, and hoping that it was all a hallucination. However, the violent assault on his senses soon convinced him that this was, regrettably, very real indeed.

"Er, what's going on?" he muttered to the nearest male, who happened to be wearing a tutu and sipping an alarmingly blue drink from a bottle.

The man grinned, then draped himself across Kester's shoulders. Kester waited patiently for an answer, realised he wasn't going to get one, and delicately extracted himself from the heavy grip. *This is down to Pineapple and Daisy,* he thought, sliding through the various sweaty bodies clogging up the hallway. *I'll kill them when I find them.*

Both of his housemates were in the kitchen, curled up by the back door like a pair of frightened kittens.

"What the hell happened?" Kester bellowed over the music.

Pineapple stood, fiddling anxiously with his vest. "Are you asking about all the people? You mean that?"

"Of course I mean that! Why are they here?"

Daisy reached up, entreating Kester to assist her. He hauled her up reluctantly, cringing as someone behind him started shaking a large bottle of cherryade. The place already looked like it'd been looted by the world's clumsiest robbers, and by the looks of things, the situation was only going to get worse.

"We didn't invite them!" she protested, smoothing down her hair.

"We didn't invite *all* of them," Pineapple corrected. "It was pure misunderstanding, right? You dig?"

"You're digging yourself further and further into trouble," Kester growled. He was aware that he sounded a bit like a cross schoolteacher but was past caring. "Who did you invite?"

Pineapple held out his hands. "Hey, be cool. I took Daisy to the pub to get her chilled, because of all the negative vibes in her life right now. And she saw some pure sweet young man who would totally take her mind off things, and—"

"And, let me guess, you invited him here, and all his mates came along too," Kester concluded.

"Yes, that's right!" Daisy beamed. "And all their mates too. So, it's quite a full house, as you can see."

Kester shook his head. He'd love to be able to say that he couldn't believe they'd done such a thing, but actually, this was the sort of idiotic exploit they seemed to specialise in. "Get rid of them," he concluded, pointing a finger at them both. "And you're clearing up all the mess, okay?"

"Maybe we could use your funds to get some cleaning help?" Daisy replied hopefully.

Kester didn't bother to reply. Instead, he stalked out to the stairs and headed to his bedroom, praying that nobody had invaded his personal space. To his relief, the room remained mercifully empty.

"Those rotten sods," he muttered, opening his laptop. There was no point trying to relax now; knowing his ineffectual housemates, it'd take them at least two hours to clear everyone out of the house.

He opened the SSFE student site and logged in, noting how many of the other students had already submitted their work. Completing the assignments was tricky at the best of times, let alone with a house party raging on below. Spotting the latest task set by the business studies teacher, he groaned loudly. *I can't keep up,* he thought, pressing his head into his hands. *Everyone else gets to focus totally on their studies. I've got a million other important things to worry about, and one of them is keeping the world safe from a dangerous spirit.*

A crash out in the garden brought his gaze sharply to the window. He took a deep breath, and then reluctantly peered out. Sure enough, a few of the partygoers were out in the courtyard garden, and, by the looks of it, one of them had smashed a garden gnome. Not that Kester was overly worried about the gnome; it'd been left there by the previous resident and no one had got around to moving it yet. He was more concerned about the inevitable complaints from the neighbours.

I've had enough of this, he thought, then without thinking too hard about it, swung the window open.

"Excuse me!" he shouted.

Three heads looked up. Two of them were shaved. There were a lot of tattoos on bare flesh. Kester swallowed hard. "Um, I meant to say, could you not smash up my garden?"

The three onlookers roared with laughter, then carried on with their conversation. *Hmm,* Kester thought, eying them with dejected acceptance. *It looks as though they're going to ignore me. Which isn't surprising. I'd probably ignore me too.*

To his surprise, one of the men started waving a small piece of paper in his direction. "Are you Kezzer?" he shouted, squinting at it closely.

"Er, Kester. Why?"

"That's what I said. This letter's for you, mate. It fell off the sill when you opened the window."

"Really?" Kester frowned. "Could you pass it to me?"

The man obligingly clambered onto the rickety bench and stretched his hand out. With a bit of awkward manoeuvring, Kester finally managed to grab it.

"Hope it's a love letter," the man leered, then returned to his friends. Kester shut the window, yanked the curtain shut, and hastily opened the envelope. He already knew who it was from, just from the quality of the envelope and the perfect handwriting.

What a way to receive an important letter from a daemon, he thought, not sure whether to laugh or sit in the nearest corner and start rocking with anxiety.

Hrschni's note was short and straight to the point.

> *Dear Kester,*
> *Meet me at Haldon Forest at 9:30 PM. Take seventy-three paces northwest from the viewing point on the shortest trail. Come alone.*

Kester placed the letter carefully on his desk, then stared at it for several minutes. Then, he turned to his laptop and searched for Dr. Barqa-Abu's Skype address.

Thank goodness she's the one spirit who doesn't have a problem with technology, he thought, waiting as the dialling tone echoed out of the speakers. A few seconds later, the screen filled with the familiar sight of his tutor's office; a room filled from ceiling to floor with dusty books and ancient antiques.

The djinn swirled into view a moment later. "Is this to do with the assignment?" she asked, cutting across his greeting.

Kester shook his head. "It's more important. It's to do with—"

"—that very important assignment that you were set more recently?" Her eyes glittered in warning.

"Yes, that's the one," Kester said, grasping the need to speak in code. *For all I know,* he thought with a shiver, *Hrschni could be in this room with me, listening into our conversation right now.* It was unlikely though; he suspected Dr. Barqa-Abu would detect a spirit presence, even through an internet connection.

"Well?" she pressed. "You do understand that we're unable to discuss much detail on this call, don't you?"

"I know. But I wanted to let you know that I've now discovered a way forward with it. If that makes sense?"

"That is excellent. However, I was aware of this already. Another student has been keeping me informed of developments."

Another student? Kester thought, blinking. He frowned, then nodded in realisation. *She means Fylgia. Of course Fylgia would know what he was up to; she's Hrschni's right-hand spirit.*

"Am I going to carry on with the assignment on my own?" He moved closer to the screen. "Or will there be support available?"

"At present, we'd like you to work independently. It's important if you're going to proceed smoothly to the conclusion."

Kester bit his lip. He wanted to ask whether or not he'd be safe but couldn't think of a veiled way to express it.

Dr. Barqa-Abu paused her relentless swirling for a moment, solidifying into view. He sensed pity in her black, fathomless eyes. "Do not worry," she said quietly. "It is an especially difficult assignment, but I would not have set it for you if I didn't have faith in your abilities. It's good to gain familiarity with the subject you're studying, do you understand? Once you've got to grips with it, you'll be in a much better position to move forward."

She's saying that I need to gain his trust, he realised. It made sense, but at the same time, he wasn't comfortable with the idea.

"Fine," he said, in a curter voice than he'd intended. "I'll get stuck into it then."

"Do not worry that you are in over your head. You are more suited for this type of study than you realise."

"Thanks," Kester said, hand hovering over the mouse to end the call.

Dr. Barqa-Abu shifted forward. "Kester?"

"Yes?"

She paused, black gaze boring through the screen, then nodded. "You are more like your mother than you know."

Without waiting for a response, she hung up, leaving the screen blank. Kester shut down the laptop, pondering over the task at hand. To his relief, someone had finally turned off the music downstairs, leaving the house in relative peace, aside from the occasional drunken shout.

Why is everyone so confident that I'm able to handle this situation? he wondered. He was convinced that their faith was misplaced. *Still,* he thought, tapping his fingers thoughtfully on the desk. *Everyone's always saying how much I'm like the great Gretchen Lanner. So maybe there's hope for me yet.*

To his surprise, the thought didn't please him as much as it usually did.

CHAPTER 16: NOCTURNAL ENCOUNTERS

Not being able to confide in the others was torturous. This was especially the case whenever Kester was near Serena, whose suspicious stares would have made even the most resilient person break down and confess everything.

The day was made worse by the presence of Larry Higgins, who turned up after lunch, then proceeded to complain about every aspect of the office layout, not to mention the lack of proper coffee-making facilities. Kester was heartily relieved that Luke had accompanied him. He and Dimitri had a knack of diluting the toxicity of Larry's comments, which helped ensure that Kester didn't snap like a rubber band from pure irritation.

Finally, the sky outside darkened to a sombre twilight. Kester switched off his laptop, tugged his jacket on, and headed for the door.

"Where the bloody hell do you think you're going?" Larry's strident tones boomed through the room like a foghorn.

He pointed at the clock. "It's five o'clock."

"Not by my watch it isn't." Larry tapped his wristwatch to prove the point, whilst making sure that everyone noticed how expensive it was. "You've got four minutes and eleven seconds to go. Nine seconds now."

For goodness' sake, Kester thought, resisting the temptation to leave anyway. Most conversations with Larry felt uncomfortably like trying to rationalise with a baby. "I'll have you know," he replied, in as authoritative a voice as he could muster, "that I'm now in charge of this company, and as such—"

"You're not bloody in charge," Larry interrupted. "Miss Wellbeloved is clearly identified as the decision-maker of the agency until she retires or dies."

There was a sudden change in the air of the room as a door swung open behind them. Kester turned to see his father, resplendent in the doorway of his private sanctum, glowering at Larry with open dislike. "It is not your place to make the decision," he growled. The cigarette in his hand skewered the air in a series of sharp jabs, scattering ash over the carpet.

"I'm now co-owner, I'll have you know, and if I say this young whippersnapper can't leave until it's the appropriate time, then—"

"Oh, I see. Mr. Pompous-Pig Higgins is laying down the law, like he is the most important man in this building, though he is a stupid slug of a man with no brains and no decency, right?"

"Oh lord, not this again," Miss Wellbeloved groaned, burying her head in her hands.

"Would you stop calling me a slug! I look absolutely nothing like a slug, it's a preposterous comparison."

"Worm, then."

"No, not a worm either! I insist that you stop antagonising me in this manner, especially as you're not meant to be here in the first place. In case you'd forgotten, your role in this agency is officially terminated. It's in the contract." Larry's nostrils flared to the point where Kester was alarmed that he'd hyperventilate.

I haven't got time for this, Kester thought, and resumed his journey to the door.

"Oi! I haven't said you could go yet!"

"Look." Kester pointed at the clock. "It's five o'clock now, isn't it?"

Luke tapped at his watch. "It says 5:02 on mine, so I think you've qualified for overtime."

Kester laughed. It was impossible not to, especially after seeing the impotent rage on Larry's face. Without waiting for a response, he sauntered from the room, aware of the argument brewing in his wake.

How this is going to work on a long-term basis I have no idea, he thought, heading outside. The atmosphere in the office was getting steadily more combustible, and he sensed that it would take only to smallest thing to blow it sky-high.

The library seemed like a more appealing place to wait until 9:30 than his home, which was no doubt still a complete pigsty from the party. Entering into the welcome warmth of the building, he hastily glanced around to see if he could spy Anya. To his regret, the only librarian on duty was a young man, who even now was smiling enthusiastically at him. Kester sighed.

"Can I help you there?" The man gestured around the library like a king presenting his castle. "You look like the sort of chap who needs directions."

"I've been here quite a few times before," Kester muttered, reading the man's name tag, which said Mo in big red letters. "I'm all right, thanks."

Mo's smile dimmed slightly before ramping back up to full wattage. "So, what are you looking for today? Do you mind me asking? We're doing a questionnaire to find out more about our readers' habits."

Kester groaned inwardly. "I'm not looking for anything in particular. Though I don't suppose you could tell me if a member of staff is working today, could you?"

"Of course, who are you looking for?"

"Anya."

"Anya? No, she only worked until lunchtime today. Do you want me to pass a message on to her?"

"Gosh, no," Kester said quickly. "It was only because I was passing, and I—"

"Are you sure? It's no problem at all. I'm meeting up with her in an hour or so anyway for a drink."

Kester felt his heart plummet like stone to somewhere around his knees.

Mo studied him with interest. "Are you okay? You look a bit unwell, if you don't mind me saying. Why don't you have a seat, take a moment to—"

"I'm fine," Kester snapped. "Are you meeting Anya alone, then? I mean like on a date?"

"Um, sort of," Mo replied uncertainly. "Why do you ask?"

Kester opened his mouth, then shut it again, realising there was no point. Whatever he said, it wouldn't change the fact that Anya had moved on. *With a much better-looking bloke than me,* he thought, aching at the sight of the slim-hipped, chisel-jawed man in front of him. Even the *thought* of standing a chance against someone like that was ludicrous.

He shook his head apologetically, then walked away.

For the next few hours, he buried himself in the supernatural section of the library, browsing through obscure texts about spirit possession and daemon activity. Anything was preferable to dwelling on the fact that Anya was, at that moment, sipping a wine or two with another man.

Why am I so upset about it? he chastised himself. *It's not as though we could ever get back together, not when so much has happened.* Still, he couldn't ignore the ache rooted in the pit of his belly, nor the desperate sense of being more alone than before.

Finally, he stepped back outside, just as the library doors were locked tight behind him. The wind had picked up while he'd been inside and now lashed with abandon against his cheeks. *Perfect weather for hanging out late at night with a daemon,* he thought, making for the nearest taxi rank. *I suppose I'd better get going. I don't want to make Hrschni wait.*

Aside from the taxi driver's frequent bemused glances in the rearview mirror, the journey to the woods passed without incident. Stepping out into the deserted car park, Kester watched as the cab drove away into the night, leaving him in darkness. It was far colder now, away from the protection of the city buildings. The trees loomed like shadowy giants, surrounding him on all sides, and a barking screech echoed from somewhere far away. He hoped it was just a fox.

"What the hell am I doing?" he muttered to himself, pulling out his phone and using it as a torch to illuminate the sign beside him. It was easy to locate the viewing point on the map, though he wasn't relishing the prospect of walking there alone.

I should have let someone know where I was, he thought, heading towards the path that led through the trees. He remembered only too well what had happened last time he'd gone somewhere isolated without telling the others. The horrors of being kidnapped in a cave were still etched firmly in his mind. However, this was different. He'd been expressly told not to share the information with anyone else in case it jeopardised their chances of success.

I've got to operate on my own, he thought, pulling his coat tightly around his body. *Whether I like it or not.*

The quiet of the woods was all encompassing. He found himself longing for a solitary owl hoot or flapping of a bat; anything to break the thick syrup of silence that surrounded him. Only the morose crunch of his shoes on the loose pebbles accompanied him, but even that noise sounded muted and somehow unreal. He wondered, not for the first time, why Hrschni had chosen such a horrible location to have a meeting.

Dr. Barqa-Abu seemed to think I'd be totally safe, he reassured himself, as the path wound onwards through the leafless trees. However, she hadn't said anything about axe murderers or other crazed lunatics that might be wandering the woods at night. He walked faster, forcing himself to focus on the task at hand.

Finally, he emerged into the open. The twinkling lights of Exeter glittered in the distance like a carpet of stars. He stood by the viewing point, then used the compass on his phone to work out which way was northwest.

"Right, seventy-three paces," he said aloud, taking a deep breath. The way ahead looked even darker than the path he was already on; a nightmare of shadowy tree trunks and uneven terrain. But this was no time to be a coward. He'd come this far, after all.

The going quickly became harder as he left the path. Breath quickening, he pushed past brambles and branches, trying not to lose count of the steps he was taking. The ground felt spongy underfoot.

"Seventy-two, seventy-three," he said finally, coming to a stop. With shaking hands, he held his phone up to illuminate the area. The light revealed a small clearing with a single tree stump in the middle. He checked his watch, noting that he was slightly late.

"Hello?" The word, muffled by the freezing night air, faltered and died.

Suddenly, the air beside him stirred. Heat rippled towards him, warming his cheek in an instant. A vague red light appeared above the tree stump before solidifying. Although he'd seen the daemon in his true form before, it was no less formidable to behold, and Kester stepped back instinctively, resisting the urge to flee.

"You came," he whispered. Fear and relief jostled for supremacy as he struggled to get his breath back.

Hrschni nodded, his slender form weaving gently to and fro. His radiating light cast an eerie glow on the tree trunks, making them seem like burning pillars. "I have been following you," he said.

Kester shivered. "Why didn't you just accompany me then? Why make me think I was out here on my own?"

The daemon's eyes glittered. "I wanted to see what you were capable of. So," he continued, in a more conversational tone, "you wanted to meet with me, and here I am."

Now what do I say? Kester wondered. His chest felt painfully tight. *I need to come up with something convincing,* he thought, racing through his options, *or risk messing this up for good. There won't be a second chance to gain his trust.*

"I've been thinking about what you said," he began slowly. "About your plans to integrate the spirit world with ours. I'm not convinced it's a good idea, but I think there might be a way to compromise. That's what I wanted to talk about."

Hrschni's mouth stretched into what might have been a smile. "Compromise," he repeated, one skeletal hand outstretched, indicating they should walk through the wood. "That's a very human concept. Except often, when humans suggest compromise, they mean that they take, while others give."

Kester swallowed hard. "I mean a genuine compromise. A slow, methodical integration programme perhaps? Let people get used to spirits first, before we go wild with it?"

"You sound like the government. I hadn't expected this from a Lanner."

He doesn't know I've read my grandfather's letters, Kester reminded himself. "What do you mean by that?" he asked innocently.

"I knew your mother very well. And your grandfather."

"You knew my mother?" Kester stopped walking. He'd wondered if that had been the case, and now here it was, confirmed for him. A dull flare of anger flooded his chest. *How many other things did she conceal from me?* he wondered. *How many lies did she tell?*

Hrschni waited for him to compose himself. "I cared deeply for your mother," he continued. "She had a deep love for the spirit world, trust me. She would want you to show the same devotion to it."

Kester bit his lip. There was so much he wanted to say, but he knew his job was to lure Hrschni into a false sense of security, not anger him. "Let's say I was willing to show that same devotion," he said, carrying on through the trees. The wind whipped around his body, but he scarcely noticed it. "What would you want from me?"

"I need to trust you before I tell you my plans," Hrschni replied. "But I can promise you, it will bring about a better, happier world."

"How?"

"Spirits will bring equilibrium. Look at what humans have become. They worship computers and television screens these days, not nature and wisdom. I observe them as they sit in cafés, staring at their phones to avoid talking to one another. I watch as couples take photos then post them on websites, rather than embrace one another. Spirits bring spirituality, Kester. That's what this world badly needs."

"How would spirits stop humans using technology?"

Hrschni laughed, a brittle sound that made Kester's skin prickle. "We would break it."

"Doesn't that hurt you?"

"It is a small sacrifice to make for the greater good. We would bring down your internet. Stop your factory machines from belching fumes. Break every car. Prevent needless plastic garbage from being manufactured. It would all stop."

My god, Kester thought, scarcely able to breathe. The sheer scope of Hrschni's vision was beyond what he'd imagined. *He wouldn't just bring chaotic spirits into our world. He'd destroy society as we know it.* "I have no particular love for technology," he said, choosing his words carefully. "But this is a lot to take in."

Hrschni smiled. "I have noticed your natural distaste for computers. You always choose to go to the library and bury yourself in books rather than spend hour after hour staring at a screen."

"Yes, but sometimes computers speed things up."

"Who needs such speed?" Hrschni whirled to face him. "That is another thing that is terribly wrong with your world today. Humans are so fixed on racing through life they fail to notice the beauty around them. Now, will you help me to make a better world, Kester? A new Eden, if you like?"

Kester struggled to maintain composure. His mind was flooded with conflicting emotions: deep-seated dread, terror, yet a strange, rebellious sense of acknowledgement. *There's truth in his words,* he thought, then chastised himself for thinking it.

"I need to think about it all," he said finally. "I can't give you an answer now."

Hrschni sighed, a hollow sound that mirrored the night's breeze. "Very well," he said. "But do not allow yourself to be swayed by others. They have been brainwashed to believe that the government's way of doing things is right. Most of them have no idea what the government are capable of."

"Do they really kill spirits that have misbehaved?" Kester blurted. He had to know the truth, somehow or another.

"Yes. Don't let them tell you otherwise."

They fell silent, pacing steadily through the cold, black night. Kester rubbed his temples, feeling the start of a headache coming on. "I'd better get home," he said eventually. "I've got work tomorrow."

"You must not tell them about this meeting," Hrschni said quickly. "I will know if you have."

Kester took a deep breath. "I'm aware of that, believe me. I've never felt so under surveillance in my life. Don't you realise how much pressure it is?"

To his surprise, the daemon raised a hand, placing it gently on Kester's shoulder. It warmed him, seeping through his clothes like hot liquid.

"I understand very well," he said. "Don't imagine that I don't recognise your suffering, or that I don't wish to make it stop. I want you to be happy, Kester. You deserve to be happy."

Kester sniffed. For a moment, he could almost imagine he was walking alongside a kindly relative rather than a dangerous spirit. "Thanks," he said quietly.

"The path is about fifty paces in that direction," Hrschni said, pointing. "You'll understand why I don't join you, I'm sure."

"You don't trust me?"

"I don't trust many; it's too risky."

Kester turned to leave. The cold was creeping through his

clothes and into his skin, freezing him to the marrow. He hoped his phone would pick up enough signal to dial for a taxi home again. "Don't you trust the other Thelemites?" he asked through chattering teeth.

Hrschni's form whirred in the air, before stilling again. "You need not be concerned with who I do and don't trust," he said. "Now, get home before you expire with the cold. I forget how vulnerable you humans are sometimes."

"Shall I pass another note to Anya when I'm ready to give you my answer?" He swallowed hard, hoping that his expression didn't betray his anxiety and guilt.

The daemon nodded. "I only hope it is the right answer, not the wrong one."

Is that a threat or a genuine wish? Kester wondered, as he started walking through the trees. Adrenalin pumped through him, which was fortunate given how leaden his limbs felt through the cold. Turning, he noticed that Hrschni had vanished, though presumably he was still around somewhere, watching him leave.

The thought didn't bother him as much as he expected. In fact, there was something reassuring about having an invisible daemon watching over him, even if his motives were questionable.

It was nearly eleven o'clock when Kester finally reached home. To his relief, the house was silent, though still covered with streamers, empty plastic cups, and discarded food from the night before. He retreated to his room and started to undress, aware of how every part of him seemed to ache. Clambering into bed, he hoped that sleep would come quickly. He closed his eyes.

A second later, he opened them again. An unmistakable green light was glowing through his curtains, turning the patterned fabric an eerie shade that reminded him of every alien movie he'd ever seen.

"You've got to be joking," he murmured, reaching for his glasses. In a louder voice, he said, "Come in, Fylgia, I know it's you."

At once, the flickering green light slid through the wall before materialising before him.

"I cannot be long," she announced, eyes piercing through the darkness.

"Good," Kester replied. "I'm knackered and I want to go to sleep."

He thought he detected a hint of a smile in the hazy glow of her face. "Hrschni has returned to the Thelemite headquarters," she continued. "He believes I am currently monitoring your whereabouts."

"Which is kind of true." He sat up straighter then blushed, remembering when he and Fylgia had last met in this bed—admittedly while she'd been in Anya's body. "Why does Hrschni want to know where I am, anyway? Is he suspicious?"

She shook her head, then edged closer, until he could feel the heat of her form radiating through his duvet. "He wanted to ensure you arrived home safely but didn't want to risk being detected close to your house."

"But it's okay for you to take that risk?" Kester said, raising an eyebrow.

"I'm not the government's primary target, remember? I'm more expendable."

Kester sighed. He was too tired to argue the point. "I presume you want me to tell you how it went?"

She nodded. Quickly, he outlined his earlier conversation. "So," he concluded, "I'll arrange another meeting with him soon."

"That will be our opportunity to catch him."

He shuddered. The choice of words didn't sit comfortably

with him. "How are you going to do that?" he asked quietly. "It'd hardly be appropriate to use one of Serena's water bottles."

Fylgia leant closer. For a moment, he thought she was going to kiss him. Instead, she pressed her mouth close to his ear. "You're going to do it," she whispered, intimate as a lover.

"Me?" Kester recoiled. "I don't think so. I have no control over when I open a spirit door. I wouldn't stand a chance."

"Haven't you worked it out yet, Kester?" She touched his hand briefly with one narrow finger, then moved away. His skin tingled in its absence. "The key is self-belief. When you have faith in yourself, you are able to do it."

"I thought it was when I thought of my mum," he replied.

"That is because she always had faith in you."

He pondered it over, remembering the times in the past that he'd been able to get the spirit door open. Her suggestion made sense, and he felt he'd always known it on a subconscious level.

"I don't feel comfortable pushing Hrschni through the spirit door," he muttered. "It's disrespectful. Also, won't he just come back through to our world? What's stopping him?"

"Don't worry about that." Fylgia rose again, hovering near the window. "We've got everything planned out. I'll make sure that Hrschni is weakened before you open the spirit door. He won't be able to resist its pull. That's when we shall have our chance. Trust me."

Everyone's always asking me to trust them, he thought irritably, watching her weave on the spot. *But they're all telling me different things. Who the hell am I supposed to trust, really?*

"What if he comes back to this world and wants revenge?" he persisted, pushing his glasses back up his nose. "What then?"

Fylgia looked down at the floor. She seemed to be searching for the right words. "Do not worry about that. It's not your concern."

"What is that supposed to mean?" Kester whispered.

She pressed a hand against his shoulder. "Never mind. Now, I must get back. Keep us informed; we need to know every detail if we're going to do this right."

He raised an exhausted hand. "Good night, Fylgia."

For a moment, her eyes glittered with light. "I miss the nights I used to stay here beside you, in your bed."

"It's probably not appropriate to talk about that, as I didn't—"

"Yes, I know. You were not aware that it was me. But you enjoyed my company, Kester. Spirits and humans have been together in the past. It can happen."

What is she trying to say? he wondered, rubbing his eyes. However, before he could ask, she'd slipped through the window, leaving the room in darkness.

CHAPTER 17: RISING SUSPICIONS

Kester arrived at the back entrance of the office, blearily rubbing his eyes. He'd had an appalling night, and the few moments that he had been asleep had been haunted by dreams of vengeful daemons throttling him to death. But it was hardly surprising really, given what he'd endured the night before. He just wanted it to end, to have life return to some semblance of normality, but he suspected normal life was still a long way away for him yet.

All I need is a quiet day at work, he thought, pushing the door open. *It's not much to ask for.*

To his surprise, the office was silent as he entered. Serena was scrutinising her laptop, Pamela was earnestly filling out some sort of form, and even Mike appeared to be hard at work melting some metal wires with a blowtorch.

"Everything all right?" Kester said uncertainly, placing his bag down on his desk.

"Fine," Miss Wellbeloved chimed, appearing from the stock cupboard armed with a pile of dusty files. "Good, in fact. Curtis

Philpot phoned a few minutes ago. They've had a lead on the Hrschni case."

Kester froze. "Really?" he squeaked, then hastily cleared his throat. "I mean, what sort of lead?"

"He was spotted last night. Heading towards Haldon Forest, of all places." She returned to her desk, dumping the files with a thud. "It's most strange; no one has any idea why he was there. Fylgia wasn't with him, nor any other human or spirit, apparently. Lili Asadi tried to track him inside the forest but couldn't get a strong enough signal."

"Whoa, hang on a minute." Kester sank down on the sofa beside the door, struggling to calm his breathing. "How did Lili know to look for him there?"

Serena peered around her computer screen. "She's had him under surveillance since he was seen at the Exeter headquarters recently. Personally, I wish Infinite Enterprises would keep us informed when they're carrying out work in our area. It's really intrusive."

What else do Infinite Enterprises know? Kester wondered. He suddenly felt nauseous. What if they knew he was involved? Or if they'd misunderstood his intentions?

"You all right, mate?" Mike put the blowtorch down and lifted his makeshift eye mask up. "It's not that much of a shock is it?"

"Do they know why he was in the forest?" Kester asked weakly. He stood, then wished he hadn't. His vision blurred and he forced himself to take a deep breath.

"No one has any idea," Serena said. "Lili parked the van and headed into the forest on foot but couldn't pick anything up. Not surprising really. Haldon Forest is huge."

Kester forced himself to think rationally. There hadn't been a van in the car park last night when he'd been there, so Lili must have left before he did. As far as he could tell, no one had any idea that he was involved.

Once this is all over, he reminded himself, *I can tell them everything. Then there won't be any secrecy or lies.*

"They've been all over the forest this morning," Miss Wellbeloved added. "Curtis said there was nothing to be gained by us going up there too. Instead, he recommended that we start putting the pressure on the other Thelemites—questioning people like Barty Melville, for example."

Kester swallowed hard. "Is Dad in?" he murmured. His mouth was dry.

"No," Miss Wellbeloved replied, frowning. "Are you all right? You really don't look well."

"I didn't get much sleep." He cleared his throat again, which felt as rough as sandpaper. "In fact, I didn't get any sleep. Can I work from home today?"

She shrugged. "You've only just got in, but you can go if you wish; it's officially your company now."

"It's not his bloody company!" Serena slammed down her laptop. "Miss W, *you're* in charge until you retire. So tell the lazy sod to sit at his desk like the rest of us."

"Don't call me lazy," Kester retaliated, without much enthusiasm. He simply didn't have the energy to argue with her.

She stood up, heels thudding against the carpet as she stalked towards him. "What's going on, eh? I mean *really.* Don't give me the fob-off version that you're giving everyone else. I want to know the truth."

Kester looked up. To his surprise, he saw that her eyebrows were furrowed with concern, not anger. "There's nothing going on," he muttered. "I've just got a headache, that's all."

"Leave the lad alone," Mike said, scooping up his tools again.

"He was probably out on the lash last night, isn't that right? Doing what young lads do."

Serena sat down beside Kester, pressing him into the squidgy armrest. "Come on," she whispered. "Something's bothering you, I can tell. You're not very good at keeping secrets."

He threw her an anguished look. *It would be so easy just to tell her everything,* he thought, his chest tightening. *To pass the problem on and let someone else worry about it.* But he knew if he told her, she'd tell the others, and then they'd probably report it to Curtis Philpot. Where the information would go after that was anybody's guess, and it would put the whole mission into jeopardy.

It's only for a few more days, he told himself, giving her a weak smile. *Then it'll all be over, one way or another.*

He remained at work until midday, then decided to take the bus across town to his father's house. He didn't quite know why, but he felt a need to be in Ribero's presence and away from the pressure of the office.

After stepping off the bus, he made his way up the winding country road until the last of the houses gave way to thick pines, some still tinged with frost, despite the glow of the wintry sun overhead. His feet crunched on the driveway as he headed towards his father's ranch, which looked even more incongruous than ever with ice tinting the gutters and windowsills.

He pressed the doorbell. A few moments later the door swung open. His father's brow was furrowed in irritation, which quickly melted away at the sight of him.

"Kester! I was not expecting you."

Kester shuffled on the doorstep. "Who were you expecting?"

Ribero ushered him inside. "The postman. He keeps telling me I must take the parcels for the family up the road. Every day I get the parcels; big parcels. What are they buying, eh? Then they leave their parcels in my house for days until—"

"Shall I go through to the lounge?" Kester interrupted. He wasn't much interested in hearing about the neighbours' parcels and couldn't be bothered to conceal the fact.

The usual fire was crackling away in the grate, and the surrounding sofas were bathed in a cosy glow. Kester threw himself onto the nearest one and let out a sigh.

"Why are you here?" Ribero asked, sitting beside him. "You are meant to be at work."

Kester closed his eyes. *If only he knew,* he thought, feeling his muscles relax in the warmth. *Then all of this would be so much easier.*

"I'm doing plenty of work as it is," he replied. "Don't start having a go at me."

"Ah, that Higgins pig has worn you out, yes?" Ribero smacked the armrest triumphantly. "I knew it would not work. I said it, did I not? That oaf of a man will ruin the agency and—"

"It's nothing to do with Higgins," Kester said quickly. "It's other stuff."

"What other stuff?"

Kester paused. The words were in his mouth, desperate to escape. He swallowed them down. "Just life in general," he said finally.

"Is it your studies? Is Dr. Barqa-Abu working you too hard? She is a tough djinn. When I was at the SSFE she was always the bully, always going on at me."

"She's not so bad." Kester watched the flames quivering around the blackened logs, then added, "What do you know about her?"

His father straightened. "What do you mean?"

"I mean, she's taught students at the SSFE for years, but does anyone know what she did before that? What about thousands of years ago?"

"These are strange questions." He held Kester's gaze. "You come to my house all jittery like a bolting horse, and then you ask these odd things. I want to know what is going on."

Kester sighed. "I can't tell you," he said finally. "And you mustn't say anything to the others, okay? I need you to promise."

His father leant back against the sofa, studying him intently. The lull in conversation stretched into a laden silence. Kester waited patiently, biting his lip.

"Are you in trouble?" Ribero asked eventually.

"What? No, I'm honestly not."

"Is someone threatening you? Is this to do with the Thelemites?"

Kester tensed. His father's ability to see through to the truth of things was uncanny at times. "I'm not allowed to say," he muttered, "and I've already said too much. But I need you to tell me something. Would you trust Dr. Barqa-Abu?"

"So, she is tied up in this, is she? I knew you saw her in Italy, but I thought that was to help with the investigation. Is she up to something? Kester, if I am right then you must tell the government, they need to know—"

"No, we mustn't tell anyone!" Kester shot him a panicked look. "Please. I need you to trust me here. Just tell me what you know about Dr. Barqa-Abu. And about Fylgia and Hrschni."

Ribero exhaled heavily, then reached into his shirt pocket, pulling out a packet of cigarettes. Kester waited patiently, noticing how badly Ribero's hand was shaking as he flicked the lighter. Finally, the cigarette was lit, and the usual plume of smoke curled slowly to the stained ceiling.

"Dr. Barqa-Abu is a very respected djinn," his father said

slowly. "I do not think she has ever been in trouble. She has been teaching at the SSFE since it was first opened, so maybe 150 years, something like that, yes?"

"What about before that?"

He shrugged. "I do not know so much. Djinn are secretive. They sometimes hibernate for long periods of time."

"In things like magic lamps?"

He winced. "No, not like the magic lamp. This is not a fairy story. The djinn sleep in tombs. Caves. Dark places."

"Was she ever working with any other spirits?" Kester asked lamely. "You know, like daemons or anything?"

"I do not understand these questions. Do you think Dr. Barqa-Abu is with Hrschni? I think that is impossible. Djinns are like daemons, they do not lie. They do not deceive. They don't even play tricks. They are very honest, yes?"

"But secretive."

"They would not mislead a human," Ribero insisted. "It is not what they do."

"What about Fylgia and Hrschni?" Kester pressed. "And what about my mum?"

At the mention of Gretchen, Ribero's hand froze, quivering in midair, just a few inches from his face. The cigarette smouldered, the length of ash stretching slowly. "What do you mean?" he asked finally.

"I know that Mum knew both the daemons."

The cigarette teetered, then fell out of Ribero's grip. He bent down to pick it up, cursing under his breath. "How do you know that?" he said, his expression neutral.

"That doesn't matter. There were a lot of things Mum didn't tell me. I think she's somehow involved in all of this, and I need to know how."

"You do not need to know."

"I do! She's my mother. And since she died, I've discovered that pretty much her entire life was a lie. She knew Hrschni, and you need to tell me what *you* know."

The thud of Ribero's hand against the coffee table made him jump. "You think I know these things?" he flared, fist still clenched. "Kester, I did not know your mother at all. No one did. She was a marvellous, exciting woman, but she was like the iceberg, yes? We only saw the tip of her, the little bit she let us see. Do you understand?"

"But you know that she encountered Hrschni?"

Ribero's face darkened. "Do not press me on this, Kester. I do not want to talk about it."

"But I do!" Kester picked up his father's hand and squeezed it. "Look, I'm in a horrible situation. I can't confide in anyone, and I feel like I'm going crazy. Perhaps if I can understand the past a bit better, I can understand what's happening right now."

"If you can, you are wiser than any of us." Ribero took a deep breath, then leant back against the sofa. "Look," he said in a softer voice. "Whatever you are mixed up in, you need to be careful, okay? I am guessing it is the Thelemites, and I am guessing that you are doing something to stop Hrschni."

"Dad, don't try to—"

Ribero held up a hand. "All right. I will not ask the questions. But you need to know that these daemons are clever. Far cleverer than you or I. As for Dr. Barqa-Abu? You can trust her, I think. She is a mean and nasty teacher but a good spirit with a good heart. She will not harm you; I am sure of it."

"What about the government?"

"What about them?"

"Can we trust them?"

"Of course. Why would we not trust them? Bernard Nutcombe is a silly man, that is true, but they are looking out for everyone, are they not?"

Kester shrugged. Beyond the patio doors, the pines hulked in a cluster, blocking out much of the watery sunlight. Already the shadows were lengthening even though it was only midafternoon. "I've heard rumours," he said carefully, "that the government was killing off spirits."

Ribero shifted in his seat. "Jennifer told me that Hrschni had said this to you. I think you worry too much. Spirits are not like us, so we do not need to—"

"What's that supposed to mean? Are you saying that the government does kill them?"

"You are too hot tempered, my boy. Take a deep breath, please. Do you want a wine? I have wine, I can get you some."

"No, I don't want wine, it's far too early in the day." Kester pressed a hand on his father's leg, pushing him back down. "I want you to tell me the truth. Do the government exterminate spirits that continually flout the rules?"

His father looked down at his lap. "I do not know," he muttered. "Jennifer would like to think not, so—"

"I'm not talking about what Miss W thinks. I'm talking about what you *know*. And you obviously know something, it's written all over your face."

"Let me make us a cup of tea. This is too much for today, and I am not feeling well."

"No, sit back down," Kester pressed, slapping his father's shoulder with more force than he'd intended. "I'm sorry you don't feel well, but you can't wriggle out of this. Tell me what you know."

Ribero closed his eyes. "There have been rumours," he murmured. "Rumours that Infinite Enterprises are paid by the government to do something like that. But I do not know if they are true," he added hastily, seeing the look in Kester's eyes, "and this was a long time ago. Things have changed since then."

"And aren't you bothered by that?" Kester asked, in a quiet voice that sounded nothing like his usual self at all.

His father paused, then met his gaze. "Sometimes we must be cruel to be kind. That is the right phrase, yes?"

Kester stood abruptly. He felt nauseous again, a sensation that wasn't helped by the fact that the room seemed to be pressing into him, the warm fire and rustic wood melting into one amorphous form that made him feel suffocatingly hot. He took a step to the door. "I need to go," he said, unable to look in his father's direction.

"You have only just got here!" Ribero rose, reaching out to Kester. "I can see you are upset. Please, sit down."

"I'm leaving." He strode towards the hallway, almost walking into the doorframe on the way out. "We shouldn't have had this conversation. I don't know what I was thinking."

With surprising speed, Ribero grabbed him by the arm. "Do not go. You are not yourself."

"You don't know me! Don't pretend that you do. You ignored my existence until a few months ago."

"Kester, that is not fair. There were reasons for that, and I—"

"I don't care." Kester marched to the front door and yanked it open, letting the cold air flood through. "I can't deal with any more than I am at the moment. You, Mum, the daemons, Anya: you're all manipulating me. Is that what I am? Some sort of tool to be used?"

He stepped outside, already regretting his words. They'd flooded from him like water escaping from a burst dam and now there was no gathering them back again. He didn't feel any better for it either. His father's stricken face was a torment to view, especially when Kester noticed how much he was trembling.

"Look," he continued in a gentler voice, "don't listen to me. Things are difficult at the moment, but they'll be okay soon. I promise."

"You are keeping secrets from me," Ribero said, leaning against the wall for support. He looked haggard in the bleak winter light. "That is what Gretchen did too. That is what she did to everyone."

"I'm not her." He held both hands out, silencing his father before he could speak. "And don't say how much I'm like her. I don't want to hear it anymore."

His father's face crumpled. "I am sorry. She and I only wanted to protect you."

Kester stalked away, hands in pockets. When he turned around again, he saw that the front door was shut.

The rest of the day passed slowly; the house unusually silent, save the occasional whistle of wind through the bedroom windowpane. Kester busied himself with research for his latest essay, but his heart wasn't in it. Instead, his mind kept wandering over the same old ground: churning up images of daemons, family members, ex-girlfriends, and plenty of other stuff that he'd rather forget.

His phone rang just as the sky outside was starting to darken, its drilling vibrations across the desk startling him from his thoughts. He took a glance at the caller ID, then slumped back in his seat.

"Hello Larry," he said wearily.

"I just tried calling you at the office," Larry began, without preamble, "but Jennifer said you were working from home. Is this going to be a habit?"

His strident tones made Kester instinctively pull the phone

further from his ear. "It won't happen very often, don't worry," he answered. "What can I help you with?"

"I wanted to run something past you. Jennifer already approves, but as you're a co-owner of the company, I need to check with you too."

Kester smiled. He could tell by Larry's voice that he'd rather do anything but acknowledge Kester's role as a joint decision-maker. "Go on," he said.

Larry cleared his throat. "A chap approached me recently, looking for some work experience. Naturally I was curious as to how he'd found us, but after extensive questioning, I'd say he seems legit. He also shows skills in ghost sighting; apparently it's something he's been able to do from birth."

"Did he go to the SSFE?"

"No. Not everyone does, you know. Some people just have raw talent. Anyway, he's asked if he can have some intern experience. I think it'd be a good idea. Lord knows we need the extra help, and he looks like the motivated sort that might help us win more business."

"How do you know he's trustworthy?" Kester pressed. "Seems a bit odd, someone turning up out of nowhere like that."

"I appreciate that. But he's been in Exeter for a while, plus we don't have to give him the details of our important cases, do we? Why don't I bring him along tomorrow morning, see what you think?"

"A formal interview would probably be a good idea."

Larry grunted. "You like all this, don't you?"

"What?"

"The power. I can hear it in your smug little voice."

Kester resisted the urge to retort. "No, I don't love all the power," he replied firmly. "I was forced to take on this responsibility by my dad. So please stop having a go at me, okay? I'm not in the mood."

He could imagine Larry's expression now, mouth opening and closing like a dying goldfish. Patiently, he waited for him to continue.

"Very well," Larry said finally. "I can understand that your idiot father was to blame for this situation, not you."

For once, Kester didn't leap to Ribero's defence. "I'll leave it with you to get the guy in for an interview tomorrow, then," he said, looking at his watch. It was later than he'd realised. "Anything else?"

Larry paused. "Everything all right, is it?" he said finally.

"What do you mean?"

"You don't sound yourself. Is there something wrong?"

Like you'd care, Kester thought, drumming his fingers on the desk. "I'm absolutely fine," he replied. "Now, if you don't mind, I've got to continue with this essay. It's due in tomorrow."

"Of course," Larry said hurriedly, then added. "Did Jennifer tell you about the latest update from Curtis Philpot, by the way?"

"No, what was it?"

"You know that recent break-in at Infinite Enterprises? The one they think was Hrschni? They've discovered that he's stolen something. Something pretty worrying."

"What?" Kester leant forward, suddenly alert.

"Classified information," Larry replied. "They wouldn't even tell me, can you imagine?"

Kester nudged his glasses up his nose. *Typical,* he thought, glaring out of the window. *Yet more secrets.*

"I presume it's something that threatens our national safety, though," Larry continued, oblivious to Kester's brooding thoughts. "So once again, it's all noses to the grindstone, trying to find out where this bloody daemon is hiding. Honestly, I'll be glad when that bastard is captured and got rid of. He's been a great big thorn up my backside since this case started."

Kester shuddered. He had no desire to think about Larry Higgins's backside. "What do you think they'll do with him, once he's caught?" he asked.

"I've no idea. Not my problem, is it?"

Kester bit back a sigh. *That's the issue, right there,* he thought. *No one knows, and no one cares.* "Thanks for letting me know," he said, keen to wrap the conversation up. "I'll see you in the office tomorrow."

"You certainly will. No working from home tomorrow, young lad." Without saying goodbye, he hung up, leaving Kester with nothing but a dialling tone.

He sat for a while, motionless in his darkening bedroom, eyes fixed on the rooftops outside. A few stars were already out, specks of brilliance in the otherwise bland, greying sky. *Timeless,* he thought, watching them gently pulse, like throbbing hearts. *Like spirits, they carry on, while the rest of us turn to dust. Is that why the government might want to eliminate some of them? Out of jealousy?*

Reaching for a notepad and pen, he started to write Hrschni a letter. They needed to meet again, and for the sake of Kester's sanity, it needed to be sooner rather than later.

Chapter 18: Brotherly Love and Hidden Footage

Somehow, Kester managed to arrive in the office before Larry Higgins; a miracle given he'd only had a few hours' sleep the night before and he'd had to drop the letter to Hrschni through Anya's letter box. He slumped at his desk, oblivious to the chatter of the others as he powered up his laptop.

Seeing his wan expression, Pamela quickly popped the kettle on and returned a few minutes later with a steaming mug of tea. "You don't look good, love," she whispered, before adjusting her sweatband.

Kester looked at her head with confusion, then surveyed the rest of her, which was currently sporting a shiny leotard and cycling shorts. "Are you going on a run or something?" he asked, sipping at his drink.

Pamela chortled. "Goodness, no. I've just had my doggy yoga class."

"Excuse me?"

"Doggy yoga. It's only our second session; Hemingway adores it. Though he did get a bit overexcited when I was trying to do the warrior pose."

"You didn't want to change, then?" It wasn't much above freezing outside, and he couldn't imagine why anyone would want to stride around in skimpy clothing.

Pamela shrugged. "I didn't have time. It's not like you lot care what I'm wearing, is it?"

He grinned. "Maybe I should join you. I could do with some exercise."

"You could do with some sleep," she said, eyes softening.

They were interrupted by the door swinging open. Larry Higgins stood resplendent in the doorway, face already screwed into a frown.

"Sodding Exeter traffic," he scowled, marching into the room. "Ridiculous road system, I don't know how you lot bear it. Anyway, glad you could make it, Kester. I trust it wasn't too hard to pull yourself out of bed today."

Kester carried on drinking his tea, determined to ignore him.

"Has this chap not turned up yet?" Larry continued. "It's four minutes past nine."

"Is this the man that wants to do an internship?" Pamela said, settling back at her desk.

"What man?" Mike added. His screwdriver slid from his grasp and he cursed.

Serena leant back in her chair. "Larry's got some unpaid chimp to help out in the office."

"We'll pay him when he gets good enough," Miss Wellbeloved added quickly. "It's not slave labour, honestly. For what it's worth, I think it's a good idea, as long as he can be trusted. Expanding the team shows the government that we're serious about growing the business."

Suddenly, a dislocated voice echoed from somewhere in the depths of the building, followed by the sound of footsteps clomping up the staircase.

Kester sighed inwardly. He wasn't in the mood to pretend to be professional. He merely wanted to roll back into bed again and blot the world out for another few hours or so.

"Aha!" Larry rubbed his hands together, standing aside to let the newcomer in. "Glad you could make it. Do come inside and meet the team."

They all looked up with interest at the person in question. Pamela was the first to react; a nervous titter that dwindled into a cough. Serena's mouth formed a perfect circle of surprise. Finally, Mike rose; a methodical, enraged action, much like a bull revving itself up to charge.

Kester gawped openly at Crispian, who stood in the doorway like an athlete celebrating a victory. *What the hell does he think he's playing at?* he wondered, lost for words.

"What are you doing here?" Mike choked, breaking the silence. His finger rose slowly before extending outwards in an accusing jab.

"All right there, bro?" Crispian grinned, then instinctively shrank backwards as Mike's fist slammed against the desk.

"You're his brother?" Larry spluttered, looking around wildly. "Crispian, why didn't you mention that?"

"Oh dear," Pamela muttered.

Mike shook his head, then started to pace around the office. "You're not working here," he muttered darkly. "No way." His expression was so apoplectic, Kester was concerned he might pass out with rage.

Crispian shrugged. "You told me the other day that I should think about my natural talents. And let's face it, when we were younger, I was the one who could see the spirits, not you."

"You can actually see them as physical entities?" Miss Well-beloved said, face brightening. "That's an incredibly useful skill."

"I may not have been able to see them," Mike spluttered, "but I was the one who got rid of them. You were always a total coward, running off to Mother and Father's room."

Serena smirked. "*Mother and Father?* God, you really are a toff, aren't you?"

"I'd be great at this sort of job," Crispian persisted, edging behind Larry as his brother started stalking toward him across the floor. "After I overheard you and Kester the other day, I couldn't get it out of my head."

"Were Mike and Kester talking about it in public?" Miss Wellbeloved raised an eyebrow.

"That's irrelevant," Mike said quickly. "This utter bell-end *cannot* work here. That's the end of it."

"Who appointed you head of recruitment?" Larry's nostrils flared in irritation. "If I say he's hired, then he's hired."

"It's our decision too," Kester reminded him, gesturing to himself and Miss Wellbeloved.

With an eye still fixed on his brother, Crispian stepped into the room. "Look guys," he said, switching on his megawatt smile, the one presumably used for wooing clients in his previous job. "I can be a great asset to this agency. I've got business experience too; I'll help you take things to the next level. You can't afford to say no."

"We can," Mike said mutinously.

Crispian's expression darkened. "You can't, actually. Because you don't want me running my mouth off about what you're doing, do you?"

Everyone gasped.

"Are you threatening us?" Pamela said incredulously.

"I don't see it as threatening, my dear Pamela. I see it as securing my future and yours."

Kester shook his head in disbelief. Things frequently took a turn for the strange in this office, but this took things to whole new levels. "Well then," he said, folding his hands over his stomach. "I guess that means we'll have to take you on. We've got no choice. We can't risk people getting curious about what we do here."

Crispian punched the air in triumph just as Mike bellowed with frustration.

"Mate, you cannot do this to me," he entreated, pressing his hands together. "He's a monumental idiot. You can't trust him."

Crispian pressed a hand to his chest. "Bro, that *stings,* it really does."

"As for living at my place, you can pack your bags and clear out," Mike snapped, whirling to face him. "I'm done with you. This is the final straw."

"Not a problem. I freed up some of my shares a few days ago, and I've already found a room to rent in town."

"You bastard! You've been planning this for ages, haven't you?"

His brother sighed. "Contrary to what you think, not everything I do is to annoy you. I really want to have a career like this, don't you see? All my life, I've lived up to what Mother and Father want me to do. Now it's time for me to achieve my dreams, just like you have."

Mike's astounded expression would have been funny at any other time. However, in this context, Kester couldn't help thinking that he looked like a dog that'd been whipped by its owner. "Fine," he said finally, stalking back to his desk. "There's nothing I can do about it anyway, is there? But if you do anything to mess up this agency, I swear I'll kill you."

"Come on, you're not going to—"

"I *will.*" The venom in Mike's voice made everyone shrink backwards.

"Right," Larry interrupted, looking more than a little ruffled. "That didn't turn out quite the way I'd hoped, but let's make the best of the situation, shall we?"

"Perhaps next time you'll vet your interns more thoroughly?" Miss Wellbeloved added wryly.

Larry had the good grace to look embarrassed.

While Crispian vanished into Ribero's office with Larry and Miss Wellbeloved to go through his contract, everyone else got back to their work. It was difficult to concentrate with Mike bashing away at his keyboard as though it were personally responsible for everything, but Kester didn't dare complain.

Eventually, Miss Wellbeloved and Larry emerged, both looking drained. By contrast, Crispian looked positively jubilant, hands shoved cockily into his suit trousers.

"You can tell them," Larry hissed, before slinking back into the office.

Miss Wellbeloved sighed. "Just to let you all know," she began, pulling Crispian forward. "As our new intern has the gift of spirit-sight, we'll be offering his services to Infinite Enterprises, for certain important surveillance tasks." She nodded meaningfully at everyone.

She's going to put him on the case with Hrschni, Kester realised, slumping into his chair. If Crispian's spirit-sighting abilities were as good as he claimed, that could cause problems, in more ways than one.

"Haven't Infinite Enterprises already got a spirit-sighter of their own?" he asked.

"No, she lost her ability a couple of years back," Serena explained. "It's one of the rare gifts that deteriorates with age."

"When your eyesight goes, your spirit sight goes too," Pamela added helpfully. "Wilsher and Sons are training a spirit-sighter, but he's only eleven. They can't legally employ him yet."

Crispian smirked. "Looks like I'm the best option, then." He turned to Miss Wellbeloved. "I'll get paid for that job, will I?"

Her lips tightened into what might have been a smile or a grimace. "The government will be happy to pay you, I'm sure. Tell you what, why don't you take the rest of the day off? You can make a start tomorrow."

Mike snorted, then hammered a fresh burst of rage upon his keyboard.

"Righty-ho," Crispian replied, looking vaguely unsettled by his brother's behaviour. He lingered for a moment by Mike's desk, caught his eye, then thought better of it. "I'll go home then."

"It's not your home," Mike snarled, angling his chair to avoid looking at him. "You've got the rest of today to clear your stuff out. I don't want to see you there when I get back."

"That's a bit harsh," Serena muttered, then blushed at the sight of Mike's infuriated expression.

Crispian bit his lip. "Mike, can't we just—"

"No we bloody can't."

He opened his mouth to continue, then shut it again, shaking his head. A moment later, he turned on his heel and headed to the door. The others watched him leave with varying expressions of amazement, confusion, and anger.

Finally, Pamela stood up and grabbed her coat. "I'll nip out to buy some cakes, shall I? I think we could all do with it after that."

Even Larry nodded in agreement.

The rest of the day passed uneventfully, which Kester was heartily relieved about. Darkness had already set in when he finally emerged from the office, and a low drizzle of rain battered his already-cold face. He was pleased to find his house empty and surprised to realise that the heating was actually working for once, bathing each room in a warm glow that was almost welcoming.

Would it be too much to hope for a relaxing evening? he wondered, heading upstairs. *A mug of hot chocolate and a nice film on TV, rather than racing around like a mad thing, getting caught up in horrible supernatural goings-on?*

He entered his bedroom, threw his bag on the bed, then suddenly noticed the envelope resting against his windowpane.

"I should have predicted as much," he muttered with a sigh. Life was *never* relaxing; he knew that by now.

Quickly, he pulled the window open and reached down to grab the letter. It was impressive how fast the daemon had penned a response; he'd only dropped the note off to Anya's on the way to work.

He pulled out the letter. A USB stick fell out too, landing on the floor with a quiet thud. He scooped it up and placed it on the desk before reading the letter. As before, it was brief and to the point.

Meet me on the tip of the dunes, where the eye gazes to Exmouth. 9:30 PM tonight.

Kester bit back a wry smile. "Typical," he muttered aloud, "there had to be a hint of a puzzle in there somewhere. He couldn't just give me a location." Quickly, he powered up his laptop and connected to the internet. A moment later, he'd pulled up a map of the area, zoning in on Exmouth, a coastal town nearby.

"Here we go," he muttered in triumph, prodding the screen. "Dawlish Warren. The dunes stick right out towards Exmouth." Studying the map more closely, he could tell it was isolated. *Still,* he reasoned with himself, *I survived a forest at night, I'm sure I can manage a deserted beach.*

He picked up the USB stick, holding it up to the light. There were no identifying marks on it. Presumably, Hrschni wanted him to plug it into his computer, though for what reason Kester couldn't imagine. Pausing, he held it in midair, unsure what to do with it.

His phone vibrated in his pocket, snapping him out of his thoughts. *Mike,* he realised, glancing at the screen. Guiltily, he slid it back into his trousers, hoping that his friend would forgive him. He just didn't have the strength to listen to Mike go on about Crispian right now.

He looked at his watch. If Dr. Barqa-Abu and Fylgia were going to be there tonight to capture Hrschni, they needed to know about the meeting place sooner rather than later. Placing the USB stick down, he vowed to view the contents straight after.

The djinn answered the Skype call after only a few seconds, her pit-black eyes alert and watchful as ever.

"Kester, how can I help?"

He shifted in his seat. "I wanted to keep you updated about my project. I think the deadline is tonight, isn't it?"

She paused, then nodded. "Agreed."

"I'm concerned about it."

"What part?"

"Will you be helping me this time?" He hoped she understood his veiled comments. Speaking in code was frustrating to say the least, especially with something as important as this.

Dr. Barqa-Abu nodded. "Help is available for this final project. Remember, you need to have a firm idea of location for this one. It's all about spirits and their localities, you see?"

He nodded. "Well, this time I'm keeping well out of the urban locations; other students were doing those, weren't they?" *I'm doing well,* he thought, with a sudden sense of elation. *Even if Hrschni was right behind me, I don't think he'd realise what I was really talking about.* To be honest, he didn't think the daemon was nearby anyway. He couldn't detect even a hint of the feeling that came over him when spirits were near.

"We weren't expecting an urban location from you," the djinn said.

"I was planning on a beach or something similar," he replied. "Though it's such a *warren* of ideas, it's impossible to know which one to choose."

Dr. Barqa-Abu's expression twisted slightly. He hoped she'd caught the drift of what he was saying.

"I suppose I've just got to *look out* for ideas," he continued, placing as much emphasis as he dared on the right words. "I feel like I'm right on *the tip* of getting there. It'd be good to have some help from you."

She nodded. "I must go," she said, moving closer to the screen. "You will be fine, I am sure. The project is due in at the same time as the last one, yes?"

Clever, he thought, going over her words. "That's correct," he confirmed, then paused. He wanted to say more but couldn't think how to phrase it. *Will you protect me if things turn nasty?* he wondered. *What will you do if Hrschni kidnaps me again? And what are you planning to do to him?*

However, she'd already hung up by the time he'd got his thoughts in order. With a sigh, he quickly slipped out of his work clothes and into something warmer, then headed downstairs for something to eat.

It was only when he was halfway through his spaghetti shapes on toast that he remembered the USB. Nearly choking, he pushed the plate away and hared upstairs, worried that it might have somehow vanished in his absence. However, when he returned to his bedroom, he saw that it was still beside his laptop, looking as innocuous as ever.

Here goes, he thought, sliding into his chair and pushing the device into the port. *Let's see what this is all about.*

There was only one folder on the USB, and in that, just one file—video content by the looks of it. Kester stared at the title. *TheTruth.mov.* "The truth about what?" he wondered, tapping his finger against the keyboard. Nervousness washed over him, a sense that he was so far out of his depth he didn't stand a chance of getting back to safety again.

I don't want to know, he thought, biting his lip. *But I need to. I have to find out.*

He double clicked and waited as the movie file opened and started to play.

At first, it wasn't obvious what he was looking at. It appeared to be CCTV footage, if the occasional hazy lines across the screen were anything to go by. A room, large, with what looked like an enormous piece of machinery in the middle. Not that he'd ever seen machinery like it before—a huge metal ring, suspended between two towering pillars.

Why are you showing me this, Hrschni? he wondered, peering more closely to check he wasn't missing anything. As he shifted forward, he suddenly caught sight of movement in the lower right-hand corner. Three people walked towards the machine, one of them carrying a metal box.

Kester frowned. The box looked familiar.

It's a spirit-catching device, he realised with a thrill of excitement. *Luke used one to catch the Fetch in Lyme Regis. Larry said they got their equipment from Infinite Enterprises.*

"Is that what I'm looking at?" he whispered, adjusting his glasses. "Infinite Enterprises headquarters?" He remembered what

Curtis Philpot had said, about someone breaking in and stealing something that threatened national security. Presumably, this footage was the stolen item.

He couldn't make out who the figures were; they were too far away from the camera. He watched breathlessly as one pressed their hand to one of the pillars. At once, the ring crackled with light, a solid sheet of sparking energy that pulsed to and fro, like the waves of a shore.

The reality of what he was watching started to dawn on him.

No, he thought, feeling his chest tighten in horror. *I don't want to see it.* However, he couldn't look away. He needed to know, for better or worse.

The person holding the metal box raised it towards the machine, then pressed a button on the top. A moment later, a drifting line of smoke emerged from the device and swiftly shifted into a glowing, quivering form.

Hrschni was telling the truth. Oh god. Kester watched, mouth open in horror, as the hapless spirit was slowly sucked towards the ring of light. Although the image was mercifully blurry, there was no mistaking its arms, flying out in desperation, nor the agony as its head connected with the sheet of light. The air around it crackled, lightning forks spreading like fingers around it, and the spirit exploded, scattering into nothingness.

Then it was over. The figures switched off the machine, the light faded in an instant, and they strolled out of the room as though nothing had happened. Kester felt sick to his stomach. He stood up, felt faint, then sat again.

How long have they been doing this? he wondered, looking at the frozen final frame on the screen. *How many spirits have been torn apart by that thing?*

He shut the video, then hovered the mouse near the Skype

button, ready to call Dr. Barqa-Abu again. Then he paused. What if she already knew about this? What if she approved of the killings? After all, her position in the human world was secure, maybe she agreed that spirits that repeatedly flouted the rules should be exterminated.

What the hell do I do? He removed the USB with shaking hands and deposited it into his pocket. His phone started to vibrate at the same time, making him jump. It was Miss Wellbeloved this time, and again, he let it ring without answering. There was no point trying to talk to her right now; his mind was racing at uncontrollable speeds, and he doubted whether his words would make any sense to her.

Downstairs, his leftover spaghetti and toast sat untouched on the kitchen table, the sauce already congealing. Kester hardly noticed it. Instead, he grabbed his jacket and scarf and headed to the door. He had no idea how long it would take to get to Dawlish Warren, nor what the walk was like to the tip of the dunes, so it was best to get an early start.

The darkness encompassed him like a shroud as he scurried to the local train station; only the occasional glow of passing car headlights illuminated the way. The station was only down the road, a tiny shack on top of the railway bridge. To his relief a train arrived soon after he did. Other than a few weary commuters fastidiously avoiding eye-contact with one another it was empty.

Kester slid into the nearest seat, pulled out his phone, then listened to his voicemail messages. Miss Wellbeloved's was a confusing babble, asking him if he'd seen his father's leather diary and something about passwords. Mike's was even more incomprehensible: a four-minute rant about Crispian stealing something from the office. Kester shook his head. Office issues had to take a backseat; they were a low priority compared to what was about to happen. Right now, Fylgia and Dr. Barqa-Abu were probably readying themselves to capture Hrschni, and he needed to put all his energy into preparing himself for it.

Does Hrschni have any idea? he wondered, studying the landscape as it slowly changed from urban sprawl to empty countryside. His breath caught at the thought of what they might do to the daemon when they caught him. They wouldn't simply send him back to the spirit realm, he knew that now. Hrschni was destined to end up like the spirit he'd seen in the CCTV footage— blown apart by a terrible machine.

He's thousands of years old, Kester thought, leaning his head against the window. *He's been around since humans were practically apes, he knows more about this world than any of us do. What right have we got to destroy him?*

But what were the options? Let him bring chaos into the world? Obliterate technology, industry, and everything humans valued in the modern age?

Without realising it, he started to bang his forehead gently against the glass. A sob rose in his throat and lodged itself there, solid and unyielding as pain itself. *I can't do this,* he thought, ignoring the strange looks he was getting from the other passengers. *I know I must do it, but I can't.*

The train clunked awkwardly to a stop, signalling its arrival at the station. Kester couldn't see much out of the window, only a strip of empty platform illuminated by a few tired street lamps. He exited into the cold and breathed in the salty air. In the distance, he could just about hear the ceaseless whoosh of waves, lapping and tugging at the beach. Instinctively, he followed the sound.

The dunes started just beyond the car park, a stretch of ghost-pale sand that meandered past scrubland and swaying trees. As he'd predicted, the place was deserted. A stiff sea breeze whisked around his body, whistling mournfully through the shifting dune and blending with the noise of the tide. He shivered and pulled his scarf over his face.

A brisk buzz from within his pocket made him yelp out loud. He quickly glanced at the screen to see a message from Miss Wellbeloved.

Kester, we've heard. You brave, crazy young man. We're on our way.

He stopped walking. "How have you heard?" he whispered, then clamped his lips together, aware that Hrschni could be here already, watching his every move. Fylgia or Dr. Barqa-Abu must have told her, but why, after all the secrecy?

Stuffing his phone back into the depths of his pocket, he started walking. Replying was too risky, though he hoped, given that he was early, that the daemon wasn't around to spy on him yet. There was something about the dunes that was eerier than he'd expected, and the breathless sigh of the sand, slipping across the ground like a caress, made him uncomfortable.

Slowly, he slipped through the shadows, leaving the trail path and heading into the wilder part of the reserve. He could see the glittering lights of Exmouth in the distance, which made him feel even more removed from the world. Between him and civilisation lay the tossing waters of the estuary, which were black as tar in the moonlight.

This must be the tip of the dunes, he thought, as he stepped out onto a narrow peninsula of sand. Under normal circumstances, the landscape would have been breathtaking. As it was, he couldn't fight his growing sense of terror. There was no way out of this situation now. He was the instigator of Hrschni's destruction, whether he liked it or not. And he'd always have that on his conscience.

He peered at his watch. Ten minutes to go until the agreed meeting time. Even waiting for a few seconds seemed unbearable.

As though responding to his despair, the air quivered before him at the spot where the shallow water splashed relentlessly on the dune. For a moment, he wondered if it was his tired eyes playing tricks on him. Then the familiar glow of red flourished into view as the light took form and grew brighter.

Kester took a shaky breath and watched as the daemon came into clearer view.

Hrschni didn't speak. Instead, he hung his head in a manner that reminded Kester of a world-weary prisoner heading towards the gallows.

They both stood in silence, each waiting for the other to start.

"I know what is about to happen," Hrschni said quietly. The words rested on the breeze for a moment, before being carried into the night. He stopped Kester's reply with a shake of the head. "There's no need to reply. Perhaps it's better if I talk now. We haven't got much time."

CHAPTER 19: A CHANGE OF HEART

"I first suspected that Fylgia was working against me when she insisted upon inhabiting the body of your girlfriend, Anya," Hrschni started, inching closer to where Kester was standing. "The plan made sense, but I couldn't help but wonder if she was trying to get closer to you, to gain your trust. When she slipped off the other day to visit you, I followed her. Then I realised the full truth of it."

Kester shivered, knowing that Hrschni must be well aware of his role in the plot as well. "Why didn't you do something about it?" he asked, trying to mask his fear. "Is it because you're meant to keep your friends close but your enemies closer?"

The daemon's face solidified into sharp focus, blazing with volcanic intensity. "She isn't my enemy. She's forgotten our true cause, that is all. It's a common problem when you live for thousands of years alongside humans. You start to see the world through their narrow eyes. The same has happened with my old friend, Dr. Barqa-Abu."

"Why are you here then, if you know they're coming for you?"

"Because of you."

Kester dared to meet the daemon's gaze. Instead of rage, he saw a glitter of something different; compassion perhaps, or hope.

"Why?" he croaked, unable to take his eyes away. "What's so special about me?"

"I can tell you, but I need time."

"We haven't got time." Kester tapped his watch. "The others will be here soon. Dr. Barqa-Abu told Miss Wellbeloved; presumably they're on their way to trap you in a water bottle."

"A water bottle?" Hrschni shuddered. "What a thing for a once-mighty daemon to endure. Did you know that centuries ago, I ruled an empire? It's written in a book, even though the world has forgotten that it was me. Still," he continued, "a water bottle is better than what would follow after. I take it you've watched the footage I sent you?"

"Would they really kill you?"

"Spirits do not die, Kester. But when you scatter their energy so thoroughly, they are unable to regroup. As such, their energy floats in eternal agony, desperately seeking that which it once belonged to. It is worse than death, because there is no end to it."

Kester bit his lip. "I don't want them to do that to you. I know you kidnapped me, and you've made my life a living hell recently, but you don't deserve that."

The daemon shook his head. "Nobody does. And you must help me to fight against it."

"I can't help you with your plans!" Kester exclaimed, stepping backwards. "I don't agree with them, and anyway, I don't see what use I can be. I'm just a small, silly man who can't help anyone."

To his amazement, Hrschni raised a hand and placed it on his shoulder. At once, a surge of heat raced through him, flushing his cheeks and quickening his heartbeat. "If they've made you believe that," he whispered sadly, "then they've been crueller to you than I ever imagined. You are worth so much more than that. In fact, I believe you are unique."

"Because I'm a spirit door opener? I know it's a rare talent, but there are others who—"

"It's more than that, isn't it? You have extraordinary powers of perception. You're sensitive to the presence of spirits. You have a knack of identifying the right course of action, of seeing the light of truth when the path leads to darkness. All your life you've been remarkable. I should know, I was there during the early days. Leaving you was one of the biggest mistakes I ever made."

"What?" Kester stumbled, the loose sand sliding around his feet. "You weren't there when I was younger. Why would you be? I know you knew my mother, but—"

Hrschni froze, alert as a fox, then started to fade. "We haven't got much time. I will tell you everything, Kester. The whole truth about your mother, your grandfather; all of it. I'll show you how you can help me create a better world, for spirits and humans alike. But I need more time. Will you give me that?"

The sound of muffled conversation travelled on the air. *The others are on their way,* he realised, shaking from raw adrenalin. *What do I do?* "Talk to them," he whispered urgently, scanning the darkness for signs of their approach. "Explain everything. Miss Wellbeloved is kind, she'll listen and—"

"There are larger forces at work here," Hrschni replied. "There is no other way. You must make your decision quickly."

On his last word, the other members of the team came into view; Serena first, water bottle already suspended in the air like a dangerous snake. As if on cue, the air shimmered close by, followed by a livid flash of green. *Fylgia,* he realised, wondering how long she had been there.

"Wait," he said, holding his hands out. "Don't do anything hasty, please."

Without warning, Fylgia streaked towards Hrschni, whirling around him and then through him, until their colours were an incomprehensible blur.

"Get out of the way!" Miss Wellbeloved shouted, stepping forward and grabbing Kester by the arm. "The resulting energy of two spirits colliding could kill you!"

"You mustn't do it," Kester whispered helplessly, watching the spirits storm around one another, filling the air with high-pitched, lionlike roaring. His words were drowned out by the noise.

Pamela's face emerged from the darkness, stricken with anxiety. She nudged Serena urgently. "You need to do it now, or else Kester needs to open a spirit door. Fylgia is the weaker of the two, she can't hold him for much longer."

Kester clutched hold of Serena's sleeve, only to be batted away again. He watched, horrified, as she started to chant; her strange, guttural words blending with the sound of the raging spirits.

"Listen to me!" he said desperately, shaking himself free of Pamela's grip. "I think you're making a mistake—"

He felt Mike's arm circling his waist, pulling him back resolutely. *This can't happen,* he realised, as he saw Hrschni's form, stretched beyond recognition, being pulled slowly towards the water bottle. *This is wrong,* he thought furiously, and instinct took over.

Without thinking, he thrust himself as hard as possible against Mike's grip, then hurtled forward. Arms outstretched, his entire weight landed squarely on Serena's back, and he wrestled her to the ground. She screamed in surprise, the water bottle bouncing down the sloping dune beside her.

"What are you doing?" she wailed. "Have you gone mad? I had him, and you stopped me!"

Blinking, Kester sat up. The world seemed to have slowed into near stasis, with every movement captured in crystal-clear clarity. Serena slapped him around the face, but he barely felt it. Instead, his eyes were fixed to Hrschni's glowing form, which flickered for a moment, before firing like a torch into the sky. He believed the daemon might have whispered his thanks before disappearing.

What followed next was a confusion of shouted questions; each of his colleagues pressing into his face, demanding explanations. Fingers jabbed in his face, words were spat out, too fast for him to hear them. Kester stared dumbly at them all, then gradually opened his mouth.

"They would have killed him," he said, in a small voice that didn't sound like his own. "But they can't. He has the answers."

The others took a step back, their expressions identical masks of rage and confusion. He waited silently, nausea rising in his stomach. He'd known this moment would be awful, but hadn't imagined just how much it would *hurt*.

Finally, Miss Wellbeloved raised a hand towards Kester, before lowering it quickly, as though she'd been burnt. "What answers were you expecting?" she asked.

He took a deep breath to gather his courage, though he still couldn't quite meet her gaze. "Answers about what's really going on," he began, praying she'd understand. "Answers about what the government are up to, and what my mother's involvement was. There's more to this than—"

"Did you really think he'd tell you anything?" Serena snapped, cutting him short.

"Daemons don't lie."

"They're bloody good at manipulating people, though. You naive idiot, look what you've done! You've ruined everything."

He had no answer. Sand blew against his body as he stared at the dark waters beyond, unable to face the others.

They'll never know why I did it, he realised, feeling the weight of it all crash down upon him. *As far as they're concerned, I've just sided with their enemy. They must hate me.*

"Don't stand there gawping like a beached fish!" Serena's voice was the first to slice through his daze, slipping with knifelike precision into his fractured mind. "Start talking; tell us what the hell we do now!"

He felt a tentative hand on his arm.

"Kester, why did you let him escape?" Miss Wellbeloved muttered. "Do you realise what this means to us? Once the government hears about this, we're finished."

"You don't understand," he replied, feeling the first tear pool in the corner of his eye. "Hrschni didn't deserve to be captured. He didn't deserve to—"

"You don't deserve a job," Serena hissed. "I've always been suspicious of you." She raised a finger, pointing it like a curse towards him. "If I had my way, you'd be sent to the government right now and imprisoned as a traitor. As it is, you'd better never cross my path again, you useless, pathetic lump."

His chest tightened. Imploringly, he looked at Pamela and Mike, who both turned away.

Fylgia edged towards them, each movement appearing like a miniature torture of its own. "I could hold him no more," she said, her glow flickering like a faulty lightbulb. "Kester, you have made a dangerous deal with an even more dangerous spirit. I should know; I have been with him for centuries. Such a great cost, for so little."

"Why didn't Dr. Barqa-Abu come?" Miss Wellbeloved said, regaining a little of her usual composure. "If it'd been the two of you against Hrschni, then you would have stood a chance."

Fylgia wove on the spot, before slumping. "I do not know,"

she said finally. "Perhaps Hrschni dealt with her already. Perhaps she changed her mind. I don't know anything anymore." With a final shake of the head, she vanished into the night, leaving them swathed in darkness.

"I'm going home," Serena spat, picking up her water bottle. "Pamela, Mike, Miss W, are you joining me?"

"What about Kester?" Miss Wellbeloved said, her voice faltering and uncertain.

Mike stepped forward, his cold expression making Kester shrink back with renewed misery. "Kester got here on his own without telling us," he said, refusing to look in his direction. "I'm sure he can get home by himself too. Oh, and by the way," he added, "I presume you're working with Crispian too, are you? Was it you that got him to steal your dad's diary, with all the passwords in it?"

"What?" Kester peered dully upwards. "What diary?"

"Mike, I doubt it was Kester, or even Crispian," Miss Wellbeloved interrupted. "It could have fallen down behind the desk; we don't yet know what—"

"We don't know what Kester is capable of, because we don't really know him," Mike said bitterly. "You know, I always thought you were a mate. I totally trusted you. Then it turns out you're working with a daemon."

"I must say, it's broken my heart," Pamela added quietly. "Though I wish you no ill will. I'm sure you had your reasons."

"Come on," Serena said. "I need to go home. Not to mention figure out how I'll manage to find another job after this gets out."

"It doesn't have to get out," Kester said weakly.

"It's already out! Miss Wellbeloved phoned Curtis Philpot on the way here. Infinite Enterprise's surveillance team are probably around here somewhere right now, no doubt listening to this conversation. Give it a few days, the whole industry will know how badly this went."

"It wasn't your fault."

"Damned right, but it's one mistake too many. Face it, you've just banged the final nail in this agency. Larry Higgins will want to distance himself as much as possible from us and—"

"Leave it, Serena!" Miss Wellbeloved shrieked, then burst into tears. "I can't take any more of this!"

Kester stood awkwardly. "I'm so sorry," he whispered, reaching out to her. "I didn't think that it would—"

"That's just it," Mike muttered, putting an arm around Miss Wellbeloved and leading her away. "You didn't think."

Kester watched, numbly, as the darkness swallowed them up. He sat back down on the sand, staring at the sea without really seeing it. After a while, he began walking, aware that Infinite Enterprise's team were probably still watching him, hoping he would lead them to Hrschni. The night passed, and his thoughts drifted through it, wild and confusing as the night itself. Finally, the sun began to rise; a milky blot on the horizon that slowly turned the landscape from ink to a steely winter's grey.

I've ruined everything. The words repeated over and over in his head, a vicious chant of self-punishment that tore his heart into pieces. He'd let his friends down, he'd destroyed months of work, and he'd put the safety of the world in jeopardy. And for what? What was there to be gained by it?

But I couldn't let them exterminate him, he realised. *It would have been terribly, horribly wrong.*

He arrived back on the outskirts of Exeter several hours later, though how, he wasn't quite sure. Stumbling along the roads, every part of his body ached, a fact that he was only dimly aware of. Finally, he reached the top of his street. It was a long way up the hill to his house, but he pressed on regardless. All he wanted to do was dive under the duvet covers and stay there for as long as possible.

As he approached, a parked car flicked on its headlights. He covered his eyes, squinting through the darkness, and then recognised the elegant lines of his father's old sedan gleaming dully in the feeble light of the forthcoming dawn.

The car door opened. "Get in," his father ordered, jarringly strident in the otherwise silent street.

"I don't want to," Kester muttered.

"They told me everything. I've been waiting here all night for you, foolish boy. Come on, you can come home with me."

Resistance was futile, he could tell. Wearily, he walked to the passenger side and climbed in. A moment later, the engine roared into life, and his father drove away.

Kester drifted in and out of sleep as the car travelled through the quiet city to the outskirts beyond. The crunch of tyre against gravel woke him fully, and he peered out of the window, momentarily confused by his surroundings. His father's house looked different in the weak light of the rising sun; bleached of colour and more forbidding than usual.

"I suppose you would like breakfast, yes?" Ribero switched off the engine then turned to look at his son. "You do not look good. Coffee will help. Good strong coffee."

"I don't want coffee," Kester said dully. "I don't want anything."

His father's expression softened. "Do not be so sad. Things may seem very bad now, but tomorrow is another day. Do not worry."

Kester shook his head. "I let Hrschni escape, Dad." He opened the car door, allowing some time to let the words sink in. They walked in silence to the front door, and then Ribero waved him through to the kitchen.

"Coffee first, talk after. And do not say you don't want it, because this is the best Argentinian coffee and that makes all the difference." At the flick of a switch, the coffee grinder lurched into noisy action. Kester watched the beans whirling around inside without really seeing them.

"Why are you being nice to me?" he whispered as his father placed the steaming mug under his nose. "I don't deserve it."

Ribero perched on the kitchen stool, motioning for Kester to do the same. "Miss Wellbeloved phoned me last night," he began, reaching for his cigarette packet. "She was very upset. She told me what happened and how angry the others were."

"I know."

"But she said that there is more to this. That you would not betray the team, that something else is going on. So, you need to tell me. And not all the nonsense stuff, yes? I want the truth."

Kester shrugged. "I suppose it doesn't matter what I tell you now." Taking a deep breath, he recounted everything that had happened over the last few weeks, right up to the conversation he'd had with Hrschni the evening before. Ribero nodded without interrupting. At the end, lit his cigarette and inhaled deeply, staring out of the window to the pine trees beyond.

"This is a lot for a young man to be taking on," he muttered. "Too much. Why did you not come to us sooner? We could have helped."

"I was told that I had to keep it a secret," Kester replied. "To be honest, I had no intention of letting Hrschni go. But then, after I'd seen that footage of Infinite Enterprises murdering the spirit, I just couldn't . . ." His voice faltered, giving way to a sob. The force of his emotions surprised him, and to his relief, Ribero didn't try to offer comfort, only sat patiently, waiting for him to finish.

Finally, he wiped his eyes and looked up. "I'm sorry," he said. "I've done a terrible thing and everyone hates me."

"No one hates you," Ribero corrected. "Well, Serena may hate you, but she will get over it, because she has a stupid temper that comes and goes quickly."

Kester managed a watery smile. "She has a right to be angry. Hrschni is still out there, ready to unleash spirits upon the world."

"You forget one thing," his father said, flicking the ash into a cigarette tray. "He needs you for that. No spirit door opener; no spirits to flood into the world. But I want to ask you one thing, Kester. Why did you *really* let him go? I know you didn't want to see him killed, but there's something else, am I right?"

"He told me he'd tell me the truth."

"The truth? What truth?"

"About my mother. My grandfather. My role in all of this."

Ribero's jaw tightened. "If there is one creature who knows, it is him."

"That's exactly what I'm talking about." Kester jabbed a finger against the breakfast table. "You make cryptic comments like that, then refuse to tell me anything else. Do you know what that feels like? To know that you're a part of a bigger picture but not be able to see it because everyone is hiding things from you?"

"Some things are better left in the past."

"That's easy for you to say; you know what those things are."

Ribero exhaled heavily and looked up at the ceiling. The exertion of staying up all night was evident in the shadow across his jaw, the dark circles beneath his eyes. Suddenly, a ringing from the living room shattered the silence. Kester jumped in his seat.

"My phone," Ribero explained, getting shakily to his feet.

"Probably Miss Wellbeloved checking that I have found you." He loped off to answer it. Kester sat in silence, sipping at his coffee.

"Hello?" Ribero answered, his voice echoing around the lounge. Then, in a more ominous tone, "You were not who I was expecting."

Kester strained to hear better, mug frozen in front of his lips.

"Yes, he is with me. How did you know that?" Ribero paused. "I see. I do not think surveillance is necessary; he is not a danger. Talking to him would not be sensible right now. Give him time."

Infinite Enterprises, perhaps? Kester sat up straighter. Perhaps it was the government, arranging to bring him in for questioning. Either way, he knew he wouldn't get out of this situation without some form of interrogation.

He waited patiently until his father returned.

"Infinite Enterprises are outside," he announced, waving towards the front door. "They want you to tell them what is going on."

"How did they know I was here?"

"They lost you during the night, so they waited outside your house. They must have followed us here." He tugged on the remnants of his cigarette, then ground it into the ashtray. The silence stretched between them as each delved deep into their own private thoughts.

"What should I do?" Kester said quietly.

His father leaned across, placing a quivering hand on his elbow. "They might take you to the government for formal questioning," he whispered, looking over his shoulder. "It may become a legal matter."

"What?" Kester pulled his arm away. "You mean, there's a chance I might get arrested?"

"No, nothing like that. But they could say that you deliberately assisted a spirit that was wanted by the law. You obstructed the justice; you know what I mean."

Blimey, Kester thought, pressing his hands against his face. He hadn't even considered the possibility that he'd broken the law. *What have I done?*

"I suppose I'd better go out and face them," he said, slowly standing. "There's no point delaying it."

Ribero's eyes shone in the glow of the overhead light. He wiped them quickly, then rose too. "Go out the back door," he whispered, clutching Kester by the shoulder.

"Why are you talking so—"

"*They are probably listening with their nosey equipment. So be very, very quiet.*"

Nodding, Kester let himself be ushered into the lounge and towards the patio doors. "Won't that get you in trouble?" he whispered back. "If you're protecting a criminal?"

"You're not a criminal, my boy." He tugged the door open, releasing the scent of pine and cold into the room. "I will say you have gone for a walk. It may give you some time to put this right, yes?"

"How am I meant to do that?" Kester stepped outside, feeling the crunch of icy grass under his feet. "I've got no way of finding Hrschni."

"He might find you," Ribero said and gave him a brief hug. "These are dark times, but light will follow; trust me. Now go."

Kester stepped across the lawn and into the trees that surrounded it. The moisture of the dawn dew clung to every pine needle, glittering in the bleached sunlight. His basic knowledge of the area was hopefully enough to ensure he'd be able to find a way out to the main road, but what then? He didn't want Infinite Enterprises to spot him, at least not yet.

If they're really using their surveillance equipment to listen to us, he thought, slipping silently through the trees, *then they'll realise I'm not at Dad's house soon enough. I haven't got long.*

Feeling clearer-headed after the coffee, he went over the events of last night. Although so much trouble had followed afterwards, he couldn't bring himself to regret his actions. Delivering Hrschni to Infinite Enterprises and the government would have meant accepting their treatment of spirits, and that was something he wasn't prepared to do.

Hrschni's right about one thing, he thought, feeling the damp start to seep through his clothes. *Things need to change. It can't carry on like this.*

His head was full of questions too. Why hadn't Dr. Barqa-Abu been there? With her assistance, Fylgia could have easily overcome Hrschni. What had Mike been talking about when he'd mentioned the lost diary and the passwords? And most important of all; where was Hrschni now?

Perhaps he's just deserted me, Kester thought glumly. *He's made his escape and forgotten all about my existence.* However, he didn't think that was the case. The daemon may love trickery, but he wasn't a liar, and he seemed a creature of his word.

Kester stopped, suddenly conscious how unsettled he felt—and how watched. Slowly, he opened his mouth.

"Are you there, Hrschni?" he whispered. There was every chance that the daemon, like Infinite Enterprises, had followed him to his father's.

The air was still and silent. He waited, aware of how small he was beneath the towering pines.

"Please," he said, his eyes misting with tears. "I've risked *everything* to help you. It's your turn to help me now, because I'm in real trouble."

Eerie quiet answered him. Kester sighed, then wiped his eyes on his sleeve. "Thanks for nothing," he muttered, then laughed. The cynical notes rang out around him before being absorbed into the wintry air.

The air rippled, barely inches from his body, and the familiar red glow swelled steadily, filling out into the daemon's form. Kester waited, head held high, as Hrschni solidified in front of him.

"How did you know I was here?" the daemon asked. He seemed vaguely amused, if the curl of his wide lip was anything to go by.

Kester shrugged. "Just a hunch. Actually," he added, musing on it, "I *felt* you. Does that sound odd?"

He waited, the weight of all the unasked questions harnessing his tongue. He didn't know where to start. Hrschni hovered beside him, strangely companionable given all that had happened to lead them to this point.

"You did a brave thing last night," the daemon said finally, breaking the quiet.

"Brave or stupid?"

"That depends on your viewpoint. However, regardless of that, I know it has caused you a lot of personal pain. Often the right course of action is also the hardest to undertake."

"Was it right?" Kester kicked at the ground. "They all think I'm a traitor. And it's damaged our agency. Infinite Enterprises were listening in last night; they know everything."

"I know, I saw them. Don't worry about that. They're the government's puppets; they always have been. Why do you think they are so well funded?"

Kester nodded solemnly. He'd always known that Infinite Enterprises were the darlings of their industry, and their links with the government weren't a secret.

"What do you think you will do now?" Hrschni asked softly, weaving in front of Kester, forcing him to stop walking.

"I'm not going to help you to bring thousands of spirits into our world, if that's what you're asking."

Hrschni chuckled. "Those words sound familiar. You're not the first to say them to me. However," he continued, inviting Kester to walk onwards, "after I tell you the truth, you might feel differently. The question is, do you want to hear the truth, Kester?"

"That's all I've ever wanted," Kester replied.

The daemon placed a skeletal hand at the centre of Kester's forehead, warming him instantly. He flinched away, but the insistent press of fingers couldn't be avoided.

"When I touch you like this," Hrschni whispered, drawing closer, "I reach for your inner eye; the part of you that connects to the spirit world."

"It's hot," Kester said, closing his eyes instinctively.

Hrschni pulled him nearer. The heat of his body radiated through Kester like bathwater, warming him from within. "*This* is how I will tell you the truth," he continued, each word soft and gentle as a lullaby. "I will *show* you."

"What will you show me?" Kester whispered.

"All of it. I will show you it through your mother's memories, which I took from her."

"How? When?"

"Shortly before she died," the daemon said. "Yes, I was with her then, just briefly. She knew that we would meet, I think. Now, the question is, do you want to see? There can be no going back if you do."

Kester felt his muscles ease into delicious relaxation under the pressure of Hrschni's finger. His head lolled to one side. *Is this right?* he wondered dreamily, casting his gaze to the treetops above.

The sun edged behind a cloud, darkening the woods around him. *Is this what I should be doing?*

He felt the daemon press more firmly against the skin between his eyebrows. For a moment, it seemed as though the bony finger was entering the centre of his skull, though the sensation wasn't unpleasant. He saw a young woman clutching some books. Although her face was unlined, her hair yet to be greyed with age, he recognised her immediately. *Mum.*

"I am the real key," Hrschni muttered into his ear. "The question is, do you want to unlock the secrets?"

The experiences of the last few months flooded over him. The scream of an unleashed banshee. The wail of a dislocated Japanese spirit. Murderous fetches, romping familiars. His father, Miss Wellbeloved; happy evenings down the pub. Holding Anya in his arms, watching her sleep. But none of it meant anything if he didn't understand the *why.*

"I want to know everything," he muttered.

With a sigh, Hrschni pressed his hands against Kester's head. There was a moment of pressure, then everything darkened to nothingness.